LEYLAH

Mists

of the

SERENGETI

PITCH73 PUBLISHING

Mists of the Serengeti
Copyright ©2017 by Leylah Attar

Editing by:
Lea Burn

Proofreading by:
Christine Estevez

Cover Design ©:
Hang Le

Interior Design & Formatting by:
Christine Borgford, Type A Formatting

10 9 8 7 6 5 4 3 2 1

ISBN: 978–1-988054-00-1

For my husband and son,
with all my heart,
except for a teeny, tiny part,
for
Nutella

Mists

of the

SERENGETI

Prologue

Jack

I F YOU HAD asked Jack Warden what his favorite things were
before that afternoon, he would have reeled off a list without
hesitation: black coffee, blue skies, driving into town with the
windows down, Mount Kilimanjaro wreathed in swirling clouds
in his rear-view, and the girl who owned his heart making up
the words to the song on the radio. Because Jack was absolute
and precise, as clear as the African Savannah after the rain. He'd
weathered his share of storms—losing his parents as a child, losing
his college sweetheart to a divorce—but he knew how to roll with
the punches. He'd learned that early in life, on dusty safaris in the
Serengeti, where hunter and hunted played hide and seek amidst
tall, swaying elephant grass.

Jack was a survivor. He got knocked down, but he always got
back up. And the times when his daughter visited the coffee plan-
tation over her summer break were golden days—mud-squelch-
ing, popcorn-munching, frog-hunting days. Jack had the kind of
presence that turned heads when he entered a room, but on those
days, he was like the sizzling crack of a thunderbolt—all lit up
from the inside.

"Lily, put that back," he said, as she opened the glove com-
partment and pulled out a bar of chocolate that looked like it had
just been dragged out of a sauna.

"But it tastes so good when it's all melted like this. Goma

leaves it there for me."

"Goma is ninety. Her brain is about as mushy as that chocolate."

They laughed because they both knew that Jack's grandmother was as quick and sharp as a black mamba. She was just full of eccentricities and marched to her own beat. It's what had earned her the name *Goma*, from the Swahili word for drums: *ngoma*.

"Lily, no. You'll get it all over your costume. Li—" Jack sighed as her chubby, eight-year-old fingers tore through the foil. He could have sworn he heard Goma laughing from the foothills of the mountain, as she sat on the porch. He smiled and turned his eyes back to the road, taking a mental snapshot of the way his daughter looked—big-eyed and curly-haired, in a rainbow tutu and sunflower hat, with chocolate smudges around her mouth. These were the moments that got him through the long months when she was back in Cape Town with her mother.

As they entered the roundabout into town, Jack rested his elbow on the window frame. His skin was tanned, much like the tourists who rolled in from the beaches of Zanzibar, but his color was permanent, earned by years of working outside under the Tanzanian sun.

"Are you going to record the dance recital?" asked Lily.

It was an unspoken agreement between them. Lily spent entire afternoons making him and Goma watch and re-watch her performances. She gave them scorecards, and the numbers slowly inched up, because she wouldn't let them leave until she got exactly what she wanted out of them.

"Watch it again," she'd say, because they had obviously missed her perfect timing here, or the double tap there.

"Can you sign me up for more lessons?" she asked.

"Already done," Jack replied. It meant an hour-long drive to Amosha and back, on half-baked roads riddled with potholes, but watching his daughter dance made his heart grow ten times its size.

"Is Mum going to enroll you in dance class when you get back?"

"I don't think so." It was so matter-of-fact, with the same kind of acceptance she had adapted after learning her parents were going to live thousands of miles apart, that Jack felt a sharp pang of sadness.

He had met Sarah at the university in Nairobi. They were both away from home—young, free, and hungry. He could still remember the first time he'd seen her—black-skinned and sophisticated—her sleek, shoulder-length braids falling around her face as she took the seat next to him in the lecture hall. She was all city-girl, he was all country-boy. She liked to jot things down—goals, plans, lists, dates. He liked to live day by day, hour by hour. She was meticulous and cautious. He was exuberant and impulsive. They had been doomed from the start, but when does that ever stop anyone from falling in love? He'd fallen hard—as had she—and what a ride it had been. In the end, the isolation and unpredictability of life at the coffee farm had been too much for Sarah. But Kaburi Estate was Jack's livelihood, his birthplace, and his legacy. Its raw, rushing beat pulsed through his veins like rich, dark espresso. He knew Lily had it in her too, that hot, frothy swirl of magic and madness. It was why she loved to dance, and there was no way he was going to stand by and watch all of her pure, vibrant essence get washed away just because she spent the majority of her time away from the farm.

"Maybe if I get better grades this year," Lily continued.

And there it was again. Structure, form, function, discipline. Not that it was a bad thing for a kid, but anything that fell outside those parameters was cut and discarded. Jack had watched it rinse his marriage of joy, until it sat like a colander full of thawed out, freezer-burned vegetables, with no color and no flavor. Sarah had left little room for joy, for simple moments to just *be*, and now she was doing the same thing to Lily. She had a plan in place for their daughter, and it did not include pursuing personal passions.

"Well, baby girl, your mum is right." Jack turned to face her. "We both want you to do well in school. Work hard on those grades when you get back. But today, you dance! And when you—" He blinked as a burst of light momentarily blinded him.

"Lily, you're going to use up all the film," he said.

"So?" Lily pulled out the milky Polaroid that was starting to develop, pointed the camera at herself, and snapped a shot.

"Give me that camera."

"No!" She squealed and pushed him away with sticky fingers.

"*Ugh.*" Jack wiped the chocolate from his face as they passed crooked shops with Coca-Cola and Fanta signs, archaic trees with bright green canopies, and patches of red, volcanic soil. "You got it all over the camera too."

"I can fix it." She took off the hat that Goma had sewn for her and wiped the camera clean. "All good!"

Jack smiled and shook his head as they turned into the mall where her dance group was performing. It was a short, informal production for family, friends, and weekend shoppers.

"Come on. Miss Temu will be waiting!" Lily jumped out of the car as soon as they found a parking spot. Saturday was the busiest day at Kilimani Mall, and there was also some kind of convention going on.

"Hold on," said Jack. He was almost done rolling up the windows when his phone rang. It was one of the staff from his farm, asking if he could pick up a few supplies while he was in town.

Lily came around to his side of the car. The window was tinted, so she pressed her palm against the glass and peered inside. She made funny faces at Jack until he hung up.

"Let's go, baby girl," he said, taking her hand.

The recital was being held on the lower level, in a small hall off the food court. As they made their way there, Lily stopped in front of a balloon vendor.

"Can I get a yellow one for Aristurtle?" She tugged on one of the helium-filled balloons.

Aristurtle was Lily's pet tortoise, who had remained nameless until Goma started calling him that because of all the grand questions Lily consulted him on.

"What is Aristurtle going to do with a balloon?" asked Jack.

"You know how he's always getting lost?"

"Because you let him roam all around the house."

"Because I don't like caging him in. So, if I tie a balloon around his shell, we'll always know where he is."

"You know, that is so absurd, it makes sense." Jack laughed and pulled out his wallet. "We'll take a yellow one."

"Sorry, they're six in a bouquet," the man replied. "I have other singles, but I'm all out of the yellow ones." He gave them a curious glance, but Jack was used to it. It had started when he and Sarah were dating, and had continued after they'd had Lily. A mixed-race couple with a biracial daughter. The contrast seemed to fascinate people.

Jack glanced at Lily. Her eyes were fixed on the bright, sunny ones. "Fine. I'll take all six."

As he bent down to give her the balloons, she wrapped her arms around him and squeezed. "I love you! You're the best daddy ever!"

A flurry of strangers milled around them, but Jack was hit with a sweet stillness in that moment, a surge of warmth and purpose in the middle of an ordinary day.

"Don't tie them to Aristurtle all at once or he'll fly away," he said.

Lily giggled and broke away, taking the escalator down, the balloons bobbing around her like golden sunburst.

"Lily!" her dance instructor called, when they got to the recital hall. "You look great!"

"It's a rainbow." Lily twirled around, showing off the tutu that Goma had made. "My favorite."

"It's perfect." Her instructor turned to Jack and smiled. "Hello, Jack."

"Miss Temu." He nodded, instinctively taking in her lithe dancer's body and smooth cocoa-powder skin.

"It's Mara," she corrected, as she had done many times before. She had made her interest in him clear, but Jack knew better than to mess with the dynamics of his daughter's dance class. In a room full of mothers, he was the only father who showed up with his child. They fawned over him, not just because Jack was a powder keg of testosterone—his voice, his hands, his gestures—but also because of how playful and nurturing he was with Lily. It drew them to him, and Jack had learned not to stir up any jealousies by keeping all his attention on Lily.

"Set up is this way." Miss Temu started ushering Lily to the back.

"Here, Daddy!" Lily handed him the balloons. "How do I look?"

"Beautiful. As always."

"Is my ponytail okay?"

Jack knelt and adjusted it. He dropped a kiss on her forehead and wiped a smudge of chocolate from her cheek. "There. All good?"

"All good!" She nodded, barely able to contain her excitement at going up on stage. "Sit in the front row so I can find you, okay?"

"I know the drill, Lily. Have I ever failed you?"

"Don't forget to record it!"

"Go." Jack laughed. "Dance up a storm."

Lily took a deep breath and smiled. "See you on the other side."

"See you on the other side, baby girl." He watched her disappear behind the curtains.

"Jack . . ." Miss Temu tapped him on the shoulder. "The

balloons. They're kind of distracting. Would you mind putting them away?"

"Of course." Jack looked around the hall. It was filling up, but the first two rows were reserved for family. "Do I have time to run to the car and drop them off?"

"Five minutes, but Lily is up third, so you should be okay."

"Great. I'll be right back."

Jack took the escalator back up to the parking lot. The aroma of freshly brewed coffee hit him as he passed the café, reminding him of the travel mug he'd left in his car. Nothing beat the taste of rich Arabica coffee beans from the farm. There was a precision that led to its distinct flavor—from planting to picking to roasting it in a rotating drum over a gas flame. Jack unlocked the car and retrieved his coffee, taking a deep, satisfying swig.

He was about to put the balloons inside when a burst of sharp, loud cracks rattled the air. His first thought was that the balloons had popped, in quick succession, but the sound had an echo, a boom that reverberated through the parking lot. When it happened again, Jack felt a bone-deep chill. His marrow congealed. He knew guns. You don't live on a farm in rural Africa without learning how to protect yourself from wild animals. But Jack had never used a machine gun, and the shots ringing out from the mall sounded very much like one.

They say that a person's true strength comes through in times of calamity. It's a strange and unfair measure of a man. Because disasters and catastrophes are absurd, freakish monsters lurking in the periphery of your vision. And when one of those formless, shapeless shadows shows itself and stands before you, naked and grotesque, it completely incapacitates you. Your senses witness something so unexpected, so bizarre, that you stop to question the reality of it. Like a blue whale falling out of the sky. Your brain doesn't know what to do with it. And so Jack stood paralyzed, holding his coffee in one hand and the balloons in the other, in Parking Lot B of Kilimani Mall on a clear Saturday afternoon in July, as shots rang out from inside, where he'd just dropped off his daughter.

It was only when the screaming started, when a stampede of panicked shoppers tumbled through the doors, that Jack blinked. He didn't feel the burn of coffee on his feet as his mug split open. He didn't see six yellow balloons drifting off into a blue whale of a sky. He just felt the desperation of a father who needed to get to his daughter. Instantly.

If someone had flown over the mall in that moment, they would have witnessed a strange sight: a mass of people scrambling, pushing, fighting to get out of the building, and a lone, solitary man scrambling, pushing, fighting to get inside.

It was more conviction than strength that got Jack through the crowd. Inside was pure chaos. Gunfire rattled through the mall. Discarded shoes, shopping bags, and spilled drinks were everywhere. The balloon cart stood, abandoned and unaffected, smiley faces and Disney princesses gaping at the havoc. Jack did not stop to look left or right. He didn't care to differentiate friend from foe. He rushed past the café, past the half-eaten almond croissants and crushed cookies, past the cries for help, with a single-minded purpose. He had to get downstairs to the recital hall.

Sit in the front row so I can find you, okay?

I know the drill, Lily. Have I ever failed you?

He was almost at the escalator when a toddler, going the opposite way, came to a halt in front of him. The boy was lost and had cried himself into a state of exhaustion. Jack could barely make out his soft whimpers over the pounding of his own heart. For a moment they stood there, the little boy with his face painted like Batman, colors smudged from tears, and the man who, for a split second, was torn between getting him to safety and getting to his own daughter.

Then Jack stepped aside. He was sure he would always remember the toddler's face, the look of expectancy in his big, round eyes, the pacifier pinned to his shirt. As he stuffed his shame into a dark recess of his soul, someone started shouting.

"Isa! Isa!"

From the way the boy turned at the woman's voice, she was obviously the person he'd been looking for.

Jack heaved a sigh of relief and rounded the escalator.

"Mister! Stop. Please. Get my son out of here."

She was lying on the floor, about ten feet from Jack, beside a stroller that had toppled over, holding on to her ankle. She was hurt. And pregnant.

"Please get him out of here," she begged.

People were still fleeing the mall, terrified blurs of motion, but of all the people, of *all* the people, she was asking Jack. Perhaps because Jack was the only person who had heard her. Perhaps because he had stopped long enough to acknowledge a crying toddler in the middle of the chaos. She had no concern for her own safety, no request for herself. And in that, they were united. They both just wanted to get their kids out.

Jack felt the escalator belt sliding under his hands as he stood at the top of the stairs.

Go down.

No. Help them.

"I'm sorry," he said. Every second he wasted was a second that kept him from Lily.

He should have averted his eyes then, but he caught the moment the boy embraced his mother, the slackening of his little body, the relief at having found her, the belief that everything would be all right—in complete contrast to the utter desolation and helplessness in her eyes.

Fuck.

So Jack did the hardest, bravest, most selfless thing in his life. He turned back. He grabbed the boy with one hand, supported the mother with his other, and got them out the door. In his adrenaline-fueled state, it didn't take more than a minute. But it was a minute too long.

As he turned to get back inside, an explosion rocked the mall, blowing him clear off the stairs. A panel of glass landed on him, trapping him underneath. Chunks of steel and concrete rained down on the parking lot, shattering windshields and headlights. The high-pitched wailing of police cars and ambulances mingled with the incessant blaring of car alarms. But those who were hurt remained eerily silent, some of them forever.

Jack stirred and fought the darkness threatening to pull him under. He had something to do. Somewhere to be. He focused on the acrid smoke that filled his lungs—sharp, bitter, and as black as the realization that hit him when he opened his eyes.

Lily. Oh God. I failed you.

As the world fell to its knees around him, walls torn, roof blown off, blood and bone everywhere—Jack felt himself rip into two. *Before*-Jack, who loved black coffee, blue skies, and driving into town with all the windows down, and *After*-Jack, whose daughter's sweet smile and cotton-candy ponytail swam before him in the heated, five-alarm blaze of the afternoon.

How do I look?

Beautiful. As always.

In that moment, as Jack struggled to lift the weight that was pinning him down, he knew. He knew there would be no escaping this, no getting back up from it. And so, like the weary antelope that bares its throat to the lion, Jack closed his eyes and let the numbing cloak of darkness devour him.

I T'S THE HAPPIEST *day of my life*, thought Rodel Harris Emerson, as she signed her name on the dotted line.

People assumed it was a man's name, until they met her. It had happened two years ago when she'd applied for a teaching position in Bourton-on-the-Water, and it happened again when she'd messaged the real estate agent to see the property she was buying now, in the same golden-hued village—affectionately known as The Venice of the Cotswolds—in the English countryside.

"Congratulations!" Andy looked over the contract and smiled. "Your first home."

"Thank you," she replied.

He had no idea. It wasn't just a home; it was a dream she had chased her whole life. And now, at twenty-four, she finally had an anchor, the kind of stability she'd missed growing up in a family that traveled wherever her father's job took them. It had been a good job, one that had afforded them the luxury of experiencing different cultures, different places, all around the world. But just as Rodel would begin to settle down and start making new friends, they would be off again. Her younger sister, Mo, thrived on it, as did her parents. They were explorers at heart, free spirits that craved new tastes, new sounds, new soil. But Rodel yearned for a rest stop, a little patch of comfort and familiarity—a *real* home.

And now she had it, in exactly the kind of place that had stirred up her imagination since she'd first watched *The Lord of the Rings* and had fallen in love with the Shire. She had been twelve then, and it had remained lodged in her mind—a fictional, improbable ideal—until she was searching for job openings after college and came across Bourton-on-the-Water. There, in the heart of England, amongst the rural idyll of peaceful rolling hills, life was unhurried. Footpaths crossed scenic fields that bloomed with snowdrops in January and bluebells in May. Stone cottages nestled alongside tree-lined streets, and low, elegant bridges straddled the river.

"Well, that's it." Andy put the paperwork into his briefcase. "There are just a few dates that we need to go over."

Rodel pulled out her phone and switched to the calendar. It rang just as Andy was about to get started.

He read the name flashing across her screen. "Montego?"

"My sister." Rodel didn't share the reason behind their unusual names. Their parents had named both daughters after the places in which they had been conceived: Rodel Harris, for the picturesque village of Rodel on the Isle of Harris in Scotland, and Montego James for Montego Bay in the parish of St. James, Jamaica.

Ro and Mo.

"Please go on." She sent her sister's call to voice mail. This wasn't the time for one of Mo's rambling chats. Besides, Rodel had big news to share. The I-bought-a-house-so-you-need-to-get-your-arse-down-here kind of news that she'd been dying to share once everything was finalized.

"I can wait if you want to take it." Andy was chatty and overly accommodating. Rodel had a feeling that his interest in her stretched beyond the professional.

"It's okay. I'll call her later."

They were seated on opposite sides of the kitchen counter in the restored seventeenth-century cottage that Rodel had just purchased. It was a tiny two-story home, but it had an open living area with exposed wood beams, a book nook, and a sunny terrace steps from the river. It was close enough to the school for Rodel to walk, but set in the secluded backwater at the edge of the village. Rodel couldn't wait to move out of the room she'd been renting for the last two years.

"The sellers have agreed to an early closing so you can have the place in a couple of weeks." Andy went over the dates.

"That's perfect." It meant that Rodel would have the summer to settle in before the school year started in September. "Thank you," she said, as they concluded their meeting.

Andy stood and cleared his throat. "I was wondering if . . . *umm* . . . you'd like to have a drink. You know, to celebrate and all?"

Another time, Rodel would have turned him down. She had been so focused on working toward her dream of owning a home that her social life was practically non-existent. It didn't help that she was a book nerd. She had book boyfriends that no flesh-and-blood man could ever live up to. She might have sought tranquility in a home, but in a man, she wanted the tempest—Strider, Aragorn, King of Gondor. Another fictional, improbable ideal. Yes, *Lord of the Rings* had quite possibly ruined her. She had found the Shire, and she had claimed her Hobbit-hole, but she was pretty sure she would have to recast the hero. Kings like Aragorn simply did not walk among mortal men.

"A drink would be nice," she said to Andy.

"Well then . . ." He looked chuffed as he led her to his car—a compact, white hybrid.

They drove to a small, rustic pub overlooking the river. The rough, hewn wooden tables were snug, barely wide enough to hold their beers, and their knees touched as they sat across from each other.

"In case I haven't been clear, I think you're very pretty," said

Andy. "You have *umm* . . . beautiful brown eyes. I like your . . ." He pointed in her general direction, searching for something elusive, and finally went in for the kill. "I like your hair."

"Thank you." Rodel drowned her face in the dimpled mug holding her drink.

Why was dating always so painful? Why were kisses always as piss warm as her beer?

"Do your parents live around here?" asked Andy.

It's just small talk, thought Rodel. *He isn't announcing his intentions to meet them.*

For once, Rodel was relieved her parents were thousands of miles away. She'd changed her mind. She didn't want to recast her hero. She would happily spend the rest of her life with fictional book boyfriends.

Darcy? *Oh yes.*

Grey? *Oh my.*

Aragorn? *Oh my, yes, yes, yes!*

"My parents live in Birmingham, but they're retired and love to travel," she said. "They're in Thailand right now."

"Well, if you need help moving, I can . . ." He trailed off and followed Rodel's gaze. She was staring at the TV. Something on the screen had caught her attention.

She stood, slowly—stiff and wooden—and walked up to the bartender. "Can you turn that up?" It was more than a simple request. There was a tight, controlled edge to her voice that drew everyone's attention. A hush fell over the pub as all eyes turned to the news broadcast.

"Gunmen stormed into a crowded mall in Amosha, Tanzania, minutes before a powerful explosion went off. Dozens are feared dead. More on this developing story from our foreign correspondent . . ."

They cut to the scene of carnage, billows of black smoke rising like dark tornadoes behind the reporter.

"My phone." Rodel backed away from the screen and stumbled toward the table. She turned her bag upside down, and got on her knees, scouring the contents for her phone.

"What's wrong?" asked Andy.

"I need my phone! My sister is in Amosha. I have to get in tou—" She pounced on her phone and started dialing. "Pick up. Come on, Mo. Pick up." Her chest rose and fell with each breath.

Someone sat her down on a chair. Someone brought her a glass of water. No one picked up at the other end. It went straight to voice mail. She dialed again. And then again. Her fingers trembled as she waited for the string of international dialing codes to go through.

She was about to hang up and try her parents when she noticed the little icon for new voice mail.

_Mo._ She must have left a message when she'd called earlier.

Rodel listened as her sister's voice filtered through the speaker, but it wasn't warm and bubbly like every other time they'd spoken since Mo had left for Tanzania. This Mo was tense and tight, and she was speaking in sharp, staccato whispers that Rodel strained to make out.

"Ro, I'm in Kilimani Mall . . . something . . . going down . . . gunmen everywhere . . ." The words were fading in and out, like a bad connection. "I'm hiding . . . there's . . . only thing . . . keeping me . . ." There was a long pause. Rodel could hear hushed voices before Mo came back on the line. " . . . going to wait . . . safe here, but if I don't . . ." Her voice dropped. "If . . . I . . . love you, Ro . . . Mum and Dad . . . don't . . . worry. We'll . . . laugh . . . my crazy stories . . . Australia. I have . . . all the chances, Ro . . ."

The recording ended. And what had started off as the happiest day of Rodel's life trailed off, just like the empty, insidious echo at the end of her sister's call.

Ro . . .

Followed by crackling dead air.

Rodel's mind raced.

Mo had mentioned Australia. She had thought she was going to die then, too, and had called Rodel while crossing a crocodile-infested river in a sinking ferry.

She had been shouting 'Ro, Ro!' but the people on the ferry thought she was telling them to 'Row, row!' The vessel had made it to safety and as Mo collapsed on the shore, the call still in progress, the two of them had laughed with giddy relief.

"Come home, Mo," Rodel had urged.

"I'm not done yet," her sister had replied. "I don't know if I'll ever be done. I want to die doing what I love."

No. I unwish that wish. Rodel clung to her phone, unaware of the invisible threads that connect wishes, actions, people, and consequences. She had no idea that the images flashing across the TV had already set off a chain of events that were heading straight for her, like cascading dominoes set into motion.

Rodel

FOR A FEW blissful seconds before I was fully awake, I forgot. I forgot that Mo was gone, that I was sleeping in her bed, in a strange room, in a strange land, where she'd spent the last few months of her life. But the guttural call of wild pigeons, the rhythmic thud of a hoe outside, the clank of a metal gate opening and closing, all reminded me that it was my first morning in Amosha.

I opened my eyes and stared at the whirring blades of the ceiling fan. Mo had left her mark on it. Bright ribbons left colorful trails as it rotated above me. It was such a vivid, painful reminder of her—her boundless energy, her spinning, kaleidoscopic life—that I felt an acute sense of loss all over again. When you lose someone you love, it doesn't end with that event, or with their funeral, or with their name on the tombstone. You lose them again and again, every day, in small moments that catch you off guard.

Almost a month since her memorial service. I had kept putting off the trip to Africa, to collect her belongings and clear her room.

"Don't go," my mother had said, looking at me through red-rimmed lashes. "There's still a travel warning in effect."

My father stood silently, shoulders hunched, bearing the weight of a man whose daughter's body was never recovered from the wreckage. We had all been denied the gift of closure, of seeing her face for the last time.

"I have to," I replied. I couldn't stand the thought of a stranger going through Mo's things, disposing of pieces of her.

And so I'd arrived, the non-traveler in a family of voyagers, at Nima House in Amosha, where Mo had signed up as a volunteer for six months. It had started out as a romantic quest to climb Mount Kilimanjaro with the love of her life. Well, the love of her life that month. When he refused to share his ration of toilet paper with her, somewhere between 15,000 and 17,000 feet, Mo dumped his arse and trekked back—no toilet paper, and no plane ticket out of there. Our parents offered to bail her out, but Mo wasn't done with Tanzania and talked them into coughing up some cash so she could stay longer. She signed up for an unpaid position, working with kids at an orphanage in return for cheap food, accommodation, and time off to chase waterfalls, flamingos, and herds of gazelles in the Serengeti.

"Do some good, see some action," she'd said, the last time we'd talked, before giving me a detailed account of how loudly and noisily lions mated. "Every fifteen minutes, Ro! Now you know why Mufasa is the motherfucking king of the jungle."

"You're a perv, Mo. You just sat there and watched?"

"Hell, yeah! We had our lunch there too. You need to get your arse down here. Wait till you see an elephant's schlong, Ro . . ."

On and on she had babbled, and I'd only half-listened, not knowing it would be the last time I spoke to her, not knowing that I would be in her room, looking up at the same ceiling fan that she had probably gazed on when she called me.

Except for the last time, when she'd called me from the mall.

When I hadn't picked up.

When she'd needed me the most.

I flipped over to my side, trying to escape the thoughts that kept haunting me.

The bed next to mine was empty and neatly made up. Mo's

roommate, Corinne, was gone. She'd let me in, the night before and hugged me.

"I'm so sorry," she'd said. "She was such an amazing soul."

Having Mo referred to in the past tense was painful. Waking up in her bed was painful. I got up and drew the curtains open. It was later than I had anticipated, but I was still adjusting to the time difference. The cement floor was hard on my feet, so I slipped into Mo's slippers. They were rabbit-faced, with pink-tipped noses, and ears that flip-flopped when I walked.

I stood in the center of the room and looked around. Mo's side had a narrow closet, but the clothes had either slipped off the hangers, or she'd never bothered to put them up.

Probably the latter. I smiled. We were so different, and yet as close as two sisters could be. I could hear her chatter in my head, as I sorted through her things.

Hey, remember when I filled a balloon with glitter and stuffed it in your closet? It popped, and all your clothes were so sparkly that you looked like a disco ball for days.

Thinking of her there beside me, sitting cross-legged on the floor, helped me get through it. It kept me from breaking down as I folded the tops she'd never wear again, her smell still alive in them.

Don't forget the drawer, Ro. I'm so relieved it's you who's doing this. Can you imagine Mum finding that dildo? I kind of debated about it myself, but it's so realistic, you know? You should totally get one, dude. No Mufasa? No worries . . .

And so the day progressed, with Mo's commentary flitting through my head, like a butterfly that went from flower to flower, saying goodbye as the sun dimmed over the horizon.

It was late afternoon when I stood back and surveyed the room. Mo's side was all boxed up, except for a map on her wall with Post-it notes in her careless, cursive writing, and the ribbons she had tied around the fan. I couldn't bring myself to remove those. Besides, I had three more weeks before I headed back to England. I wanted to see the places she'd mentioned, understand the magic that drove her, find some resolution in the place that had claimed her.

Kilimani Mall was still a wide, gaping hole in the ground, but the civilians had been collateral damage. The gunmen's target had been a government minister who was speaking at a convention that day. His security team was moving him to safety when a car bomb exploded, killing them all. It had gone off in the underground parking lot, and large parts of the mall had collapsed. No one had claimed responsibility, and investigators were still sifting through the rubble. It was one of those tragic, senseless things, like when a sinkhole appears without warning and swallows up your car, your home, the people you love. There's no one to blame for it, so you carry your pain and anger with you, all the while waiting for an epiphany, a kernel of understanding that would help you move on, because surely it all *meant* something.

I sank on the bed and hugged Mo's pillow, wishing I could feel her arms around me. Something solid slid beneath my fingers. I slipped my hand under the cover and pulled out an eyeglass case. Her spare pair was still in there—orange cat-eye frames. Mo had a habit of stashing things in her pillowcase. I was surprised I hadn't discovered them the night before. Then again, I had been too overwhelmed to notice.

"I wish you could see the world through my eyes," she'd say to me, whenever I couldn't understand the allure of her lifestyle.

Well, here I am, Mo. I put on her glasses and scanned the room through the distorted lens of her frames.

The sun was setting and its golden light filled the room, falling on the wall. The metal tacks that held the map over her desk shone like the glitter Mo had spewed all over my clothes.

I got up and traced my fingers over the yellow Post-its she had stuck on it. Taking off her glasses, I leaned closer to read them.

April 14—Miriamu (Noni)

May 2—Huzuni (Pendo)

June 12—Javex (Kabula)

July 17—Juma (Baraka)

Aug 29—Sumuni (Maymosi)

Sept 1—Furaha (Magesa)

The notes were strange and hard to decipher. The first three were crossed out with black ink. They were scattered around the map, some close to Amosha, some farther away.

"Wow. You got a lot done," said Corinne, as she entered the room and tossed her bag onto her bed. "Have you been cooped up in here all day?"

I looked down at myself. I was still in my pajamas.

"Did you get anything to eat?" she asked.

I shook my head, realizing that the last thing I'd had was a snack on the plane.

"How are you Mo's sister? We called her Woe-Mo when she hadn't eaten. She got real mean when she was hungry." Corinne steered me toward the bathroom. "Freshen up so we can grab some dinner."

I stared at my reflection as I brushed my hair. The warm chestnut waves parted naturally to one side and swept softly across my forehead. My eyes still held that startled look people get when you snatch something away from them, something precious. They seemed a darker brown, as if the pupils had opened wide and remained that way. Mo had looked like that when she was excited about something, although her eyes had been far from plain brown. They reminded me of warm driftwood and golden sand. Our parents had named us aptly. Mo was the laid-back heat of the Caribbean, the cool, carefree beat of reggae. I was quiet inlets and ancient mountains. I didn't dress too bright or speak too loud. I was more comfortable blending into the background. My averageness made it easy. Average height, average weight, average job, average life.

It didn't take long to change into a pair of jeans and a long-sleeved T-shirt. Corinne gave me a quick tour of the place. The Nima House volunteers' compound was located away from the orphanage, with modest rooms that opened to a shared courtyard.

The other volunteers were already gathered around a long table outside.

"You have to try the *wali* and *maharagwe*," said Corinne, as we joined them. She ladled my plate with rice and what looked like bean stew.

"Don't let the Swahili fool you," someone piped in. "She's just reading it off the board."

"I'm trying to make a good impression." Corinne sat down beside me. "I'm sorry, I forgot to introduce you. You guys, this is Mo's sister, Rodel."

There was a noticeable lull in the conversation before everyone started talking all at once.

"Hey, so sorry."

"It's quiet around here without her."

"I still can't believe she's gone."

They shared their stories of Mo. They had all signed on for different terms, some for a couple of weeks, others—like Mo—for the full six months. It was a small, informal group from all over place. Corinne was from Nigeria. The guy next to me was German. A couple of them had traveled from towns that were not too far from Amosha. Not everyone spoke English or Swahili, but somehow, everyone understood each other. My heart grew full as I listened to all the ways they remembered my sister: sweet, adventurous, loud, bold.

"She was freaking hot," said one of the guys before someone kicked him in the shin.

It wasn't until Corinne and I were back in our room that I realized just how exhausted I was. I was always on edge when I traveled. That, combined with an emotional roller coaster of a day had me yearning to sink into bed. But I had one more thing to cross off my list.

"Corinne?" I said. "What do these notes mean?" I pointed to the Post-its on the map.

"Oh, those." She stood next to me, surveying them. "Mo worked with at-risk children in her spare time. She picked up a kid from one of these places every month and got them to a safe place. See, she's listed the date she was expected there, the name of the child, and this here, in brackets, is the name of the place. She was aiming to round up six kids in six months. She did the first three." Corinne pointed to the ones that had been crossed out.

"What about the rest? Who's going to look after them?"

"I guess the guy she was working with. Gabriel something. One of the locals. Nima House has nothing to do with it. It's already at full capacity. It doesn't have the resources to look after the kids they were rounding up."

"So where were they taking them?"

"I'm not sure. Mo might have mentioned it, but I don't recall." Corinne crawled into bed. "Goodnight, Rodel. Try to get some sleep."

I turned off the light and slipped under the covers. The ceiling fan turned slowly over me. I could barely make out the ribbons in the dark. My mind was filled with all the bits and pieces I'd learned about Mo. While I had been looking for heroes in books, my sister had been one—a silent, probably accidental one, who would have gagged if anyone had referred to her as one. She wasn't out to save anyone. She was just greedy for life—for fun, for food, for colors, for experiences. She couldn't see past what was directly in front of her, and she only did the things that made her happy, but that made her even more of a hero to me.

I thought of the notes that she had not been able to cross off the map—the part of her that remained undone—and resolved to fulfill her wish. Six kids in six months. That's what she'd aimed for. There were still three kids left.

I'm going to get them for you, Mo. I'm going to cross off every one of the notes before I head back home.

I PAUSED AT the foot of the palatial stairs that led up to The Grand Tulip, a legendary hotel in Amosha, known for its tradition of hosting discerning celebrities. I was still jittery after taking a local mini-bus, a *dala dala*, to get there, but it was where Corinne had sent me. She didn't know Gabriel's last name—the man my sister had been working with—but she knew where he lived.

And no, it was not at The Grand Tulip.

It was in a village on the outskirts of Amosha.

"You could take a *dala dala* there, but they're kind of chaotic and not too safe —okay for a quick hop on and off. To get to Gabriel's place, I would recommend getting a driver," said Corinne. "I've used one a couple of times. His name is Bahati. He doesn't venture too far out of town, but he knows the area and he's fluent in English. He's usually at The Grand Tulip in the mornings."

So there I was, climbing the stairs to the grand dame of hotels. Massive pillars that resembled giant, gnarled trees supported the shaded entrance at the top. Two uniformed men guarded the open lobby, but what caught my eye was the life-sized statue of a Maasai warrior, set against the stark, white expanse of the outside wall.

It stood in a proud pose, spear in hand, hair embellished with ochre mud. The ebony wood had been polished so smooth that his skin looked like it was smeared with animal fat. His red toga billowed and flapped in the wind. He looked like a young biblical prophet in a time that had moved on, like something that belonged in a museum.

I moved closer, examining the fine details—the red and blue beads that adorned his body, the eyelashes with tips so fine, they caught the morning sun. I pulled out my camera and framed his face.

"Eight thousand shillings," he said.

"What?" I jumped back.

"To take a picture."

"You're real!"

"Yes, Miss. I make it six thousand shillings for you."

"That's okay," I said, backing off.

"You are from England? I can tell from your accent. Two pounds sterling. Cheaper than a Starbucks coffee."

"No thanks. I'm actually looking for someone. His name is Bahati. Do you know him?"

"A thousand shillings. I'll take you to him."

"Never mind." I shook my head and walked away. He was obviously a hustler. "Excuse me," I said to the doormen. "Do either of you know where I can find Bahati?"

They exchanged a glance and then pointed behind me.

You have got to be kidding me. I turned around slowly.

Sure enough. The Maasai was grinning at me.

"You found me. Commission-free. You are a smart haggler. What can I do for you?"

"I was looking for a driver, but it's okay. I changed my mind." I started walking down the stairs.

"My friend. My friend!" he called after me, but I didn't look back.

Great. I thought. *I'll have to take the dreaded* dala dala *all the way to Gabriel's village.*

I trekked a dusty twenty minutes back to the bus stop. It was a dizzy cacophony of charter buses, tour operators waving maps in my face, and people wanting to sell me bracelets, bananas, and roasted corn.

The street resembled an orchestra between motorcycles, cars, and *dala dalas,* all going at different speeds—starting and stopping with no order or warning. Conductors hung out of minivans shouting their destinations, slapping the side of the van when they wanted the driver to stop for passengers. Each *dala dala* was brightly painted with a decal or slogan, honoring some type of celebrity. Beyonce, Obama, Elvis. I waited for the call to Gabriel's village, Rutema, but none of them were going that way.

"My friend. I found you!" A 4x4 screeched to a halt beside me, narrowly missing a man on a bicycle. The driver was wearing a crisp white shirt, sleeves rolled up, and aviator shades that reflected my frazzled face. "It's me." He removed his glasses and shot me a cheeky grin.

Bahati.

"What happened to your . . . costume?" I shouted over the honking.

"It's not a costume. I am a real Maasai."

"Your hair is gone too?"

"The braids? They are extensions. I dress up for the tourists. They take pictures with me. I am also a tour guide, but it's all temporary. I am really an actor—an action hero—waiting for my break. One day, you will see me on the big screen. But that is for the future. You said you were looking for a driver. Where do you want to go?"

"Rutema," I replied.

"Get in. I'll take you there."

"How much?" I asked, narrowing my eyes.

"For you, same price as the *dala dala.*"

I hesitated. I wasn't one to hop into a car with a stranger, let alone a stranger in a whole different part of the world.

Someone pinched my bum. It could have been the old woman trying to sell me the bracelets. I didn't check. I hopped into Bahati's car as a conductor with a megaphone blared something in my ear.

"You know Corinne from Nima House?" I said. "She told me to come see you."

I have friends, buster, and they know where I am.

"I know Miss Corinne. She gave you good advice. I am an excellent driver." Bahati made a sharp left, while I clutched the dashboard with white knuckles.

"You have no seat belts?" I reached for mine but came up empty-handed.

"No one wears seat belts around here." He laughed. "Don't worry. You are in good hands. I have an impeccable record. No accidents."

I watched as two pedestrians swerved out of the way just in time to avoid being clipped by him.

"You didn't tell me your name, Miss . . . ?" He left the question hanging.

"It's Rodel."

"Miss Rodel, you are lucky I found you or you would be on that." He pointed to the *dala dala* overtaking us. "Most of these mini-vans are supposed to hold ten people. If there aren't at least twenty, it isn't a real *dala*. If you're comfortable, it's not a real *dala*. The driver has absolute authority. Never ask him to turn down the music. Never expect him to stop where you're supposed to get off. Never make fun of all the pictures on his visor. Once you step out of the *dala*, you waive all your rights. He can run you over, take off with your other foot in his van, your luggage, your—"

"I get it. I'm better off with you."

"Absolutely. And I offer many special packages. Packed lunch. Banana beer. Free African massage. No. Not that kind of massage, my friend. I mean this, see?" He glanced my way as we bounced over a pothole-riddled street. "African massage. Hehe. It's good, no? You will leave me a review? I have a 4.5-star rating on—"

"Bahati?"

"Yes, Miss?"

"You talk too much."

"No, Miss. I only give you important information. Today is a good day to go to Rutema. Tomorrow there is rain. The roads get very muddy. I am happy we are going today. Tomorrow I would have to charge you extra for a car wash. For Suzi, my car." He thumped the steering wheel. "She likes to keep clean. But if you want to go tomorrow, that is okay, too. I have an umbrella in the trunk. It is from The Grand Tulip. Very big, very good. Oprah Winfrey used it. You will see the logo. The Grand Tulip logo, not Oprah's. They gave it to me because—"

"Today is fine. Isn't that where we're headed?"

"Yes, yes. That is where I am taking you. You already told me. Did you forget? That's okay. I have a good memory. But I don't understand why you want to go there. There is nothing to see. If you ask me, you should go to . . ."

We passed bustling markets and colonial buildings that stood like stubborn, dusty historians among the modern shops. Bahati droned on as we left Amosha and followed a dirt road through small farms and traditional homesteads. He trailed off on a hill with sweeping views of the area and stopped the car.

"Look," he said, pointing beyond the canyons, to the horizon.

Rising above the clouds, like an ethereal crown of glory against the jewel-blue sky, was the snow-capped dome of Kilimanjaro. I had imagined its vast splendor whenever Mo talked about it, but nothing had prepared me for my first sighting of its lofty, powdered peaks.

Bahati seemed to share my sense of awe. For a few moments, there was a lull in his commentary. He had no words to share with me, no litany of facts to impress me. We gazed at the surreal giant that loomed in the distance, towering majestically over the golden plains of the African Savannah.

"Why do you want to visit Rutema?" asked Bahati, once we were back on the road. "It is just a bunch of local homes and a few shops."

"I'm looking for a friend of my sister's." I explained what had brought me to Amosha, and why I needed Gabriel's help.

"I am sorry to hear about your sister. It was a terrible thing," he said. "This man—Gabriel—you don't know his last name?"

"No. Just that he and my sister worked together."

"Don't worry, Miss Rodel. We will find him."

It was a simple reassurance, but I was grateful for it.

As we entered Rutema, barefoot children raced behind us on the dusty street, chanting, *"Mzungu! Mzungu!"*

"What are they saying?" I asked Bahati.

"Mzungu means a white person. They are not used to seeing many tourists around here." He parked the jeep under a ficus tree. A group of grease-stained men were working on a tractor beneath it, muttering like surgeons around a patient. "I will ask them if they know Gabriel."

The kids encircled our car as Bahati talked to the men. They gawked and giggled. "Scholastica, Scholastica!" they shouted, pointing at me.

I had no idea what that meant, but they disappeared when Bahati returned and shooed them away.

"Lucky for you, there is only one Gabriel in the village with a *mzungu* lady friend. But he travels a lot, and they haven't seen him for a while. His family lives over there." He motioned to a large compound. It seemed out of place amongst the row of small huts. A perimeter of walls with sharp, broken glass, set into the mortar at the top, surrounded it.

My heart sank. I had not considered the possibility that Gabriel might not be around. "Can we go ask when he'll be back?"

We honked at the gate and waited. The men stopped working on the tractor and watched us with curiosity. A woman wearing a dress made of colorful, local *kitenge* fabric came out to greet us. She spoke to Bahati in Swahili, through the metal bars, but her eyes kept drifting back to me.

"You are Mo's sister?" she asked.

"Yes. My name is Rodel."

"I'm happy to see you. *Karibu.* Welcome," she said, unlocking the gate. "I am Gabriel's sister, Anna." Her smile was warm, but her eyes held ghosts. She was beautiful in the quiet way that people with broken hearts are. She led us into a courtyard with fruit trees and a small play area for kids. An empty swing creaked, still swaying, as if it had been hastily abandoned.

Inside, the curtains were drawn—a shame, because it was such a beautiful, sunny day. Boxes lay scattered on the floor, some empty, some taped shut.

"I am sorry to hear about your sister," said Anna, after we were seated.

"Thank you," I replied. "I don't want to take up too much of your time. I was wondering if you could tell me how to get a hold of your brother."

"I wish I knew," she said, staring down at her hands. "I haven't heard from him in a while. He's never been gone this long. I'm afraid he's not coming back. Or worse, that something bad has happened to him."

"Something bad?" I looked from her to Bahati, but he was staring over my shoulder at something behind me.

I turned and saw a girl standing by the back entrance. Her dark silhouette was outlined against the light streaming in through the open door. She seemed around six or seven years old, but her posture was stiff and wary, as if she was unsure whether she should come in.

"It's okay, Scholastica," said Anna. She switched to Swahili and coaxed the child to come inside.

When the girl stepped into the light, I flinched. It might have been the unexpectedness of it, the shock of seeing a pale ghost appear out of the shadows in broad daylight. Her skin was a strange shade of white, with patches of pink where the sun had touched it. She looked at us through otherworldly eyes—milky and blue. Her hair was shorn close to the scalp, a muted shade of blonde, but without the softness or delicacy. The absence of color was jarring, like a painting robbed of pigment. I had seen people with albinism before, but this girl had scabs all over her lips and face, like little black flies feasting on her. I couldn't help the shudder that ran through me, though it was Scholastica who visibly shrank away from me, from the knee-jerk response that she was no doubt familiar with. Disgust. Horror. Revulsion.

I averted my gaze, ashamed of myself. She was just a little girl, born without color.

"This is Gabriel's daughter," Anna told us. "She doesn't speak English. Gabriel stopped sending her to school because they can't promise her safety, so she stays home with me."

I nodded, thinking of the kids chanting, 'Scholastica, Scholastica!' when they'd seen me. To them, she probably looked more like me than them. As a teacher, I was well aware of how kids could gang up and react to something they didn't understand.

"She's sensitive to the sun, but I can't keep her indoors all day." Anna touched her niece's face. "These are scabbed-over sunburns." Her voice quaked when she spoke again. "I want you to take her with you."

"I'm sorry?" I leaned forward, convinced I must have heard wrong.

"Your sister helped Gabriel get albino children to the orphanage in Wanza. They have a school there, for kids like Scholastica, a place where she'll be safe, where she doesn't have to feel like she's any different."

"You want to send her away? To an orphanage?" I was astounded. "Shouldn't you discuss this with Gabriel first?"

"Gabriel has been gone too long this time. He said we were going to move to Wanza when he got back." Anna's chin trembled, and she took a deep breath. "I can't look after Scholastica alone. I have two children of my own. Gabriel took us in and rented a bigger place when my husband and I divorced. Without him, I can't afford to pay the rent. I just received an eviction notice." She gestured to the boxes around us. "I have to move, and once we leave this compound . . . Bahati, you understand, don't you? Tell her to take Scholastica to the orphanage."

At the mention of her name, Scholastica looked from her aunt to Bahati.

She has no idea what we're talking about, I thought.

"The orphanage in Wanza—that's the place Mo was taking all the kids?" I asked.

"Gabriel was taking them. He asked Mo to help him get them there. They had an arrangement. Gabriel offered to drive Mo anywhere she wanted to go—the national parks, lakes, lodges—for free. In return, Mo passed the kids off as her own."

"I don't understand. Mo passed the kids off as her own?" I asked.

"Albino children stick out in Africa. They are special. Different. There are people who would not hesitate to pick on them or harm them. When you put a big hat and the right clothes on these kids, you can fool people into thinking they are tourists—at least from a distance. It is much easier when people think they're seeing a *mzungu* mother and a *mzungu* child, traveling with a local guide. Once a month, Mo ensured safe passage for one of the kids that Gabriel tracked down, and Gabriel returned the favor by showing her around."

"But now he's missing," I said. "Have you reported it to the police?"

"Yes, but there are many men who leave for the city and never return. They think Gabriel abandoned us."

"Is that a possibility?"

"I don't know. I don't think so. He wouldn't just leave Scholastica like this. Her mother left after she was born. She wanted to give her away because she believed albino children are cursed, but Gabriel wouldn't have any of it. If you could get Scholastica to Wanza, I'd feel so much better, at least until I'm more settled. When Gabriel resurfaces, he will know where to find her."

It was all too much to absorb. I had come to Rutema on a simple mission: to find the man I thought was helping my sister. Instead, I was the one being asked for help.

"I'm sorry, but without your brother, I'm in a bind myself. I came looking for him because my sister left the names of three other children who need to get there. I can't help them, or you, on my own." I felt like crap. I didn't like the shame and guilt that crawled under my skin every time Scholastica looked at me. She was sitting on the floor, by Anna's feet, tugging on the edges of her skirt to cover her toes. I assumed it was a habit, from having to protect herself from the sun every day.

"What about you?" Anna asked Bahati. "You can't take Miss Rodel to Wanza?"

"To get to Wanza, we'd have to cross Maasai land, and I don't go there."

"Why not?" Anna appraised his tall, lanky frame. "Aren't you Maasai?"

"Yes, but my people have disowned me. I have no wish to see them." Bahati's jaw clamped, signaling the end of the conversation.

Anna stroked Scholastica's hair absently. She had a faraway look in her eyes, part despair, part resignation.

"I know someone who might be able to help," said Bahati, after a while. "He is also *mzungu*, but his family has lived in Tanzania for three generations. His grandfather was a British soldier, stationed here during the Second World War. Maybe Miss Rodel can convince him to get Scholastica and the other kids to Wanza."

They looked at me expectantly—both Bahati and Anna.

"How much do you think he would charge for it?" I asked. I had limited resources. My bank account was dry after I'd made the down payment on the cottage, and the trip had drained the rest of it.

"Oh, he wouldn't do it for the money. He has a coffee farm, one of the largest estates in the area. He's a big man—not the kind of person anyone would want to mess with. And he has a big heart. You and the kids would be in good hands."

"What's his name?"

"Jack," replied Bahati. "Jack Warden."

The name hung suspended in the air between us, like a bridge waiting for me to cross over. I got the sense that if I did, there would be no turning back. I would be bound by whatever I decided in the next few seconds. I felt the weight of the moment as the clock on the wall ticked on steadily.

"What about Scholastica?" I asked, indicating the little girl whose head was bowed as she traced invisible patterns on the floor. "Doesn't she have a say in any of this?"

"Gabriel promised to take her to Wanza so she could be with kids just like herself. She's always wanted to go to. She misses her father, but if I tell her that he will meet up with her there, she will go."

Scholastica looked up at me then. It was as if she sensed we were talking about her. I saw myself walking out into the sun, leaving her there, making patterns on the pale cement floor, with all the curtains drawn.

"I'll do it," I said.

"Bless you!" Anna clasped her hands over mine.

Bahati was not as enthusiastic. "Are you sure you want to do this?" His face was different, like he was once more that solemn statue, carved out of wood, spear in hand.

"How hard can it be? Getting a bunch of kids to Wanza?" I had promised to cross the remaining names off Mo's notes, and that's exactly what I was going to do. "Anna, get Scholastica's things ready. We are going to see Jack Warden."

3

BY THE TIME we reached Jack Warden's place, it was late afternoon. Stone pillars etched with the words "Kaburi Estate" led us down a winding, bumpy road to the main building—a white-washed manor surrounded by green gorges, banana groves, and endless rows of berry-laden coffee plants. It stood like a rebel, in the shadow of the mighty Kilimanjaro, with electric blue shutters that stood out against the dark clouds now gathering in the sky.

"I thought you told me there would be no rain today, Bahati," I said, as I got out of the car. "Looks like a storm is coming."

"I told her to dance up a storm." It was a man's voice, deep and rumbling, like low thunder. But there was no sign of him.

"It's Jack." Bahati tilted his head toward the covered porch. "Come. I will introduce you."

"No. You stay in the car with Scholastica. I'll go talk to him." I didn't want to drag Scholastica into the situation until I had spoken to Jack myself.

Lightning split the sky as I stepped onto the veranda. "Jack Warden?" I asked the man who was sitting on a kiwi green porch swing.

He didn't respond. It was as if he hadn't heard me. He was holding his phone out, eyes trained on the horizon, recording something. The storm. The lightning. When the thunder hit, he got up and walked to the railing, still recording.

He stood tall and rawboned against the rolling expanse of the farm—square faced and square shouldered—wearing a dark hooded sweatshirt and dusty work pants. He had the kind of beard I imagined would grow on a man if he hibernated all winter. It was shorter around the side and fuller on his chin. His hair was thick and tawny—darker at the roots, with ends that were bleached blond from the sun. It hung around his shoulders, wild and forgotten, like a jungle of beautiful chaos.

As the first drops of rain started falling, he tucked his phone away and braced the railing, staring up at the sky. I was about to try to get his attention again when he started laughing.

"I told her to dance up a storm," he repeated, but he wasn't saying it to me. He was talking to himself.

He held his hands out, letting the water slip through his fingers, and he laughed again. It was a heavy, heaving laughter with big, gasping breaths in-between, unlike anything I'd heard before. Then the gasps grew louder, longer, and I realized why it sounded so odd. I had never heard someone laughing in pain, and Jack Warden was doubled over with it, weeping and laughing in the same breath.

"Jack?" I called again. "Are you okay?"

He whipped around, seeing me for the first time. I sensed all the loose, unraveled threads of him getting reeled back into his core. It happened so quickly, I felt like I was facing a different man: detached and emotionless—every nuance, every expression locked away. The air around him crackled, as if he had just thrown up an electric fence. Against the backdrop of dark, stormy clouds, he stood like Thor, glaring at me with lightning in his eyes.

"Who are you?" he asked.

"I'm . . ." I trailed off, knowing that I had just intruded on a very private, unguarded moment. That was the only reason he was eyeing me like that, like he was about to chew me up and spit me out. "My name is Rodel Emerson."

"What do you want?" He kept his eyes trained on me.

Cat eyes, I recalled Mo saying, from some unbidden memory. *Because cats don't hide their utter hatred and disdain for all mankind.* I had laughed then because it had been funny, but I wasn't laughing now. I was miserable and self-conscious, wishing I'd opted for something more substantial than a gauzy top and washed out jeans.

"Maybe this isn't the best time," I said. "I'll come back tomorrow."

"And tomorrow will be better because . . . ?"

He took a step toward me, and my first instinct was to turn and run. But this wasn't about me. It was about Mo, Scholastica, and the other kids. Still, I hated that I needed anyone to do what I had to do, man or woman.

"I need your help getting some kids to Wanza," I said.

"You need my help," he said slowly, chewing on the words. He turned around and called to no one in particular, "She needs *my* help." Then he started laughing. Not the gut-wrenching type of laughter like before, but mirthless, without any humor.

"Get off my property," he said. "You're trespassing. You're also barking up the wrong tree. I am in no position to help you or anyone else. And more importantly, I don't care to."

"You're Jack Warden, right?" I held my ground. I had promised Anna I'd get Scholastica to Wanza. I wasn't about to crumble at the first sign of a challenge.

"I am." He straightened to his full height, and I was tempted to take a step back. Holy crap, he was a big man.

"Then you're the man who is going to get me to Wanza."

"And why exactly should I give a fuck about you? Or Wanza?"

I stared at him, the schoolteacher in me wanting to reprimand him for his manners, his uncalled-for attitude. He hadn't even bothered to listen to what I had to say.

"You hear that?" he said, cupping his hand to his ear. "That silence is exactly how many fucks I give."

My face burned a bright red. "You know what? Whatever was tearing you up earlier, you damn well deserve it." I pivoted on my heel and marched into the pouring rain, water running down my hot, inflamed cheeks.

"Let's go, Bahati." I slammed the car door shut. "I'll have to figure out some other way."

But Bahati was looking at the man staring into the rain. "Something is not right with his eyes, Miss Ro. That is not the Jack Warden I know."

"Well, it's the Jack Warden that I talked to. And he's a . . ." I bit back the words even though Scholastica wouldn't understand me. "Let's just go."

We were almost at the gates when a red jeep, going the other way nearly careened into us. Bahati slammed on the brakes and we skidded to a halt barely a few feet from it. The other driver pounded on the horn, a loud, blaring, continuous beep.

"Crazy lady," mumbled Bahati, as he put the car in reverse. It was a one-lane road, and she was bearing down on us, giving us no choice but to back-up as she advanced.

The rain was coming down in sheets and I could barely make out the road as Bahati reversed the car to the main building. But instead of parking, the jeep kept coming at us until we were backed up in a tight corner. The driver got out and rapped on Bahati's window.

"Where do you think you're going in this god-awful weather, young man? Driving like a maniac on that washed-out road?" She peered into the car, raindrops trickling down her plastic hood. She must have been at least ninety, but her blue eyes shone bright and clear.

Bahati and I exchanged a look. She was the one that had come barreling at us like a bat out of hell.

"With a lady and a child, no less," she continued, looking at Scholastica and me. I had to hand it to her. She didn't bat a wrinkled eye at the girl's appearance. Then again, given her age, she'd probably seen it all.

"Get out. All of you." She clapped her hands and made for the house, leaving her car parked exactly where it was.

"That's Goma, Jack's grandmother," Bahati explained. "You can't argue with her."

We made a beeline for the porch, our shoes squelching in the mud. I was relieved that Jack was gone. The screen door shut behind Goma as Bahati, Scholastica, and I shivered in our wet clothes, under the awning.

"Well? Are you coming in or should I send my homing pigeons to deliver an invitation?" Goma hollered from inside.

We stepped into a charming living area with large windows, plump sofas and faded pine floors. The house was as eccentric as the lady who had invited us in—a blend of colonial design and African heritage, with mismatched pieces and earthy textures.

Goma was standing in the middle of the room, trousers around her ankles, stepping out of her soggy clothes. Bahati and I averted our gazes while Scholastica watched with wide eyes.

"Brave girl," said Goma. "Not afraid of old skin. You don't speak English, do you?" She switched to Swahili and soon Scholastica was giggling. "Come on." She held a hand out to her. "Let's get you some dry clothes."

I snuck a peek out of the corner of my eye, relieved that Goma had left her underwear on. They returned, wearing colorful muumuus—long, loose dresses that covered them from head to foot.

"I make these out of *kitenge*. You'll never want to wear those jeans again," said Goma, handing me a muumuu.

Bahati looked at her like she'd lost her mind when she gave him a green and yellow one.

"Oh, go on." She shoved it into his hands. "You're dripping water all over my floors."

They faced each other for a few seconds, battling silently. Then Bahati snatched the muumuu from her.

"Bathroom's over there." She inclined her head and watched as he ambled towards it, his feet shuffling like he was heading off to a sacrificial altar.

"I'm Katherine Warden," she said, turning to me. "Everyone calls me Goma."

"Rodel Emerson." I shook her gnarled hand. "And this is Scholastica."

"Rodel and Scholastica," she repeated, looking at us with curious eyes. "So what brings you here?"

I explained the situation as concisely as I could.

"I'm sorry Jack was so rude to you," she said, when I was done. "It appears you are both bound by the events of a tragic afternoon. Jack hasn't been the same since he lost Li—" She stopped as Bahati returned, wearing the muumuu. It barely skimmed past his knees.

Goma pinched Scholastica—a quick, sharp nip on the back of her hand to stop her from giggling. Bahati in a muumuu was a very quiet man, nothing like the Bahati who rattled on and on.

"Excuse me." I needed to get out of there before Goma pinched me too. "I think I'll go change."

When I came back, they were all in the kitchen—Bahati and Scholastica huddled around the table, while Goma ladled hot soup into their bowls.

"You can hang those up in the laundry," she said, pointing to the wet bundle rolled up in my arms.

The rain was still falling hard as I made my way down the hallway to the laundry room. I found some clothes pegs and was hanging up my things when lightning illuminated the back of the house. I thought I saw Jack momentarily through the window, standing outside in the middle of a full-fledged tropical storm. I was about to chalk it up to my imagination when another flash lit him up again. He was just standing there, under a tree that looked like it was hundreds of years old, staring at the ground, while the rain whipped hell and fury all around him.

"I think Jack is still outside," I said when I stepped into the kitchen.

Goma nodded and continued having her soup. "He does that. Sits with her whenever there's a storm." She pushed a bowl toward me. "Eat."

"Sits with who?" I asked, taking the chair across from her.

"Lily. His daughter. She's buried out there. They all are. This place sure lived up to its name."

"Kaburi Estate?" I recalled the sign at the entrance.

"Yes. It was supposed to be Karibu Estate. *Karibu* means welcome, but I was still learning Swahili back then and I wrote *Kaburi* on the work order. It means a grave. Sam—my husband—thought it was hilarious. He refused to correct it. He always said he'd love me to his grave." Goma stared into her bowl. "And so he did. He loved me to the end."

I sensed the beginning of an epic love story, the kind I was always hungry for, but she didn't say anything more. She just smiled wistfully and swirled her spoon around the bowl in little circles.

"Should we . . . should someone go get Jack?" I asked as lightning pierced the sky again. I was starting to feel terrible about what I'd said to him.

"He'll come in when he's done. And he'll keep doing it, until one day, he doesn't need to anymore. It's what you're doing too, aren't you? Miles from home. Mourning your sister in your own way. You've got to let it run its course. Give in until it's spent and quiet, until you've learned to breathe through the loss."

I had a spoonful of my soup and thought about what she'd

said. Mo's death was like a door that had been sealed shut forever. I could never walk through it, never listen to her go on about all the inconsequential things that I missed so terribly now. There is an invisible threshold of possibilities when someone is alive. It contracts when they're gone, swallowing up all the worlds that hover around them—names of people they'd never meet, faces of kids they'd never have, flavors of ice cream they'd never taste. Losing Mo hurt like hell, but I couldn't imagine what it would feel like to lose a child.

"I thought I told you to leave."

I jumped at the sound of Jack's voice. He was drenched to the core, standing by the back door in a puddle of water. The hoodie was gone and his T-shirt was molded to the kind of muscles that came with hard, physical labor. We were high up at the foot of the mountain, where the air held a touch of frost in the evenings, but he showed no sign of being cold. Perhaps that was the point— standing in the rain past the point of numbness.

"I invited them in," said Goma.

Jack followed her eyes and noticed Bahati for the first time.

"*Habari*, Jack," said Bahati.

Jack nodded in acknowledgment. He had no reaction to seeing a muumuu-clad man at his grandmother's table. Then his eyes fell on Scholastica, and everything changed. If he had been harsh with me before, he was positively hostile toward her. His hands clenched into tight fists by his sides, hackles rising until the air bristled with unspoken tension.

"That's Lily's," he growled.

"So it is." Goma didn't seem perturbed by his reaction. "Scholastica needed a change of clothes, so I gave her Lily's dress."

Jack's jaw clenched, like he had just stopped himself from biting someone's head off. Scholastica huddled closer to Goma, shriveling under his biting glare.

"I think we should go now," I said to Bahati. I had no idea if they'd let Scholastica board with me at the volunteer's hostel until I figured something out. All I knew was that I didn't like the way Jack Warden made me feel. I was used to constants with people—a nice, smooth line, with maybe a few blips here and there. But with Jack, it was like a polygraph test gone wild, the recording needle jumping all over the place. I went hopeful to insulted, from being sympathetic about his loss to infuriated by his attitude.

"No one's going anywhere in this weather. In case you haven't been listening to the forecast, the storm isn't going to clear any time soon," said Goma. "There are no streetlights for miles and the roads are treacherous in the rain. Besides, you have Scholastica to think about."

"I'm sure the hostel can accommodate her for one night," I replied. "I can call ahead and—"

"That's not what I—"

"It's not safe," Jack declared. "You leave in the morning."

I stared at him in silence. What made him think he had the right to call the shots on what I did? Or when? Maybe if he'd said it differently, like he gave a damn, I would have considered it, but he clearly didn't want us there, and I wasn't about to accept any grand favors from him.

"You can't make that decision for us." I lifted my chin and met his gaze.

His eyes narrowed, but he didn't say anything. I was pretty sure I was seconds from combusting into a pile of smoldering ash when his scrutiny shifted.

"Bahati." He held out his hand. "Keys."

Bahati cast a furtive glance at me, but he clearly didn't want to lock horns with Jack.

The keys disappeared as Jack closed his fingers over them and slid them into his pocket. "You leave in the morning." He looked pointedly at me.

"Well. It's settled then." Goma shot me an expression that left no room for protest. She got up and filled a bowl of soup for Jack. "Now sit down and have a bite to eat."

"Later. I'm going to take a shower," he announced, peeling off his T-shirt and wiping his face with it. He was tanned all over, with no lines marking his skin, except for the dark cuts sculpting his washboard abs. He started heading upstairs and then turned around. Trickles of water ran down his back from hair that was still glistening from the rain. "Bahati, come with me. I have something you can borrow. You need to get out of that . . . *thing.*"

Bahati glared at Goma before following Jack out.

"What?" She glared back. "You wear that tribal robe all the time. Same thing, just with sleeves."

"You know Bahati?" I asked, when the men were gone.

"Yes. Anyone who's been to The Grand Tulip knows him. Jack used to take his wife there on weekends—his ex-wife, Sarah. She wasn't made for life out here. They met while Jack was studying in Kenya. The farm seemed like a romantic notion to her then, but once she got here, it drove her nuts. She missed the shops and restaurants. The spa at The Grand Tulip was her favorite haunt, so Jack drove her to town whenever he could. He'd take her to see a show afterward. Sometimes they stayed over. He ran into Bahati there. The staff there is nice, but they all make fun of him. He stands out front like a brave warrior, but he'll squeal if a ladybug lands on him. He's the first to abandon post at the slightest hint of trouble. They laugh because, in spite of all that, he wants to be an action hero. Not Jack. Back then he was all about chasing your passion. He took one look at Bahati and told him he wasn't qualified. The Maasai walk everywhere, but that wasn't going to cut it. How was he going to handle a high-speed car chase, if he broke out in hives at the thought of getting behind the wheel? So, while

Sarah was getting her massages, Jack taught Bahati how to drive."

"I don't know if I'd be taking credit for that," I mumbled, thinking of my white-knuckled ride with him.

"What's that?"

I shook my head and looked around. "You have a lovely home. I hope we're not imposing."

"Not at all. I can't remember the last time we had company. It's just Jack and me in this big old place. Sarah moved back to Cape Town many years ago. They divorced when Lily was a few years old. I can't tell you how much I looked forward to having her over. I miss her dearly, and having a little one under our roof again makes me happy." She wiggled her finger at Scholastica, "We have lots of spare rooms. You can take your pick." She pointed me down the hall. "There's a linen closet on the left with bed sheets and extra towels. Help yourself."

"Thank you," I replied. "Would it be all right if I made a quick call? I need to let my friend know not to expect me tonight."

"Of course." Goma waved me in the direction of the living room.

There was an old-school rotary phone on the console. I dialed the number to Nima House and asked for Corinne.

"Where are you?" she asked.

"At Kaburi Estate."

"Where?"

"It's a coffee farm, run by Jack Warden and his grandmother. I couldn't get a hold of Gabriel. Bahati said Jack might be able to help."

"Jack Warden? The same Jack Warden who lost his daughter in the mall attack?"

"Jack lost his daughter in the mall attack?"

"Yes. That's him. I remember now. He was at the memorial for victims of Kilimani Mall."

"I didn't know." I sat down, realizing what Goma meant when she said we were bound by the events of a tragic afternoon. He had lost Lily, the same place, same time, as I had lost Mo.

"Yes. He got some kind of recognition award for saving an expectant mother and her son. Never got up to receive it. He just sat there, looking like he wasn't seeing or hearing any of it. His daughter's dance teacher received an award too, for getting the kids to safety. It's a shame his daughter wasn't one of them. How is he now?"

"Intimidating. Sad, angry, bitter. I think he might have a death wish. He was standing under a tree in the storm, by his daughter's grave, like he wanted to be struck down right next to her. He didn't want to hear anything I had to say about the kids or Wanza."

I stayed on the phone long enough to catch Corinne up on Scholastica.

"You won't be able to bring her back to the hostel with you," she said. "It's for volunteers only. They made an exception for you, because of what happened to Mo."

"I'll figure something out. Maybe Jack's grandmother can point me in the right direction." I said goodbye and hung up.

"If you think getting Goma involved will convince me to help, you're wrong."

I spun around to find Jack watching me from the doorway, sipping a bottle of Coca-Cola. The shower had brought the warmth back into his face, but his voice sent cold shivers up my spine.

"You've made it clear you're not interested, but if you think I'm giving up, you're the one who's wrong," I replied.

He regarded me across the room, eyes glowing with something inscrutable, not moving, not saying another word.

"I'm sorry about your daughter," I said, when the tension became too much to bear. "And about what I said earlier."

He nodded and stared into his bottle.

"I'm sorry about your sister," he said. "Bahati filled me in. Take my advice." He shifted and pinned me down with his gaze. "Pack up and go home. You're in way over your head. You have no idea what you're getting into."

I flared up. For some reason, Jack Warden got under my cool-as-a-cucumber skin. Every. Single. Time. "You know what? I am getting tired of you assuming you know what's best for me. You can't help me? Fine. But I didn't ask for your advice, and I sure as hell am not going to let it stop me."

"Tell me something." His voice was calm and unaffected. It irritated me. *He* irritated me. "Exactly how much did your sister tell you, about these kids that you want to get to Wanza?"

"I . . . she . . ." I cursed myself for not paying closer attention to all the things that Mo had chattered on about. "What does it matter? What exactly is it that you think I can't handle?"

Seconds ticked by before he answered. "You don't want to know. Trust me. Some things are better left in the dark, where they belong." Then he drained his bottle of Coca-Cola in a long chug and left the room.

THE PIERCING CALL of a rooster woke me the next morning. It crowed every ten minutes, telling me it was dawn, even though it felt like I had only just fallen asleep. I rolled out of bed, shivering in Goma's muumuu, and walked to the window.

There was just enough light to make out a figure in the fields. It was Jack, on a tractor, plowing through a bare patch of earth. I tried to imagine what it would feel like, grieving for someone in a place where things kept growing, where new life burst through the soil with bright, green shoots every day.

Where have you brought me, Mo? What are you showing me?

I made my way to the laundry room and found my clothes washed, ironed and ready to wear. I slid them on, savoring the warmth that was still folded into them.

"Oh good. You're up," said Goma, when I entered the kitchen. "Breakfast is ready. Be a dear and go get Bahati and Scholastica. They're in the library."

The house was a rambling structure, new rooms extending out of the original building over the years, nooks and crannies everywhere. It took me a while to track down Bahati and Scholastica, and when I did, I stopped dead in my tracks.

They were seated on the floor, across from each other—one of them tall, lean, and dark as night, the other soft and silver, like moonlight—watching the strangest sight: a tortoise with a yellow balloon tied around it, crossing the floor between them. They looked at me from the corner of their eyes, then back at the tortoise, and then at each other. The tortoise plodded along on round, stumpy feet, squinting at them—left, then right—like a crusty old man shaking his head in somber disapproval. We all started laughing at the same time. Scholastica's giggles filled the space, even after Bahati and I stopped to catch our breaths.

"Come on, you two. Breakfast is ready," I said, making eating motions for Scholastica. I headed for the door but stopped short for the second time that morning.

Jack was standing there, his eyes fixed on Scholastica. His boots were muddy, sleeves rolled up, one foot forward, but going nowhere, as if he'd been frozen by the sound of her laughter—a little girl in his daughter's dress, giggling over a tortoise and a balloon.

Scholastica clammed up as soon as she saw him, still wary of his reaction to her from the night before. She kept her head down as he strode into the room toward her. Seconds ticked by in uncomfortable silence as his shadow loomed over her. Then he said something to her in Swahili. She nodded and went back to staring at the tortoise. Jack reached into his pocket for something and popped the balloon.

BANG.

The tortoise snapped its head and limbs into its shell so fast, the air expelled out of its lungs in a long, hiss. It lay on the floor, vexed and disgruntled, with the balloon in tatters around it, like little yellow flags of surrender.

"And that's the fastest you'll see Aristurtle move," observed Jack, before repeating it in Swahili for Scholastica. He knelt beside the spooked tortoise and stroked his shell. "You okay, little fellow?"

Aristurtle poked his pebbled head out warily and looked at Jack with grizzled contempt.

Scholastica burst out laughing. She laughed so hard, she rolled over, holding on to her stomach. Jack sat back and watched her, his Adam's apple bobbing as if the sound of it was piercing his heart with the sweetest shrapnel. He rose and headed over to the corner where a bunch of other yellow balloons were bobbing and handed one to Scholastica. She took it and pointed to the turtle.

"No." He shook his head. "For you."

"Lord." Goma walked in and gave all of us the stink eye. "I send one to get the other and lose all of you. Everyone in the kitchen. Come along now."

She marched us to the table and filled our plates with food. "Coffee from our farm," she said, pouring Bahati and me a cup before sitting down.

"It's delicious," I said, after the first hot sip. "Thank you. And thanks for looking after my clothes this morning. I hope I'm half as active when I'm your age."

"It's the farm," Goma replied. "Clean air, hard work, fresh food."

Scholastica tied her balloon on the chair next to Jack, and sat down beside him. He buttered a piece of toast, slathered it with jam, and put it on her plate. He blinked when she thanked him, as if it was something he'd done out of habit, not realizing until after he was finished.

"I heard you saved an expectant mother and her child during the mall attack," I said, as Bahati and Goma conversed at the other end of the table. "That's incredible."

"Is it?"

I put my fork down and looked at him. "What's your problem? Every time I try to be nice, you throw it back in my face. Every time I think there's another side to you, you go back to being a jerk."

"That's because I *am* a jerk. I'm the jerk who let his daughter die. I was in the mall that day. Right there. And I stopped to get a couple of strangers out first. I was too busy saving other lives."

"Did you ever think that maybe they saved yours?"

"You think they saved me?" Jack laughed. Yet another kind of laugh. This one filled with deep, dark irony. Did he ever just laugh, like normal people? *Really* laugh?

He leaned across the table, so close that I could make out the gold rings around his icy blue irises. They were the color of parched Savannah grass, waiting for rain. "In a thousand lives, I would die a thousand deaths to save her. Over and over and over again."

I believed him. Every word. Because of the way he said it.

I had no comeback, so I watched as he got up, opened the fridge and reached for a bottle of Coca-Cola. He placed the edge of the cap against the counter and hit it with the palm of his hand. After discarding the cap, he pulled up a chair, tilted his head back and drained the bottle in one go.

What an odd man, I thought. A coffee farmer who didn't drink coffee.

Most people drowned their sorrows in something stronger. Jack chose a bottle of Coca-Cola. Maybe he wanted to be fully aware, fully awake to the pain. Maybe Jack Warden *liked* the pain because he believed it was exactly what he deserved.

"Have you decided what you're going to do next?" Goma asked me.

I turned my attention away from Jack and focused on her. "I was hoping you know someone who'd be willing to take Scholastica and me to Wanza, with a couple of stops along the way."

"I know the perfect man for the job. He's sitting right at this table, and he knows it too, but he's too wrapped up in himself to give a damn."

"You didn't lose a daughter," growled Jack, keeping his eyes on his plate.

"No, I didn't," replied Goma. "I lost my only son, your father.

And I lost his wife, your mother, in the same accident. I lost my husband. And I lost Lily, my great granddaughter. That's four generations I've buried out back. And I'm still standing. You think I didn't want to go to sleep and never wake up from the loss? Each and every time? You think my heart and yours are so different? They're not. I hurt as much as you do, Jack. But I get up because *you're* still here. You're the only one left, and you know what? You're enough. You're reason enough to keep me standing. And it kills me to see you like this, alive on the outside but dead and hollow on the inside. You hear me? It kills me."

The silence that followed was thick and heavy, like the knot that clogged my throat. I knew I should excuse myself, but I couldn't move. Bahati was staring at his hands, no doubt feeling the same way. Even Scholastica, who had not understood the words, sat stiffly in her chair.

Jack looked at Goma and started to say something, but turned to me instead.

"I'm sorry to disappoint you." He tossed his napkin onto his plate. "I can't help you. I couldn't even help my own kid. I wish everyone would just leave me the hell alone!" His chair scraped against the floor as he got up and stalked out of the room.

Goma remained seated and finished her breakfast. When she was done, she wiped the breadcrumbs off the table, her skin stretched tight over translucent knuckles. "Growing old isn't for sissies," she said softly. "You lose the people you love. Over and over again. Some get taken away from you. Some walk away. And some you learn to let go."

Bahati, Scholastica, and I cleaned up in silence as she sat there, staring out of the window. The previous night's storm had cleared to reveal glorious blue skies.

"Where to now?" Bahati asked, when we were done.

"Back to Amosha," I said. "Someone at Nima House must

have an idea of what I can do."

"I'll get my keys," said Goma. "My Jeep is still blocking Bahati's car. I'll meet you out front."

I tidied my room and left Goma's muumuu folded at the foot of the bed. When I stepped outside, Bahati was already waiting by his car.

"Ready?" he asked.

I nodded and gave him a small smile, but I had no idea what I was going to do.

"Sorry it didn't work out," he said.

"I'm sure we'll find another way." I wasn't sure at all, but with Scholastica in tow, there was no turning back. I slid into the car and shut the door.

Goma was putting a hat on Scholastica's head. "She has no pigment," she said. "That makes her sensitive to the sun. Pick up some sunscreen when you get to Amosha."

"I will," I promised. "Thank you for your hospitality."

"You're most welcome. *Kwaheri*, Rodel. *Kwaheri*, Scholastica. Goodbye."

She opened the car door for Scholastica to hop in, but Scholastica went running to the porch instead. Jack was standing there, holding out her forgotten balloon. She gave him a wide smile as she took it, but he didn't notice. His eyes were focused on the hat she was wearing.

"Where did she get this?" he asked.

"Not again, Jack." Goma walked up to the porch. "I found it in your car."

"Lily was wearing it. She left it in the car when we went into the mall."

"It's just a hat, Jack. There's no part of Lily in it. She's here—" Goma touched his heart "—where she'll always be."

"It's the last thing I have of hers. Her sunflower hat. You have no right to give it away."

"I made her that hat. I can give it to whoever I choose."

"It's not just a hat. Not to me!"

They went back and forth, hurling sentences at each other.

Scholastica's eyes darted from Jack to Goma. It didn't take much to figure out what they were arguing about. She took off the hat, sliding it slowly from her head. For a moment, she admired the big, floppy flower in the center that looked like a little burst of sunshine. Then she folded it in half and held it out to Jack, squinting up at him with her bizarre, milky blue eyes. He stopped mid-sentence, staring at her. She nudged the hat closer and when he continued standing there, stiff and frozen, she placed it in his palm and curled his fingers around it.

My throat clogged as the sun beat down on her exposed head. Somewhere down the line, she had become my ward, my responsibility. I had moved beyond her startling appearance and saw her for the little girl she was.

Jack saw something too, something that made him grab her hand as she turned to go. He held his daughter's hat tight in his other hand and knelt before Scholastica.

"Her name was Lily. *Jina yake ilikuwa Lily,*" he said.

"Lily?" asked Scholastica.

Jack nodded. "*Mtoto yangu,* my daughter. She liked rainbows and chocolate. Melted chocolate. See?" He pointed to the stains and slid the hat onto Scholastica's head. "She liked dancing. And singing. And taking photos." He adjusted the hat so that the sunflower was centered in the front. "She died," he said. "*Alikufa.*"

"*Pole,*" replied Scholastica. Sorry.

Then she put her arms around him and gave him a hug. They embraced under the gable of the house, Scholastica's balloon bobbing over them, and Kilimanjaro watching silently from the clouds.

It was a moment of big and small—the man, the girl, the

mountain, the manor. I couldn't see Jack's face, but I knew something was happening—something powerful, yet tender. When it was done, they spoke to each other without any words. Jack straightened and led Scholastica to the car, where Bahati and I were waiting.

"You said you'll come back tomorrow," he said to me.

"Pardon me?"

"Yesterday. You said, 'Maybe this isn't the best time. I'll come back tomorrow.'"

I stared at him blankly.

"It's tomorrow, Rodel Emerson. Come back inside. I'll take you and Scholastica to Wanza."

"You will?" A small thrill shot down my spine. "What about the other kids?" I had other names to cross off. I needed a commitment.

Jack opened the car door and waited for me to step out. Then he extended his hand out. When I put my hand in his large, rough grip, he held it for a moment, as if allowing me the opportunity to back out.

Then he squeezed.

It was a silent handshake, an unspoken agreement. And although I had only just met him, I knew I could trust Jack Warden to keep his promise. Come what may.

I FOLLOWED JACK into the library after lunch and watched him unroll a map across the polished walnut desk. He took the three Post-its I handed to him, and laid them out on the map:

July 17—Juma (Baraka)

Aug 29—Sumuni (Maymosi)

Sept 1—Furaha (Magesa)

"We'll make one trip to Wanza," he said, after studying Mo's notes. "The last two stops are on the way there and the dates are close. Your sister and Gabriel probably planned it that way. Instead of driving back and forth, we'll go to Baraka and get Juma first." He tapped the location on the map. "We can leave tomorrow and bring him back to the farm. The next pickup isn't for another week. We'll set out with him and Scholastica then, stop at Maymosi and Magesa, and head on to Wanza from there." He looked at me for confirmation.

He was silhouetted against the window, dust motes dancing around him as beams of light slanted in through the pane. The edges of his hair shone like pale gold where the sun touched it, making him look like a dark, charcoal drawing, infused with light. He was still walled up, still barricaded from the inside, but something had cracked open.

Jack had no desire to be pulled back into a world that had taken his daughter away. He had done his part, played the hero, been lauded for saving three lives—a woman, her unborn child, and her little boy—but he found no comfort in the fact that they were alive, or that *he* was alive. Lily was gone, and he was in pure agony. And yet, there he was, waiting for a reply, looking at me as if acknowledging for the first time that I existed, that what I thought *mattered*.

"That sounds great." If he could see me from within that vortex of pain, if he could see beyond himself, I sure as hell could look past his rough, harsh edges. Besides, there was something to be said for a man who kept a bunch of balloons in his all-dark library.

"They remind me of Lily," he said, when he noticed my eyes lingering on them. "I pick up a new batch whenever I'm in town. It was the last thing she asked me for. Yellow balloons. She wanted them for Aristurtle, so we wouldn't have to keep looking for him," he explained, before returning the Post-it notes to me.

I thought about how Mo and Lily were still so present in the yellow paper I held, in the yellow balloons that Jack held on to, and the tortoise that was somewhere behind the desk—invisible, but with a burst of color trailing him.

"I hope we all go like that, leaving something bright behind," I said.

We watched in silence as the balloons bobbed gently in the corner, as if touched by soft, invisible breaths—rising and falling.

"This was her. My sister." I searched through my phone and showed Jack a picture of Mo. She was getting her hair braided. A comb was sticking out in the undone part of her hair. She looked so happy, sitting in the shade of a tree, on an upside-down plastic crate, wearing a turquoise dress and polka dot glasses. "We didn't look much like each other." Mo was the kind of person who sprang out at you in pictures and crowds. Your eyes just automatically picked her out.

"My daughter and I, we didn't look much like each other either."

I didn't think he was going to share anything further, but then he seemed to changed his mind.

"This is her." He pulled out his wallet and gave me a Polaroid of Lily.

She had honey-colored skin and was smiling into the camera with pure mischief in her eyes. Strands of flyaway hair were peeking out from under a sunflower hat—the one that Jack had given Scholastica. She looked different from Jack, but I could see him in the arch of her brows and the defiant turn of her chin. She would have broken rules and hearts, and loved every minute of it.

As we held the photos, side-by-side, I felt a sense of loss that goes with the disappearing of smiles, of vibrancy, of voices, and warmth, and choices. And yet there was a sweetness of having shared and known, of having loved, even though it seemed as fleeting as the flutter of a bird's wings.

I handed Lily's photo back, and stooped to retrieve something that had landed on the floor. It was another Polaroid, one of Jack, that had been stuck to the back of it. He looked like he'd been caught mid-speech, his skin over-exposed as if the flash had gone off right in his face. Perhaps that was why he seemed so different—his eyes so clear and startling, they captivated me. They had an iridescence that was not easily forgotten, like icy glaciers ringed by golden, summer light. They held no hint of the storm clouds that they did now. I'd pegged him for being around thirty, but he looked much younger in that photo.

"She took both of these," said Jack, when I handed him back the second Polaroid. "We were driving to the mall that day." He stroked the edge of Lily's photo absently. "I told her to stop wasting film." He slipped the prints back into his wallet and stared at the leather.

"I didn't answer my sister's call that day." I hadn't told anyone that, not even my parents. I had shared Mo's final message, but not the fact that I'd ignored her call. I was too ashamed to, but somehow, I felt all right sharing it with Jack. "I was too busy signing papers for my new home."

Jack remained silent. Maybe he was running over the same things I was: the what-if scenarios that you go through over and over again.

"Is that why you're doing this?" he asked. "Taking on her unfinished business? Because you feel guilty?"

"I don't know," I admitted. "We don't always understand the things we do. We just do them and hope we'll feel better."

"I don't know about feeling better." Jack took a deep breath and straightened from the desk. "All I know is that when Scholastica handed me back Lily's hat, I couldn't shut her out. It was the way she looked at me—with no expectation, no judgment. I have no qualms saying no to you, or to Goma, or to anyone who asks anything of me, because I don't owe anybody a damn thing, including explanations. But when that little girl looked at me, without asking, without speaking, something in me answered."

Scholastica's voice mingled with Goma's in the kitchen as we stood in the library. It was probably what Kaburi Estate had sounded like when Lily was alive—a mix of young and old, with the hum of a distant tractor, and the muted conversations of the staff drifting in through the windows. The breeze picked up the scent of Jack's skin—green coffee beans and soft earth. It was both light and dark, elusive yet rooted, just like the man. I could have gone on breathing the moment, but I had an odd sensation, like I was standing at the edge of something deep and vast, and needed to pull back.

"Is this Lily's mother?" I walked over to one of the shelves and picked up a frame. It held a photo of Jack with a beautiful black woman. She had a swan's neck, elegant and smooth, and the kind of face that needed no makeup to accentuate it. Her features radiated an intelligent confidence. Jack had his arm around her shoulder as she held a younger Lily up for the camera.

"Sarah." Jack took the frame from my hands and gazed at it. "She wanted to take Lily to Disneyland, but I insisted she come here, like she does every year."

He left the rest unspoken, but it was clear that Sarah blamed him for what had happened to their daughter. From the expression on his face, he didn't begrudge her that, because he did too.

"Lily was our last link, the one thing that kept us connected. I haven't spoken to Sarah since the funeral." Jack carefully placed the frame back on the shelf.

He did that a lot. Every movement was concise and deliberate, like he was focusing on the things he could control, to keep from getting sucked into a dark, spinning void.

The shrill ring of a referee's whistle came from the living room, where Bahati was watching a football match. It jarred the strange spell that seemed to have woven around Jack and me.

"I should get going," said Jack. "I'm needed outside." He slipped on his sunglasses and paused at the door. "We'll leave for Baraka in the morning."

I sat down after he left and watched Aristurtle take little bites of lettuce from his feeding dish. Shafts of sunlight fell on the dark shelves around me. It was only then that I realized I was surrounded by books. Yet not one of them had clamored for my attention while Jack had been in the room.

I RUBBED MO'S note between my fingers as we left the farm. Dewdrops were still glistening on the leaves, like morning diamonds scattered in the field.

July 17—Juma (Baraka), it said.

It was the first of Mo's Post-its that had not been crossed out, and though it was now August, we were headed for the place she was supposed to have picked up a kid named Juma. It took us half the day to get there, on dirt roads that meandered through tall, yellow grass.

Baraka was a collection of thatched-roof huts surrounded by thorn bushes and footpaths that led to small fields of corn and potatoes. The villagers pointed us in the direction of Juma's family's hut and then huddled outside, listening in.

I tried to follow the conversation between Jack and the woman who was squatting by the fire, but they were speaking in quick, short bursts of Swahili.

She had a baby tied to her back, and was cooking something that looked like thick porridge. Chickens pecked around her feet, while another toddler slept in the corner.

The conversation was getting heated. Jack sat next to me on a wooden stool, his earlier cordiality gone. He was hunched over, trying to fold his frame into the small, smoky space. The woman, Juma's mother, seemed to be deflecting his questions and ignoring us. Gabriel's name was thrown around. The woman shrugged, shook her head, and kept her back to us.

"Has Gabriel already been here?" I asked.

"Apparently, he never showed," replied Jack.

"And Juma? Where is he?"

Jack gave the woman a black, layered look. "She says she doesn't know."

Just then, a man walked in and started talking to us, his voice raised, arms waving wildly.

"What's going on?" I looked from him to Jack.

"It's Juma's father. He wants us to leave." But Jack showed no sign of getting up. "Not until they tell us where Juma is."

The villagers outside peeked in, as the conversation got louder. Jack's hard-nosed tenacity fueled the other man's rage. Juma's mother started wailing, startling the sleeping toddler. His cries mingled with hers, as the men continued arguing. The dark hut turned into a madhouse of clucking chickens, and weeping, and yelling.

"Stop!" I couldn't take it anymore. "Everyone, just stop!"

The outcry was met with stunned silence. I guess they had all forgotten I was still in the room.

"Please." I got up and clasped the woman's hands. "We're just here for Juma. That's what you wanted, right? That's why Gabriel and Mo arranged to stop by. To take him to Wanza. If you've changed your mind, just tell us and we'll leave."

She didn't know what I was saying, but as she stared at our hands, joined together, big, fat tears started splashing down on them.

"Juma," she said, her throat convulsing around his name. Then she was talking as if she'd bottled up the words for so long, she couldn't stop them from tumbling out. She held my hands tightly when she was done and sobbed. And sobbed.

"Jack?"

His eyes held a tortured dullness as they met mine.

"Let's go." He pulled me away from her, clamping his fingers around my wrist. "There's nothing for us here." He led me through the door, past the crowd gathered outside, and toward the car.

"What did she say?" I asked.

"Get in." He was already starting the car.

"Not until you explain what just happened in that hut."

"Get in the car, Rodel," he growled. His jaw was ticking, and he stared straight ahead, not looking at me. This was the Jack I had met on the porch that first time—harsh, detached, unyielding.

"I'm not going anywhere until you answer me."

"You really want to know? Fine." He slammed the steering wheel with both hands. "They sold him, Rodel. They sold Juma. They were going to hand him over to Gabriel in exchange for some necessities, but when Gabriel and Mo didn't show, they sold him to someone else. Juma is gone."

"Gone where? What do you mean they sold him?"

"I mean that his parents sold him because they have too many mouths to feed. Two little ones in there, and three more out in the fields. They sacrificed one kid so the others could live. They got seeds for their farm, a bunch of chickens, and enough food to get them through for a while."

"I get it," I said, even though it shook me. I had seen a lot of things on my father's foreign assignments. The good and the bad. "It's awful that his parents felt compelled to do something like that, but Juma is with a good family, right? I mean, they must really want him if they came all the way here to get him."

"Juma is an albino kid." Jack was still furious. Not angry-furious, but a heartbroken, choked-up furious. He chewed out the words like he couldn't stand them. "He's worth more dead than alive. Albinos here are hunted for their body parts because people believe they hold magical powers. Witchdoctors make talismans out of them: teeth, eyes, internal organs. Fishermen weave albino hair into fishing nets because they think it will lure more fish. Politicians hire albino-hunters to get their limbs and blood so they can win elections. Wealthy buyers pay big money for them. Three thousand dollars for an arm or leg. Fifty thousand for the whole body, maybe more." Jack looked at me for the first time since he'd dragged me out of the hut. "So, no. Juma is not with a good family because Juma is dead."

His words came as a jarring shock. I knew albinos were in danger, but I had assumed it was because they were picked on, bullied, ostracized, or physically assaulted. I had not conceived of anything as brutal as their cold-blooded murder for profit and greed and superstition.

Some things are better left in the dark, where they belong. Jack's words came back to me.

It was what he had tried to shield me from. I had thought I could handle whatever it was. I was a big girl. I lived in a big world. But in that moment, in the barren compound of Baraka, in the blazing heat of the afternoon sun, I felt small and dizzy—sick at the thought of a hacked up little boy, betrayed by his own parents. I turned away from the car and stumbled to the nearest hut, thankful for the darkness of its shadow, which shielded me from the villagers.

They all knew.

The villagers. Jack. Goma. Bahati. Scholastica.

Mo had known too.

It's much easier when people think they're seeing a mzungu *mother and a* mzungu *child.*

Once a month, Mo ensured safe passage for one of the kids that Gabriel had tracked down.

The words were making more sense now. Mo had taken on a dangerous mission, but she had known.

Had she retched into the ochre soil like I was doing? Had she gone limp against the wall and slumped to the ground when she'd first heard about it?

No. Mo was strong. She always kept her guard up and her knees strong. She didn't dwell on things that broke her heart. Like boyfriends who cheated on her, or people that disappointed her, or events that shattered her illusions. She accepted, assimilated, and moved on.

The world will screw you over. It's a given. Once you accept that, it gets easier, she'd said after a particularly rough breakup.

What happens when you want to break-up with the world, Mo? When it throws something at you that's so unforgivable you curl up in the shadow of a mud hut and never want to see its face again?

There was no answer, just the idling of Jack's car as he drove up to me and waited. I stared at the wheels, caked with mud and grime from our trek. I had brought extra bottles of water, a hat, sunscreen, and snacks for Juma. We'd be taking them back unused.

"How old do you think he was?" I asked, still sitting on the ground. He could have been two, or five, or ten, or twelve.

"We'll never know," he replied, weary and spent.

"Can't we go to the authorities? Have them do something about it?"

"If the police could do anything about it, this wouldn't be happening. You can't fight an army of nameless, faceless ghosts. Even if you catch up to them, they're just the middlemen, working for witchdoctors, who are in turn funded by rich, powerful patrons. It's not a person you're dealing with, Rodel, or a group of people—it's a way of thinking, a mindset. And that is the most dangerous enemy of all."

"So we do nothing? Just accept it and move along? Because it's not personal? Because it doesn't affect us?"

"Yes! Yes, you accept it! Just like I've had to accept it." Jack's eyes raked over me with scalding bitterness. "There is nothing more personal than losing a daughter. You think I haven't wanted to punish the people responsible for killing Lily? You think I haven't tried to picture their faces? I lie awake every night, grasping at smoke and ashes, breathing the stench of my own helplessness. So don't preach to me about being unaffected. And if you can't handle it, you might as well pack your bags and go home, Rodel, because this is not a fucking tea party in the cradle of Africa."

I kept my chin up even though it trembled. He wasn't the only one who had lost someone. I had lost my sister. And by some crazy twist of fate, our paths had crossed—two people with fresh, tender grief, thrown into a hopeless situation, trying to save a bunch of kids when we could barely keep our own heads together.

I laughed at the irony of it. And then I laughed again because I was beginning to understand the hollow, mirthless ways that Jack laughed. But my laughter turned into soft, silent sobs. It was the stoicism that got to me, the acceptance of tragedy—self-inflicted or perpetrated. I had seen it in Jack's eyes, and then again in the hut, in Juma's mother's eyes. Perhaps when you've watched the lion bring down the gazelle, time and time again, when you've felt the earth tremble with the migration of millions of wildebeest, it comes naturally. You make friends with impermanence and transience and insignificance. Whereas I had never entertained tragedy or failure or disappointment. I resisted it. I forged ahead with the deep conviction that happiness was the natural state of things. I believed it. I wanted to hold on to it, but it was slowly being wrangled away from me.

Jack let me cry. He didn't try to coax me or comfort me. There was no rushing me, or telling me to stop crying. When I finally got into the car, he gave me a curt nod, the kind I suspect one soldier would give another—an acknowledgment of respect, of kinship, of having survived something big and ugly.

As we drove into the shimmering blue of the hazy horizon, I

caught a glimpse of his soul. So many pieces of him had been fed to the lions. And as dark and bitter as it had turned him, he was a gladiator for standing where I would have surely fallen.

B EYOND THE ISLANDS of flat acacia trees, wisps of crimson and violet seeped into a waning sky. Even as night fell upon the vast plains, the light was dazzling and clear. This was the Serengeti, a region of Africa extending from northern Tanzania to southwestern Kenya. Renowned for its magnificent lions and herds of migrating animals, the Serengeti encompassed a number of game reserves and conservation areas.

"We'll have to stop somewhere for the night," said Jack. "It will be dark soon. Time to get off the road. We took longer than expected in Baraka."

Because of my breakdown, I thought.

We were still hours from the farm, driving along the edge of the Ngorongoro Crater, the crown jewel of the Serengeti. Once a gigantic volcano, it had erupted over 3 million years ago and collapsed into a 2,000-foot drop crater. Now the world's largest intact caldera, it shelters one of the most expansive wildlife havens on earth. Another time I might have paid more attention, but I stared vacantly at the road ahead. I kept thinking of Juma, and how he'd still be alive if Gabriel and Mo had made it—how we're all connected in strange, mysterious ways. Pull a thread here and a life unravels there.

Jack turned into a campsite as the sun started to set. The sign at the entrance said "Luxury Safari Tents". Small, dark forms slipped through the grass as the car bounced on the dirt track leading up to the reception. Nights in the Serengeti belonged to the animals, and I was grateful for Jack's sturdy, enclosed Land Rover.

"Can we get something to eat?" Jack asked at the counter, after we'd checked in.

"Dinner is in a couple of hours, but there are still some snacks from this afternoon in the dining room."

We headed to the open canvas enclosure and got a table facing the crater. The western sky was turning a pale violet in the sun's afterglow.

"Would you like something to drink?" one of the staff asked.

"Tea, please," I replied.

"Coca-Cola," said Jack.

"I'll bring them out right away. There is no menu. Please help yourself to the buffet." The waiter pointed to the table.

I hadn't thought about food all day, my appetite curbed by the brutal reality of what I'd learned, but my stomach growled as I picked through the leftovers of what must have been afternoon tea. Cucumber sandwiches, little cakes and pastries, sugar-sprinkled cookies.

"Thank you," I said, when the waiter brought my tea.

I grinned when Jack returned to our table, his plate piled higher than mine.

"What?" he asked.

"Nothing." But even as I tried to contain it, something broke loose.

"What?"

"This." I raised my cup and motioned toward the crater. "A fucking tea party in the cradle of Africa."

At first, he didn't react. He just looked at me, shocked at having his own words thrown back at him. Then his eyes smiled, and it took a few seconds for the rest of him to catch up.

It felt good to laugh. And have Jack laugh with me. His real laugh was warm and deep, like something that had been unearthed on a sunlit day.

"Not just the cradle of Africa," he said. "Quite possibly the cradle of mankind. One of the oldest pieces of evidence about mankind's existence was found out there, in Oldupai Gorge."

We stared into the space. It was dark now, and so vast that it seemed to stretch out forever.

"*Zinjanthropus,*" I said. "The Nutcracker Man."

Jack tilted his head and assessed me. "You're full of surprises, Rodel Emerson."

"I'm a teacher." I shrugged. "And you can call me Ro."

He sipped his drink straight from the bottle. Coca-Cola by the crater. "I like Rodel," he said. "I've never met a Rodel I didn't like."

"Is that a roundabout way of saying you like me?" We both knew he'd never met a Rodel before.

"I'm not a roundabout kind of person." He put his bottle down and pinned his cat eyes on me. "I like you. I like that you stand your ground and see things through. I like that you can fall, dust yourself off, and get on with it. I like that you have this . . . this innate faith. That no matter how dark it is, you hold out for the light. I like sitting at this table with you, being called out on my own bullshit. I'm sorry if I was harsh earlier. I was pissed about Juma. With his parents for what they did. With the circumstances that go with it. With you for bringing me out here. With myself for not being able to do anything about it. I felt just as powerless as I did the day I lost Lily."

I stared back, tongue-tied. Jack Warden was an ever-changing enigma. He complimented, apologized, and bared himself, all at once, with a directness and sincerity that left me speechless. My ticker-tape of emotions went haywire around him, regardless of whether he was happy, angry, sad, or contrite.

"I get it," I replied. It was all I could manage. I hadn't realized exactly what I'd been asking him to do, but it was clear why he'd shut me out the first time. The last thing Jack needed was someone banging down his door, asking him to shoulder the responsibility of another child's life, when he believed he had failed his own. What man would willingly face the reality of his worst nightmare yet again?

We finished the rest of our food in silence.

A watchman with a rifle and a flashlight lead us to our tent. It was nothing like the average tent at a camping ground. It sat on large wooden pallets, with a high ceiling supported by wooden beams. There were two beds with small night stands, a trunk full of blankets, and a wardrobe rack to hang our clothes. A connecting door led to a sparse, but functional bathroom.

"Dinner is in an hour. Signal me with your flashlight when you want to be escorted to the dining room," said the guard.

"I don't think I can eat again," I said, after he left.

"You might change your mind. It's not like there's a vending machine if you get hungry in the middle of the night." Jack tossed his shoes off and reclined on the bed.

When they'd told us there was only one tent left, I hadn't thought it would be a problem, but the small space seemed dwarfed by his presence.

"I think I'll go freshen up." I grabbed my handbag and disappeared into the bathroom.

I was out two minutes later and heading for the exit.

"What are you doing?" Jack watched as I tried to pry the zip open.

"The toilet won't flush. I'm going to let them know."

"You can't just walk to the lounge, Rodel. This place isn't fenced in, which means there are wild animals roaming around. And that's not an automatic toilet. You need to pour water into the tank when you want to flush."

"Ah. Got it." I marched back into the bathroom and looked around. "*Umm . . .* Jack?"

"Yes?"

I startled to find him right behind me. "There's no tap on the sink."

"You get the water from here." He lifted a flap and pointed to the row of buckets filled with water. He removed the lid off the toilet tank, poured water into it, and flushed.

If I had thought he took up all the space in the tent, I could barely breathe in the cramped bathroom. There was something about Jack that brushed against the boundaries of my awareness— the way he moved, the way his arms tightened when he lifted the bucket, the way he radiated heat and warmth. But that was just Jack. I was pretty sure it was the response he drew from most women—the chance gaze, followed by a pause; the appreciation of something magnificent, no matter how fleeting. I would have to be six feet under not to react to him. It wasn't just about the way he looked. He had something more. Solidity. Substance. The kind of thing the moon does to the tides, making the waves rise to attention. Jack could give you goosebumps simply by circling past you. I shuddered to think what it would be like if he deliberately decided to slay you.

"Thank you," I said, as he returned the empty bucket. "I think I'll hop in the shower now." I practically shoved him out the door. I liked goosebumps, but I liked them on my own terms. And this was not a goosebump-approved situation. With a goosebump-approved man.

I was halfway undressed when I realized there were no taps in the shower either. And no showerhead. Just a drain in the floor.

Crap.

I slunk back into my sweater and opened the door.

Jack was standing there, arms folded, leaning against the beam, like he'd been waiting for me.

"It's a bucket shower," he explained, anticipating my question.

"No hot water?"

"Only in the morning. But they'll heat some water for us if we request it."

"I can wait. I'll just use a wash cloth for now." I shut the door again and heard his footsteps recede.

When I came out, I grabbed a blanket and wrapped it around myself. It was nice to be wiped clean of the grime and dust, but the water had been cold, the temperature had dropped, and I was freezing.

"You all right?" Jack opened one eye. He was lying on his tummy, fully clothed under the covers.

"*Uh-huh.*"

"Cold?"

"No."

"Want to go for dinner?"

"Yes." *If only to warm up in the heated dining area.* "Can we go now?"

"Hungry, so soon?" His voice carried the slightest hint of a smile.

"Famished," I replied.

Jack signaled the watchman with his flashlight.

"Here." He removed his hoodie and draped it around my shoulders as we stepped outside.

"What about you?" I asked, sinking into its warmth. It smelled like him, and I found it oddly comforting.

"I'm not so hungry," he said.

A bubble of laughter surfaced and got lodged in my throat. He'd caught on to the fact that I wasn't about to admit I was cold, so he was playing along.

I swallowed the chuckle because I couldn't afford to like Jack Warden. Not that way.

Dinner tables were assigned by tent number in the dining area. Jack and I ended up sharing a table with an elderly couple.

"Hi, I'm Judy. And this is my husband, Ken," said the woman. She had platinum blonde hair, and was wearing a brightly patterned dress.

"I'm Rodel."

"Jack."

We shook hands before taking our seats.

"Is that an English accent I detect?" asked Judy, when the starters arrived.

"Yes. I'm from the Cotswolds," I replied.

"But you're not," her husband remarked, taking in Jack's tanned skin. He had silver hair and eyes that twinkled when he spoke.

"No. I was born here," replied Jack.

"Well, it's nice to see a couple that didn't let a little distance get in the way."

"Oh, we're not . . ." I gestured between Jack and me.

"We're not together," both of us said at the same time.

"That's what I used to say all the time, didn't I, Ken?" Judy laughed. "We're not together, we're not together."

"And here we are," said Ken.

"Over forty years later."

"Only because you want to see the world and need someone to carry your bags."

"We pick up knick-knacks from around the world, for our vintage shop in Canada," Judy explained.

"A place called Hamilton."

"It's by Niagara Falls."

"Look us up if you're ever in the area."

"It's called Ken and Judy's."

They completed each other's sentences and entertained us with their stories for the rest of the night. Jack and I hung around after they left, watching the flickering lanterns sway in the night breeze.

The watchman did not need his flashlight to show us back to the tent. Someone had built a roaring fire in the center of the semi-circle of tents. A few of the guests sat around on blankets, while one of the guards played a harmonica.

"Stay a while!" Judy patted the empty blanket beside her. "There's no heating in the tents."

I wove through the small boulders around the circle of guests and sat down next to Ken and Judy. Jack followed, taking the vacant spot beside me. Above us, a spray of stars hung suspended in the velvet sky. The fire crackled, like leopard eyes in the night, reminding me of ancient men who had come and gone, in the rolling grasslands and volcanic highlands around us.

The warmth from the fire softened my bones. The harmonica played in long, slow drags, lulling my senses. Another guard started beating a drum to the same languid beat. Ken and Judy got up and swayed to the music. The couple sitting next to them passed me a pipe.

"What is it?" I asked.

They said something, but it wasn't in English.

Another time, I would have declined, but thoughts of Juma and Mo and Lily were starting to crowd my mind. I took a deep puff of whatever it was and handed it back to them. It warmed my lungs and left a woody, astringent taste in my mouth. We went back and forth a few times, exchanging the pipe.

The wood smoke, soft voices, ember light catching on gleaming foreheads, the slow warmth, the cold stars—all melded into a throbbing night sorcery. The music slid under my skin, its drunken notes pulsating through my veins. The valley quaked, the sky glowed in a flame. I felt like a forgotten galaxy in a vast universe, like I was about to float away.

"Dance with me, Jack." I gripped his hand. It hung heavy, until I got up and tugged.

I couldn't remember the last time I had danced, let alone asked someone to dance. It was good to be held in Jack's arms, to shuffle around the fire with his warm hands circling my waist. I lay my head on his chest and heard the drum beat through his heart. I felt like an oracle listening to it. It said I was equal parts earth and stars, equal parts animal and soul. I was hope. I was calamity. I was love. I was prejudice. I was my sister. I was his daughter. I was Juma. I was *Jack, Jack, Jack, Jack.*

"I like the way your heart beats," I said. "And I like the way you say my name. *Rodelle.* It makes me sound pretty."

"You *are* pretty." He paused mid-step, like I'd thrown him off. He lifted my chin gently and watched the play of golden light across my face. "You're insanely beautiful."

They were not words I would have used to describe myself, but in that moment, I believed him. I felt insanely beautiful, even though I wasn't wearing a lick of makeup, and my clothes were wrinkled, and my nails were bare and ragged. I believed him because he said it with the simplicity of an observation, one that seemed to hold him arrested, as if he had just noticed it himself.

The blood rushed to my cheeks, my lips, the arch of my brows, the tip of my nose—everywhere his eyes seared my skin.

"No." I averted my gaze. It felt wrong to feel so alive, wrong to feel this burst of exhilaration. "Mo was beautiful. And fun. And funny. I miss her. So much."

Jack didn't move away, but it was as if we both took a step back from whatever had momentarily blazed between us, turning instead to our private thoughts, our private grief. As we swayed in silence, I found myself burrowing deeper into the comfort of his arms. He was so warm—warmer than the fire.

"Is that Bahati laughing?" I mumbled, my cheek pressed flat against his chest. Jack was tall, the tallest guy I had ever danced with. "What's he doing here?"

"I don't know what you smoked, Rodel, but that's not Bahati. It's a hyena. Somewhere out there." He laughed.

"I like it when you laugh. I mean, when you *really* laugh. It starts here." I touched his throat. "But I feel it here." I splayed my fingers across his chest.

We both felt it then—the flare of something wild and combustible, like a flickering ember leaping from the bonfire. Our eyes locked and Jack turned stone-still, every muscle in his torso locking down in taut, tight tension. His chest was red hot under my hand, as if all of our senses had fused there, in a scorching, molten mess. Then he cleared his throat and stepped away.

"I think we better get you to bed," he said.

I nodded, feeling a bit like I was standing in quicksand. My legs were wobbly and my heart was pounding. It must have been from the pipe, because I stood there, limp and drained, like a stewed noodle.

I can't remember if I walked, or if Jack carried me back to our tent, but he tucked me into bed and wrapped the blanket tight around me.

"Goodnight, Rodel."

"'Night, *Jack, Jack, Jack, Jack.*"

I heard the soft thud of his shoes and the creaking of his bed. The buzzing of night beetles and the drunken warmth of the bonfire had almost lulled me to sleep when there was a loud roar.

"Is that a lion?" I mumbled. It sounded like it was just outside our tent, but I was too gone and too tired to care.

"Yes. But it's not as close as it sounds. A lion's roar travels a long way."

"Are they doing it?"

"Doing what?"

"Mufasa." I yawned. "That's why he's the motherfucking king of the jungle."

"Mufasa?"

I turned around to face him, but I was sliding into a deep fog. "Nevemrind."

I heard Jack chuckle in the dark.

"You make me laugh, Rodel," he said softly. "I haven't laughed in a long, long time."

MY EYES WERE heavy as they fluttered open. It took a moment to focus on the beams running across the ceiling. There was a bitter taste in my mouth, and my tongue felt like it was coated in thick wool. Something wasn't right.

Then I remembered. The tent. The pipe. Dancing with Jack. The fire. The drums. His heartbeat. *Jack, Jack, Jack, Jack.* Something roaring between us.

I flipped to my side and moaned. I was hungover from whatever I had smoked.

"You all right?" Jack's morning voice was raspy and rough.

We were lying in our beds, facing each other.

"I'm fine." Mine came out like I had sucked on helium. It wasn't every day that I woke up in the same room as a big, lumbering man. Or a mid-sized one. Or anything that can grow stubble overnight.

The pale light played up his hair, giving it a soft, bluish cast. One hand was under his pillow, while the other dangled off his bed, his fingers close enough to touch. Even through all the layers, it was easy to make out the solid sinew of Jack's body.

When I get home, I am going to get a life, I promised myself. *Meet some hot men. Date. Have lots and lots of sex, so I'm not so miserably ill-equipped around a male body.*

Now you're talking! Mo popped into my head.

Really? This is when you choose to show up? When I'm having

R-rated thoughts?

You owe me. Big time. You never had any juicy stories to share when I was around.

Well, nothing juicy is happening here right now.

Not yet.

Mo! He just lost his daughter, and I'm still getting over you.

So? There's nothing more life-affirming than sex.

You know I'm not about a quick romp in the hay.

No. You want more. You've always wanted more. But you don't always get what you want. Sometimes you get exactly what you need. And good God, look at him! Don't tell me you don't want a slice of that.

I sighed and closed my eyes. *Tell me something, Mo. Are we really having these conversations or am I making you up in my head?*

Whatever floats your boat.

You're absolutely no help.

Anytime, dude.

A bittersweet knot lodged in my throat. *I miss you, Mo.*

No answer.

"Rodel? You sure you're all right?"

My eyes flew open.

Jack was watching me across the small space that separated our beds.

I nodded and wiped the stray tear that had escaped. "Just having a moment."

He didn't take his eyes off my face, and I was strangely comfortable with that, with him seeing the part of me that no one else got to see. He was so achingly familiar with loss that sharing it with him didn't feel foreign. There was an acceptance, an understanding, that lifted me and held me steady in his gaze. Perhaps he found the same in me because his face turned soft—the shape of his lips relaxed, the bottom one falling slightly open.

The clang of something outside the tent shook us out of the moment.

"I think they just brought the hot water," he said. "You want to take that shower now?"

"That would be nice."

But neither of us moved. We lay there for a few beats, while the water turned cold outside, wisps of steam rising in the chilly morning. We had found a pocket of quiet, where all the ghosts in our minds had gone to sleep, and we were the only two people awake.

Then Jack blinked, and the moment drifted away. I watched as he brought the buckets in and carried them to the bathroom. I went first, making sure I left enough hot water for him. Then again, maybe not. There was a hell of a lot more of him to cover.

I stepped out of the tent while he showered. A hazy sun was just peeking over the horizon. Wisps of pink clouds were saying goodbye to a pearlescent moon. The watchmen were gone so I figured it was safe to walk around in the daytime. The camp was perched on the rim of the crater, with sweeping views of the landscape below. Keeping a respectful distance from the edge, I peered over and saw patchwork colors in the grassy plains. As I watched, they changed and moved. Then I realized they were herds of wildebeests and zebras, grazing on the floor of the caldera. They were barely discernible from this height, like blocks of little marching ants.

It was a beautiful, surreal sight. I crept closer, but thick clouds that were sweeping down from the rim and covering the crater obscured my view. The air was noticeably colder, and there was a fine drizzle on my face. I zipped up Jack's hoodie and headed back to the tent.

I didn't get too far. Everything had turned thick and gray. The mist rolled around me in smoky swirls, giving me a tiny peek before shrouding it again. I walked one way, saw something, and started walking in that direction instead. After a few minutes, I was completely lost, completely disoriented. I didn't know if I was walking toward the crater or away from it.

"Hello? Can anyone hear me?" My hair clung dankly to my head as I held my hands out, trying to steer my way out of the heavy, silver labyrinth.

Something shifted in front of me.

"Jack? Is that you? Anyone there?" I turned to follow the movement.

A gigantic, dark figure rose ahead of me. It had the ghostly outline of a person but with arms and legs elongated way beyond proportion. Its head was sheathed in a shimmering ring, like a hazy, rainbow halo. I blinked, pretty sure I was imagining the unnerving apparition, but it stood there, as real and chilling as the droplets of water clinging to my skin. I took a step back, and it moved with me.

Motherfucker.

I turned and sprinted blindly, stumbling over the uneven ground. I thought I heard my name, and then the fall of heavy footsteps behind me. I picked up my pace, high on the fumes of adrenaline, but it was no use. A strong grip clamped around my wrist and spun me around.

"What the hell, Rodel? Didn't you hear me? Why are you running?"

"Jack!" I let out a soft gasp. "Thank God. That thing." I looked over his shoulder, my chest heaving. "Did you see?" I broke away from him, searching for it.

"Listen to me." He pulled me back with such force that I crashed into him. "Stop moving. You hear me? Stop. Fucking. Moving."

The urgency in his voice shackled my floundering footsteps.

"You were this close to the edge." He left an inch between his thumb and forefinger. "This close. What the fuck do you think you're doing?" He was furious, his face a glowering mask of rage.

"Listen to me!" I yanked my hand away, my heart still black

with fright. "I saw something. A ghost. A dark figure. I don't know what it was, but it was following me."

Jack ran his hand through his hair. It was damp from the mist. Or maybe his shower. His hair was darker when wet, the ends curled up to an almost decent length.

"Was it big?" he asked. "Long arms, long legs?"

"Yes."

"Rainbow colors around the silhouette?"

"Around its head. Yes."

He let out a deep breath. "Rodel?"

"What?"

"Don't go wandering off without me, okay?" He started walking away from me. He seemed to know exactly where he was going.

"Wait." I wasn't about to lose sight of him. "Are you going to tell me what it was?"

"We'll talk inside."

I followed him into the dining room and waited until we were seated.

"How did you do that?" I asked, after the waiter brought our food.

"Do what?"

"Find me. And then find the dining room in the mist."

"When you spend a lot of time in the wild with no markers, no buildings, no road signs, you learn to keep track up here." He tapped his temple. "How many paces, which way. As far as you're concerned, I just followed your voice and footsteps. It's not hard once you know what you're tracking. I just didn't expect you to start running toward the cliff."

"It was that *thing*." A shiver went through me that had nothing to do with the cold. "What the hell is out there, Jack?"

"Nothing." He buttered a piece of toast and handed it to me. "You just witnessed an optical illusion called the Brocken Spectre."

"The broken what?"

"Brocken Spectre. B-R-O-C-K-E-N. It was your own shadow projected in front of you through the mist." He took a bite of his toast and washed it down with a swig of Coca-Cola.

"That was no shadow, Jack. It was huge, and there were these colored lights around it."

"I've seen it." Jack nodded. "Once. While climbing Kili— Mount Kilimanjaro. It doesn't happen too often. Only under specific conditions. The sun must be behind you, low in the horizon, to cast that kind of shadow. The rainbow-colored halo is produced by light backscattered through a cloud of water droplets. Depth perception is altered by the mist, so it appears distant and larger than expected."

"But it moved. I don't just mean with me. It did that too, but it was . . . it wasn't just dull and flat like a shadow. It was changing."

"That's because the mist is thicker in some parts and thinner in others, so there's a play of light involved." Jack finished his plate and signaled to mine. "Are you going to eat your breakfast?"

"I'm just . . . it's fascinating." It made sense when I thought about it. "I wish I'd known. I'd have taken the time to study it instead of freaking the hell out."

"What we don't understand always scares us."

"Yes, but now that I know, I find it rather beautiful. I mean, I was something much bigger for a moment. With the longest arms and legs, everything within my reach. And let's not forget my spectacular rainbow halo. I may look ordinary, but I am freaking magical!"

Jack smiled and regarded me over the steeple of his fingers.

"What?" I asked, digging into my plate.

"There is nothing ordinary about you. I thought we established that last night."

I flushed as I recalled his words. *Insanely beautiful.* In spite of the haze of last night, that one moment still sparkled through. And the crazy thing, the thing that made it matter, was that he meant it about all of me—not just the way I looked.

"I have to admit," he continued. "I'm kind of glad you had the living daylights scared out of you."

"That's awful. Why would you enjoy something like that?"

"Sometimes we need to be jarred out of our own reality. We base so much of ourselves on other people's perceptions of us. We live for the compliments, the approval, the applause. But what we really need is a grand, spine-chilling encounter with ourselves to believe we're freaking magical. And that's the best kind of believing, because no one can unsay it or take it away from you."

I nodded and sipped my tea. "And what about you, Jack? Do you believe in your own magic?"

"I stopped believing," he said. "After Lily." He stared out into the gray vastness of the crater. "All the Brocken Spectre means to me now is a dark projection of myself. Grotesque. Eerie. Contorted. It's what the world does, you know? It distorts you until you can't recognize yourself."

My heart squeezed at the pain that flickered in his eyes. "You're a good man, Jack," I said. "You saved my life today. I might have ended up at the bottom of that crater if you hadn't shown up when you did."

His eyes came back to me, like he'd been far away and I had just pulled him back. "What were you doing so close to the edge?"

"I was looking down over the rim. It was beautiful. The animals, the lake, the forest. That was before the mist rolled in and blanketed everything."

"You should see it up close before we leave. Do it now. You never know if we'll be passing this way again."

I nodded. A few weeks ago, I had no idea what this trip would bring. New faces, new places. A few weeks from now, they would all be left behind. A twinge of sadness hit me, but this time it had nothing to do with Mo.

"Have you heard from Goma?" I asked.

Jack had asked Bahati to stay with Goma and Scholastica while we were away. After what had happened to Juma, I understood why. I thought of the walled perimeter of Gabriel's house in Rutema, the broken glass on top, the hastily abandoned swing.

They can't promise her safety, Gabriel's sister, Anna, had said, explaining why Scholastica didn't go to school. I had chalked it up to kids being mean because she was different, but it was much bigger than that.

And now I was responsible for getting Scholastica to safety, and I had dragged Jack, and Goma, and Bahati, into it too.

"The mobile phone reception is sporadic out here," said Jack. "I'll have to use the landline at the reception. I'll let Goma know not to expect Juma. You have anything in the room?"

I shook my head and patted my handbag.

"Okay. You stay, finish your breakfast. I'll go check us out."

When he returned, I was talking to Ken and Judy. The mist was lifting, and guests were slowly drifting into the dining room.

"If you want to see the crater, we need to get moving," said Jack.

"Listen to the man. He knows what he's talking about." Ken poured tea for himself and Judy. "We had a late start yesterday, and it was filled with cars."

"Here." Judy handed me a business card. "If you're ever in our corner of the world, and still 'not together.'" She made hand gestures around *not together*.

"Thank you." I laughed. "Enjoy the rest of your visit."

We said goodbye and headed for the crater. Jack stopped at the gate to look after the permits and paperwork.

As we took the winding road that descended into the caldera, the clouds that covered the rim gave way to a sweeping, surreal landscape. The haziness dissipated and the world came into sharp focus again. The first animals I spotted were . . .

"Cows?" I turned to Jack in surprise.

Against the soft, pastel grasslands, a red cumulus of dust marked a line of cattle, inching down the steep, narrow track to the crater floor. A scrawny figure was guiding his herd into the mouth of the lion's domain.

"The Maasai," he explained. "They are free to roam the Ngorongoro Conservation Area, but they cannot live in the crater, so they bring their cattle to graze here. They have to enter and exit daily."

"But what happens if he's attacked? Or one of his cows?"

"Cattle are the Maasai's greatest wealth. A Maasai man will do anything to sustain or defend his livestock. He is trained for it from the time he's a little boy. When he passes the ultimate test of bravery, he earns his warrior name. Killing a lion used to be the final rite of passage to becoming a warrior, but things have changed. There are government rules and regulations to be followed now. Still, that there—" Jack motioned to the lone man, marching to the clang of cowbells, spear in hand "—is the ultimate warrior."

"Is this what Bahati would be doing if he lived here? Is Bahati his warrior name?" I asked as we left the man behind.

"Bahati is his nickname. He never received his warrior name."

"What happened? He told me his family disowned him, but he didn't say why."

"That is something you should ask him." Jack switched gears as we reached the floor of the caldera.

Patches of forest edged around steep cliffs, providing a soaring backdrop to the sea of grass, dappled with herds of grazing buffaloes. Sharp-eyed vultures scanned the morning from above. A skittish warthog ran across the plain, tail upright, the tuft of bristles at its end waving like a little black flag. Ostriches surveyed us with bright eyes, their bald heads bobbing up and down. The view was flat and clear for miles and miles.

I took a deep breath. So much earth. So much sky. Vast and infinite. It was humbling and awe-inspiring, like the roof had been lifted and I could see the dawning of the world.

It's beautiful, Mo, I thought. *I wish I'd come when you'd asked me to. While you were still here.*

"There." Jack turned the car off and pointed to something behind us in the knee-high, golden grass.

There was an almost imperceptible shift in the blades. Then they parted and a pride of lions ambled out, tails swishing as they walked down the road towards us. I watched them approach in the rear-view mirror, and held my breath as they prowled by us with long, powerful strides. There were ten lions, including two males with thick, black manes. Their massive, padded paws made no sound as they passed the car. One of the cubs broke away, but his mother went after him. She picked him up by the scruff of his neck and didn't let him down even after they'd caught up with the rest of the pride. He swayed back and forth, dangling out of her mouth, mewling apologies.

"Not a very regal send-off for a prince." I laughed as the lions retreated into the bush again.

"That was me and Goma when I was little," said Jack, starting the car. "I was always chasing something, and she was always pulling me back."

"What happened to your parents?"

"My father loved to fly. My parents were on their way home when his two-seater crashed. I was seven. Goma locked herself up in her room for a week. When she came out, she was just as fierce as she's always been. Although, sometimes I think it was more for me. She didn't have the luxury to fall apart. Like I did with Lily."

She didn't blame herself for what happened to her son, like you're doing with Lily, I thought, but held my tongue. "Your grandfather wasn't around?"

"He died before I was born, but I feel like I knew him. Probably because of all the stories Goma told me about him. I used to think she was making them up, but I still meet people who talk about him. He was larger than life. An extraordinary man."

We passed herds of wildebeest and zebra. Jack explained that zebras grazed on the harder parts of the vegetation, while the wildebeest preferred the softer parts, so they were perfectly paired. Roaming the plains together heightened awareness of predators, and the zebra's stripes confused the big cats.

"Where we see black and white, the lion sees only the patterned stripes because it's pretty much color blind. If a zebra is standing still in the wavy lines of the grass around it, a lion may completely overlook it."

I'd always been attracted to men who had brains to back up their brawn. Jack fit the bill perfectly, but I was only half-listening to his words. It was his voice that held me entranced. He didn't speak much, but here in the vast, unobstructed space, he seemed to be opening up to me. And his voice was delicious. It set my skin vibrating like a tuning fork—the perfect pitch, the perfect timbre, making the tiny hairs on the back of my neck stand on end. I wanted him to go on and on.

He might have sensed the shift in the air because he trailed off and looked at me. Directly at me. And it wasn't with the softness of his earlier morning gaze. It was different. Heart-poundingly different.

There's an unspoken rule about how long you can stare like that at another person. No one says it, but we all know it. There is the quick glance we give to strangers, the acknowledgment we exchange with people we know, the private joke, the silent acceptance, the lover's gaze, the parent's concern. Our eyes are always different, always speaking. They meet and look away, a thousand nuances expressed without words. And then there's this. Whatever was passing between Jack and me in the middle of that ancient caldera. Perhaps it was because we didn't know exactly where we fit—two people bound by a sunny, tragic afternoon, retreating from the edge of attraction—lives that were oceans apart, breaths that lingered in the space between us.

A jeep blaring loud music rattled past us, leaving a film of fine dust on the windshield. Jack drew away and started the car.

"They're beginning to come in. We should head to the lake before it gets too crowded. There's a salt lake, not too far up ahead, in the center of the crater."

I let my breath out and nodded. Something was always crackling between us, waiting to catch fire. It wasn't something either of us wanted, and so we resorted to distance and distraction.

I stared out of the window, at herds of Cape buffalo, so tame that they didn't budge as we drove past.

"They are one of the Big Five," said Jack.

"The Big Five?"

"Lions, leopards, elephants, rhinos, and Cape buffalo. They're called the Big Five. It's a term that originated with big game hunters. It has nothing to do with their size, but because they were the fiercest and most dangerous animals to hunt. Now no safari here is complete without spotting all five."

"I've seen two so far. The lion and the buffalo." I missed Mo in that instant—so much that it suddenly hurt to breathe. I'd been so wrapped up in my goals, I'd let the important things slip. I had my cottage, but I would never have the memory of going on a safari with Mo.

"I'm sure we'll see elephants, closer to the forest, but leopards tend to be shy, and rhinos have dwindled from all the poaching," said Jack. "Rhino horns are in high demand, mostly due to the myth about their medicinal value. Truth is, you might as well chew on your own nails for all the difference it makes."

"Rhino horns. Albino body parts. You ever wonder who starts these myths and how they gain their power?"

"We all want magic, Rodel. We want to wake up rich. Or healthy. Or beautiful. We want to make the person we love stay with us, live with us, die with us. We want that house, that job, that promotion. And so we create the myths, we live them, and we believe them. Until something better comes along, something that suits us better. Truth is that you and I are creating a myth ourselves. With Scholastica and the other children. We think if we get them to Wanza, we'll save them. And, yes, they'll be safer, but it's still a lie. Because it will just keep them cut off from the rest of the world. Eventually, they'll have to leave, and the world will still be the world. They might be better equipped to handle it, not quite as vulnerable, but they will still be targets."

"I know." I followed the swooping flight of a brightly plumed bird before turning to him. "I know it's not a solution. Nothing will change until the superstitions about them disappear. And who knows when that will be? I don't have the answers, Jack, but sometimes the only things that keep us from falling off the edge are necessary lies. The kind we tell ourselves, so we can keep going."

"Necessary lies," Jack repeated. He took his eyes off the road and glanced at me.

Suddenly, we weren't talking about the kids anymore. We were talking about the sweet, necessary lies we could tell each other in that moment. We could pretend—exchange phone numbers, promise to stay in touch, to visit, to remember birthdays—just to allow ourselves a taste of whatever was beating hard and fast between us. It would be like sucking on chili pepper candy balls. It would buzz and sting when it was gone, but it would be so, so good. And maybe that was it—the allure of something wild and indulgent to jump-start us back to life. Except we were not those people. We were Jack and Ro. And the last thing we needed was to connect and then let go of yet another person.

I turned away and gazed out of the window as we approached the lake. It sat like a shimmering jewel in the center of the crater.

"A pink lake?" I asked.

"Look again," said Jack.

"Flamingos!" I exclaimed, as they came into view.

Thousands of pink-feathered birds lined the shore. Their serpentine necks dipped in and out of the water, as if pecking at their tall, slender reflections.

"You'll get a better view through there." Jack slid the roof open, and I scooted to the back so I could stick my head out.

As Jack drove closer to the shore, the flamingos scattered around us, like pink petals in the wind. Some soared into the air, unfolding their wings and displaying the red plumage beneath.

My heart lifted with unexpected gladness, for Mo. That she'd seen this incredible sight, that she hadn't listened when I'd lectured her about finding a *real* job or renting a *real* apartment. She had packed so much into her life, living every single day on her own terms, it was as if she'd known there was no time to waste. Some people are like that. They listen to their inner voice even if it's mad and feral and doesn't make sense to the rest of us.

It was short, Mo. But it was full and bursting with flavor.

Are you talking about my life or those chili pepper candy balls?

I laughed as the flamingos danced around me, honking like geese. They were so close that I could see the yellow of their eyes and the curve of their beaks. The sky was a stark blue now, except for a few salt clouds whipped up from the lake. It was much warmer and my skin felt sated from the sun.

"Ha!" I thumped the roof with my fist, loving the wind in my hair. "It's a beautiful day!" I called to the birds.

We left them behind and passed swamps and marshes where hippos wallowed in thick, wet mud pools. A pack of narrow hipped hyenas circled the remains of a kill. They nipped at the black-backed jackals that were encroaching on them. Vultures and Marabou Storks hovered above, looking to get in on the action. Two gray-crowned cranes watched a group of aggressive buffaloes chase a lion around the water hole.

Jack veered off the dirt track and stopped the car. A few minutes later, he popped up beside me and handed me a set of binoculars.

"See that group of birds over there?" He waited for me to spot them. They had creamy white throats, and were picking at the ground with their bills. "They're Kori Bustards. The males are amongst the world's heaviest flying birds. Now look up into that tree. The tall one with the branch extending off to the right."

He stood behind me, his chest to my back, pointing it out. His other hand rested on my shoulder, warm and heavy.

It took me few minutes to find what he wanted me to see.

"A cheetah," I said.

It was stretched out on the branch, eyes closed, tail flicking away the flies hovering around it.

"Not a cheetah. A leopard." We were so close that Jack's breath stirred my hair as he spoke. "They're easy to confuse because they both have spots. Cheetahs have solid black spots and black tear lines that run from the corner of their eyes. Leopard spots are clustered, like rosettes. Leopards are also bigger and more muscular. They're not built for speed like cheetahs, but what they lack in speed, they make up for in stealth and power. They'll often carry their prey high up in the trees to prevent other predators from eating them."

I watched the leopard's belly rise and fall with each breath. I thought of it slipping through the tall Savanna grass with scarcely a ripple, lunging on its unsuspecting quarry, and exerting a lethal hold with its powerful jaw.

"Number three of the Big Five," I said, with a bit of shudder.

"You still cold?"

"I'm fine," I said, tilting my face to him.

The sun was directly behind him, framing his thick, untamed hair like a golden mane.

I wonder if he goes at it like Mufasa, Mo.

"What's so funny?" Jack caught my grin.

"Nothing." I glanced away. "Sometimes I have these weird conversations with my sister."

"It had something to do with me, didn't it?" he asked, as if talking to my dead sister was a completely normal thing to do. Then again, maybe it was something he could relate to.

"Do you do that?" I asked. "Do you ever speak to Lily?"

"I can't." The fences came back up around him, like I'd wandered in too far and touched something he didn't want anyone to see, something personal and raw and painful. "I can't . . . face her."

My heart constricted. Jack was too guilt-ridden to have a conversation with his daughter. Even an imaginary one. Because he hadn't been able to get to her in time. Because she had died alone. I wanted to say something, but I kept my mouth shut. Telling someone to get over something like that was bullshit.

"If you can't speak, just listen," I said. "Maybe one day you'll hear what she's saying."

I squeezed past him through the open roof and took my seat. We drove in silence until we got to a patch of tall, yellow-barked trees. Vervet monkeys swung from the dense canopy, and birds flitted through the branches.

"The Lerai Forest," said Jack.

"Oh, Jack. Look!" I squeezed his arm and pointed into the shady thicket.

A massive elephant was rubbing itself against a tree, its large tusks dragging in the dirt.

"It's an old bull. Most of the crater elephants are male," said Jack. "The large breeding herds only descend here occasionally."

"Why is he doing that? Rubbing up against that tree?"

"Probably scratching himself. Or getting rid of parasites on his skin." He leaned forward and squinted through the binoculars. "Maybe he's just horny."

He said it so matter-of-factly, I burst out laughing. "Are you checking out his schlong?"

Jack glanced at me sideways. "Did you just snort, Rodel Emerson?"

"It was a chortle."

He sat back and folded his arms. "You snorted. And you call a dick a schlong."

"Mo said I should come down here so she could show me an elephant's schlong."

"In that case, mission accomplished." He made an imaginary check mark in the air and passed me the binoculars. "Go on. Don't be shy."

"No, thank you. I don't need to see his . . . his schlong." I was pretty sure my cheeks had turned beetroot red, or maybe a bright shade of scary cherry.

"Oh, my God. You're shy. You're coloring up like the Serengeti sunset." Jack was grinning. A full-fledged ear-to-ear smile that was completely dazzling.

"Can we just go?" I handed him back the binoculars.

"Hang on to those," he said, starting the car up again. "We'll probably see some more schlongs up ahead."

The color receded from my cheeks as we drove through the dappled forest, but the buzz remained—the high I got from seeing this man smile.

We sighted baboons, waterbucks, and more elephants tearing

off branches and stuffing them in their mouths.

"It doesn't look like we're going to get all of the Big Five today," said Jack, as we approached the ascent back up to the rim. "No rhino sighting."

"Four out of five isn't so bad," I replied, looking down at the crater.

Lines of cars traversed the plains below, whipping dust clouds in their wake. A pride of lions sprawled under the shade of a tree, while a Maasai grazed his cattle within stone's throw. A few paces away, a newborn zebra nuzzled up to its mother on unsteady legs. With the mist now gone, the crater was visible all the way up to the forested rim. A handful of white clouds lingered, casting dark shadows on the floor.

Had Mo stopped here to take in the same view? I wondered. Even though she was gone, I felt closer to her for having been there. It was like touching the shadow of her soul.

"Thank you," I said to Jack. "I don't think I'm ever going to forget it."

The blue of his eyes held me for a heart-skipping instant. Everything seemed hushed and bare.

It was a while before he spoke, and his voice was soft but loaded. "Me neither."

Losing someone you love tunes you in to the fragility of life—of moments and memories and music. It makes you want to embrace all the foolish, inarticulate longings that pull at your heart. It makes you want to grasp un-played notes of un-played symphonies. Perhaps that was why Jack and I clung to that moment, eyes locked, breaths stilled, listening to something that only we could hear, something that lived in the fleeting space between hello and goodbye. It made me want to freeze-frame the rippling grasslands below us, and the play of light across Jack's face.

A S WE DROVE away from the crater, the towering trees gave way to a high, windswept plateau.

"One more stop before we head back," said Jack, turning into the entrance of a Maasai village.

It was a collection of thatched-roof huts surrounded by a circle of thorn bushes to keep out wild animals and predators. Jack retrieved a duffel bag from the trunk and swung it over his shoulder.

"You don't travel light, do you?" I said, when I saw all the stuff stashed in his car.

Spare wheels, coils of thick rope, a washbasin, pots, pans, utensils, a portable stove, spare gallons of petrol, water, electrical tape, mosquito netting, camping gear, flares, a first aid kit, a paraffin lamp, matches, tins of food, pliers, tools, gadgets. And a rifle, with what looked like a long-range viewer.

"I come prepared when I'm out in the reserves."

"So, what's in the bag?" I asked, following him down the path to the village.

"Coffee, from the farm," he said. "For Bahati's father. He's also the village elder. Interesting guy. Wise, stubborn, insightful. He's set in some ways, but incredibly progressive in others. Eight wives, twenty-nine children, and counting."

"Seriously? So, the Maasai are polygamous?"

"Yes. They determine a man's standing first by his bravery,

and then by the number of wives, children, and cows he has. Each wife usually has a home within the same *boma* or village. Bahati's village is not as traditional as some of the other Maasai *bomas*. It's a designated cultural *boma,* which means a lot of tours stop here so people can visit the homes, take pictures, buy souvenirs. That kind of stuff."

A group of Maasai men emerged to greet us. They were draped in brilliant reds and blues, their skin the shade of acacia bark. They were as tall as Jack, at least six feet, but with slim, wiry bodies, and eyes that looked permanently yellow—probably from wood smoke. They wore long braids, dyed with red clay, and had distended earlobes adorned with beads and ornaments. Upon seeing Jack, their stiff gaits loosened and their smiles widened.

"Jack Warden, no entrance fee," one of them said. "Your girlfriend? Also no fee."

"*Asante.* Thank you," Jack replied. "Come along, girlfriend. Let's follow the *moran.*"

"The *moran?*" I ignored the 'girlfriend' part.

"It's what they call their warriors."

We maneuvered around piles of cow manure, stirring up the flies, and stopped outside a loaf-shaped hut. The *morans* presented us to a dignified looking man with a checkered red and black sheet draped over his shoulders. Loops of silver and turquoise earrings hung from his earlobes. He sat on a low, three-legged stool and flicked a fly whisk back and forth across his face. Men and women squatted around him. The *morans* stood to the side, leaning on their spear shafts, some of them balancing like storks, on one leg.

"Jack Warden," said the man, spitting into his palm and holding it out for Jack.

"Olonana." Jack shook hands.

I tried not to think about the gob of spit sealing their greeting.

"This is my friend, Rodel." Jack steered me forward until I was standing before the chief. "Rodel, this is Bahati's father."

Oh God. Please let this be a spit-less hello.

I smiled and gave the man a curt bow, keeping both hands plastered to my sides. He nodded, and I let out my breath. Apparently, his spit wasn't just for anyone, only those he held in great affection. And he was obviously fond of Jack because he summoned another stool for him, while I was waved away.

"She sits with me," said Jack, grabbing my hand and pulling me back.

No other stool made an appearance and after a few beats, I realized that Jack really did mean for me to sit with him. Or rather, *on* him. And so I perched awkwardly on Jack's lap, while the women and children laughed at me.

"*Kasserian ingera.*" Olonana didn't use the familiar Swahili words for hello that I had grown accustomed to—*habari* or *jambo.*

"*Sapati ingera,*" replied Jack.

I wondered if anyone else greeted the chief this way—solemn and sincere, while balancing a squirming woman on his thigh.

They exchanged a few words. Then Olonana raised his whisk to a man whose bent, wizened form was barely discernible against the dark entrance of the hut. He was dressed in a long green cloth, but what stood out was the leather pouch hanging around his neck. It was adorned with white beads and cowrie shells, different from the ornaments that everyone else was wearing. He also had a necklace of crocodile teeth that rattled when he moved.

"That's Lonyoki. The *oloiboni,*" Jack explained in a hushed voice. "I guess you could call him their spiritual leader. A vision seeker and medicine man. The *oloiboni* is charged with divining the future. He oversees their rituals and ceremonies."

"So he's like *Rafiki.*" I stopped shifting and decided to suck up my ridiculous lap-sitting stint as gracefully as possible.

Jack blinked before catching on. "You're talking about the

shaman in that movie, *The Lion King*. What's with you and all *The Lion King* references?"

"What do you mean?"

"You were babbling about Mufasa last night."

"What?" *Oh God.* "What did I say?"

"Something about him being the king of the jungle."

I was glad that Rafiki, a.k.a Lonyoki, a.k.a. the medicine man, chose that moment to pound his club into the ground. It had a polished wooden shaft with a heavy knob at the top, carved in the shape of a serpent's head. Puffs of red dirt stirred at his feet. Everyone turned their attention to the woman who rose from the crowd and disappeared into the hut.

"What's going on?" I asked Jack, realizing that we had interrupted some kind of a village gathering.

"A coming of age ceremony," he replied. "No matter what happens next, I want you to remain expressionless. Do not show any emotion. Do not look away. Do not flinch. You hear me?"

"Why? Wha—" I broke off as the shrill screams of a girl filled the air. It was coming from inside the hut. Whatever was happening to her was excruciating—painful and agonizing. And yet no one made a move to help her. They all waited, huddled outside, blank faces turned to the dark, open doorway. A chorus of women started humming, as if to drown out the sounds, or maybe to offer her comfort.

"Jack, what is going on?" I whispered.

"The transition from girlhood to womanhood. Female circumcision." He clamped his arm around me as he said it, containing my burst of outrage. "Listen to me." He leaned close and spoke slow and steady in my ear. "It happens, even though the government has banned it. It is a deeply rooted tradition, but Olonana and his people are moving away from it. What's happening in there is symbolic. The girl is receiving a ritual nick on her thigh. It's nothing compared to cutting out part of her genitalia. The screaming is important. She must scream loud enough for everyone outside to hear, or they won't feel like she has earned the status being conferred on her. They circumcise the boys too, in their teens, except they are not allowed to make a single sound. Doing so would bring shame to them and their family."

The whole thing was tough and harsh to take. When the girl's cries stopped, I realized my fingers were squeezing tightly around Jack's.

"Do you know them through Bahati?" I asked, letting go of him like I'd touched a hot stove. "Olonana and his people?"

"Olonana's family saved my grandfather during the war when he was injured in hostile territory. They sheltered him until he recovered from his wounds. Goma and I always stop by and pay our respects whenever we're in the area."

"That's why you took Bahati under your wing and taught him how to drive?"

"I didn't know he was Olonana's son at first. Most of his kids live out here, in the *bomas*."

Everyone stood as the girl emerged from the hut, flanked by two women. One was the lady who had entered the hut earlier, probably to deliver the ritual cut, and the other, I assumed to be the girl's mother. The girl was given traditional beads and a ring made from animal skin as a sign of her passage into womanhood. The *oloiboni* presented her to the village, ready for marriage, and all the responsibilities that went with it.

"She is so young," I remarked.

"She is one of the lucky ones," replied Jack. "A few years ago, she would not have been able to walk out of there for days."

"So, what convinced them to do away with it? With female circumcision?"

"It's not something that happened overnight. Eventually, it

came down to persuading the men that sex with an uncircumcised woman is more pleasurable—that far from promoting promiscuity, having an intact clitoris makes a woman more receptive to their advances."

"It's a patriarchal society," Jack continued, catching the expression on my face. "Their way of life may seem strange and harsh, but every culture evolves with its own set of values and practices that change with time and circumstance. The women are pushing back and becoming more independent. A lot of them have started working with overseas organizations, selling their bracelets and jewelry. They're turning their traditional bead-working skills into something that generates an income."

We merged into the shuffle of villagers that were heading for the livestock enclosure in the center of the homestead. Most of the cattle were out to graze, but there were a few left behind, along with some goats and sheep. A cow was held down and shot in the jugular with a blunt arrow. The blood that spurted from the neck was caught in a calabash and served to the girl that had just undergone the ceremony.

"The Maasai rarely kill their cattle," explained Jack. "But they will extract some of the blood and staunch the wound right away. The cow will be no worse for the wear, and the blood is used as protein to help the weak regain their strength . . ." He trailed off because the blood-filled calabash was being passed around and Olonana offered it to him next.

I watched as he took a sip and passed it on. Thankfully, he skipped me and for that, he had my eternal gratitude. Sushi was about as adventurous as I was willing to get, but hats off to him for going all Dracula on it.

"You drink when you're offered," he said. "It's a sign of respect."

"Between the blood and the spit, the exchange of bodily fluids is clearly a winning theme," I remarked under my breath, but Jack heard me nonetheless. I'd always thought I was fair and open-minded, but my prejudices were starting to surface, and it was making me irritable and uncomfortable.

"Maybe I shouldn't have accepted the invite to the communal orgy we're headed for?"

"What?" I stopped in my tracks.

The little boy walking behind me nose-dived straight into my bum. It was a cushioned landing for him, but he had a hard head, and I rubbed my arse as everyone passed us by.

"It's part of the celebration." Jack checked out my tush with great interest, so I glared at him, even though a part of me ached whenever I caught a glimpse of this Jack—the fun, laid-back Jack who'd been buried under the rubble of a mall.

"It's an eating orgy, Rodel," he said. "They're going to slaughter a goat in honor of today's ceremony."

"And I'm supposed to eat it?" My bum was sore, I was tired, and the flies seemed to have a thing for me. I was hungry, but not *that* hungry.

"They're going to roast it." Jack laughed. "But first, they dance," he said, as we found ourselves at the edge of a circle of villagers.

A *moran* entered the circle, poised and regal in his scarlet sheet and turquoise cape. He started jumping, spear in hand, while the rest of the men emitted a low-pitched drone. As he jumped higher and higher, they raised their pitch to match his leaps, until he got tired and another warrior took his place. Then the women took over the singing. A lone woman crooned a line, and the rest of the group answered in unison. A lot of the ladies wore ornate, beaded collars around their necks that rocked up and down when they flapped their shoulders. As the men jumped, fierce and proud, attaining impressive heights, everyone heaped praises upon them. It was a very male display of muscle, virility, and stamina. I sneaked a look at the women to see if they were taking notes.

Holy crap, they were. They were totally into it. Especially the girl who had undergone the symbolic circumcision ceremony. She was being nudged and elbowed by the other girls. She was The Bachelorette, the debutante, the Belle of the *Boma*. I wondered if she got to choose her husband, or if it would be decided for her.

I was about to ask Jack when Olonana pulled him inside the circle. A high-pitched trill ran through the crowd as Jack kicked off his shoes. Apparently, it was a call to battle—to see who could jump higher. Olonana and Jack leaped facing each other, rising and falling. I caught glimpses of a sheathed dagger under the chief's clothes as they rose higher and higher. It was a duel between the chief and his visitor, and Jack was all in.

There was an unrestrained fluidity about his movements, a rawness that stirred something hot and electric in me. He was muscle in motion. Dynamic, dominant, compelling. I could make out the warm lines of his body through his clothes—the expanse of his chest, the cut of steely thighs, the arms that had brushed past me in the bathroom last night. I dug my nails into my palm, hoping to wake myself up from the madness consuming me, spreading through my nerves like wild grass fire. There was something in the dust, something in the dry, low humming around me, that settled in my stomach and writhed like a fish gasping for a drop of water.

I suspected Jack held back in the end, out of respect for the chief. And the older man was wise enough to know it, because he invited the other *morans* to join them, declaring a shared victory for all. When the group broke, Jack found me. I avoided his gaze, acutely aware of the way his breath had turned quick and shallow, the fine sheen of sweat on his forehead, the heated glow of his body.

"Everything okay?" he asked, taking a big glug of water from a gourd someone handed him. No Coca-Cola here. "You seem flushed."

"Just . . . from the sun."

He passed me the water, and I took a sip. And then another. I wanted to douse myself with it. I had no business thinking sexy thoughts about this man. I didn't *want* to, damn it.

We were invited into Olonana's *inkajijik*, a traditional Maasai house. The entrance was a long, narrow arch with no door. After the bright afternoon sun, it took a few minutes for my eyes to adjust to the dark. I felt around and found a knobby chair.

"Rodel." Jack cleared his throat.

It was at that moment I realized I was clutching an old woman's knee. Not a chair.

"I'm so sorry." I jumped on Jack's lap instead. It was turning out to be my safe haven.

Olonana and Jack conversed, while the old woman eyed me from her stool. She rummaged through a burlap sack then held something out for me. As I reached for it, something landed on my head. It was wet and warm. I was about to touch it when Jack grabbed my wrist.

"Don't," he said.

"What is it?" I could feel it settling into my scalp.

"A drop of rainwater from the roof." His spoke the words softly, in my ear. "The gods have favored you. Just smile and accept the gift she's holding out for you."

I did as I was told, retrieving a bracelet from the old woman. It was a string of small, round beads threaded through a leather cord. Jack tied it around my wrist.

"It says something." I held my hand up to the light. There was a letter seared into each bead.

"*Taleenoi olngisoilechashur,*" said Jack.

"*Talee*-what?"

"There is a saying among my people, that everything is one," said Olonana. "We are all connected. *Taleenoi olngisoilechashur.*"

I was momentarily taken aback that he spoke English, but it made sense that he would use the local dialect when he spoke to Jack since they both understood it.

"We are all connected." I touched the beads, feeling their cool, smooth surface. "Thank you," I said to the old woman, touched by her simple, meaningful gift. "*Asante.*"

She smiled back, revealing two missing teeth, a gap that made her look like a wrinkled baby.

"My mother speaks Maa, not Swahili," said Olonana. "The word *Maasai* means the people that speak Maa."

"Please let her know I love it."

As I admired the blue, green, and red beads on the bracelet, a platter of hot, roasted meat was brought into the hut, along with a gourd filled with some kind of fermented drink.

"You will accompany my mother to the other hut now," said Olonana, looking at me.

Clearly, the men and women ate separately, so I followed Olonana's mother to a smoky *inkajijik*, similar to the one we'd left. A large wooden pole held up the roof. The walls were made of branches, plastered over with dirt, cow dung, and ashes. There was a sick calf being tended to by one of the women. All the other women were gathered around a large wooden bowl, chewing diligently on the meat. It was nothing like the prime cuts that Jack and Olonana had received.

Olonana's mother offered me a piece of charred, marbled fat. I knew better than to refuse. The kids touched my hair and picked at my clothes as I ate. Flies bunched around their mouths and eyes, but they didn't seem to notice. Someone passed me a horn filled with soured milk. I dipped my lips into it but didn't drink. There wasn't a single loo in sight, and there was no way I was making a mad dash for the bushes in case it didn't agree with me.

You're such a wuss, Ro.

Thanks, Mo. Like I need to feel any worse about myself right now.

I always said you need to get out more. You meet yourself when you travel.

I ignored her but she persisted.

Wuss.

Fine! I bit into the meat ferociously. *Happy now?*

When I was sure she was gone, I spit it out, but didn't want to risk offending anyone. I thought about dropping it in a dark corner, but my covert operation turned out to be unnecessary. A dog entered the hut, sniffing around the women and children. I scratched his ear and fed him the charbroiled lump in my hand, turning his face to the wall until he finished eating.

I'm so sorry. I'm so sorry it's kind of pre-chewed.

My stomach growled because I hadn't eaten anything since we left the campsite that morning. Olonana's mother smiled and handed me another piece of goat meat.

Crap.

Thankfully, a busload of tourists arrived, and everyone headed out to greet them. Jack emerged from Olonana's *inkajijik* with the chief and joined me. Olonana grabbed a handful of coffee beans from a pouch and threw them into his mouth.

"He chews the coffee beans raw?" I asked.

"They're roasted. But yes, he eats them whole. For energy," replied Jack. "Sometimes the *morans* use them on long treks, or when they want to stay awake at night."

Olonana took Jack aside while I wished his mother goodbye. The rest of the villagers were putting on a welcome dance for the tourists. A few were trying to sell them bracelets and other handicrafts.

"What was that about?" I asked, when Jack returned. "It looked pretty intense."

"He was giving me a message for Bahati."

"He wants to reconcile?"

"He just had two words for him: *Kasserian ingera.*"

"Isn't that what he said to you earlier?"

"Yes. It's a Maasai greeting. It means, 'How are the children?'"

"I didn't know Bahati had children." I stopped by the stall at the entrance to the *boma*. It was filled with colorful, hand-made souvenirs.

"Bahati doesn't have kids. It's not about his children, or mine, or anyone else's. You always reply '*Sapati ingera*', which means 'All the children are well'. Because when all the children are well, everything is good and right with the world."

"That's beautiful. And profound. What strange, wonderful people they are." I might not have been able to relate to their customs or lifestyle, but I admired them for the pride and authenticity with which they held on to their rich, fierce heritage.

"You like that?" Jack motioned to the wooden figure I was holding. It was about the size of my palm, carved in the shape of a boy playing a flute.

He paid for it without waiting for an answer and handed it to me after the woman wrapped it up for us.

"Thank you. You didn't have to do that."

"I kind of did. My way of saying sorry." He rubbed the back of his neck sheepishly.

"Sorry? For what?"

"You know when that drop of water landed on your head?"

"Yes?" I walked faster, trying to keep up with him as he made a beeline for the car.

"I didn't want you to freak out, but the old lady spit on you."

"The old lady . . ." I stopped in my tracks. "She spit . . ." I touched the spot on my head. My hand came back dry, but I stared at it, horrified.

"She liked you." Jack's mouth wobbled, like he was trying to keep from laughing. "It was her way of blessing you."

Most people are uncomfortable with silence, especially the kind when you know someone is about to erupt. Jack was not one of them. He ignored the steam coming out of my ears.

"This is not going to make any difference." He opened the trunk, poured some water on a rag, and patted my scalp with it. "But it'll make you feel better."

I glared at him without a word.

"This?" He offered me a packet of biscuits.

Silence.

"This?" He threw in a bottle of pineapple juice.

My outrage dissipated, because yes. Yes. I was starving, and that made me feel much, much better.

"Friends?" he asked, holding the door open for me.

I was going to come back with a sharp retort, but my stomach chose to answer instead. With a wild growl. To his credit, Jack kept a straight face.

I ripped into the biscuits before he got in the car.

"Not a fan of the local cuisine?" he asked.

"Not a fan of roasted entrails, local or otherwise. And you're one to talk. You got all the good stuff."

"Hey, I came bearing gifts for the chief. We caught him just in time. He'll be heading out soon with the cattle."

"But he's the chief. He can get someone else to graze the cattle."

"He's a nomad. When he feels the call of the land, he goes. Sometimes he'll trek clear across the plains with them, following the water."

"Wow." I stuffed my mouth with chocolate-coated biscuits. "I'll have a lot of stories to tell my students when I get back."

We left the bleak plateau behind, and the landscape changed once again. Huge fig trees lined the road, draped in spools of trailing moss. Starry bursts of sunshine sparkled through the leaves as we drove by. I could see Mo in them—her warmth, her dazzle, her sharp, bright energy. For a moment, I was transported back to a time when we were kids, playing peek-a-boo.

. . . *5, 4, 3, 2, 1 . . . ready or not, here I come!*

I remembered the thrill of hiding. The rush of seeking. Hearts racing. Bodies squirming. The squealing when you find someone, or when someone finds you. Maybe that's what life was about. Seven billion people playing hide and seek, waiting to find and be found. Mothers, fathers, lovers, friends, playing a cosmic game of discovery—of self, and of others—appearing and disappearing like stars rotating on the horizon.

Maybe Mo was still playing hide and seek in these beams of sunlight, in the dance of elephant grass, in the fragrance of wild blossoms, waiting for me to find her again and again. Maybe Jack found Lily in thunderstorms, under the tree, by her grave. Maybe he looked for her in raindrops, because she felt like redemption pouring down from the heavens. Maybe when he recorded thunder and lightning, he was capturing bits of her, to carry with him on his phone.

"Can we stop here?" I asked, as we rounded a rocky outcrop. A lone fig tree grew on the patch of soft earth at its edge.

We got out and stretched our legs. It was late afternoon, and the shadows were getting longer on the plains below. I dug a small hole under the tree and buried the wooden statue we had picked up from the *boma*.

"What was that about?" asked Jack, when we got back into the car.

"For Juma," I replied. "Every kid needs a lullaby. Now he can listen to the birds in the trees, and the wind in the valley."

We sat in silence for a few minutes, as the sun slipped slowly behind the silhouette of the giant tree.

Then Jack took my hand, lacing our fingers together. "We'll get the next one."

Something sparked and buzzed in the stillness between us. It felt like hope, like life, like my heart galloping away from me.

"We'll get the next one," I repeated, thinking of the other two kids on Mo's list.

Maybe it was a necessary lie, one we were trying to convince ourselves of, but in that moment, with my hand resting in Jack's warm, solid grip, I thought anything was possible. Because that's the way holding hands with Jack made me feel.

B Y THE TIME we got back to the farm, the lights were off and everyone was in bed. For the first time in weeks, I fell asleep the moment my head hit the pillow.

The shot rang out in the early morning—a single, jarring crack that echoed through the stillness like a clap of thunder.

Scholastica! It was my first thought as I bolted out of bed. I flung her bedroom door open, but she wasn't there. I checked for Jack, but he wasn't in his room either.

"Scholastica!" I called, spinning around and running straight into Goma. "I can't find her," I said, steadying her tiny frame.

"She's fine. She's been sleeping with me, in my room." Goma held her door open, and there was Scholastica, snuggled peacefully under the covers.

"What was that noise?" I asked, trying to keep my voice down. "Did you hear it? And where's Jack?"

"It was a rifle. And Jack is probably out already." Goma belted a thick gown over her muumuu. She unlocked her wardrobe, parted the clothes, and reached for a shotgun tucked in the back. She loaded it calmly, propped it against her hip and racked the pump. "Never piss off an old bird. We're cranky, constipated, and we need our beauty sleep."

She signaled me to stay behind her as we made our way down the hallway. Had I caught sight of myself, creeping behind Goma's frail form, I might have laughed. But she held the gun like she meant business, and my heart was still caught in my throat. I had no idea what was waiting for us downstairs. And neither did she.

The floorboards creaked as we checked out the ground floor. When we got to the kitchen, Goma pushed the sheer curtains aside with the tip of her shotgun.

"There." She motioned to the glow of light in the fields. "Someone's in the livestock pen."

We stepped outside and made our way toward it, two dark figures against a violet dawn sky. Goma kicked the corral gate open, keeping the rifle pointed firmly ahead of her. Something was on the ground outside the barn, barely discernible in a weak pool of light.

My mind played out all kinds of scenarios. What if someone had come for Scholastica? What if Jack had gotten in the way? What if he'd been the target of the shot we'd heard?

Oh God. Please don't let it be Jack.

"No!" I rushed toward the figure sprawled out by the barn. The ground was dark and wet around it.

Blood.

"Step away from there." It was Jack's voice. Gritty and raw. I turned towards it with the kind of relief that couldn't be contained.

"You're okay," I said. Nothing else mattered, just that he was standing there.

I didn't realize that I was running to him until I was a few feet away, when I caught a glimpse of Goma's expression. She was watching me with a mix of curiosity and astuteness that made me stop short.

You care for him. She didn't say it out loud, but she might as well have. *You care for Jack.*

Of course, I care for him. I stumbled and came to a halt. *If anything happened to him because of me, I'd feel awful about it.*

Right. Goma lowered her shotgun. *And that's all there is to it.*

But her sharp eyes stayed on me, making me feel like she could see clear to my soul.

"We . . . we heard a shot," I said to Jack.

"A pack of hyenas on the prowl. They were after one of the calves. I shot one." He motioned to the prone figure. "The rest took off."

"And the calf?" asked Goma.

"A few cuts and scrapes, but she'll recover."

Goma nodded. "I'll go find her a blanket."

She disappeared into the barn, leaving Jack and me standing by the dead hyena.

"Does this happen often?" I asked.

Jack had shot the hyena dead center, in the middle of its forehead. How he'd managed that in the bleak light of dawn, was beyond me.

"Mostly when the rains fail. That's when the animals tend to stray from their turf. Luckily, the horses got nervous and alerted me."

"You have horses too?"

"And cows and hens. We try to be as self-sufficient as we can. Eggs, milk, fruit trees, a vegetable patch. Even our alarm clock is organic."

I smiled as the rooster crowed again. "You like to keep it au naturel?"

"One hundred percent."

I knew the nuances in his voice now. And from the way he was looking at me, he wasn't talking about the farm. My throat went dry as I realized I was completely back-lit from the light, that my every curve was exposed to him. My nipples were puckered from the morning chill, but a rushing warmth flooded through my every pore. My heart fluttered wildly, like a kite in a whirlwind. There was a magnetism and self-confidence about Jack that made me want to hand him all my strings. I wanted to know what it would feel like to have his hands wrapped around my hair—pulling, tugging—

"You two should get a barn."

We both jumped at the sound of Goma's voice.

"Seriously, with a carcass at your feet?" She looked from me to Jack. "No. I don't want to hear it." She held her palm up as Jack started to say something. "You can deny it all you want. Both of you. But you're not fooling this old crone. There's some major ogling going on here. Sparks and all."

We stared at her in awkward silence. What do you say to something like that?

"Get back in the house, Goma," said Jack.

"With pleasure," she replied, giving us a sly, haughty look.

Oh God. Could the ground just part now and swallow me whole?

We stared at our feet when she was gone.

"I'm sorry she—"

"It's okay." I cut him off. "I should head to town today and pick up my things from the hostel." *So I'm not wandering around in your grandmother's muumuu, which is the furthest thing from sexy, so it's kind of insane that we even had that moment, and maybe if I just keep talking to myself long enough, I'll be able to heckle this embarrassing incident right out of my head, and then we can just go back to—*

"You hear that?" Jack swiveled around, shielding me with his large frame. "Something's out there," he said.

"It's just me." Bahati emerged from the shadows. "I heard a gunshot."

"That was half an hour ago. Where have you been?"

"Watching. From my window." He pointed to the upper floor of the house.

"And you let Goma and Rodel check out the situation first? You make a lousy guard, Bahati."

"I am not a guard. Never claimed to be. I am an actor. You paid me to stay here until you returned. You got back last night. The way I see it, my contract ended then. Besides, I am only playing the role of a guard. When people see me, they see a fierce Maasai warrior they don't want to cross. That's all that matters. Their perception. They don't have to know I wouldn't harm a fly. So, you see, everything gets resolved peacefully. No combat, no fighting. But hyenas in the middle of the night? They're all yours."

"Well, you can help me bury this one," said Jack. "And then I'm hoping you can drive Rodel to Amosha so she can pick up her things. It turns out that I need you a little longer. I've been gone a couple of days, and I need to catch up. I could do with some help until Rodel and I leave for Wanza. You think you can handle that?"

Bahati rubbed his chin and glanced at the hyena. "Same pay?"

"Same pay."

"No bonus for disposing of dead bodies?"

"No bonus. It's still a lot more than what you make from your trips and The Grand Tulip," said Jack. "You want in or not?"

"Yes, yes. Of course. Just checking. But I think we should have a code. For emergencies, you know? In case I need you. Your farm is a dangerous place. Yesterday, I saw a snake. It crossed the path right before me. Maybe I should get a whistle. What do you think? And all this stuff with Scholastica gives me heartburn. I hardly slept a wink while you were away. Goma forgets to lock the front door. And your house is old. It makes a lot of noise at night. I keep having panic attacks. And then this shooting. Wild animals sniffing around. I should get some kind of compensation. Health and hazard . . ."

I retreated slowly as he prattled on. I wanted to slink away and pretend that my insides weren't jangled, that the tingling in the pit of my stomach was from the early morning scare, and had nothing to do with Jack's scorching appraisal.

When I got to the house, I turned around.

I could have sworn Jack was still watching me.

"I AM GOING to town with Rodel and Bahati," announced Goma.

"What for?" Jack refilled his water bottle and leaned against the counter. He'd been out all morning, and his face was flushed from the sun.

"Someone needs to follow up on that girl's father." She gestured to Scholastica. "He's missing, and no one seems to give a damn."

"His sister already filed a report with the police."

"Yes, I spoke to her. Rodel left me her phone number in case of an emergency with Scholastica. Anna said the police think Gabriel's abandoned his daughter. If that's the case, fine. But I want to hear it from him. I've jotted down all his details. I'm going to visit my friend at the police station and have them track Gabriel down."

"Just be careful, okay?" Jack couldn't hide the concern he felt for his grandmother. "Don't let them know we have Scholastica here. In case someone knows he has an albino daughter."

"I'm no fool, boy." Goma put on a pair of mirrored, rainbow sunglasses. They covered most of her face and reflected the world in two colorful, round saucers. "You'll keep an eye on Scholastica?"

"We'll check in on the calf," replied Jack. "Would you like that, Scholastica?" He switched to Swahili and sat down beside her.

Jack and I were avoiding gazes, which was fine with me. Dealing with the high voltage zinging between us was one thing; having it pointed out by Goma just served to amplify the whole situation. We were both feeling guilty for it because desire has no place at grief's table, and yet, there it was, sitting between us like a shameless, uninvited guest.

"Well, we're off," said Goma, as we stepped out the door.

"*Kwaheri!*" Scholastica waved goodbye. She seemed to have grown closer to Goma while Jack and I were away.

"Look how my Suzi is shining today!" Bahati preened as Goma and I got into his jeep. He had waxed and polished her to a dazzling gleam.

"If you spent half as much time paying attention to a nice, young lady, as you do to your Suzi, you'd have a family by now."

"Family is fickle. My Suzi—" he thumped the dashboard "— she is solid. Reliable. Jack said you met my father, Miss Rodel?"

"It's Ro." It was funny how he called Jack and Goma by their names, but was more formal with me. I was learning it was his way of distancing himself. "And yes, I met Olonana. Your grandmother gave me this." I held up the bracelet so he could see it in his rearview.

"They were nicer to you than to me. You know what my father gave me? My nickname. Bahati. Bahati Mbaya."

"You don't like it?" I asked. We had left the stone pillars of Kaburi Estate behind and were driving down the main road to Amosha.

"You wouldn't like it either if you knew the meaning. *Bahati* means luck. *Mbaya* means bad. My father thinks I am bad luck. When I was born, Lonyoki, our *oloiboni*, had a vision. He saw me riding the back of a giant, black serpent. I was fighting my own kind, helping the white people. Many years ago, the colonialists took our land. We are still trying to recover and hold on to our way of life. Lonyoki believed I was a threat to the village, but my father loved me. He listened to Lonyoki on all matters except that, and it displeased the *oloiboni*. He blamed every misfortune on me. If the rains didn't come, it was my fault. If his spells didn't work, it was my fault. If disease wiped out our cows, it was my fault.

"Maybe if I had been like the other *morans*, if I had proved my worth, it would have passed. But I was not a good hunter or herdsman. I liked hanging out at the village. I liked putting on shows for the tourists. I liked gadgets and music and movies. So, the elders urged my father to send me away. I thought he would stick up for me, that he would tell them to stop believing outdated superstitions, but he caved. He thrust a few shillings in my hand and saw me off. He told me to never step foot in Maasai land, that if I did, the prophecy would come true. I tried to reason with him, but my father said we would all be better off if I just went away. I have not been back since."

"I'm sorry to hear that," I replied. "I hope you're able to reconcile with him someday."

"Olonana is a stubborn old coot. Just like me. We don't come around easy." Goma rifled through her purse and passed me a bar of chocolate. "Here." She handed Bahati one too. "Chocolate makes everything better."

It was warm and soft, and I rolled it in my mouth like a sweet piece of comfort.

When we got to the Nima House volunteer's hostel, I went inside and packed my things. I sat at the foot of Mo's bed after I'd stripped it clean, thankful that Goma and Bahati had stayed in the car. I needed a moment, one last moment to occupy the space that Mo had been in, to breathe the air she had breathed.

I was glad I had come, but there was no denying the pockets of emptiness where she was supposed to be. I realized these moments would always creep up on me, always echo with her voice, her face, her smile, like an empty room in my soul. I was overcome with a sudden sense of gratitude and connection to Jack, and Goma, and Scholastica, and Bahati. They were all showing me different aspects of what it meant to be strong, at a time when I was struggling with it myself.

I left a note for Corinne, letting her know I would be at Kaburi Estate for the duration of my stay. Then I slipped my sister's orange cat-eye frames into my handbag and picked up my suitcase. The streamers she had attached to the fan fluttered when I opened the door to leave. I couldn't bring myself to untie them, so I hoped that whoever took her place enjoyed the whirl of bright colors whenever they turned the fan on.

Goodbye, Mo, I thought.

You wish, she replied.

It was such a Mo thing to say, at such a Mo moment, that I wanted to smile and sob at the same time.

I was thankful for Bahati's chatter as we drove away, through the congested streets of Amosha. A motorcycle stopped beside us, the passenger on the back sitting sidesaddle as she read a book. Our eyes met briefly as she looked up, over the din of traffic and street vendors. Then the lights changed, and Bahati turned into the local police station.

"I have to pick up a few things from my place," he said, dropping Goma and me off at the main entrance. "I'll see you in a bit."

I surveyed the shabby building while Goma breathed on her psychedelic sunglasses and wiped them with the edge of her caftan. Her silver hair popped against its vibrant, fuchsia print.

"Let's go light some fires," she said, sliding her glasses back on.

I had to hand it to her. She knew how to make a dramatic entrance. She was loud, demanding, and colorful, like a whirlwind of pink energy in the drab setting.

"Goma, you're still alive?" One of the policemen grinned at her.

"And I will be, long after you're gone, Hamisi." She plonked down a stack of bills on his desk. "This is for the chairs."

"What chairs?" He slid the money into his drawer without waiting for an answer.

"The ones you're going to get for me and my friend so we can sit down and discuss business."

And that was how we jumped the line of tired, ragged people waiting their turn. No one batted an eye or questioned it. Goma kept her rainbow lenses on as Hamisi took down Gabriel's details.

"I believe a missing person's report has already been filed by his sister. I need this man found."

"Sounds personal," said Hamisi.

"It's for my friend." Goma tilted her head my way. "Her sister died in the mall attack. She knew this guy. If we can talk to him, we can tie up some loose ends."

Hamisi shifted his gaze to me. "Sorry about your sister. It's unfortunate, but most of our resources are tied up in the investigation. This could take a while. Was there a romantic connection, perhaps?" He tapped his pen on the form.

"How about this for a connection?" Goma snatched the pen from him and scribbled a figure on the paper. "Personal enough to free up some of your resources?"

"Maybe." Hamisi examined the number. "It's a start."

"A start, my bony ass. You agree to that sum right now, or we leave. I'm sure I can find someone else who would be happy to help."

"Goma." Hamisi held his arms out in a placating gesture. "Always like *pili pili mbuzi*. You know *pili pili mbuzi*?" he asked me. "Crushed chili seeds, so hot they burn your tongue. Even in their old age."

Before he could go on, four police guards stopped by his desk. They were holding a man between them. He appeared to be in his early thirties, but he was bald, and not in a clean-shaven way. He had little hairy tufts growing in odd patches on his scalp. A red tribal bandana was wrapped around his wrist. The two ends stuck out like a stiff *V* as one of the guards held on to him. He wasn't particularly big or burly, nor was he resisting them, so it seemed odd to have so many guards on him. He wore an expression of utter nonchalance, as if he were waiting for a bus on a summer day.

"K.K." Hamisi sighed. "Back so soon?"

K.K. smiled, as if something good was about to happen.

There is nothing creepier than a person whose emotions don't match the situation. His eyes fell on me, and I couldn't help but think of the scavenger storks I had seen in the crater, with their hollow leg bones and spotty, featherless heads.

"Take him to the holding cell," said Hamisi.

"When are you going to tire of this game, Inspector? I'll be out of here before you can start the paperwork."

"Maybe so, but it's not going to stop me from doing my job."

"Your job is a joke," said K.K, as the guards led him away. "Hey old lady. You!" he called Goma from across the room. "I want those glasses!"

Goma glared at him over the rim of her frames. "Over my dead body."

"That can be arranged." The man cackled, before the bars slammed shut on him.

"Sorry about that," said Hamisi, turning his attention back to us. "Where were we? *Ah*, yes." He circled the bribe Goma had offered. "I think we can work with this. I'll be in touch."

"Thank you," I said, as he shook our hands.

"I'll be waiting," Goma said to Hamisi.

We found Bahati waiting for us in the car park. He had changed into a button-down shirt and trousers, and was standing by the boot of the car, rifling through his backpack.

"I forgot to pack my moisturizer," he said, staring forlornly into it.

"It seems like you packed everything else." Goma poked the two suitcases he'd loaded into the car. "You're not moving in, you know. Just until Jack and Rodel get back from Wanza."

"I take my assignments seriously."

"Apparently. And your skin care too." Goma slid into the front seat.

"You could do with a good moisturizer." Bahati shut the boot and started the car. "What do you use? The spa at The Grand Tulip passes me all their extra stuff. Here. Feel my skin. Smooth as a newborn baby. I am going to get some headshots done soon. For my portfolio. I was waiting for my hair to grow out a bit . . ."

We were driving past a part of town I had not seen before. It looked like the commercial center, with newer buildings and wider streets. A huge construction zone interrupted the line of shops and offices. At least, that's what it looked like until I saw the wreaths of flowers, stretching across the fenced-off area, from end to end.

"Wait," I said. "Stop here."

Bahati broke off his ongoing commentary. He and Goma exchanged a look.

"It's fine. Really. I just have to see." I stared out of the window, at what was left of Kilimani Mall.

The cleanup crew had removed all the debris and shattered glass. The plumes of smoke I had seen on TV were gone. What remained was the shell of a half-collapsed building, its steel beams sticking out like sharp, fractured bones. At its center was a dark, gaping pit, where the roof had been blown off the underground car park. Police-tape fluttered in the wind, its bright yellow color clashing against the somber, ashen scene.

I got out of the car in a trance. This was where it had happened, where Mo had lost her life. But she wasn't the only one. Photos were taped to the wire fence—names, notes, dates, pleas for information on people that were still unaccounted for.

Sleep in the arms of angels, Morgan Prince.

Taken too soon. Salome Evangeline, my baby girl.

Beloved husband and father. Always with us.

Have you seen this man?

I walked past the long line of candles and flowers and toys. People leaving their tributes, perhaps some who came every day, whose souls were anchored to this place of lost loved ones.

Where were you, Mo? I peered through the crisscross of the fence, to the rubble beyond. *What were you doing?*

I would never know the answers to my questions, but the one that hurt the most, the thing I tried not to think about, was that she had died alone.

"Excuse me." A woman brushed past me. She stopped at a particular spot, removed a dried-out wreath, and replaced it with a new one.

Her face looked oddly familiar. As she made her way back toward me, I realized where I'd seen her before. We had stopped next to each other at the traffic light earlier. She'd been the passenger, reading a book on the motorcycle.

I reached for the beads on my bracelet, thinking of the words on them.

Taleenoi olngisoilechashur.

We are all connected.

How many times do we pass people on the street, whose lives are intertwined with ours in ways that remain forever unknown? How many ways are we tied to a stranger by fragile, invisible threads that bind us all together?

She paused by a street light and looked at the flyer taped to it for a few seconds. Then she tore off a strip of paper, walked by me, and crossed the road.

"Everything all right?" asked Bahati. "Goma asked me to check on you."

"What's on that pole?" I made my way to it and read the sign.

Lost a loved one you would like to contact?

Need a promotion at work?

Want to rid yourself of disease or evil spirits?

For a small contribution, I can make it happen for you.

Best Mganga, *from Zanzibar.*

Call now!

And then a name and phone number.

"What's a *mganga*, Bahati?"

"Traditionally, a doctor, healer, or herbalist. But the term applies to witchdoctors and potion makers too. The ones from Zanzibar are particularly revered. Zanzibar is an island off the coast with a rich history of local voodoo."

"And people believe in it?" There were just two strips of phone numbers left on the flyer.

"If you are desperate enough, you do."

I nodded, thinking of the woman who had just left fresh flowers at the site. I could see how the first line in the flyer would appeal to friends and families of victims of the mall attack. "These *mgangas*—are they also the ones that perform spells using albino body parts?"

"Some of them. It's impossible to tell unless you're in their trusted circle."

"Have you ever been? To a witchdoctor?" I asked, as we walked toward the car.

"No. Unless you count our *oloiboni*, Lonyoki. A lot of people don't have access to doctors or health care in the rural areas. Healers and herbalists are usually their first line of defense. Many healers have legitimate knowledge of how things work, passed down to them from their forefathers, but there are an equal number of quacks. Personally, I shun local superstitions. Maybe because I fell victim to them myself, and had to leave my home and people."

"Just like Scholastica."

"Yes." Bahati paused before getting into the car. "I never thought of it like that, but yes. I guess Scholastica and I have that in common."

I rested my head against the window and listened to Bahati chatter on. It had become strangely comforting, like familiar background noise. Goma must have felt the same way because she dozed off and her head rolled from side to side as we drove past patchwork fields and shacks with corrugated iron roofs.

When we got to the farm, Bahati backed Suzi into the garage. It was a sloping structure, extending from the house, open on all sides, but sheltering the cars under its roof. A hose was lying next to Jack's car, with a stream of soapsuds trickling toward the drain on the floor.

"You're back." Jack was in his car, one long, tanned arm leaning out the window.

"Are you going somewhere?" asked Goma.

"No. Scholastica and I were washing the car, and out of the blue, she just started crying. I think she's homesick and missing her father. She's all right now, but exhausted. She fell asleep a few minutes ago."

I peered into the car and saw her curled up on the passenger seat, her head resting on Jack's lap. "How did you manage to calm her down?"

"I told her a story that Lily used to love." He stroked her hair absently, as if strumming a beloved, forgotten lullaby.

"I'll take her inside." Bahati scooped her out of the car, careful not to wake her.

"I think I'll lie down for a bit too," said Goma. "These rough roads rattle my bones."

We watched them open the door and disappear into the house.

"I don't know how any man can abandon his daughter," Jack said softly. "If I could squeeze in one more moment with Lily—one tiny, fleeting moment—I would do it. No matter the cost. I'd trade my soul to the devil for it."

"I don't think Gabriel's abandoned Scholastica. It doesn't make sense. Here he is, getting all these kids to safety—putting himself at risk in the process. And then he just takes off and leaves his own daughter? It just doesn't fit."

"How do we know he was really getting those kids to safety?

All we know for sure is that he was rounding up albino children, using your sister. Did she ever say they actually delivered the kids to the orphanage in Wanza? Did they physically lead them in through the doors, get them registered, and settled in?"

"Mo never brought it up, but I've never questioned Gabriel's motives. He has an albino daughter himself."

"Yes, but that doesn't automatically align him with the cause. We know nothing about him as a person. We're assuming he's a good guy. What if he's not? What if he's just been using Scholastica to get the families of other kids to trust him? We know he offered Juma's family some sort of compensation. Is it out of his own pocket, or is he working for someone else?"

"Are you saying that Gabriel could be an albino hunter? That he duped my sister into helping him?" I felt sick to my stomach at the thought of it.

"I don't know, but it's a possibility we need to consider. We won't know for sure until we get to Wanza. Once we're there, we can check the records and find out if he really delivered those kids to the orphanage."

"Why don't we just call them?"

"I don't want to tip anyone off—in case Gabriel has someone keeping an eye out for him there. I'd rather just show up and check it out myself."

"What about the police? Goma has Hamisi searching for him."

"Hamisi keeps his mouth shut. His discretion is what earns him a second income."

I nodded, but it felt like the ground was shifting from under my feet. Everything I had based my decisions on seemed to be illusory, like a distant mirage. "I stopped at the mall today."

We were talking through the window, with Jack still sitting in the car. For the first time since our early morning exchange by the barn, our eyes met and held. There was something indefinable in his, something he didn't want me to see. And then like a curtain, it dropped, and he cupped my face. The rough pad of his thumb brushed against my cheek in a gesture that was so tender, the breath stilled in my chest.

My lashes spiked from unspilled tears, though I didn't know exactly why I wanted to cry. It could have been from seeing the mall, or the possibility that I might have totally misjudged Gabriel. But a part of it was also because of *this*. This sense of fitting so easily into the curve of Jack's palm, the rightness of it, the ripeness of it, like a fruit—sweet and heavy—waiting to be plucked. I knew I would have to leave it hanging—untainted, untasted—like a perfectly round echo of what could have been.

I don't know how to say goodbye to a sister, and then to a lover, all in one breath.

And so I stepped back, and Jack withdrew his hand. He rolled up the window and got out of the car.

"You missed a spot," I said, pointing out the smudges on the glass.

"They're not smudges," he said. "They're Lily's fingerprints. She was eating chocolate that day. When we got to the mall, my phone rang. She came around to my side and put her hand here. Like this . . ." He hovered his fingertips over the marks. "One, two, three, four, five. See? Five perfect little chocolate prints. I haven't washed them since. Every time I look out of the window, I see Lily there, holding her palm to the glass, making faces at me."

Whenever Jack spoke of Lily, his entire profile softened. In those moments, his innately captivating presence was like a flame, kindled from within. For a second, I was completely jealous, because I had never lived in someone's heart like that. And I wanted to. I wanted to make someone, someday, glow like that when they thought of me.

As Jack put the hose away, I realized that it wasn't true. I didn't want someone, someday. I wanted now. Today. And I wanted it with Jack.

No matter how many reasons I gave myself not to, I was falling for Jack Warden, more and more, with each passing day.

11

THE DAY STARTED early at the farm. The best time to pick coffee was before it got too hot. It had to be done by hand because coffee cherries on the same branch ripen at different stages, so the harvesters pluck only the mature cherries and place them into their baskets, one by one.

"It takes around seventy cherries to make one cup of coffee," said Goma, when I asked her.

"Wow." I cradled my cup with a new sense of appreciation.

"*Hapana*, Scholastica. Not for you," said Goma, as Scholastica swiped her coffee. "*Watoto wana kunywa maziwa.*" She pointed to the glass of milk on the table.

"*Sitaki maziwa.*" Scholastica pushed it away and stared at us sullenly.

The back door creaked open, followed by two heavy clunks as Jack removed his boots.

"What's going on here?" He eyed Scholastic and then Goma.

"A standoff," said Goma. "She's acting up, refusing to drink her milk. She wants coffee."

"Of course she wants coffee. She's on a coffee farm. It's all around her. You're all having it. It's only natural that she wants to try it. I suspect she's also looking for a reason to piss you off. She's probably thinking it'll get her sent back to Rutema. It's the only home she's known."

He circled the table, stirring up the smell of green leaves and dark earth in his wake. "You want *kahawa*? Coffee?"

Scholastica nodded. "*Harufu nzuri sana.*"

"Yes, it *does* smell good, doesn't it? How about you finish everything on your plate, and I'll show you how to make your own cup of coffee?" Jack repeated his offer in Swahili and got an even more enthusiastic nod.

"Take Rodel with you, too," said Goma. "I'd like the place to myself for a while. I can only take so many people for so long."

I had the sneaking suspicion that Goma was trying to play matchmaker, but I kept my mouth shut. I slathered sunscreen on Scholastica before we went outside. She squirmed and giggled as I applied the cool lotion to her skin. The scabs on her face were healing, and her eyes had lost some of their wariness. The fear was still there, deeply ingrained, and her eyes darted nervously as we followed Jack through the rows of coffee plants.

"Coffee beans are actually the seeds of coffee cherries," he explained, as Scholastica and I tied baskets around our waists. "See these bright, red ones? These are the ones you want." He cracked the red skin and picked out the seed beneath. It was gooey and slimy. "The cherries from your baskets will get dried in the sun, raked, and turned throughout the day, so they don't spoil. They're covered at night or when it's raining, to prevent them from getting wet. Depending on the weather, it can take a while until they're dry enough, when the beans 'rattle' inside the cherries. Then we separate the beans from the rest and sell it as raw coffee. We save some for the farm and the workers, so we can roast it for our own use."

"That's so cool," I said to Scholastica when she plucked her first cherry and held it up for us to see.

The farm was a balanced grove of banana trees and coffee bushes. The banana leaves provided shade and shelter for the coffee. The rows were tight, and as we moved between them, Jack slid by me to help Scholastica. It was barely a brush, but his entire body tightened in reaction. I felt the quickening of his breath on my face, the jolt of his thigh against my body, the crackle of awareness where his bare arms touched mine. I felt the kind of chemistry I'd been holding out for, the kind that ignites all your senses, so that you're more alive in that one second than in all the moments, in all the days before. Then Jack stepped past me, from under the shade of glossy banana leaves, and into the sun.

"Good job!" He peered into Scholastica's basket and high-fived her. "*Safi sana.* I think you guys have earned your coffee." He combined our baskets and headed for the collection site.

"Come on," he said, as I trailed behind them, still trying to catch my breath. "Time to make your first cup of coffee from scratch."

He dumped our cherries into a giant bin, scooped an equivalent amount from the ones that were drying on large, flat containers, and poured them into a giant, wooden mortar.

"We use a machine for this part, but this works great for small batches. Here." He handed the pestle to Scholastica.

We took turns pounding the berries. Once the husks were off, we poured everything into a shallow basket and winnowed, leaving only the inner bean. Jack roasted the coffee in a small clay pot over an open fire, until it turned dark. Then we pounded the beans and brewed them in boiling water.

"Ready?" He handed Scholastica a cup.

She blew on the hot liquid and took a big gulp.

"*Kaaaaa!*" She spit it out and wiped her mouth with the back of her hand. "*Mbaya sana!*" She handed the cup back to Jack.

"You don't like it? *Hupendi?*" He feigned surprise.

"Ah-ah." She shook her head and said something in Swahili.

"Bitter like medicine?" Jack tsked. "But it smells so good. *Harufu nzuri sana.*"

She turned her nose up as he held it out for her. "*Ninapendelea maziwa.*"

"*Maziwa? Jamani.*" He sat down with an exaggerated sigh. "All this hard work and you want milk? Go on. Go ask Goma for *maziwa.*" He pointed her toward the house.

She didn't need further prompting.

"You knew she wouldn't like it," I said, as we watched her race away in her sunflower hat.

"I guess I could have offered her milk and sugar." Jack gave me a sheepish smile. "But it's not really coffee she wants. It's having some kind of control over her life, even if it's something as small as choosing what to eat or drink. All we really want is to feel that we matter—that we're seen, that we're heard."

"You're really good with her," I said. "I feel like I'm at a bit of a disadvantage because I don't speak Swahili."

"If you can't speak, just listen. That's what someone once said to me." He poured me some coffee and sat down on the wooden log across from me.

"Good advice." I accepted the cup and smiled. He'd remembered my words, and for some reason, that made me happy. "You don't like coffee?"

"I love coffee," he replied, watching me take a sip.

"Really?" I prodded. "I've never seen you drink it."

He leaned back, picked a cloud, and fixed his eyes on it. I didn't think he was going to answer when he finally spoke.

"I was drinking coffee in the parking lot when it all started that day. At the mall. The taste of it was still in my mouth when the building collapsed. I retch every time I have coffee now because it takes me right back to that moment."

I didn't know what to say, because I had no idea what it was like to be surrounded by acres and acres of something that you loved, but could never taste. Instead, I cradled my coffee and followed his gaze toward the sky. We watched silently as the clouds drifted past the majestic face of Mount Kilimanjaro, like wispy veils of silver.

"THIS ONE, SCHOLASTICA." I pointed to the letter *A* in the book and encouraged her to copy it on the sheet of paper before her.

She seemed to have trouble understanding, so I went ahead and wrote a small *A* at the top of the page.

"Your turn," I said, handing her the pen.

She looked at me, then at the paper, and scribbled something completely different in the corner.

"Like this: *A*," I said, as I wrote the letter.

She repeated the sound perfectly, but her *A* was nowhere close to mine.

I flipped to a blank sheet and filled the entire page with a big *A*, exaggerating the strokes. "Can you do it like this?"

She copied my letter slowly and held it up.

"Yes!" I clapped my hands. "That's it! How about this one?" I asked, indicating a *B* in the book.

Her expression was blank, so I wrote a big *B* and showed it to her.

She bent over the desk and replicated it perfectly.

"Well done! This is *A*, and this is *B*." I pointed out the letters in the book. She peered at them but had no reaction.

"Here." I pulled the book closer to her. "Can you see them now?"

Scholastica looked at the pages and brought them even closer, until her nose was inches from the center crease. Then she smiled.

"*A*." She showed it to me, before picking up her handwritten one and waving it gleefully.

"Good!" I beamed at her. "Can you find a *B*?"

Once again, she held the book near her face and examined

the words.

"B!" she exclaimed, when she found one.

We were still celebrating when Goma entered the library.

"Scholastica is learning the alphabet," I said. "But I think she needs glasses."

"That doesn't surprise me. Poor vision goes hand in hand with albinism. I'll make an appointment for her to see Dr. Nasmo. He's the optometrist we use in Amosha."

"That's great! You hear that? You're going to get fitted for glasses." I made hand gestures for Scholastica. It's strange how much we can communicate with expressions and body language when words are not an option. And stranger still, is how much more authentic the conversation can feel.

"Oh, wait!" I rummaged through my bag and pulled out Mo's spare frames. "Let's see if these help. They won't be perfect, but . . ." I placed them over her ears and stepped back. "How's that?"

Scholastica blinked a few times and looked around the room. Then her mouth opened in pure awe. She stared at Goma and me for a few seconds, before whirling around to the bookcase.

"B!" She pointed it out on one of the book spines. "A!"

She went down the entire row, stopping to greet every _A_ and _B_ like they were her new best friends.

"I haven't seen a girl so happy since we bought Lily that tortoise," said Goma. She had a wistful look in her eyes until she noticed the little droppings Aristurtle was leaving by her feet. "That's it! You're getting a box. I'm not taking any more shit from you, you hear?" She picked him up and said something to Scholastica in Swahili.

I followed them outside and watched Scholastica race off with Aristurtle tucked under her arm. She pushed Mo's glasses higher to keep them from sliding down her nose.

"Where is she going?"

"To find Bahati. Maybe he can clear up one of the crates we have in the barn. It'll make a fine home for Aristurtle." She retrieved the laundry basket and started hanging the clothes out to dry.

"Here. Let me do that," I said, taking the clothes from her. "You go on inside. It won't take me long."

I alternated between the basket and the clothesline, hanging up the smaller items before moving to the bigger ones. It was a perfect, sunny day. The clouds had cleared, leaving a blue satin sky. There were a few more days before we left for Wanza, and I was getting used to the daily routine on the farm.

As I moved between the lines of fluttering laundry, I caught a glimpse of Jack. He was standing shirtless between the berry-laden rows of coffee, his body glistening in the afternoon sun. I looked away but couldn't help stealing glances at his strong, golden body. I might have been able to ignore my attraction to him, even though it flared up constantly, if it wasn't compounded by my affection for him. It was a deadly combination—one that made me dream about being crushed in his embrace, even as I focused on the mundane task of hanging clothes up to dry.

I was almost done when the wind picked up. I struggled with the last bed sheet, trying to keep it steady so I could secure it, but it flapped wildly around me. I dropped a clothes peg and bent to retrieve it, pinning the sheet down with one hand on the line. That's when Jack's strong, long fingers closed over mine. My knees lurched at the unexpected impact of his warm grip. I fumbled as I picked up the peg, my heart hammering in my chest. Our eyes held across the damp sheet as I straightened.

For a long, breathless second, we found ourselves in a laundry-scented bubble of suspension. Jack's gaze fell to my lips as the wind whipped my hair across my face. The touch of his hand was sudden—electric—but it lingered, gently brushing the strands away. I felt myself swaying wildly, like the clothes on the line. The only thing holding me steady was Jack's other hand, anchoring mine.

The clothesline bucked between us as another gust picked up. The bedsheet slid off at the other end. We picked it up and stretched it across the line, like a curtain between us. Jack held it down while I clamped a peg over it.

"Any more?" he asked.

"No. All done."

Thank God, my knees declared. *This guy makes it hard for us to do our job right. We don't like him.*

"Thank you," I said to Jack, gathering the empty basket. "I'm going to . . ." *head back inside,* but I was tongue-tied, so I pointed to the house, and started walking toward it.

If there's ever an occasion to carry off the nonchalant, graceful, catwalk stride, it's when you're walking away from someone, and you know they're still watching. Ironically, that's also about the only time when you become painfully conscious of every single step you're taking. And so I kept my back straight and put one foot in front of the other until I made it to the door.

When I got inside, I caught Goma ducking from the kitchen window with a sly smile on her face.

It wasn't long before she asked me to call Jack in for supper.

I found him in the barn with Scholastica, tending the calf that had been attacked.

"*Mfalme! Mfalme!*" said Scholastica, pointing to Jack when she saw me. She was still wearing Mo's glasses and even though I was the one that had given them to her, my heart contracted a little, missing Mo's eyes looking back at me through them.

"What does that mean?" I asked. "*Mfalme?*"

"It means king," Bahati answered from the corner. He was sanding the box he'd made for Aristurtle. "She's made Jack a crown out of twigs and hay."

"Oh?" I noted her lopsided creation on Jack's head.

"I just finished telling her the story I started the other day, when she fell asleep in the car," he replied. "She seems to have cast me as the lead character."

"Well, if it pleases Your Majesty, supper is ready. You've all been summoned by Goma."

"You go ahead," Jack said to us. "I'll be in shortly. I'm almost done with her." He patted the sleeping calf in the stall.

"*Twende*, Scholastica." Bahati held his hand out for her. "Let's put Aristurtle in his new home and see if Goma approves."

"How is the calf?" I peered into the stall as Bahati and Scholastica headed back to the house.

"She's fine. Just making sure this cut doesn't get infected." He flushed it with some kind of medicinal solution, applied salve, and bandaged it up again.

"Poor thing." I knelt beside her and stroked the abrasions on her skin. She stirred and opened her big, brown eyes.

"Thankfully, those are superficial. She'll be good as new in a few days. Won't you?" Jack nuzzled her. "But you need to rest right now. That's right. Close your eyes. You're safe now." He rubbed her hide in broad, gentle strokes, as the light of the setting sun fell in golden beams around them.

Suddenly I was in the presence of a flesh-and-blood man that no book boyfriend could ever live up to. He wore a crown of dried twigs and hay, but he was more royal, more magnificent than all the jeweled kings in all the fairy tales because he walked in real life—mortal, vulnerable, broken, jaded, but still a king—with the heart of a lion, and the soul of an angel. I ached to touch him, to feel his golden energy. My hand moved heedlessly toward him, the sides of our palms touching briefly as he soothed the calf. It was the softest sweep of skin against skin, a little nibble for my hungry heart before I withdrew.

Anyone else would have brushed it off as accidental, but not

Jack. He *knew*. Perhaps because he was just as acutely aware of the currents that spiraled between us. His gaze shifted to my face, searching my eyes. I don't know what he saw in them, but the air between us felt locked and loaded, like it was rigged with dynamite—one false move and we'd both get blown to bits. I didn't care though, not in that moment. His closeness was like a drug, lulling me to euphoria. I drifted toward him, slowly, helplessly, until my lips tasted the full, intoxicating essence of his.

Kissing Jack was like kissing a slumbering lion. He barely moved, but I could sense the raw power behind his restraint. And deeper still, lurked something wild and dangerous, something that could obliterate me if unleashed. But I wanted it, because it was magnificent, because it swirled over the loss and pain running through his veins, because it was the part of him that was alive. It made me want to thread my fingers through his thick, tawny hair even though I knew it was a bad, bad idea.

Jack didn't respond, but he didn't push me away either, and that was okay with me. There is special kind of hell that comes with remembering, in full-blown Technicolor detail, a kiss that never happened. And I had just freed myself from it. I pulled back, my eyes still closed, knowing that I had just stolen an epic moment from life. Someday when I looked back, I would smile in the middle of the street and no one would know why, because it was just for me, so that I could say to myself:

Once in Africa, I kissed a king . . .

I got up, smoothed my dress, and walked away, leaving Jack kneeling by the calf.

"Rodel," he said, just as I was about to step outside.

Rodelle. Another thing I would always remember—the way he said my name, *elle*-vating it beyond the ordinary.

He was between me and the exit before I could turn around. He swung me into the circle of his arms and kissed me—not softly or tentatively, like I had kissed him, but hungry and demanding, crushing my body to his. His mouth moved wildly over mine, his tongue exploring the recesses of my mouth, as if I had stolen a piece of him, and he wanted it back. I tasted the whole universe in Jack's kiss—the blue heat of spinning stars, the birth of distant suns, atoms buzzing and colliding and fusing.

And just like that, in an old red barn at the foothills of Mount Kilimanjaro, I found the elusive magic I had glimpsed only between the pages of great love stories. It fluttered around me like a newborn butterfly and settled in a corner of my heart. I held my breath, afraid to exhale, for fear it would slip out, never to be found again.

When Jack lifted his head, my pulse was beating hard and fast at the base of my throat. He traced it tenderly, in gentle fascination, before meeting my eyes.

"Rodel," he said my name again.

I tried to mask the swell of emotions running through me, but he caught the flicker of something, because his expression turned grim.

"Come with me," he said, leading me outside by my hand.

We walked past the house, in the soft half-light between afternoon and evening, to the giant acacia tree I'd seen him standing under, the night of the thunderstorm.

"Everyone I love ends up here," he said, pointing to the four tombstones at the base of the tree. His grandfather. His father. His mother. His daughter. "And this here is my spot." He marked out an area next to Lily's grave. "I was born here, and this is where I'll die. God knows, there are days when all I want is to be with Lily, wherever she is. When I met her mother, I was young and naive. I thought we could make it work. But not many women are cut out for life on the farm, removed from everything and everyone. At first Sarah was taken by it, then she tolerated it, then she hated it. It took away everything good between us. After she left, I vowed never to put anyone else through that again." He shoved his hands into his pockets and turned around.

"This thing between us—" his shoulders heaved as he took a deep breath "—it'll just hurt us both. When it's all said and done, we belong in different worlds. My home is here, yours is there. I could never ask you to stay, and you can never ask me to leave. It wouldn't be fair. And I don't have what it takes to let you in and then let you go. I can't handle any more goodbyes, Rodel." He stood at the foot of Lily's grave, as twilight descended and shadows melted under the canopy of the ancient acacia tree. "The last one destroyed me."

My fingers ached to straighten the crown on his head, but I stood next to him, my hands by my side, fighting the strangest pull of emotions. My heart was heavy with a sense of loss: his, mine, *ours*. At the same time, something beautiful had come alive at Jack's declaration, his acknowledgment of our connection. It was as if a tiny seed filled with magic had taken root. And even though it would never see the light of day, just the fact that it had formed, where there had been nothing before, made me feel like infinite blossoms were blooming inside me.

N IGHTS AT THE farm were slow, welcome pauses when everything hung suspended under the canopy of a star-freckled sky. Goma sat at her old sewing machine, her foot on the pedal, filling the library with a soft whirring. Occasionally, she would get up, measure the fabric against Scholastica's form, and either nod or get her scissors and tailor's chalk.

"What are you making?" I asked.

Jack, Scholastica, and I were leaving in the morning to pick up the next child on Mo's list, and from there we had one more stop before we headed for Wanza.

"I'm sewing some wraparound skirts for Scholastica," replied Goma. "They'll last her a while."

Scholastica looked up at the mention of her name. We were practicing how to write her name. Ever since she had seen it on paper, she'd developed a fascination with it.

Scholastica
Scholastica
Scholastica

She scribbled it on every blank piece of paper she could find. It was as if she was discovering her identity, solidifying it every time she wrote it.

This is me.
This is me.

This is me.

"She looks exhausted," said Jack. He was seated at his desk, working on some invoices.

"She does, doesn't she?" I stroked her hair, wondering how much of her apparent tiredness came from knowing it was her last night on the farm. "Are you feeling okay?" I asked.

She might not have understood the words, but she took her glasses off and laid her head on my lap.

"Well, I'm all done for the night." Goma snipped a thread and held the skirt up for inspection. She folded it and placed it on the pile of other clothes she'd stitched for Scholastica. "I'll take her upstairs. Come along." She held her hand out for Scholastica. "Let's get you to bed. *Twende kulala.* Big day tomorrow."

Bahati let out a long sigh as they left the room.

"What's wrong?" I asked.

"There is absolutely nothing to do out here," he moaned. "I'm bored out of my mind, and it's only 8 p.m. Don't you crave the lights and action, Jack?"

Jack glanced up, and then went back to what he was doing.

"How about we play book charades?" I asked.

"What is book charades?" Bahati perked up.

"It's charades, but with these." I pointed to the shelf. "We pick a book and see if the other person can guess the title."

"I've never played charades with two people. That's silly."

"Oh, come on! I'll go first." I pulled a book off the shelf, read the spine, and placed it, cover down, on my chair. "Okay. Here goes." I held up three fingers.

"Book, obviously. Three words."

I nodded and tried to communicate the first word, holding my nose up and walking haughtily around the room.

"Fart! You smell a fart!" exclaimed Bahati.

I glared at him and shook my head.

"Sounds like . . ." Bahati interpreted my ear-tugging gesture. "Cowboy!" he said, as I pranced around.

"*Pride and Prejudice*," said Jack, without looking up.

I turned to him with my mouth hanging open. "That's right. First word sounds like *ride*. That's what I was trying to convey," I said to Bahati. "Okay, your turn."

"So, who wins?" he asked, removing another book from the shelf.

"Jack, I guess," I replied.

"But he's not even playing."

"It doesn't matter. Just get on with it, Bahati."

Bahati made a face when he checked the book he was holding. He put it aside and thought about it for a while.

"Book. Two words. First word . . ." I hesitated as he pointed to his butt. "*Umm* . . . rump, rear end, backside, tush."

Bahati motioned for me to keep going.

"Bum, arse . . ." I stopped when he jumped on it. "Arse?"

He nodded, but wanted me to expand.

"Butt?"

He shook his head.

"Derriere, bottom . . ."

"No, what you said before!"

"You're not allowed to speak. Stick to the rules. So . . . arse?"

"God, you English! Never mind. Moving on to the second word." He sashayed like a diva across the room, hips swinging, fanning his face, and fluttering his lashes.

I was about to take a guess when Jack piped in again.

"*Don Quixote*," he said, head still bent over his desk.

"That's right!" said Bahati, holding the book up for us to see.

"How the hell is that *Don Quixote*?" I asked. "You pointed to your arse."

"Ass, as in donkey. But you say *arse*, which doesn't work. So then I moved on to being a hottie. Donkey hottie." Bahati clapped his hands together. *"Don Quixote."*

"That's just . . . there's just no way in hell . . ."

"You try to pull off *Don Quixote*. Besides, Jack got it." Bahati gloated.

I glanced at Jack. He was busy writing something, but I caught the slight upturn of his mouth.

"No." I walked over to him. "I don't believe it. Something's not right here."

Jack put his pen down and sat back, regarding me with eyes that looked like rain on wild, blue forget-me-nots. "What are you saying, Rodel?"

"I don't know, but I don't like it." My eyes narrowed on him. I grabbed my book and swiveled on my heels.

"Where are you going?" he called after me.

God. That voice. It made me feel like I should be marching straight to his bedroom.

"Out. With Mr. Darcy," I replied, heading for the porch. It was my favorite thing to do at the end of the day—snuggle up with a good book on the swing.

I wasn't too far into my date with Mr. Darcy when Mr. Warden showed up, blanket in hand.

"I thought you could use this," he said. "It's chilly out tonight."

I ignored him and kept my nose stuck in my book.

"Yep, definitely some frost in the air." The porch swing creaked as he sat down next to me.

"All right, fine," he said, after he got tired of listening to the crickets chirp. "No one ever touches those books, except for you, so everyone pretty much has its own spot. I could tell which books you and Bahati picked."

I kept my eyes on my book for a few moments. Then I reached for a corner of the blanket Jack had brought and tugged it across my lap. Jack might have smiled, and maybe I did too, but it was just the tiniest bit. Book nerds find that kind of thing sexy—a man who knows his book shelves like the back of his hand.

Oh, my dear, dear Darcy, I thought. *I'm in so much trouble. I know I'm in deep when even you can't hold my attention. I hold my breath every time I pass his door. My skin tingles every time he sits next to me.*

I flipped my book shut and cast my glance at the crescent moon. It hung amongst clusters of stars, its halo bright against the charcoal sky.

"I'm scared, Jack."

"Of what?"

Of never feeling about anyone else the way I feel about you.

"Of tomorrow," I replied. "After what happened with Juma, I don't know what to expect."

Jack was quiet for a moment. Then he reached into his pocket and pulled out his phone.

"I want to show you something." He flipped through it until he found a video. "This is the last dance performance I have of Lily's. I recorded it a few weeks before she died. The look on her face—it's pure joy."

Lily lit up the small stage. She hopped off her right foot, then her left, swinging her arms in fun, upbeat moves. It was half cho-reographed, half free-style, and she couldn't stop smiling through it. When she finished, she pointed to the camera and sent her dad a flying kiss before taking a bow.

"She always told me to sit in the front row, so she could find me."

"She's amazing." I couldn't bring myself to use the past tense, not with her energy and enthusiasm coming through so clearly.

"She wasn't always easy with it. This was her, the first time she got on stage." Jack showed me another video.

It was a different Lily, younger, but also unsure and nervous as hell. She was part of a group, and she lagged behind everyone because she was taking her cues from them. Her moves were small and stilted, as if she were dancing in a box that restrained her. She didn't make it all the way through. Instead, she walked off the stage and slipped behind the curtains, while the rest of the group completed the performance.

"She was terrified because she looked different from all the other kids. Being biracial isn't easy for a kid. She seemed to be okay in class, but up on stage with all those people watching, she lost her nerve. I didn't think she'd want to go back. But she did. She watched this over and over again. And each time she accepted herself a little more, saw her own beauty, practiced the moves, gained more confidence. She asked me to record her next performance. And the next one. Then she watched those. Over and over again. Until she could go back and laugh at her first attempt." Jack put his phone away and turned to me. "It's okay to be scared, Rodel. I'm scared too. I stood in that parking lot, paralyzed by fear. I haven't been able to shake it off. I don't know if I ever will—if I'll ever believe that the world is a safe place. Then I watch Lily's videos, and you know what she says to me? That fear is a liar. Don't let it whisper in your ear. Turn that shit off. Do what scares you. Over and over again. And one day, your fear will become so small, you'll be able to laugh at it."

"Big lessons from a little girl," I replied. "I wish I'd met her."

"You would have liked her. I lived for the times when she came to visit. I loved watching her race across the plains, in grass that was almost as tall as her. She was my flower, my rising sun. Blue jeans and a rainbow T-shirt." He rocked his foot, setting the swing into a soft, lulling motion. "Nothing's going to hurt you or those kids, Rodel. I've been at war ever since I lost Lily, only I don't know who with. And it kills me. Because every fiber of my being wants to find them and destroy them, and I can't. But if anyone . . . if anyone touches a hair on your head or tries to harm those children, I will rip them apart. I don't want to play by the rules anymore. I don't want to see them behind bars. I don't want them getting a fair trial. I want them dead. I will put them six feet under, Rodel, so help me God."

He clasped my hand under the blanket and threaded his fingers through mine. He'd held my hand once before, but this felt different, possessive—like he was staking his claim. A curious swooping pulled at my insides. We both knew there was a line we couldn't cross, but it didn't stop Jack's arm from going around me or my head from leaning on his shoulder.

For a few hours that night, Jack and I sat out on the porch, with the scent of wild jasmine in the air, and nothing but the squeaking of the swing, and the buzzing of night insects breaking up the silence.

S OMETIME DURING THE night, I had fallen asleep on the swing, and Jack had carried me to bed. I might have awoken when he scooped me up, but the feeling of being wrapped up in his arms was so delicious that I'd faked it. And then replayed it over and over in my head until I'd fallen back to sleep.

This is it, little sis, I thought, when I got up the next morning. *We're going to pick up the last two kids on your list and get them to Wanza.*

There was no answer, and for a while, I wondered if it was some sort of sign from her, a warning not to go. I shook off my unease and got out of bed. I was making things up—my conversations with Mo, and now the silences too.

I had filled my parents in on what was happening. They weren't too happy that Jack and I would be away for the next few days. They had lost one daughter and they wanted the other one back, safe and sound. A part of me longed to head home to them, and to my little stone cottage by the river, but another part, the part that had shifted and changed, felt a sharp pang at the thought of leaving. It was also the part that leaped to life when Jack opened his door, at the opposite end of the hallway, with sleep-rumpled hair, and nothing but his boxers on.

Good God, imagine waking up to that every day.

He was half-shadowed as he stood in the corridor, but it turned his body into a sculpted study in light and dark. For a quick, satisfying beat, his self-contained demeanor slipped, as his eyes raked over my bare shoulder, grazing the skin where my top had slipped off.

"Thank you for *umm* . . . carrying me up the stairs last night," I said, attempting to cut through the crackling that happened whenever we got within a few feet of each other.

Jack didn't say anything, but he must have caught the flush on my face, because a corner of his mouth turned up, but just barely, as if he'd been in on the whole thing all along.

Well, I'm not sorry. Not sorry at all.

"Good morning." Bahati came out of his room, looked left at me, looked right at Jack, and then made a beeline for the bathroom.

"Hey, I was going to—"

"You snooze, you lose," he taunted, shutting the door on me.

"*Shh.* Keep it down!" Goma stuck her head out of her room. "Scholastica and I have been up all night."

"Everything okay?" asked Jack.

"She's running a fever. I've given her something for it, but she's in no condition to go anywhere today."

Goma held the door open so Jack and I could step inside. Scholastica was sleeping with the covers thrown off.

"Her skin feels clammy," said Jack, sitting down beside her.

"We can't leave without her." I pressed my palm to her forehead. It was hot to the touch.

"We have to. Today is the day Mo and Gabriel are supposed to be picking up the kid in Maymosi."

"Sumuni," I said. I had memorized all their names. "But what about Scholastica? I promised Anna I'd get her to Wanza."

"And we will. Correction. I will. You have to catch a plane when we get back. I'll make another trip after you leave. In the meantime, we'll let Anna know there's been a delay. I don't think it matters, as long as she's assured that Scholastica is safe."

"What's going on?" Bahati piped in, checking in on us.

"It's Scholastica. She's sick. She can't go with Ro and me today," replied Jack. "Can you stay a little longer? Until I get back?"

"But Jack, it's so bori—" He stopped mid-sentence as Jack announced a figure. "I can get new tires for Suzi with that amount. And then all she'll need are new seats. Don't get me wrong. It's not that I don't like it here, but I miss The Grand Tulip. The guests, the pretty girls, the movies, the resta—"

"You want in or not?" asked Jack.

"Fine," replied Bahati. "I'm in."

"I don't need a babysitter," huffed Goma. "I'm perfectly capable of looking after myself and Scholastica. But if you're staying on, no more hollering for me or Scholastica to check for lizards under your bed at night. Clear?"

Bahati had the decency to look slightly ashamed. "Anyone want breakfast?" He dashed out without waiting for an answer.

By the time I went downstairs, he had coffee brewing and was helping Jack load the car.

"You'll be all right?" Jack asked Goma when she came to see us off.

"Fine. And so will Scholastica." She wasn't one to hug or kiss goodbye. "It's this one I'm worried about." She tipped her head toward Bahati.

"What do you mean?" he said. "No one takes me seriously around here. This is why I—"

Jack started the car, drowning out the rest of his comments.

"Bye, Goma." I waved as we backed out of the garage. "Bye, Donkey Hottie."

The clouds hung low that morning, muting the trail of dust we left behind. We passed riverine forests and wooded hills with towering termite mounds. Other times, the landscape turned dry and brown, with nothing but scruffy bush for miles. Then the road snaked around the Great Rift Valley, offering sweeping views that took my breath away. This vast trench in the earth's crust stretches from the Middle East in the north to Mozambique in the south. It is also the single most significant physical detail on the planet, visible from space. To be driving along it, hugging the steep walls, where I had once pointed it out on the map to my students, was completely surreal. Across the horizon, not too far in the distance, colossal thunderclouds trailed shawls of rain across vistas as wide as the sea.

As we approached, the rain washed over us in thick, diagonal sheets of gray. The wipers squeaked, double tempo, but it was impossible to see more than a few feet ahead.

"We'll have to wait it out." Jack pulled over and turned the car off.

Mother Nature was in full drama, knocking on the roof, the windowpanes, the doors, as if trying to smudge everything into a Monet masterpiece. It was a day of inescapable wetness.

Jack's mood shifted, turning as somber as the sky. In the thunderous roar of the rain, I almost missed his words.

"She's leaving me," he said.

"Who's leaving you?"

He kept his eyes fixed on his window, watching the droplets trail down the glass in fast, furious rivulets.

"Lily." He pressed his palm to the pane, meeting the fading chocolate prints on the other side. "I'm losing the last of her." If torment could be grasped, it would be in the pauses between his words. "My baby's out there, under that big tree. I always watch over her. Every time it rains, I stand by her side. I think of her little body getting soaked by the rain and I can't stand the idea of her being cold and alone. But today, I'm not there, and she's leaving me. I'm losing my baby girl."

He fell apart slowly, his walls crumbling brick by brick, as if the house he'd been living in was being swept away by a mudslide. When he cried, there was a rawness to it, an agony that spoke of denial, of an open wound that had gone untended. The sobs were stifled at first, like he was trying to hold his grief at bay. How deep he'd buried it, I didn't know, but it washed over him in waves. He hunched over the steering wheel, his hands clasping and unclasping, as if searching for something to hold on to, to keep from getting sucked into the next surge of pain.

"Jack," I said. But he was in his own world, lost to me.

It didn't stop until he gave in to it, until he let himself drown in it, until his whole body shook as it ripped through his skin and bones. When he finally lifted his head, he was a picture of complete devastation.

I witnessed, for the first time, how someone can radiate pure strength from a place of pure pain. Sometimes the most heroic thing we can do is fight the battle within and just emerge on the other side. Because it's not just one battle, one time. We do it over and over again, as long as we breathe, as long as we live.

Jack pressed his forehead to the windowpane, his breath steaming up the glass. Lily's fingerprints were gone, washed away by the silver streams cascading down the sides of the valley. The thunderclouds had passed over us, and there was a watery sheen to the world. Everything was wet and slick and new. Rods of soft, luminous light shimmered in the puddles as a muted sun appeared through the haze.

"Remember when you told me that if I couldn't speak to Lily, I should just listen?" said Jack.

"I didn't realize you'd never truly let her go until just now—"

"I'm listening." He pointed to the other side of the valley.

There, against the graphite horizon, a soft arc of colors hung suspended across the washed-out sky.

"A rainbow."

"Lily loved rainbows. Everything was rainbow colored. Her tutu, key chain, socks, pencils . . ." He drifted off, as if rediscovering its beauty in the newborn light. "I told her to dance up a storm. And that's exactly what she did. She got my attention. All this time I've been searching for her in the wrong places—in the rain, and in thunder, and lightning. And all this time . . . there she is, hiding in rainbows."

We sat in silence, witnessing the miracle of sun and rain and color. Then Jack took a deep breath and started the car.

"See you on the other side, baby girl," he said to the rainbow across the valley.

THE VILLAGE OF Maymosi was perched by a river, in a meadow strewn with baobab trees. Bare of leaves and fruit, they arched into the sky like masses of clawing roots, looking like they'd been planted upside-down.

Maymosi was much bigger than I had imagined, with a wide road lined with modest stalls. It was muddy from the rain, but that didn't stop everyone from squelching around in their rubber flip-flops. Women with shaved heads picked through fruits and vegetables, bargaining loudly over the price. A butcher in a red baseball cap hung slabs of glistening goat meat, surrounded by an audience of hopeful dogs. Thin smoke rose out of charcoal burners as vendors brewed milk tea and fried *mandazi* bread for their customers.

We parked by the river and got out. Women sat on their haunches, washing clothes and hanging them to dry on thorn trees. Children lugged buckets of water home, leaving a trail of wet splashes behind them. Herders waited in line with donkeys and cattle for their turn at the stream.

"*Bongo Flava! Bongo Flava!* Come see!" A procession of kids banging on pots and pans surrounded us—beautiful children with their faces dusted gray from hearth ash.

"What's *Bongo Flava?*" I asked them.

They looked at me like I'd grown two heads and started laughing.

"Music!" one of the girls explained. "You will like it."

"Thanks, but I'm not here for that." I tried to extract myself from the tangle of arms as they started dragging me along with them. "We are looking for Sumuni. Do you know Sumuni?"

"Yes! Come to *Bongo Flava!*"

I shot Jack a questioning look as they tugged me past him.

"We should check it out," he said. "Looks like all the kids are heading there." He pointed to the circle of kids already seated before a makeshift stage. It looked like a boxing ring, with a rope strung around on four wooden posts. The orchestra entered—three kids with handmade instruments. One of them had an upside-down gourd lodged in a bucket of water. A drum, I assumed. The other one held a shoebox with rubber bands wrapped around it. I couldn't imagine what that was for. The last kid rattled two tin cans filled with stones to get everyone's attention.

"*Nyamaza!*" she said.

In the silence that followed, a short figure, wearing a hooded robe entered the ring. It was actually a blanket, tied at the waist with a floral sash that looked like it might have been swiped from a woman's dress.

"Awright! Let's get this party started!" he said, dropping his hood and turning to the audience, Michael Jackson style.

"Sumuni! Sumuni! Sumuni!" the other kids chanted, throwing their hands in the air for him.

"Well, I'll be damned," said Jack. "Sumuni is a motherfucking superstar."

Sumuni bopped around the stage, a pale demi-god with flaming orange hair, rapping lyrics that were half English, half Swahili. He had no microphone, but his voice carried effortlessly, pulling in the other villagers around us. They laughed at his moves, his words, but most of all, at his over-the-top attitude. It didn't matter that the music was off, or that the shoebox with dirty rubber bands was a valiant yet lacking substitute for a guitar.

Everyone cheered at the end of the performance. Sumuni and his band took a bow. Some of the adults dropped mangoes and oranges into a box by the stage before shuffling off.

"I should have known," said Jack, shaking his head in amusement.

"Known what?"

"Sumuni. It means fifty cents in Swahili. I guess he's named himself after 50 Cent, the rapper." He pulled out a couple of bills from his wallet and handed them to Sumuni.

"Thank you." Sumuni put the money into his hat before putting it on. "You're tourists?"

Our presence didn't seem to arouse much curiosity. Maymosi was obviously a place that saw its fair share of visitors.

"We're actually here for you. To take you to Wanza," said Jack. "Are your parents around?"

Sumuni paused and squinted at Jack. He must have been twelve or thirteen, but his eyes were those of an old soul. They were different from Scholastica's—more pink than blue. "Yes, but there must be some kind of a mistake. We're expecting Gabriel."

He led us to his home and asked us to wait in the courtyard while he went to get his parents. They greeted us warmly, though they were quick to inquire about Gabriel.

"We're not sure where he is," I said. "I found Sumuni's name on some notes my sister had made, and we decided to come get him."

They nodded as I explained the situation, but I could tell they were busy assessing Jack and me.

"We are very grateful that you made the trip, but the thing

is, we know nothing about you. We cannot just hand our son over to you." Sumuni's father spoke with a finality that left no room for argument. And yet, it was Sumuni's mother he looked to for direction every time he spoke. She was clearly the one in charge.

"We are in no rush to send Sumuni to Wanza. It is mostly for school," she said. "There is no high school here and he will need one soon, but we will wait for Gabriel—whenever he shows up. Sumuni's situation is not like that of most other albino kids. He is loved and protected here. The whole village would rise up if anyone tried to hurt him."

"We understand," I said, even though it felt like an anti-climax, having come all this way, only to be turned away. "It's totally your call."

"And if Gabriel doesn't show anytime soon?" Jack interjected.

"Then no school for me!" Sumuni fist pumped. "I get to be a Bongo Flava star."

"We'll see about that," his mother said, hushing him. "If Gabriel doesn't show, we'll just have to save up for a train ride to Wanza, by private coach. Taking Sumuni there by bus is too risky. You never know who you're traveling with."

"We hope it hasn't been too much trouble coming this way." Sumuni's father shifted in his chair. "Where are you headed next?"

"To Magesa, but we have a couple of days before we're expected there. Or rather, before Gabriel is expected there."

"Why don't you stay for supper?" Sumuni's mother asked. "We planned a big meal. We thought it would be Sumuni's last night with us before he left for Wanza with Gabriel. We've invited some of our friends and family too. Consider it a token of gratitude, a little something for coming out this way. We would be honored if you ate with us."

A LITTLE SOMETHING' turned out to be a major feast. Half the village gathered under a tall baobab tree. Pots filled with stewed chicken, and peas in coconut, simmered in the fire. Potatoes baked on hot coals, and the aroma of milk tea drifted late into the night.

Sumuni and his little band put on another show for everyone. His father watched proudly, a wad of tobacco tucked behind his ear, while his mother threaded beads on long strands of fiber from the baobab.

"What's wrong?" asked Jack. "It feels like you're somewhere else."

We were sitting shoulder to shoulder by a warm spot near the fire.

"I'm just . . . I feel like I'm failing Mo. I'm not getting anywhere with these kids. We got to Juma too late, and now . . ."

"Now what?" He turned to study my face.

When Jack looked at me, it didn't matter where I was, or what I was thinking. I came right back to the present. To his eyes. To his voice. I could be drowning in torment, and all he had to do was look at me, just like he was doing then.

"You see that?" He tilted his head toward Sumuni. "Look at him. Look at his parents. That's love. That's happiness. They're glowing with it. How can that ever make you feel like you failed Mo? Besides, it's not like she entrusted you with anything. You took it on yourself. Your decision. Your mission."

"It's a stupid mission," I said. "I wanted to honor her memory, I wanted to make a difference, but I feel like it's all been for nothing."

A cool breeze rustled around us and blew dry leaves into the embers. We sat there, watching the women sweep the ground clean with hand brooms of grass and twigs until most of the guests dispersed.

"You did make a difference," said Jack, as they started dousing the fires, one by one. "To me."

He got up, boots spread, and held his hand out for me.

Around us, the night sky grew shrouded with clouds of smoke and blowing dust, but that moment, that moment shone with clarity so sharp and poignant, I knew it would remain lodged in my heart like a diamond.

You did make a difference. To me.

14

THERE WERE NO hotels in Maymosi, but one of the wealthier villagers rented rooms in his private villa. Jack and I spent the night in adjoining rooms that were sparse, but functional. The walls were paper thin, so I knew he'd been up most of the night. He was as bleary-eyed as I was in the morning.

Glad I wasn't the only one tossing and turning all night, I thought.

It was getting harder to keep things platonic between us. I wondered if the same thoughts had been running through his mind—to tear through the flimsy partition that separated us, give in to the crazy pull between us, and fall asleep to the sound of spent breaths.

We were both quiet as we drove away from Sumuni's village, lost in our own thoughts. I held Mo's final note in my hand:

Sept 1—Furaha, (Magesa)

The edges were curled up from all the times I had flipped through her Post-its. *Furaha* meant happiness. I wondered if her parents had named her that so it would always stay with her . . . happiness . . . no matter what the world threw at her. I was realizing that the situation with albino children in Tanzania was complex—Juma at one end, sacrificed by his own family, and Sumuni at the other—whose parents and friends would do anything to protect him. I wondered where Furaha fit within the spectrum.

"We'll go through the park, and on to Magesa through the

western corridor," explained Jack, when we got to the Serengeti National Park.

"Oh, look!" I said, as soon as we entered. "Giraffes! I didn't spot any at the crater."

"No, they find it too difficult to negotiate the cliffs there."

With their legs half-hidden by a sea of golden grass, they appeared to be floating gracefully across the horizon.

"What are those?" I pointed to a pair of wide-eyed animals that looked like overgrown hares on spindly legs.

"Dik-diks. They're a type of antelope."

"So tiny. So cute."

Just then, something spooked them, and they skittered away in zigzag patterns, whistling through their noses.

"You missed the annual migration," said Jack. "It's an extraordinary sight."

"I can't imagine it getting any better than this," I replied, staring out the window.

It was easy to get lost in the setting, almost as if something primal kicked in, peeling away the inner static and sharpening the senses. Everywhere around us, animals roamed the plains. Lions, elephants, impalas, wildebeest, zebras, warthogs, birds with iridescent feathers that shimmered like rainbows in the sun. There was a spectral magnificence to the ever-changing landscape. As we drove through the center of the park, the grassy plains gave way to patches of woodland and riverbeds lined with trees. Outcrops of granite stuck out like rocky islands on the horizon.

"Kopjes," said Jack. "That one looks exactly like the rock where Rafiki presented Simba to everyone in *The Lion King*. You want to check it out?"

"I doubt we'll find them there." I laughed.

"Maybe. Maybe not." Jack smiled. "But it's the perfect place for a lazy lion to warm up."

As we rounded the rocky outcrop, Jack slowed down and turned the car off.

"It's your lucky day, Rodel." He pointed to one of the rocks.

"Wha—" I halted when it moved. "Oh, my God. A rhino."

"Number five of the Big Five—the black rhinoceros. Now you've seen them all."

It was facing away from us, plucking on the bushes that sprouted between the boulders. Its body was thick and gray, like a round, armored tank. Red-billed birds perched on its back, feeding on what I assumed were ticks on its hide. We spent a few minutes admiring its imposing bulk, the large, lethal horns, and its surprisingly slim legs.

When Jack started the car, the rhino whirled around and turned its mud-crusted face to us. For a moment, it did nothing. Then it bellowed until a smaller figure appeared at its side.

"Fuck!" said Jack, backing away slowly. "She's got a calf."

Shielding the baby with her body, the rhino lowered its head and snorted loudly.

"Easy, big momma," said Jack, as he continued reversing.

For a moment, it looked like the hefty beast had been placated by our retreat. Then she came at us, so fast and furious I had to blink to believe something that size could move so quickly. The ground rattled as she exploded into motion—hot anger, cold, dark eyes. My skin turned to ice, all the blood pumping desperately to keep my heart from collapsing. She was close, and looming closer, so close that I could see her breath—heavy with moisture exhaled from her lungs—the thick, dense fiber of her skin, the menacing iron horn lowered as she headed straight for us.

Shit. Shit. Shit. Shit.

It was like watching a hellish, Jurassic nightmare flash before my eyes. And there was nothing I could do to get away from it. The violent sound of crushing metal ripped through the air as she rammed into us. All the air expelled from my chest. The sheer, brute force of the attack sent us skidding across the sandy dirt, uprooting scrub and foliage. The car teetered on its edge, and for a heart-stopping moment, it felt like we were going to tip right over.

"Jack!" My arms and legs flailed wildly as the world tilted around me.

"It's okay. We're okay," he said, as the car righted itself.

The rhino stood back in a display of dominance, but she looked like she was getting ready to charge again. Jack changed gears and the car leaped forward, wheels spinning as she crashed after us. We hurtled ahead, tearing through grass and shrubs until we lost her.

"Are you hurt?" Jack glanced my way.

"No." My stomach was still clenched, and I knew I'd be bruised all over, but it sure beat the alternative. "You?"

"I've been through worse," he replied. "Next time, grab the oh-shit handle."

"The what?"

"The oh-shit handle." He pointed to the handle over my window.

"Is that what it's called?" I laughed, in spite of the close call. My heart was hammering loud and fast, as if trying to flee my chest. "I always thought it's to hang up the dry cleaning."

"City dwellers." He shook his head.

"Safari maniacs," I shot back.

We found our way to the main road, along the western edge of the Serengeti National Park. It was like we had the whole place to ourselves. I couldn't spot a single car, probably because the road was horrifically corrugated, and the animals were few and far between. Against a hazy mountain range, ribbons of tall trees lined the banks of a flowing river.

"That's the Grumeti," said Jack. "It empties into Lake Victoria, Africa's largest freshwater lake. Wanza is located right on the shores of Lake Victoria."

"One more stop before we get there."

"That's right. First Magesa, then Wanza," replied Jack, as we exited the park.

After a few potholed miles, we approached a bustling center, nestled at the foot of green, craggy hills.

"I'm assuming we're coming up to the town of Bunda now?" I looked up from the map.

"That's right." Jack stopped to check the car and refuel. There was a sizable dent on the passenger door in the back, where the rhino had attacked. The door wouldn't open or close, but apart from that, the Land Rover seemed to have weathered it well.

After a quick lunch of *pilau* and stewed fish, we drove on through the gravel road that led out of town. The clusters of homes and shops soon gave way to cassava fields and banana plantations. Mango trees edged the street, bows heavy with fruit. There were few travelers on the road to Magesa, and the trees closed around us as we followed the dirt track leading to the village. The path was wet from rainfall, and the car fell into a constant rhythm of gas, brake, gas, brake, as Jack navigated around ravines and boulders. We ran into trouble after hitting a particularly deep pothole. The Land Rover gave a hellish clang and lurched to a halt.

"Damn it." Squatting on his heels, Jack peered under the car's carriage. Two of the wheels were mired in thick, black mud, but he seemed more concerned about something else. "We broke an axle. It probably came undone with the rhino attack, but this just sealed the deal."

"What do we do now?" I asked.

"Well, we're not going anywhere until we get it replaced."

"How far to Magesa?"

"Too far to walk. We won't make it before nightfall, and there's no way we're going through that forest in the dark." He pointed to the thicket of trees ahead. "I'll call for a mechanic. See if they can come help us out." He turned on his phone and shook his head. "There's no signal out here."

"Shit. We're screwed."

"Not yet. But we will be when the sun sets and the lions come out. Don't worry," he said, when the color drained from my face. "We'll take turns keeping a look out. I'll keep watch on the roof while you sleep, and then you can do the same for me. Here." He tore off a branch from the tree, stripped the leaves, and handed it to me. "Start whittling. A long, sharp point is best."

I held the stick, speechless, as he ducked into the car to get a knife. It took a moment before I caught on.

There are no lions prowling about here.

Sure enough, when I marched over and swung the door open, there he was, doubled over. Laughing. The sound of it was like ripples in a still pond, after a stone has been thrown into it. It radiated outward, enveloping me, until I couldn't help but join in.

It was in that state of intoxication, that release from self-consciousness, between peals of laughter, that I realized I was totally, completely in love with Jack Warden. It hit me like a ton of bricks, that you could feel so alive, even though your heart was nowhere in your possession, and you knew that you were going to walk around without it for the rest of your life. I stepped away from him, the laughter dying on my lips like he had speared my chest with the stick I was holding. I dropped it and turned on my heel, but my shoe was entrenched in the mud and I lurched, face forward, into the ground.

My downfall was complete. Quite literally. Absolute embarrassment. Absolute humiliation. Because Jack could read me like an open book—my *whys*, *ifs*, and *buts*; my starts, stops, twists, and turns. It was exhilarating because it was effortless—no explanations needed. It was terrifying because it left me transparent, with no blanket of pretense. There was no way to hide my feelings for him.

When Jack helped me up, I avoided his gaze. When he wiped the mud away from my face, I kept my eyes on the ground. When he sat me down and poured water over my palms, I watched the dirt wash away.

"Rodel."

Damn him. Damn his voice. Damn the way he said my name.

He lifted my chin so I had no choice but to meet his gaze. He wasn't smiling or laughing. It wasn't the face of a man who was amused. He was looking at me with a mix of such intense tenderness and yearning, I choked back a sob, because beneath it all was an apology. For the things he stirred up in me, for the things I stirred up in him, for the bittersweet journey that had brought us together, and for the parting that was yet to come. And then very softly, very gently, with one finger still under my chin, he kissed me—once, twice, three times—like he was picking a bouquet of flowers from my mouth.

"Your hair is a mess," he said, running his fingers over my mud-coated tresses

"*I'm* a mess." I took stock of myself—my feet, my clothes, my nails.

"It's an easy fix. Stay right here."

He got a kerosene stove out of the trunk, and before long, he had heated up two big pots of water, set up soap, a bucket, and a folding chair.

"Welcome to Jungle Jack's Salon." He bowed with flourish. "Sit. Lean back."

"What are you doing?" I asked, settling into the chair.

"Washing your hair." He adjusted the angle, so my head was hanging over the edge of the chair.

"Shouldn't we be figuring out what we're going to do next?"

"*Shhh.*" His breath fanned against my forehead, sending little shivers down my spine.

And there, on the road to Magesa, beside a car stuck in the mud, Jack Warden washed my hair with a bar of blue soap, as I sat on an old chair that he carted around in his trunk. When he poured warm water over my hair, I closed my eyes and thought how there really ought to be a word to describe the sensation when your lungs fill up with the sweetest air, and yet you're left completely breathless.

It was more intimate than a kiss, Jack's hands trailing through my hair, the rough pads of his fingers massaging my scalp, making slow, steady circles as he worked the lather from my roots to my tips. He started at my temples, moved on to my head, and down to my nape. Massaging the back of my neck, he kneaded the muscles until my head fell back, relaxing into the cup of his palm. My skin tingled from his touch, from the sensual rhythm of his strokes, from the deliciousness of an unexpectedly submissive moment.

I don't know how long we spent in that clearing, Jack washing my hair like it was the only thing he wanted to do, the sun on my face, little peeks of his body silhouetted over me. When he was done, he poured more water, pulling his fingers through my hair until all the soap had been rinsed out. And then again, just because. I was ready to get up when he grabbed my hair with both hands and gathered it at the crown of my head. Then he twisted it and squeezed out the water. The sensation of rough after soft sent a tingling to the pit of my stomach. I shuddered as little rivulets trickled down my neck and back, but it wasn't from the water. It was because I could feel Jack's eyes on the back of my ears, my nape, the curve of my exposed jawline. Then he let my hair go, and watched it tumble over my shoulders.

"Towel," he said, handing it to me. He strung up a sheet between two trees and heated some more water. "You can finish off over here."

"Nice." I stepped behind the barrier and peeled off my clothes.

"Jungle Jack's is a full-service salon. A gal could get used to this."

"A rhino attack, car trouble, face planting in mud, and a bucket shower?" He laughed. "You're a strange one, Rodel Emerson."

It was strange when I thought about it—that I'd be okay with things that were so far removed from my comfort zone. But things didn't always have to make sense. The most profound, most memorable moments of life are the ones that make you feel. And that's what I'd been missing. That feeling of being alive. I had come with a heart full of grief for my sister, never expecting to find love or life budding out of it. It was like Mo was showing me the possible in the impossible.

I wish you could see the world through my eyes, her words echoed in my mind.

I'm starting to see, Mo. I'm starting to see.

I peered over the sheet. Jack was dragging the tent out of the truck. It struck me then that I would be all right, no matter what. Sometimes you come across a rainbow story—one that spans your heart. You might not be able to grasp it or hold on to it, but you can never be sorry for the color and magic it brought.

15

NIGHT DESCENDED AROUND us with flat and complete
blackness. The moon hung above, but not a single dot of
light flickered on the horizon. Yellow-winged bats flitted
off to meet the darkness as Jack stoked the fire.

"We'll set off for Magesa in the morning," he said. "Once
we find Furaha, we can come back for the car with a mechanic.
Hopefully, the phone will pick up a signal too."

"Have you ever been? To Magesa?" I rinsed out our dinner
plates and sat next to him.

"I haven't been to any of the places on Mo's list." He was
sitting close to the flames, his face toasty and warm.

"They're all so different—each town, each village. I never know
what to expect." Night eyes glittered around us. A porcupine? A
mongoose? I couldn't be sure. All I knew was that I felt completely
safe with Jack.

"You miss home?" he asked.

"Yes. And no." I shifted on the mossy log we were sitting on. "I
just bought my first home. I miss that. I miss its worn, honey-hued
walls. The sound of the river as it flows by. I miss my little book
nook. The sheep-dotted hills. Fields of lavender. June roses tumbling
over the fences. Small, wild strawberries growing through cracks
in the flagstones. I miss the church bells, the tall, elegant spires. It's
home, you know? We traveled a lot when I was younger. I've looked

for a place like that my whole life, a place that spoke to my soul."

"It sounds beautiful." Jack turned to me, elbows resting on his knees.

In the silence that followed, I smiled ruefully. After Sarah, he had vowed to never ask another woman to live on the farm with him. And I had just ensured that even if he changed his mind, that woman wouldn't be me. We both had places of permanence that we weren't willing to give up.

"And Africa?" he whispered, staring into the flames. "What do you think of Africa?"

I will always think of you when I think of Africa.

"It's beautiful and heart-wrenching. It heals you, it destroys you. It's the place that claimed my sister." *And my heart.*

The fire threw our flickering shadows against the tree trunks. The heat of the day had dissipated, and our breaths were turning to vapor.

"We should turn in," said Jack. But neither of us moved. Because there was only one tent, and it had been flashing in our faces all evening, like a big neon sign on the Vegas strip.

I went in first, while Jack secured the fire. It was a fair-sized tent—until Jack entered because everything just seemed to shrink around him. I closed my eyes and huddled under the blankets as he slid in, next to me. I kept my back to him, but the air-inflated mattress shifted under his weight, so I ended up clinging to the edge, to keep from rolling toward him. I really was on a slippery slope when it came to him.

"Rodel?"

"Yes?"

"If you dig your nails into the mattress any harder, you're going to rip a hole through it."

"I . . . I'm not—"

"Let go." He propped himself up on his elbow and loosened

my grip. "What are you so afraid of?" His eyes searched mine. "This?" He swept me into his arms and held me snugly. "See? It's not so bad," he said, as his warmth seeped into my body—so male, so bracing.

"They're just arms." His fingers trailed slowly up and down my arm. "And legs." He traced the curve of my thigh. "And this spot right here, that I've been dying to taste since I washed your hair." He kissed a spot under my ear lobe. "I crave you, Rodel. In the most innocent ways. I lie awake in my bed at night, thinking of you down the hallway, wanting nothing more than to hold you. I want to stroke your hair until you fall asleep. I want to give you forehead kisses when you're down. That's all I allow myself. I don't go any further."

He stopped trailing patterns over my skin and shut his eyes like he was struggling with something wild and powerful.

"But right now, Rodel, now that I'm holding you, and touching you, and breathing you, all I want to do is take you like no one's taken you before." His gaze burned when he looked at me. "I want to take you like I *hate* you. Fiercely. Completely. Because you resurrected me, only to relinquish me. I don't think you have any idea what you've done. You see this?" He rubbed his hand over the scruff of his beard.

"After Lily died, every time I picked up the razor, I thought of ending it. The only thing that kept me from doing so was the thought of Goma having to bury me. When you showed up that stormy afternoon, it was like grace stepping on my porch. I didn't want to look at you, I didn't want to see you or hear you because there was no place for grace, or hope, or virtue in my world. They had been snuffed out."

I held my breath as he continued baring pieces of himself. I couldn't have spoken even if I'd wanted to. Lying next to him, our bodies touching under the blanket had turned me into a mess of quivering sensations.

"I thought you were well intentioned but naive." His eyes were on my lips, and I marveled at how he could make them throb with a glance. "And that day, by the fire, I thought you were beautiful. But then you were more. You were smart and funny. And brave. And every time I look at you, I see something new, and interesting, and compelling. You make me feel like I want to go on long trips with you. To the sea. To the mountains. You make me feel things that I had stopped feeling, and I don't know what to do with them, or where to put them. Every time you're around me, I feel like I'm going to explode, trying to contain it all. You opened me up again, Rodel, and you had no right to, damn it! You had no right." His grip changed, all the wound-up tension snapping in a hot breath.

Everything shattered as he took my mouth with savage intensity. One large hand gripped my waist, drawing me to him as if he couldn't stand the distance anymore. Blood pounded in my brain as his hand glided under my top and fondled my breast, turning its pink tip marble hard. His body was rough and insistent on top of mine, our breaths uneven, limbs entwined.

"Touch me." He pulled his T-shirt over his head, heat rippling off his skin. My pulse raced to my fingertips, as I traced the corded muscles on his chest, the light mat of hair in the groove between his pecs. When I slipped my hands into his boxers, he reclaimed my mouth, surging into my palms with a groan.

"Tell me you want this." He slid down my stomach, to the swell of my hips. "Show me."

And then he was uncovering me, fingers hooked in my panties, dragging them over my legs. He slowed down then, sat back on his haunches, and touched me—a soft, single brush of his thumb over my clit. The moan that escaped me pierced the stillness around us.

"I'm going to make you come, Rodel." He said that part in my ear, partially covering my body with his because I was shivering. "I want to know what you sound like when you orgasm."

I hadn't expected Jack to be dominating, mostly because I had seen the other side of him—broken, nurturing, vulnerable. But Jack in bed was a different man. He had the Art of Manliness down to a precise skill. And it thrilled me, excited me.

"On your side." He flipped me over and pulled the blankets over us, spooning me from behind. His rock-hard erection twitched against me as his fingers circled my clit. His other hand roamed over my breast, kneading the soft flesh with tantalizing possessiveness. My body squirmed against his, our contours nestling into each other, as hot, swift currents of desire stirred up inside me.

"Jack . . ." I half-turned to face him.

He knew what I wanted before I said it. He crushed my mouth hungrily, his tongue seeking mine, demanding it. My lips parted on a ragged sigh as he buried his face in the hollow of my neck, intensifying the rhythm of his fingers. Pleasure radiated outward, like jolts of liquid fire. I clutched the tendons in the back of Jack's neck. He was a biter, grazing my neck with just enough force to command all of my attention, and then letting go, like a lion playing with his prey. I slid my fingers through the thick tufts of his hair, pulling him back, and then we were kissing again, leaving soul sonnets deep inside each other's mouths. That was when he sent me over the edge, sliding his thigh between my legs, shifting his lean, hard frame over me. It was a simple act, but I shattered into a million glowing stars.

The contrast of rough against smooth, the anticipation of penetration, of being taken by Jack, the way our bodies were already locked in a hungry, primordial rhythm, his fingertips coaxing my pleasure points, his lips devouring mine. It was a sensual onslaught that rocked the very core of me. My breath came in long, shuddering moans that unleashed something hot and raw in him.

"I can't hold back, Rodel." He rubbed the tip of his shaft against me. "Tell me you want this."

I knew what he was asking. He wanted to be sure I could handle it. This night, maybe a few more before I left. Nothing less, nothing more.

"I want you, Jack." My body rose instinctively to meet his. The thick, hard length of him on my thigh was both electrifying and intimidating. "But you should know . . . I . . . I haven't done this before. You're my first."

He stilled and sucked in a long, ragged breath. "This . . ." He took in another soul-deep breath. "You haven't—"

"It's okay," I whispered. "Look at me. Look at me, Jack. I want you to be my first."

And my last. And all the times in between. But I can't have that. So I'll take this. What we have right here. Right now.

But Jack wasn't listening. "I'm too far gone, Rodel," he growled, taking my hand and guiding it to him. His head fell back as my fingers closed around him, and he let out a soft gasp.

Against the flickering light of the fire outside, he was the glowing image of passion and raging desire. It was only when he started thrusting into my hand, his rhythm urgent and frenzied that I realized what he meant. He was too far gone to deny his release, but he was still in control of how it happened. I felt a stab of sadness, but it didn't stand a chance against the heady eroticism of the man before me, the way he was watching me, making love to every curve, every inch of my body with his eyes, as my fist moved up and down his throbbing shaft.

"Fuck, Rodel." His voice had a raw, brittle edge, like he was about to snap. His lips clamped down on mine as his body convulsed with sharp waves of pleasure.

He leaned his forehead against mine, catching his breath. When he rolled on his back, taking me with him, I thought how incredibly warm his arms were, how perfectly they wrapped around me.

"Rodel? Why are you crying?"

"Because." I snuggled deeper into him. "It feels good."

"This feels good . . ." He squeezed me tighter. "Or the crying?"

"Both." I sniffed.

He propped himself up on his elbow and looked at me. "These tears—" his thumb swiped my cheek "—they have nothing to do with you thinking that I rejected you, do they?" A shadow passed across his face when I didn't answer. "God, Rodel." He swore. "Your first time. The possibility didn't even register on my radar. Just the fact that you've waited this long—that has to mean something. It has to be special. Not in a tent, on a flimsy air mattress, in the middle of nowhere. And not with me, not with a man who can't offer you all the things that should go with it. I did the only responsible thing I could, and let me tell you, it still feels like hell."

"Good. Because I don't want responsible, Jack. I've done responsible things my whole responsible life. I want reckless. I want mindless, ruthless, heedless. I want to be swept up in madness. I want your passion. I want your pain. I want you to tell me that you can't bear the thought of me leaving, that it feels like you can't breathe, that you want me, that you'll miss me."

His gaze traveled over my face for a long, still beat before falling on my neck. "I can't bear the thought of you leaving," he said to the mark his teeth had left there. "I stop breathing every time I think about it." He found another one, closer to my collarbone, and pressed his lips to it. "I want you in ways you can't even begin to imagine." His voice was muffled, vibrating against my flesh with deep, soft resonance. "Will I miss you?" He lifted his head and looked at me. "Like a dream that starves and curls up beneath my bones."

I thought his touch was the only cure for my crazy, heated senses, but I found myself being pulled beyond the circle of his arms, to a place where souls go to kiss—lipless and formless and free. I knew that whenever I thought of love, it would have a face, a name, a voice. And I would hear its heart beating from inside a tent in the wilds of Africa.

I WOKE UP with my nose lodged in the dip between Jack's collarbones. Steel arms were wrapped around me, one crooked under my neck, the other around my waist. I shifted, and he loosened his hold the tiniest bit. That was when I realized Jack was awake and probably had been for a while. We untangled ourselves slowly, with little prickles of awareness—me lifting my hair so he could slide his arm out, him untwisting his legs from around mine.

Every time his gaze met mine over breakfast, my heart turned over. I couldn't help but think of where his hands had been, what his eyes had seen. As we got ready to leave for Magesa, I caught him watching me, as if he were taking little snapshots and storing them away.

"You think we need that?" I asked, when he got the rifle out of the car.

"I hope not, but I'm not leaving it behind." He slid it into a discreet carry bag and rolled the sleeping pad around it.

It was amazing how many things Jack managed to fit into his backpack. He folded the tent fabric inside, squeezed in the rest of the supplies, and secured the poles outside.

When everything was packed and loaded, he tightened the straps and locked the car. "It will take us a couple of hours to get to Magesa. You good to go?"

I nodded and then looked away. His eyes were so impossibly

blue, it was like he had the whole sky inside of him.

We hiked through a small patch of forest with trees so dense they blocked out the sky. Vines wrapped their tendrils around gray, scaly bark and moss grew like a carpet under our feet. I had to squint when we emerged from the dark canopy, even though a blanket of cotton wool clouds obscured the sun. The dirt track we were on veered and merged with a wider road up ahead.

"One more check," said Jack, turning his phone on. He searched for a signal and shook his head. "We're still out of range."

I adjusted my backpack as we marched on. It wasn't as heavy as Jack's, but the load was starting to take its toll.

"Do you hear that?" Jack shielded his eyes and peered behind me. "There's a car coming. We might be able to hitch a ride."

I turned and followed his gaze. A white van was rattling down the road, music blaring.

"Is that a *dala dala?*" I asked.

"No. Looks like a private vehicle." Jack stood in the middle of the road, flagging it down.

It was hard to see anyone through the dirty windshield, but there was yellow text emblazoned on the side—something about repairing air conditioners. The van slowed as it approached, but just as Jack lowered his hands, the driver suddenly hit the accelerator. The wheels spun as he came at Jack, head on, at full speed.

It was a blatant, deliberate disregard for his life, almost like he was road-kill trophy to the lunatics in the car who were cheering to run him over. I caught a glimpse of them—grinning and banging the sides of the car, windows down, as they hurtled toward him.

"Jack!" I gasped as they zoomed past me in a flash of dust and hot metal.

He dived to the side of the road, dodging the front bumper by a hair's breadth. The van careened down the road, and I heard the loud, raucous sound of laughter.

Keh keh keh keh.

The driver gave a blaring victory honk, celebrating his dangerous, infantile prank.

"Fuckers!" Jack got up and dusted himself off.

"Are you all right?" My stomach was in knots. "Who runs a person off the road for fun?" I stared after the van as it disappeared around the bend, the beat of heavy bass fading with it.

Jack rubbed his shoulder, rolling it forward and then back. His eyes had a burning, faraway look. "I hope we never see them again." His gaze refocused on me. "The sooner we get to Magesa, the better. Come on."

My fingers threaded through the warmth of his outreached hand. They were shaky and stiff.

"Frightened for me, Rodel?" Jack raised my hand to his lips.

"No." I swallowed. His hot lips on my skin were breaking down my brain-to-mouth connection. "Just wishing we'd packed the oh-shit handle."

"Here." He laughed, hooking my finger through one of the belt loops on his jeans. "Hold tight and don't let go."

He might have meant it as a joke, but I took him up on it. We must have walked another mile like that when a rusty pickup truck came into view.

"Don't even think about it," I said, as it approached.

"Chicken," he muttered, under his breath.

"Really?" I stopped, hands on my hips. "You would chance it? After what just happened?"

"Really." He grinned. "Chicken."

The truck bounced by, wheat colored chickens squawking at us from its cargo hold. We stood by the side of the road, staring after it in a cloud of exhaust fumes.

"Come on." He nudged my elbow. "You know you want to laugh."

I kissed him then, suddenly and without warning, standing on my tiptoes to reach him.

"What was that for?" His mouth quirked higher.

I wanted to know what your lips taste like after a smile. I shook my head and grinned like I was holding a big secret.

Everything seemed sharper and clearer after that, even though the day was gray and painted in a dull, desolate light.

Magesa was little more than a collection of crumbling mud homes in the shadow of a tall, rocky hill. It was a hot, sweltering dust bowl—dry brush, a dried up well, and dry, bony people. It seemed like a place that rain clouds skipped over, probably because the hill soaked up most of the precipitation.

"Give me sweet. Give me sweet. I am school child. Give me sweet." A doe-eyed boy came running up and tugged on my top.

"A school child, huh? Why aren't you in school then?"

He looked at me blankly and held out his hand. He had no idea what I had said, but he'd had memorized all the English he needed.

I laughed, and he smiled shyly, before turning to Jack and repeating the same four lines.

"Give me sweet. Give me sweet. I am school child. Give me sweet."

Jack said something to him in Swahili. The boy ran off and returned with a woman who I assumed was his mother. They talked to Jack for a few minutes. Furaha's name was mentioned. The woman shook her head. Jack asked a few more questions and got the same response.

"Thank you." He handed her some things from his backpack. Then he pulled out some granola bars and gave them to the boy.

"*Asante sana!*" they said.

"So . . ." Jack turned to me after they left. "You want the good news or the bad?"

"How bad is it?"

We were standing next to an empty oil drum behind a tin-roofed hut. Small, green bugs hovered at the bottom, atop what remained of the rainwater it had collected. It was thick now, with dust and debris.

"Furaha isn't here. But—" Jack held up his hand as my shoulders sagged "—the good news is that she moved with her family a few weeks ago. Her father inherited some property. The lady said he's a rich man now."

I stared at him for a few seconds. "So that's it? They're gone?" I looked up and down the row of sagging huts. "I mean, good for them. Really. But this is just so frustrating! Three kids, three strikes. What are the chances? I didn't even get to one of Mo's kids. Not one! And now we're stuck here—no car and no phone service. Tell me they have a mechanic, Jack. Someone who can fix the car?"

"No mechanic, but there's a bus that comes around. We can take it to go get the spare parts."

"Okay. That's good." I wasn't just dealing with the crushing disappointment of having let my sister down, I also felt terrible for dragging Jack away from the farm. It had amounted to nothing but a wild goose chase. "How long before it gets here?"

"Three days."

"_Three_ days?"

"It comes by once a week."

"There's got to be another way. Do they have a landline? A phone box? Some kind of roadside assistance?" I flung my hands out in despair.

"Rodel." His long, tapered fingers slid down my arm and tightened around my wrist. He didn't have to say anything. He was doing it again—bringing me back to the moment. He had an artless way of communicating with his eyes. He could blur everything in the periphery, so all that remained was his calm, commanding presence.

"You do that to the calves when they get skittish."

"Do what?"

"What you're doing now."

"Does it feel good?" His thumb slid back and forth over the pulse in my wrist.

"Like I'm being hypnotized."

"Good. Now come here." He pulled me into his arms.

My eyelashes fluttered shut as I rested my cheek against his chest.

"Unbelievable," I mumbled. *From all wound up to Zen mode in under ten seconds.*

"Are you talking to your sister again?" asked Jack.

"I don't hear her anymore. She's stopped talking to me." My throat ached as I said it. "I think I've let her down."

"Or maybe she's said everything she needed to say."

"She never said goodbye." The swell of pain was beyond tears. "I wish I'd picked up her call." I had failed Mo. And I had failed at getting whatever closure I thought I would find in Tanzania. And I had royally buggered up my heart in the process.

"Hey," Jack whispered into my hair. "Come back to me."

We stood there for a few moments, locked in each other's arms. A black bird watched us from the thin grass, hopped closer, and then vanished in a dry scatter.

"Jack, I—"

We both froze as his phone rang.

"It's working. Holy hell, we have a signal! Hello?" he answered. The person on the other end started talking. And continued talking. And talking.

"Bahat—" Jack intervened, but was cut off. "Stop. Bahati. Listen. *Listen!*" It came out like a lion's roar.

Pin drop silence from the other end. Even the brown leaves around us seemed to stop rustling.

And then, I heard a tinny voice through the phone.

"I'm not shouting at you, Bahati. You have no idea how glad I am that you called." Jack paced back and forth as a stream of words came through.

"There's a spare key in my desk. Top drawer, right-hand side. But that's not—" Jack shook his head as Bahati rattled on. "Just tell Goma to wait until I get home. There's someth—" Jack threw his hands up and went silent.

"Are you done?" he asked, when the chatter at the other end stopped. "Yes? Now I talk, you listen. Deal?" He must have got an affirmative because he continued. "Ro and I are stranded in Magesa. The car broke down. No. It's just us. No kids. I'll explain when you get here. Yes. I want you to come get us. I know . . ." He held the phone away from his ear as Bahati squeaked at the other end. "I know you don't. But you won't be making any stops in Maasai land. You'll be driving straight through. Who cares about Lonyoki's vision? You don't believe in those superstitions, do you? Okay, so now's your chance to prove it. Prove his prophecy wrong."

There was more protesting before Jack spoke again. "Look, I'll make it worth your while. I don't know. New seats for Suzi? It doesn't matter. Black leather, red leather, pink fucking zebra. Whatever you want. Yes. Yes! And one more thing. How's Scholastica?" Jack paused and nodded. "Good. That's great. Bring her too. We're close to Wanza. We'll take her to the orphanage, get her settled in, and sort out my car on the way back. If you leave now, you can make it here by morning. Rodel and I will set up camp tonight. No, not Magesa." Jack scanned the village. There was a latrine pit at one end, and when the wind blew the door open, a foul stench filled the hot, humid air. "Meet us on the other side of the hill. You'll see it when you get here. We'll wait for you there. Right." He hung up and exhaled.

"Bahati's coming?"

"He is." Jack shook his head like he couldn't quite believe it. "And Scholastica's feeling better, so he's bringing her too. We just ha—" His phone rang again.

"Yes?" he answered. Then he laughed. "Really, Bahati? No gas money? That's the best you can come up with? Put Goma on the line. Oh? You don't want to get her involved? That's right. Or she'll make you drive through Maasai land in her muumuu. I know you don't want to. Do it for me, okay? No, you still get the seats. The seats stand, plus, I will be forever indebted. Yes? Okay."

We watched the phone for a few more moments after Jack hung up, but it didn't ring again.

"You think?" I asked.

"I think." Jack put the phone away. "He's going to come through."

WE SENSED THE rain before it came, in racing clouds that thrummed with charged energy. I was securing the poles at the base of the tent when it started falling, rolling over us in thick, warm sheets.

"Get inside," Jack shouted over the rumbling of the sky. "I'll finish off."

"I got this one. You fix the other side."

By the time we crawled into the tent, we were wet and soggy but exhilarated from racing against the storm.

"No, leave it open," I said, as Jack went to zip the door shut. "I want to watch." I leaned back on my elbows, trying to catch my breath.

We lay beneath the raining canvas, gazing through the tent flaps. In the distance, thorn trees stood in iron silhouette against the gray sky. Water mingled with the cindery soil, filling the air with the sweet, earthy fragrance of rain.

Jack grew still. Too still.

"Are you okay?" I asked. His hair was wetly draped over the bones of his chiseled face.

"It'll take some time," he replied, staring into the light. "I can't shake off this feeling—of wanting to stand by Lily's side, so she's not alone out there, in the rain. I know it doesn't make any sense, I know she's gone, but a part of me still wants to protect her."

A train whistled in the far distance, and somewhere on the water-washed plains, a solitary jackal whined at the flash of lightning.

"I'm sorry." Jack blinked and tilted his head to look at me. "Sometimes I get so wrapped up in it, I don't see the whole picture. At least I got Lily back. They never recovered your sister's body. That had to be tough."

"It was. It is." I folded my arms around my knees and rested my chin there. "But then I think that maybe Mo would have wanted it that way. She never wanted to stay in one place. She felt boxed in. And now she's . . . free. She would have laughed at my thwarted mission. First, that I crawled out of my comfort zone for her. And then at how wrong everything went, how I couldn't get even one of her kids to Wanza. If there's a lesson behind things, I wonder what I'm supposed to learn from it."

"Maybe the lesson is not for you but for me. So you can teach me that it's okay to sit in the rain without Lily, and not feel like dying."

He leaned in and something wild swirled in the pit of my stomach. It wasn't just a kiss. It was a lesson—a fierce, burning imprint, so that my lips would always know the difference between being wanted and being craved. The world washed away in a blurry, wet painting. All that was left was Jack's hot breath, the firmness of his lips, the way his drenched clothes clung to his body. When he pulled back, he was breathing hard, like he'd run a long, long way.

"Stop running, Jack." I took his beautiful face in my hands as lightning flashed in the distance. "Stop running away from us. I want you. I'm not asking you for forever. Yes, it's what I wanted—it's what I was waiting for. But then I took a trip. And I realized I'd been living in a delicate, made-up world. No, not living. Hibernating. Crossing off the days, one after the other. So what I want—what I really want, is this one rainy afternoon. I want to go back home drunk and intoxicated, filled with ecstasy and white heat. So love me tenderly, Jack. Or love me recklessly. I don't care which. But do it now. You never know if we'll be passing this way again." His expression was so galvanizing, my heart fluttered wildly in my chest. "Your words. Remember?"

"I was talking about a trip to the crater, not—"

"Not this?" I tossed off my wet top in a passionate challenge.

My invitation pushed him over the edge. Something intense flared through him—instant, electric, as if I had just unleashed him.

Shit. I'm in for it now. My pulse pounded with a dizzy cocktail of desire, rimmed in gritty bits of trepidation. He gazed at me intently, cranking up the anticipation until it was almost unbearable.

"Take it off," he said, his command thick with longing.

My fingers faltered as I slid off one strap, and then the other. He didn't wait for me to unclasp my bra. He was done waiting. His tongue flicked my nipple through the wet fabric before he latched on, sucking it into his mouth, rasping the edges with his teeth.

"*Ohhh.*" My breath escaped as he brought my untried senses to life, pulling down the lace on the other cup and flicking the puckered peak with his thumb.

He lifted me into his lap, straddling my legs on either side of him. He was hard, and he wanted me to know it. "Last chance, sweetness. I've never wanted anyone the way I want you. So if you're having second thoughts, now's the time, because in a little while I'm going to take you, gently at first, and then to all kinds of dark, delicious places."

His breath left hot, phantom kisses between my breasts, his

words making me squirm. His husky bedroom voice sent delightful shudders through me. My insides jangled with excitement. Without breaking the intense gaze we were locked in, I tugged at the hem of his T-shirt. He lifted his arms and let me peel it off. His skin was slick with rainwater, but the heat coming off his body was palpable. Our breaths came in unison as we paused at the edge, that exquisite swell of silence between the crack of lightning and the roar of thunder.

And then the space between us exploded.

He covered my mouth hungrily, devouring its softness, his long fingers buried in my hair. He tugged a fistful, exposing my neck and left a trail of tantalizing, beard-brushed kisses. My back arched at the feel of them—unexpectedly silky against my flesh. Goosebumps rioted over my skin as he unclasped my bra and tossed it aside. My eyelashes fluttered shut when his tongue swirled over a taut, dusky pink nipple, whispering his adoration in gruff, short breaths.

"Hold tight, sweetness." He gazed up at me when my hands clutched his shoulders. His eyes held the most intoxicating kind of threats and promises.

I gasped as he pushed me onto my back, his hand searing a path down my abdomen and onto my thigh. He rubbed slow circles over the wet, clinging fabric of my jeans, moving closer and closer to the junction between my legs.

My nerves thrummed, like the rain falling on the canvas roof over us, but he denied me and tugged at my zip instead. I held my breath as he pulled it down slowly, watching me with a look that was so potent, so compelling, he might as well have been unfastening my soul, bit by quivering bit. He slid my jeans off and sat back on his knees, drinking me in.

It had been different in the dark, but in the gray, muted daylight, my insecurities kicked in. It wasn't as if I'd been naked in front of many men before. A hand under my blouse, a feel up my skirt, but never so exposed. And certainly not with someone who looked like Jack. My hands moved instinctively across my breasts and stomach.

"Don't." He clamped my wrists above me as his hooded eyes roved over my naked body. My flesh trembled, my toes curled, but when I opened my eyes and caught the expression on his face, everything melted. He was looking at me like I was stardust and light.

"Jesus." His eyes darkened with stark sensuality. "You are so fucking beautiful."

He paused to kiss me and then started planting worshipful caresses with his hands, and his lips, and his tongue, and his teeth. He moved slowly, relishing every inch, until the hot flush of desire rippled in waves under my skin, making my hips surge in an age-old rhythm.

"That's it, baby. Now let me ride it with you."

I bucked at the first brush of his tongue between my slick folds as he buried his face between my legs.

"*Mmm.*" He lifted his head for a second to savor the wetness on his lips. "God, I've been dying to taste you. You're . . ." The rest of his words were muffled, but they melted into hot, sweet vibrations against the very core of me.

Jack was not a quiet lover. He voiced his pleasure with thick, throaty sounds. He threw my leg over his shoulder and nipped my inner thigh before plunging his tongue into me. I held onto his wild, thick hair as involuntary tremors of arousal shot through me. He seemed to sense the awakening flames because his movements intensified, carrying me to the peaks of pleasure.

"Yes." He lifted my hips off the floor, bringing me in full, carnal contact with his mouth. "Fuck, yes."

His raw sensuousness sent me over the edge. I gasped, and yielded to the twisting, gasping sweetness that burst through me in whirls of electric sensation.

I was still panting when he gathered me against his warm, pulsing body. My breasts crushed against the hardness of his chest as he rubbed the bare skin of my back and shoulders. It was as if he knew I needed that, to ground me because I felt like I was going to float away.

I don't know exactly when we started kissing, or when his soft stroking turned my skin to liquid fire. Something dormant had awakened in me, and I was greedy with it. I tugged on his jeans, sliding them off. I touched him, explored him, aroused him, worshiped him—the moon-curve of his lips, the pleasure groves behind his ears, the valleys between his hard, chiseled abs. He was like a piece of living, breathing, responsive art—melting when I touched him here, turning rock hard when I teased him there. I learned his taste and his curves, the sweetness of his breath, the indents of his back, the rough hair on his leg. I reveled in his moans, his grunts, his shivers of delight, the way his head rolled back when I took him in my mouth, the look in his eyes as he lowered his body over mine, imprisoning me in a web of mounting arousal.

He held still for a second, though I could feel him throbbing with need before he pushed in. My body stretched to accommodate him, inch by slick inch—slowly, impossibly—until he came to a barrier. He withdrew slightly and brushed a strand of hair off my face.

"Kiss me," he said, smoky and raw.

I touched my lips to his, my focus still on the point where our bodies were melded.

"A *real* kiss," he growled, grazing my bottom lip with his teeth. "Like this." His mouth swooped down to capture mine until my senses were spinning. My breath escaped through softly parted lips. "Give me your tongue." His words were a spell I had fallen under. I shivered as the velvet warmth of his tongue tangled with mine, losing myself to the mastery of his kiss.

That was when he thrust deep into me—one hard, firm push that made me gasp and break free of his lips. I clutched his shoulders, my nails leaving crescent shaped indents as the pain tore through me.

"*Shhh.* I've got you." He dropped kisses on my forehead, my nose, the corner of my mouth. He stayed inside me, not moving, until my body adjusted to him and the pain subsided.

"Not gonna lie." His Adam's apple bobbed as he started to rock gently inside me. "It's taking everything in me not to take you hard and fast. You feel like heaven." He laced his fingers through mine, as if to anchor himself.

My body melted around him, and the world was filled with him. We found a tempo that bound our bodies together.

Jack, Jack, Jack, Jack, it sung to me, each thrust of his hips carrying me higher.

I clung to him, riding out the raging storm that was building up inside me.

"Rodel." The words were strained as he buried his face in my neck, his hot breath scorching my skin. Passion flamed through my veins as his rhythm changed. His fingers dug deep into my hipbones as he started tipping over the fine edge of control. His thumb found my clit and he drew out a moan. My thoughts fragmented as he teased it, stroked it, flicked it.

"Jack." My entire body clenched and then peaked as he freed me in bursts of shuddering rapture.

Lighting flared around us as his breath hitched and his thighs tensed. In a moment of blinding clarity, I realized that every time the thunder rolled, I would think of Jack—the essence of him clinging to my senses, the turbulence of his passion around me, our boundary lines dissipating. Skin and bone and breath tangled up in a sizzling bolt of ecstasy.

We lay there, chests heaving, Jack's forehead resting on mine until our breathing slowed.

"You okay?" he asked, running his thumb along my jaw.

I sighed in pleasant exhaustion and snuggled closer. I ached, but it was nothing compared to the satisfaction that came from yielding to the searing need that had been building up in me.

"When do you think we can do it again?" I asked.

"You little minx." Jack smiled and wrapped me up in his arms. He was warm. So deliciously warm.

My eyelids drooped, but I didn't want to miss any of it—the way his fingertips were tracing the outline of my lips, the way his beautifully proportioned body felt against mine, the flecks of harvest gold in his sky-blue eyes.

"Remember this." He brushed the hair off my neck and breathed a kiss there. "When you're curled up with your books on a rainy afternoon in England, remember how you painted my world with your colors. Remember your rainbow halo."

"I will." A hot ache grew in my throat. He was already saying goodbye. "I'll remember. For the rest of my life."

Outside, the thrumming of the rain softened as the clouds passed over. Inside, we held each other, burning bittersweet poems in the silence.

"Jack?" I propped myself up and looked at him, brows softened, eyes half closed, defenses down. Spent and happy, like a big cat lounging on a rock.

I wanted to remember him like this, exactly like that.

"What?" He was measuring my palm against his, fingers splayed, all five touching each other.

I wish I could explain to you what that voice does to me.

I wish I could explain to you how you make me feel.

I don't think I'll ever fall as hard and as fast for anyone, the way I fell for you.

I don't think I'll ever love anyone the way I love you.

"Nothing." I took his face in my hands and kissed him.

"You think I don't feel it?" he whispered, under the curtain of my hair. "Every beat of my heart is taking you away from me. I want to stop here forever. This tent, this kiss, this moment." His fingers sunk into my hair as he pulled me to his lips.

I was drinking in the sweetness of his kiss when my stomach growled.

"I think your stomach wants in on the action." Jack slid down and put his ear to my belly. "Are you talking dirty to me?" He proceeded to have a makeshift conversation. "What? No shit." He came up and gave me a grim look. "Good news or bad?"

"How bad is it?" I played along.

"Death threats. If I don't feed you, I'm done for."

"And the good?" I laughed.

"You get a bite to eat, and then we get to pick up right where we left off."

"And what about you?"

"Oh, I plan to eat my fill, sweetness." He bit the slope between my neck and shoulder and held it between his teeth before soothing it with his tongue.

I fidgeted with a bag of milk chocolate squares while he rummaged through his backpack.

"This can or this one?" He held out identical tins.

"Both." I popped a piece of chocolate into my mouth and grabbed another one. Apparently, sex made me hungry.

"Do you hear that?" asked Jack, sitting up straighter.

There was a faint, metallic clanging coming from outside.

"What is it?" I asked.

"Sounds like . . . cowbells."

We got dressed and pushed the tent flaps aside. The rain had stopped, but a thick mist rose out of the damp, heated ground.

"Why would anyone bring cows to this godforsaken place?" Jack stepped outside.

I crawled out after him and squinted into the dense, colorless haze.

"They may not see us," said Jack, picking up the two cans he'd just emptied for our lunch. "We need to keep them from trampling over our tent." He hurried ahead, striking the cans together as an alert.

The cowbells got closer but seemed to still as the other party heard us. We stopped and peered through the humid vapor. Groves of monumental rock rose on either side of us. The mist gave everything a fey-like quality, like we were standing at the threshold of an otherworldly place, still and suspended, except for the muted clink of the odd cowbell.

A figure appeared through the fog, shrouded in veils of phantom gray. He planted his spear in the soft, sodden soil and stood before us like a velvet-black shadow. A checkered sheet hung around his shoulders and loops of silver jangled from his earlobes.

"Olonana." Jack stepped forward as the chief came into focus.

"*Kasserian ingera.*" He lifted his spear in greeting. *How are the children?*

Jack was about to reply when the ribbons of mist around Olonana shifted. Moon white faces appeared soundlessly, one by one, around the chief's dark figure. I watched breathlessly, as they materialized, like silent notes summoned by a conjurer's symphony. One, two, three, four . . . they kept stepping out of the mist, until they were all standing, like a line of vapor-cloaked wraiths on either side of Olonana.

Thirteen albino kids, flanked by a pair of red-garbed Maasai warriors.

My hair stood on end. Against the backdrop of distant, blurry mountains, the group stood before us with an air of expectation.

Behind them, cows sniffed the wet, barren ground, searching for whispers of grass.

"Jack Warden," Olonana prompted him for a response. "I have come a long way to bring you these children."

"What . . . ?" Jack paused. "How . . . ?"

"The last time we met, you told me you would be in Magesa, end of the month. I am glad I caught up with you. I cannot go any farther with the cattle, so I leave them with you." He gestured toward the children that were huddled around him. "Where are the other kids, the ones you were transporting to Wanza?"

"It didn't work out, but you . . ." Jack scanned the faces before us. "How did you end up with all these children?"

"We found them in the back of a cargo van, not far from the town of Bunda. The car was parked outside a restaurant. We heard thudding from the inside, so we stopped to check it out. Salaton here—" he pointed to one of the *morans* with him "—he jiggled the lock with his spear. We found them bound and gagged inside. Some of them have been abducted from their homes, others traded. They tell me there were more kids, but . . ." Olonana shook his head. "The men who had them are dangerous people. They trade in black magic. They are delivering these kids, one by one, for sacrificial rites. It won't be long before they track us down. We made the children walk between the cattle to hide them and distort the footprints. The rain hasn't helped though. We've left a trail in the mud. A good tracker will be able to find us. And they will. These kids are worth a lot of money to them. You must get them to Wanza as soon as you can."

Jack did not respond. His face was like a blank slate—emotionless and expressionless. Silence loomed, gray and heavy as the mist. The gravity of the situation was not lost on me. Neither was Jack's predicament. We weren't prepared for this. We had no car, no supplies, and no way of safeguarding thirteen kids against whoever was chasing them down.

"The van you found the kids in—" I said to Olonana. "What did it look like?"

"It was white," he replied. "And yellow."

My heart hammered in my chest. "With an air-conditioning logo?"

"I think so. Yes." Olonana's brows drew together. "You saw it too?"

"We did. On the way to Magesa. They must have been searching for the kids. They almost ran Jack over." I turned to him, waiting for a response, but he looked like the Jack I had seen on the porch the first day, the one who had closed himself off to everyone and everything. Something was very wrong.

"Can you give us a minute?" I asked the chief.

He nodded, and I pulled Jack aside. The mist shrouded us from the rest of the group.

"Jack?"

He stared at me with the kind of detachment that made me flounder.

"Jack! Snap out of it." My panic seemed to get through to him. His eyes changed and then darkened with unreadable emotion.

"I can't," he said. It came out choked, like his breath was being cut off. "I can't. Dear God, not again." He hunched over, holding his sides as if he was in excruciating pain. "It comes at you from nowhere. One minute you're buying balloons for your daughter, and the next . . . she's gone, and you can't even get up. Because something's pinned you down in the parking lot. The weight of it. I can feel it all over again. Right here." He held his hand to his chest and took long, staggering breaths. "I wish I could do this, but I can't, Rodel. I'm not the person everyone thinks I am. I'm not the strong, selfless hero. I'm just a guy trying to get over his daughter's loss. I came prepared—in my head—for three kids. I

would lay down my life for them and for you. But this . . . escort-
ing thirteen easy targets with a bunch of bloodthirsty maniacs on
our trail . . . it's got disaster written all over it. I have no way of
protecting them. And I can't stand to have any more blood on my
hands, Rodel. I can't."

I reached for his hand, because I was breaking with him, *for*
him, and holding hands with Jack always made me feel like I was
reaching for solid ground. Something became unstuck from my
palm and fell to the ground. It was the small square of milk chocolate that I had been holding when we'd left the tent.

"Here." I picked it up and gave it to Jack. "Chocolate makes
everything better." They were Goma's words, and for a second she
was there, standing over us, strong and stalwart, like the gnarled,
guardian tree that watched over the graves behind the manor.

"Melted chocolate." He held it in his palm for a long moment.
"Lily's favorite." He seemed lost in his thoughts as he unpeeled
it from its sticky wrapper. "I hear you, baby girl." It was barely a
whisper, but he stood taller as he said it. Bit by bit, his body seemed
to fill with new breath. "I hear you. Louder than all the crap in
my head. Louder than all the things that scare me." He broke the
chocolate square in half and popped it into his mouth. He closed
his eyes and savored the taste like it was some sweet memory.

"I haven't forgotten how brave you were when you danced in
front of all those people. I lost you, my sweet angel, but I'm not
going to let those kids down. I need to face up to my own demons.
I need to stop feeling like I failed you. God, Lily. Wherever you
are. Daddy misses you so much. So, so much." His voice cracked,
and he shut his eyes in silent tribute. When he looked up, his eyes
were glinting like diamond blue points of clarity in the diaphanous
veils of mist that swirled around us.

He held out the other half of the chocolate for me and
smiled. "Goma knows what she's talking about. Chocolate makes

everything better."

Our fingers brushed as I took the candy from him. I couldn't help the alarm bells that went off in my head. I could see danger coming, its gleaming edge sheathed in the mist. And though I had started this, sitting in a pub miles away, watching horrific images flash across the screen, I wanted Jack to walk away. How could I have known that in trying to do something for my sister, I would end up putting the man I loved in danger?

NIGHT HAD FALLEN by the time I finished tending to the kids. I put away the first aid kit and plopped down beside Jack.

"Are they all right?" he asked. But his eyes held concern for me too. We'd been slipping in and out of these moments all afternoon, where everything faded and it was just the two of us, in spite of the chaos—the kids, the cattle, the trio of Maasai men, around us.

"They're survivors," I replied, drinking in the comfort of his nearness.

The children had trekked a long way. They were hungry, hurt, exhausted. They had lacerations from being bound by cable ties. The ones who had fought back had more—bruises, sprains, and worse. They let me tend to their wounds, some with detached gazes, others with anger, fear, confusion, gratitude.

"What's wrong?" I asked, as Jack fidgeted with his phone.

"I wanted to contact Bahati. Ask him to gather a couple of drivers on his way here, ones that can be trusted. We won't be able to fit all these kids in his jeep. But my battery is gone."

"We'll figure something out when he gets here. Have you told Olonana that he's coming?"

Olonana knew we'd had to ditch Jack's car, but he didn't delve any further. He'd done his part, and as far as he was concerned, the rest was up to us to figure out.

"If Olonana learns that Bahati is driving through Maasai land to pick us up, he won't be too pleased. He's planning to leave at dawn. Bahati won't get here until later. There's no point stirring things up."

The chief and his warriors had offered one of their cows to feed the children. They were grilling pieces of meat, skewed on long sticks, which they stuck into the ground at an angle over the fire. Most of the kids had eaten. The younger ones were sleeping in the tent, while the older kids stretched out by the fire, on pieces of cowhide that the Maasai were carrying.

"What is it?" I asked, when I caught Jack staring at me.

"I love watching you in the firelight. The way your skin glows, the way your eyes dance, the way your hair comes alive." He drew me into the crook of his arm and pulled a blanket around us. "The first time was that night we stopped over by the crater. Dancing with you around the bonfire. I thought you were the most exquisite thing I'd ever laid eyes on. It was the first time I'd paid attention to anything or anyone after Lily. I felt like I'd been punched in the gut."

A warm glow spread over me as he spoke. It was like being wrapped in a cloak of invisible warmth. "Is that when you decided to play hard to get?" I poked him with my elbow.

"Doesn't matter what I decided, or which way I turned. There was no denying this thing between us." He shifted so I could lean my head on his shoulder. "Get some rest, sweetness. You must be exhausted."

We stared into the inky black plains around us. A train whistle blew in the distance, followed by the *chuggah-chuggah-chuggah* of its engine, and then a vast, deep silence. The kind reserved for oceans and mountain peaks and the craters of the moon.

"Do you think the men in that van will backtrack or keep going?" I asked.

"I'm pretty sure they'll be back, but I don't know when." He stroked my hair softly. "Don't worry. We'll figure something out in the morning."

The crackling of the fire lulled me into a strange dream. I was flying over coffee farms with a flock of dove children. We were racing a storm that was brewing on the horizon. Clouds of blood rain broke loose, splattering their ivory wings. I screamed as they fell from the sky. And then I was on the ground, ankle deep in scarlet mud, when something sharp pierced my foot. I picked it up and held it to the sky. It was a mangled crown of twigs and hay.

"Jack!" My eyes flew open, heart racing.

"Jack!" Olonana's voice echoed mine. "They're coming." He pointed to twin spotlights in the distance. They were faint, almost impossible to make out, but they left a telltale glow in the dark.

"How can you be sure it's them?" Jack got up and reached for his rifle.

"It's them." Olonana turned to Jack, his eyes full of ancient wisdom.

"We can take them. You, me, the two *morans*." Jack gestured to Salaton and the other Maasai warrior. "How many can there be?" He peered through the lens of his rifle.

"No," replied Olonana. "My men and I do not fight. Ironic for a tribe of warriors, but peace is our way of life now. Every time my people get involved in a confrontation, it affects all of us. We get branded as savage and barbaric. I won't play into that anymore. I'm sorry, Jack. We can delay them for you. Maybe even throw them off. It's possible that they've turned around because they're calling it quits, in which case they might just drive right by. And if they're tracking us, that's who they'll expect—us, not you. Take advantage of that. Take the children and go."

"I can't just leave you here," countered Jack. "This could get ugly. Especially if they figure out you took the kids."

"It could. Either way, I'm responsible for my men, and you're responsible for the children. That's two versus thirteen. I'm pretty sure I'm getting off easy. You need to get the kids as far away from here as possible. Go. Take down your tent and go."

We woke the children up while Olonana and his crew rolled up the cowhides and righted the campsite.

"It will be a while before they get here," said Jack, heaving his backpack over his shoulders. "You have some time." He gazed at the flickering lights snaking their way through the night terrain. "Traveling in total darkness is slowing them down. Or maybe they're stopping to check for tracks."

"Don't worry about us," said Olonana. "Do you have a plan?"

"The train," replied Jack. "I heard it pass through a couple of times. If we follow the track, we can get on at the next station, and then head to Wanza from there."

The chief nodded and spit into his hand. "God walk with you, Jack Warden."

"And with you." They sealed their goodbyes with a spit-filled handshake.

Then Olonana turned to me and extended the same hand. *"Taleenoi olngisoilechashur."*

Well, shit.

He was showing me the same honor he reserved for Jack.

I spit in my palm and shook his hand, all the while thinking *hand sanitizer, hand sanitizer, hand sanitizer.*

Olonana seemed to see right through me, because he laughed and said to Jack, "I hope she doesn't make this face when you do the . . . what do you call it? The French kiss."

Jack grinned and hooked his arm around my hip. "I love all her faces. Every single one of them."

"Then you should marry her and keep all the children." Olonana and the *morans* laughed.

That was how we left them that night—Olonana grinning with

his two bottom teeth missing, the fire silhouetting his perfectly round head, and the *morans* standing by his side. That night, my definition of *hero* grew bigger and wider. Sometimes heroes were found between the pages of a book, and sometimes they stood on a hill, their checkered togas fluttering in the wind, holding fort for the rest of us.

NIGHT VISION SETTLED in as we moved away from the campsite. The sky was dark and clear, speckled with asters of silver. We moved silently over the barren plains, guided by the light of the moon. It was eerily quiet, considering we had thirteen children in tow. Except these children were no ordinary children. They had all been touched by death, and now it was stalking them. A survival instinct had kicked in and they moved collectively, not asking, not talking. Even the youngest of them clamored to keep up, holding on to my hand, or Jack's, when the going got tough. There was an urgency about their movements that broke my heart.

"Not far now," said Jack. "We should be coming up to the railway tracks soon."

It was progress, but we still had a long way to go. The next station was miles away, and once the sun came up, it would be easy for anyone to spot us.

"You think Olonana and his crew are all right?" I scanned the area behind us. The flickering light of the fire had long disappeared.

"*Ona!*" One of the kids that Jack had hoisted on his shoulder pointed to something.

There was a faint glow in the distance, a few miles away. It appeared and disappeared.

The headlights of a car, lurching through shadow and shrubbery.

Panic rioted through me. There was no other reason for anyone to be there at that time. They had found us, out in the open, with nowhere to run, nowhere to hide. They wouldn't let the kids slip away this time, and worse, they might not even try to get them back into the van. It wasn't the kids they were after. It was their body parts. They could massacre every single one of them and still collect their blood money. And they wouldn't leave any witnesses behind either.

As the lights moved closer, my nightmare flashed before me.

Blood rain.

Dove children.

A mangled crown.

The sound of my own pulse throbbed in my ears.

Oh God, talk to me, Mo. Say something. Say anything.

There was nothing but silence.

Vast and deep.

And then, from across the plains, on the other side, a shrill cry pierced the air.

The whistle of a chugging train.

"There's a train coming! We need to get on it. Fast!" I said to Jack, but he was gazing at the train and then at the car. "Jack? What are you doing? There's no time to waste."

He shifted the child off his shoulder and started unzipping his backpack. "Do we have any rubbing alcohol left in the first aid kit?"

"Yes, but—"

"Catch." He hurled the bottle my way. Then he pulled out a couple of his T-shirts and started ripping them apart. "We need to stop that train, and there's no way the driver is going to see us in the dark. We need to light some torches."

He gave some of the cotton strips to a couple of the kids and pointed to a dead thorn tree that had fallen victim to the harshness of the plains. "*Leteni tawi.*"

They rushed off, gathering branches from the tree, wrapping the ends with the strips, so the thorns didn't scratch them.

"Jack. Look!" I exclaimed. Another car was now trailing the first one, its headlights glinting like snake eyes in the dark.

"Fuck. They've brought reinforcements." Jack was whittling the thorns off the branches, all except for the ones at the top. He wrapped those in cotton and doused it with the rubbing alcohol. He assembled more torches in quick succession, racing against the cars that were getting closer and closer. The air was thick with urgency and desperation. It soaked through my skin, leaving a thin film of sweat. The kids stood by, still and silent, as if their voices had already been muted.

"Hold them high," said Jack, handing out the torches to the older kids. "Don't be afraid." His thumb struck the wheel of the lighter as he set them on fire.

One by one, the flames came to life, ten hot, swirling suns illuminating the night. The ground around us ebbed and flowed in waves of flickering, golden light.

"They can see us now," I said, turning toward the cars.

"And so can they." Jack pointed to the train. It was still a distance away, but approaching fast. "The question is, which one's going to get to us first?"

We weren't too far from the railway tracks, and yet they seemed like an eternity away. My breath came in short, shaky bursts as we raced across the brittle ground. One of the kids ahead of me tumbled and fell. I weaved and grabbed her, hoisting her up on my hip. My lungs were on fire, my legs trembled under the extra weight, but I kept running. I would run until the skin on my soles wore off because that's what you do when monsters are gnashing at your feet. You lock up your screams, your panic, your fear, and you outrun the suckers.

I fixed my eyes on Jack and kept going. His torch shone ahead, white smoke drifting skyward. The kids were flocked on either side of him, radiating out in a *V*, the older ones in front, the younger ones trying to keep up. They *were* a flock of birds—homeward-bound—on wings of fire. It was such a surreal, powerful spectacle, that it slipped through all the chaos and panic, and became forever seared in my mind.

We stumbled upon the tracks, our eyes skimming the horizon for the cars. They were gaining on us.

"Quickly now." Jack positioned the kids, shoulder to shoulder, on both sides of the track. "You can let go now," he said to me.

I realized I was still clutching the little girl I had picked up. My grip loosened and I let her slide slowly to the ground. She took her place with the other children, her alabaster skin flushed with the heat of their torches. Together they formed a wall of bright, blazing light.

I stood with Jack in the middle of the railway track. The gravel under my feet pulsed as the train thundered closer.

Oh God. Please stop, please stop, please stop.

Jack threaded his fingers through mine. It was as if he could sense the tension building up in me.

"Hold tight and don't let go," he said.

He was holding the torch over us with his other hand. His eyes blazed and glowed with the light of the flames, but there was something more—something driven, and solid, and purposeful. At first, I couldn't put my finger on it. And then it hit me.

Do you believe in your own magic? I had once asked Jack.

I stopped believing. After Lily.

But I was watching the profile of a man who believed, and I gloried in the moment we were sharing, come what may.

"Jack's back," I said.

"What?" His voice was swallowed by the metallic squealing of the carriages as the train's headlights bore down on us. The tracks thrummed as the locomotive came hurtling along the tracks, full speed ahead.

Jack swore under his breath. "It's not going to stop."

"Why not?" I started waving my hand over my head. "I'm sure they can see us. We're all lit up."

"It's a freight train. If the driver's fallen asleep, or they don't have eyes up front, we're screwed."

The train was approaching us at an alarming rate. And so were the cars. We could make out the rectangular patch of light reflecting off the number plate on the first one.

"Here." Jack handed me his torch. "Get yourself and the kids out of the way."

"What are you doing?" My stomach churned as he got his rifle out.

"Stay on the other side. All of you. It will take a while for the train to pass. The men won't be able to get to you."

"And you? Jack, you need to get off the track!" I was shouting so he could hear me over the rumble of the train.

"Go, Rodel. Now!" His command moved me to action.

"Keep your torches up." I huddled the children to one side. "Keep them up there," I said to thirteen kids who'd had to hide all their lives, and who, in that moment, needed desperately to be seen.

My eyes darted from Jack, to the train, to the van that was barreling for us. Pale ribbons of dawn were bleeding through the eastern sky. Jack pointed the rifle skyward. He fired a shot, opened and closed the breech to eject the casing, and fired another. The sound reverberated across the open plains like a boom of thunder.

The van came to a slow halt, its lights staring at us like a predator stalking its prey.

That's right, you fuckers. We've got firepower, so BACK OFF!

The crack of gunfire seemed to have alerted someone on the train too because its powerful thrusts slackened. There was a loud screeching as the brakes hit, but it was still going way too fast to keep from slamming into the man on the tracks.

"Jack!" I cried out. There was a collective gasp from the children as it hurtled by us in a blur of rust and metal, snuffing out some of the torches in a blast of air. It came to a standstill, the front car stopping several meters from us.

The silence that comes after something loud and thunderous ceases is grand. It magnified the emptiness of the surrounding plains. The beast we had chased so hard to catch, groaned and creaked like a dragon that had run out of steam. Jack had managed to flag it down, but all I felt was a sick hollowness in my heart. I stood there frozen as the minutes ticked by, staring at the bright blue cargo that had halted before me, trying to remember how to breathe.

The sounds of metal sliding against metal jarred me out of my shock.

"Rodel. Over here!" It was Jack.

Relief. So profound that it jump-started my heart; the blood started flowing in my veins again.

The kids found him before I did.

"*Haraka! Haraka!* Quickly." He put out the torches that were still lit, snuffing them in the ground as he lifted the kids into a boxcar. It had louvered sides, with slits instead of solid metal on all four sides.

"I talked to the driver," he said. "I've paid him to get us to Wanza." He was in full-on adrenaline mode, clueless about what he'd just put me through. He held out his hand, waiting for me to take it so he could hoist me into the car. "Come on, Rodel. Stop dallying around. I told him to get going. There's no time to waste."

"I'm not dallying around!" I wanted to weep, and I didn't know if it was from anger or relief. "I thought that you . . . you—"

There was a sharp whistle, and then the train lurched.

"Rodel?" Jack rubbed his shoulder, rolling it forward and then back.

"You hurt the other one?" It wasn't the shoulder he'd landed on when we'd encountered the van.

"I really need to stop getting out of the way like this."

He said it so earnestly, the corners of my mouth tilted. "How do you manage to make me smile, even under the worst circumstances?"

"I'm glad my injuries amuse you." He lifted me into the boxcar before hopping on beside me.

"There are goats in here!" I exclaimed. The floor was covered in hay, and goats were crammed in the pens around us.

"It's a livestock car."

"It smells like one too," I noted. Jack had left the door open, so the stench wasn't too overwhelming.

I did a quick head count of the children. All there, all accounted for. The little girl I'd carried had bloody knees, but apart from that, they seemed all right. They stared out through the slits, their pale eyes on the van that had inched closer, clearly visible in the early morning haze. It was the one we'd seen on the way to Magesa. The second one was coming up behind it, covered in dust.

"You scared them," I said, as Jack leaned against the open hatch, rifle slung over his shoulder.

"I took a gamble. Two shots were all I had."

"So if they get on the train right now—" We were moving at snail's pace, the engine straining to get the cargo going again.

"They won't. They don't know I'm out. They want the children, but not enough to put their selves at risk. Once the train picks up, we're golden. We'll be in Wanza long before they can catch up."

I was about to heave a sigh of relief when the car that had been trailing the first started speeding up. It didn't look like the driver had any intention of stopping.

"What the fuck?" Jack straightened as it approached.

"He's going to crash into us!"

But the driver rammed straight into the white van. Then he backed up and slammed into it again.

"Shit," said Jack, when the clouds of dust settled. Both cars were banked up against the gravel mound by the tracks. "It's Bahati."

"Oh God. He must have come looking for us. But what's he doing? It's not like him to provoke anyone."

We watched in horror as three men got out of the van and dragged Bahati out of his car. The driver stayed in the van, an ominously dark silhouette against the tinted glass.

"Scholastica." Every muscle in Jack's body tensed as he said it. "She's not with Bahati. I told him to bring her. They must have her. It's the only reason Bahati would follow them this far."

"Jack." I clamped his arm. He had to go. But I held on a few seconds longer. "You have no bullets. You have nothing."

"It doesn't matter," he replied. "There's a little girl out there who needs me."

In a thousand lives, I would die a thousand deaths to save her.

It wasn't Lily, but Jack wasn't about to let it happen again.

"Listen to me," he said. "No matter what happens, you stay on the train. You get these kids to Wanza. You hear me?"

"I don't . . . I can't . . ."

"You can. You're my rainbow-haloed girl, and you're freaking magical. Don't you ever forget that." He took my face in his hands and kissed me like I was the most beautiful thing he'd ever tasted.

And then I heard the crunch of gravel as he hopped off and headed for the circle of men who were kicking and hitting Bahati as he lay on the ground.

"Let him go," he said, pointing his rifle at them. His tone left no room for argument. He knew he had no bullets, I knew he had no bullets, but as far as they were concerned, he meant business.

The men backed away from Bahati and lined up against the side of the van as Jack swung his rifle from one to the other, keeping them in check.

"Bahati, get on the train," said Jack, as Bahati lay curled up. He was in bad shape, but he staggered to his feet. One eye was swollen shut, and he held on to his knee as he limped toward the train.

"You." Jack tapped the driver's window with his rifle. "Come out with your hands up and open the back door."

At first, it seemed like the man hadn't heard him, but he stepped out, one foot first and then the other. My heart contracted when I caught a glimpse of his face. There was a raw slash running across his forehead, splitting his eyebrow, and down to his cheek. The blood had just started to clot, a river of jagged purple against his skin. There was something wrapped around his wrist. A red bandana that flapped in the breeze. I'd seen him before.

Where?

When?

And then it hit me. At the police station. When I'd gone with Goma. He'd creeped me out. His eyes had said something completely different from his smile.

K.K. That's what Inspector Hamisi had called him. I shuddered as I recalled the laughter I'd heard when he'd tried to run Jack over.

Keh keh keh keh. Like a hyena digging around dead bones.

I held out my hand as Bahati approached and helped him climb on board. A trickle of blood leaked from his nose.

"Open the back door," Jack said to K.K.

K.K. walked to the rear of the van like he was taking a Sunday stroll, slowly and leisurely. "I don't know what you think you're—"

"Shut up." Jack prodded him with his gun. "Let her out."

"Let who out?" K.K. unlatched the door and stood aside.

I couldn't see inside the van because it was angled off, but Jack didn't look too happy.

"Where is she?" he asked. "What have you done with Scholastica?"

"Jack," Bahati interrupted, nursing his jaw. "Scholastica's at the farm. Goma wouldn't let her leave until she got her glasses. I came alone."

Jack shot him an incredulous look. "Then why are you locking horns with these fuckers?"

"Because they hurt my father. I came to get you, and I found him at the campsite instead. He wouldn't tell them where the kids were so they tortured him and the *morans*. If I hadn't got there in time . . ." Bahati squeezed his eyes shut. "Something in me just snapped, Jack. I didn't think. I just came after them."

"They're scum." Jack started retreating slowly from the men, his eyes staring down the barrel. "We're leaving now. We don't want any trouble. So get back in your car and turn around."

I had to strain to hear him over the huffing of the train. It was picking up pace.

Come on, Jack. Wrap it up.

"Sure," said K.K., his hands still up. "We don't want any trouble either."

He turned to get back in the van but stooped as if to tie his shoe laces. Something flashed as he straightened. By the time I realized it was the steely glint of a machete, it was hurtling toward Jack with a sickening *whoosh*. I gasped as he swerved to avoid it.

Two seconds later, he lurched. A blot of crimson stained his T-shirt and spread over his sleeve. Blood poured in red rivulets down his arm and dropped to the ground from his knuckles. He'd been sliced.

His knees hit the ground with a sickening thud. The rifle slipped from his hand as he clutched his shoulder, trying to stave the flow of blood.

"We don't want any trouble either," K.K. repeated. He walked over to Jack and picked up the rifle. Then he placed the sole of his shoe on Jack's face and slowly, slowly, put his weight on it until Jack fell back under the mounting pressure. "What I want is to get my boots licked, for all the shit you've made me trudge through to find you. You see this?" He pointed to the gash across his face. "This is from that Maasai chief who stole my cargo. You know what I did to him? I broke his legs. My men asked me: 'Why, K.K.? Why not kill the bastard?'" K.K. rubbed the spotty tufts of hair on his head, slanting his head one way, then another, as if listening to voices in his head. "See, that's something most people don't grasp. The intricacies of suffering. I suffer when I kill. Killing is easy, like putting out a cigarette butt."

Jack flinched as K.K. rubbed his heel back and forth on his face.

"But to prolong it . . . *ah*. To transform it. That's art. I made art out of that chief. A statement piece. What good is a nomad who can't wander?" He broke into a spine-chilling gaggle. His men joined in. They stood in a semi-circle over Jack, laughing as they recalled what they'd done to Olonana.

"Fuck you," Jack spat at K.K. A pool of blood was starting to stain the ground under him.

Get up, Jack. Run! Every fiber of my being screamed. *It's now or never.* But I didn't know if he could get up, or if he could run. All I knew was that with every second that ticked by, we were moving farther and farther away from him.

"Oh my," said K.K. "There's no need for that kind of language. You don't want to lick my shoes? That's okay." He dropped the sinister mask of amusement he'd been wearing. He looked like the vulture he was, inside and out. "I'll just cut your tongue out and polish my shoes with it while you watch. But right now, my goods are leaving, and it's pissing me off. You—" he snapped at one of his team "—stop the driver. And you two, get the kids. Take the machete. Do it on the train. Slaughter them like the goats they're hiding out with. The girl too."

"You touch them and I'll—"

"You'll what?" K.K. ground his shoe into Jack's wound and watched him writhe in the dust. "You can't even get up." He patted Jack down and retrieved his wallet. "You're no good to anyone, Jack Warden." He read the name off Jack's driver's license before throwing it back in his face. "You know why? Because you're dead, motherfucker." He pulled the trigger.

For a second, he just stood there, blinking, when nothing happened—no splash of red on his shoes. "Your cock," he said, pointing the gun at Jack, "has no balls." He laughed deliriously. "All decoration, no bullets. And you . . . you walked up to us like you owned us. *Keh keh keh keh.*"

He was still laughing when Jack grabbed the barrel and hit him with the butt of the rifle. K.K. staggered back, holding his nose. Jack shouted something I couldn't hear, the words eaten up by the growing distance between us.

He surged forward to hit K.K. again when one of his men clamped Jack in a chokehold. It was the guy K.K. had sent to stop the driver.

Fuck. He'd backtracked and come to K.K.'s aid.

Something caught the edge of my eye, and I swore again. I had been so concerned about Jack, I hadn't noticed that the other two men K.K. dispatched to get the children had climbed on board the moving train. They were hanging on the rungs, a few cars down, and making their way toward us.

Everything was moving way too quickly to process. On the one hand, Jack was being pounded by K.K. while his accomplice held him up. On the other, death was coming for the children, shirts flapping in the wind, machete in hand. My heart raced like it was going to explode. I gripped the edges of the doorframe, my knuckles turning white as I tried to figure out what to do.

"Bahati." I shook him. He was lying slumped against one of the pens, his body lurching with the motion of the train. "Shit." He had passed out, and I had no idea if he was going to be okay.

I ran to the open hatch and looked out again. The men were clinging to the sides of the train, proceeding when they had secured a sure footing. Jack was slipping from view. There was something wild and tempestuous in his punches now. He wasn't just fighting two men, he was fighting the monsters that had taken Lily away from him. He was pouring all his rage and hurt and pain into it. But he was injured, and he held his wounded arm stiffly as they came at him from all sides.

No matter what happens, you stay on the train. You get these kids to Wanza.

I choked back a sob. I had to shut the door and lock it. I had to stop those men from getting to the children.

I slipped my backpack off and pulled on the hatch. It didn't budge. I put all my muscle into it and tried again.

Nothing. It weighed a ton.

The kids watched me, eyes wide and overly bright. One of them had his hands jammed into his armpits and was hugging himself.

"It's okay," I said. "You're going to be all right." I was a liar. A dirty, filthy liar. "Come on. Give me a hand," I asked them. "We can do this!"

I held on to the latch and pulled, tendons sticking out in my neck, while the kids pushed from the other end. It held for a while, and then it slid out of its rut with a great big jerk. The goats bleated as the carriage turned dark. The only light streaming in now was through the louvered sides.

"Good job!" I said to the kids, even though a part of me was dying to fling it wide open again, in the desperate hope that Jack would make it on, somehow, some way.

I looked for a way to secure the door, to keep it from sliding back, but there was nothing.

Shit. It locks from the outside. It's a livestock car.

I wanted to pound my head against the door. My arms were shaking. I didn't know how long I could hold on. I peered through the louvers. I couldn't see the men, but I knew they'd be upon us soon. Sweat beaded on my lip.

Think! There's got to be something.

A light bulb went off in my head. It was a long shot, but it was all I had. I let the door go. It slid open with a grating *thump*. I looked out. I couldn't see Jack anymore. We had left him far behind. But I could see the men. And there was now only one car left between us.

I snaked my foot out, searching for a notch in the louvered sides. My fingers hooked around one of the pipes that ran overhead, and I swung myself around to the outside of the car. The ground under the train rushed by in a blur of gray. I squeezed my eyes shut, the wind beating against my face.

Shit. Shit. Shit. Shit.

My fingers trembled as I unhooked them from the pipe and grabbed on to the slits from the outside, first one hand, and then, very slowly, the other.

"What are you doing, miss?" asked one of the kids.

I was clinging to the side of the train, scared shitless, my jaw clenched in fright, but I summoned up my best classroom voice. "I'm going to uncouple the cars behind us, so the bad men can't get to us. I need you to stay inside. Okay?"

My bones were rattling with the motion of the train, but I held steady until he nodded. I heard him translating for the kids that didn't speak English. I shut out the part of me that was screaming: *Uncouple the cars? Are you out of your freaking mind? You have no idea what you're doing. You're going to die out here!*

I'm dead either way. At least I'll die trying.

I inched along, slipping my foot into one opening, then the other, all the while clinging on to the slits above me. I swallowed the fear that was beating thick and heavy in my throat as the gap between me and the men closed. They had seen me. The one in front had the machete tucked in the back of his pants. The other one was glaring at me through wind-blasted eyes. The only thing slowing them down was the fact that their car didn't have louvered sides like mine, so they had less to hold on to. I made it to the edge before they did. There was a metal ladder, soldered to the side, so I swung around to it and held tight as I tried to figure out the coupler.

Fuck if I know how to do this.

I felt sick. I felt dizzy. I didn't know if it was from the sense of impending doom that was fast approaching, or from watching the ground disappear between the two cars.

I can't do this. I don't know how.

My composure was cracking in fragile shells around me. The mask of bravado I'd put on for the kids was slipping off.

I've lost Mo.

I've lost Jack.

And now I'm going to lose these kids.

A suffocating sensation tightened my chest as I heard a thud. And then another. The men had hopped onto the adjacent car. It was only a matter of time before they got to us. The endless night had turned to day. We had fought and fought and fought, but it was going to end here. The only thing standing between those men and the kids was me.

You're my rainbow-haloed girl, and you're freaking magical. Don't you ever forget that.

I wiped my tears with the back of my hand and straightened. *That's right. I'm freaking magical.*

I could tell the lock from the pin on the coupler. I just had to figure out how to unlink them.

"The lever."

I whipped around to find Bahati. He was clutching the edge of the car. "The kids told me what you were doing when I came around." He swung around beside me, still shaky and unsteady.

"Are you all right?" I asked. "God, Bahati, I could kiss you!"

He grimaced. "I'm the reason you're in this mess, Miss Rodel. I'm bad luck. They don't call me Bahati Mbaya for nothing. You and Jack would have gotten away if I hadn't shown up and buggered it all up." He put his foot out, trying to span the gap between the cars, his fingers wrapped around one of the rungs of the ladder for support.

"Bahati, stop! What are you doing?" I yanked him back by his shirt and for a moment we both teetered over the gap between the cars. My stomach churned at the thought of what it would feel like to be crushed under those thundering wheels of steel.

"The lever can only be pulled from the other side," Bahati said, after we steadied ourselves. "I'll have to jump."

"Wait!" I stopped him again. "If you get on that car, you won't be able to get back once you unlink us. You'll end up with those men, and God knows they won't be too happy about losing the kids."

"I know." It was the shortest sentence he'd ever spoken. I wanted him to fill the silence that followed with his ramblings, but we lurched ahead to the rhythm of unspoken things—unexpected circumstances, unexpected sacrifices.

"Bahat—"

"It's time I earned my warrior name, Miss Rodel." And then the man who hopped on his bed at the sight of a lizard, who squealed at crickets, and ran from moths, leaped. His lean, long legs closed the gap, even though he faltered when he landed on his battered knee.

He attempted a smile, one eye swollen shut, and pulled the lever.

"*Kasserian ingera*," he said, as the cars unlinked and I left him behind. *How are the children?*

"*Sapati* . . ." I swallowed hard and bit back the tears. K.K.'s men were almost upon him. "*Sapati ingera.*" *All the children are well.*

As the rear of the train fell away like the severed body of a giant python, I lost sight of him. "Thank you, Bahati," I whispered, hoping the wind would carry it to him.

Lonyoki's vision had come true. He had seen Bahati riding a giant serpent, fighting his own kind, helping the white people. But Lonyoki had not interpreted it right. The serpent was the train, and Bahati was fighting K.K.'s men to get the albino children to safety. At the same time, if Bahati had listened to them, if he had stayed away like his father had told him to, he would still be safe.

A war of emotions waged in me. So many delicate threads held us all together. The endless plains stretched out on all sides, vast and empty, as I held on to the last car, on the last leg to Wanza, nursing the last images I had of Bahati and Jack.

"THIRTEEN?" A WOMAN screeched from behind the closed door. "She brought thirteen kids in? Why were we not notified?"

"She just showed up at the gate," said the guard who had escorted us inside the orphanage. "We told her she has to speak to the Regional Commissioner, but she refused to budge. And to be honest, they look too exhausted to go anywhere."

I sat on the bench outside the office as they went back and forth. It had been a harrowing ordeal, huddled up with the kids in a car full of goats, for hours and hours. There had been a long delay when the train arrived at the next stop. I assumed it had to do with the freight cars that had been left behind. We didn't dare get out or make a sound. We didn't know friend from foe, so we stayed put until the train rolled into Wanza.

We must have been quite a sight when we climbed out of that boxcar. An off-duty police officer spotted us and offered to get us to the orphanage. I left my name and his badge number with the stationmaster before getting on the private *dala dala* he arranged for us. I wasn't going to take any chances this close to our goal, but my choices were limited. I couldn't exactly walk out of the station and hit the streets with them.

The policeman turned out to be another kind soul. The kids and I would never have made it without Jack, Olonana, and Bahati.

I mentally added him to the list of all the people who had made it possible.

Wanza was fresh lake breezes, beautiful water, and a rapidly rising skyline. It sat by the shores of Lake Victoria, surrounded by hills that were strewn with enormous boulders. The orphanage was a bit of a drive from the railway station, encased with barbed wire, with guards patrolling the gate. It wasn't the kind of sanctuary I had pictured. There was a stale, dank odor coming from the dorms. Children were bunked two to a bed. The ones playing in the courtyard were wearing threadbare blue uniforms, their milky-pink skin contrasting sharply against it. And yet they seemed happy—the kind of happiness that comes from feeling safe. They were free to run and play and shout.

"*Chui, chui, simba!* Leopard, leopard, lion!" they chanted, running in circles and tagging each other in a game.

My kids watched from the sidelines—thirteen of them, standing against the scuffed-up wall. The place was overcrowded and underfunded. I could understand the reaction of the woman I was waiting to see.

"Miss Emerson?" She opened the door and read my name off the note the guard had scribbled for her. "Welcome. My name is Josephine Montati. I run this orphanage. Please . . ." She indicated the chair by her desk. "I understand you've brought some children you'd like to leave in our care. Thirteen, if I'm not mistaken?" She was magnificent and imposing in spite of her small frame. At least sixty, if not more. Her brow was furrowed, and she wore her hair in cornrows.

"Yes. That's right, but some of them were abducted. I'm sure their families are looking for them and will be happy to have them back."

"And how did you end up with all these kids?"

I relayed the story as concisely as I could while she watched me over her half-moon glasses. When I finished, she sat back and sighed.

"I won't lie. I'm not happy to see them. We don't have the resources. You can see for yourself." She gestured out the window, to the crumbling building outside. "A lot of these albino kids are legally blind. We need special textbooks. Bedding. Hats. Sunscreens . . ." She stopped and shook her head. "I'm sorry. I apologize. You saved thirteen lives. You risked your own. You're worried about your friends. And I'm going on about supplies. Do forgive me. I will get the children settled in. We just need to fill out some paperwork and then you can go. Why don't we get you and the children something to eat before we get started? I'm sure you're all very tired and hungry."

"That would be nice," I replied. Food was the last thing on my mind. I was too worried about Jack and Bahati to care, but the kids had been on the go for many, many hours. "There's just one other thing I was hoping to talk to you about. Do you know someone named Gabriel?"

"I know a couple of Gabriels." She removed her glasses and placed them on the table.

"My sister was working with him, to get some kids to you."

"*Ah*, you mean Gabriel Lucas. So that delightful young lady he brought around . . . that's your sister?"

"You knew her?"

"Yes, but I haven't seen her for a while. Did she complete her volunteering term?"

"No. My sister . . . she died in the Kilimani Mall attack."

"Oh." Josephine came around and engulfed me in a hug. "I am so sorry to hear that. What a terrible thing to happen to such a beautiful soul."

"Thank you." I stayed in her arms a little longer. Some people have an amazing capacity to soothe and comfort. Josephine Montati was one of them.

"I was hoping you could tell me something about Gabriel," I continued, when she stepped back. "His sister and daughter haven't heard from him in a while."

"Well, let's see . . ." Josephine put her glasses back on and walked over to the register. "He was last here in June. I haven't seen him since. I figured he was busy getting his house built in Wanza."

"He has a house in Wanza?"

"That's what he said—that he was moving so his daughter could attend school here. He doesn't want her to board at the orphanage. He knows what it's like here. He's brought in twenty-four children in all. Over the years, of course. Not all at once, like you." She laughed. "Good man, that Gabriel. Heart of gold. He's on the road a lot, but I'm surprised he hasn't been in touch with his family. I'll have to give him a good tongue-lashing next time I see him."

I sat back, relieved. Gabriel was a good guy. He'd delivered the kids to the orphanage, just like he'd promised their parents. He hadn't conned my sister. In fact, he'd brought her here, too. But where the hell was he?

"Would it be all right if I used your phone?" I asked Josephine.

"Yes, of course. I'll take the children to the dining hall. Come find us when you're done."

"Thank you," I said, as she shut the door behind her.

I picked up the receiver and put it down again. My hands were shaking. I felt like a tall pile of blocks, stacked haphazardly on top of each other. One nudge and I'd come tumbling down. I had held it together all this time, but sitting in an empty room, alone with my thoughts, I was starting to fall apart.

The last couple of days had been a roller coaster of emotions: the incredible high of making love to Jack, the unexpected encounter with Olonana, watching thirteen kids materialize out of the mist, the overwhelming responsibility of getting them to safety, the thrill of outrunning our pursuers, the awful, bitter taste of having to leave Jack behind, Bahati looking at me from the other side of the carriage . . .

And there I was, in Josephine Montati's office, staring at the scratches on her desk, about to call Goma and tell her I didn't know where her grandson was. Her only living family member.

"Hello," she rasped, when I finally dialed the number.

"Goma? It's me. Rodel."

"Rodel." She chuckled. "I guess Jack is too pissed off to talk to me."

"No, he's . . ." *Missing.* But I couldn't bring myself to say it. "Why would Jack be pissed off with you?"

"For not sending Scholastica with Bahati. Is everything all right? You sound . . . off. Don't tell me you're still waiting for Bahati. Did that boy chicken out on—"

"No, Bahati . . . he came to pick us up. It's just . . . it's just—"

"Spit it out, girl. My Zumba DVD is rolling."

"Goma, I don't know where they are."

"Where who are?"

"Jack and Bahati." I explained what had happened—from the time Jack and I left Magesa and crossed paths with Olonana, to how Jack, Bahati, and I got separated. When I finished, I waited for Goma's response. The line remained silent.

"Goma?" *Shit.* Maybe I shouldn't have called.

"I'm here. I'm just thinking happy thoughts. My dear Sam always did that when we ran into trouble. 'Happy thoughts,' he used to say. 'Happy thoughts.' So right now, I'm thinking how much I'd like to string that bastard, K.K. to the back of my Jeep and drive him through the thorn bushes. *No one* lays a hand on my grandson and gets away with it. Not while my lungs still breathe fire. I will burn his ass to a crisp. He'd better pray no harm has come to Jack or Bahati. Are you and the kids all right?"

"We're fine. I was wondering if you could contact Inspector Hamisi. Maybe he knows someone at the police station here who can send out a search party."

"Oh, don't you worry. I'm going to mobilize them all. As soon as I get off the phone. And then I'm going to get in my car and head straight for Wanza. You just hold tight. We're going to get our boys, you hear me? If I have to turn over every pebble and stone myself."

I thought she'd crumble, but she'd risen like a dragon, talons bared, ready to lacerate her enemies into ribbons of flesh and bone. Her reaction lifted me. It lit an inferno of hope within me.

"Yes, Goma," I replied. "Let's go get our boys." For a second, I wondered if she was really that strong, or if she'd sit with her head bowed afterward, staring at the gnarled veins on the back of her hands, wondering how they would find the strength to leave flowers on yet another grave, if it came down to that.

I hung up and walked out of the office. Outside, kids were still playing in the courtyard. The ones that had accompanied me were out of the dining room and waiting to be fitted for their new uniforms. A few of them dragged me to a cardboard box that had been set up as a table, with square bits of newspaper for place mats. I sat on a stool as they pretend-poured tea for me in a chipped miniature cup.

"*Asante.*" I took a sip and feigned burning my tongue, fanning my mouth.

"*Moto sana!* Too hot!" They laughed, plying me with invisible food.

A shadow fell over us as I offered a cup to the straw doll sitting across from me.

"I turn around for two seconds and you're in the middle of a tea party."

My breath caught mid-fake-pour. His voice was like balm over my aching heart.

"Jack! Jack!" The kids flocked around him.

"You're late," I said, trying to stem the swell of tears in my eyes. His arm was bandaged in a dirty fabric, beard thick with congealed blood, lips cracked and swollen. He stood stiff as a board, covered in dust and tatters, looking as if all his muscles had seized up.

I'd never seen a man more beautiful than him.

I would have run to him, wrapped my arms around him, but my circuits were so overloaded with relief, that I just sat there, holding a miniature teapot.

"My date ditched me," he replied, taking the kiddie stool across from me, and sitting the doll on his lap. He was saying one thing, but his eyes were saying another.

You're okay.

You made it.

God, let me just look at you.

And so we sat there, staring at each other across an upside-down cardboard box, as the kids milled about around us. He unclasped my fingers from the little teapot I was holding and pretended to fill two miniature cups with it. I picked up mine, he picked up his, and we clinked them in a silent toast.

We pretend-ate and pretend-drank. The air thrummed between us, heavy with words we couldn't wrap our tongues around.

"I thought . . . I thought you . . ." A tear spilled like a raindrop on the cardboard box.

"*Shh.* You're here. I'm here. Everything is exactly as it should be."

"Jack, Bahat—"

"He's fine. He's in the car, outside. We're all right." He stood, unfurling his long legs and held out his arms. "Come here, sweetness." His voice was hollow with longing.

Jack Friggin' Warden. He'd survived. And Bahati had made it too.

I crushed my face into his chest, maybe a little too enthusias-
tically, because he winced under his breath.

"Sorry. Am I hurti—"

"Shut up, Rodel." He claimed my lips, his kiss singing through
my veins.

My arms looped around his neck as I melted against him.
I wanted to heal the cracked lines of his lips with the softest of
kisses, lick all the sore, tender parts of him. I wanted to love him
like he was mine.

"Miss Emerson?" I tore my mouth away and found Josephine
Montati watching us with a raised eyebrow.

"Sorry." I smiled sheepishly at her. The kids were watching
us with amused fascination. "My friends made it. Both of them.
I'm so happy!"

"I can see that. I'm glad you're all right," she said to Jack.

"We'll be right in to fill out the paperwork." I nodded at the
stack of forms she was holding. "Could you give us a few minutes?"

"Of course. I'll be in my office."

"We?" said Jack, after she was gone. "I like how you dragged
me into that. I'm not sure my penmanship is up to filling out any
forms." He flexed his raw, bloody knuckles.

"Well, I'm not letting you out of my sight. But first, I want to
see Bahati. And I want to know exactly what happened."

"What happened was that K.K. and his goon beat me up pretty
bad." He reached for my hand as the guards swung the gate open
for us.

"Yeah. I was there for that part," I replied, thinking how ridiculously happy my hand was, holding his. And my heart. "Get to
the good stuff. You know, when you whooped their sorry arses."

"That's not exactly how it played out." He chuckled. "So,
there I am, flat on my back, pretty sure I'm done for when they
start arguing. K.K. is mad because he told the other guy to stop the

driver, but now the train is leaving and the kids are still on it. The other guy's yelling that he turned around to save K.K.'s ass when he saw that I was getting the upper hand. So K.K. shoots back that he's doesn't need anyone's help, and that's just disrespecting him.

"Meanwhile, I'm on the ground by Bahati's car. The door is open from when they dragged him out, and what do I see? Bahati's bag—the one he uses when he puts on his full Maasai garb at the Grand Tulip. It's toppled to the floor, and sticking out of it is his spear. So while K.K. and his friend are bickering, I'm inching my way toward it.

"The rest happened so fast, it's all a blur. I got his friend first, swung the spear around and slashed him in the leg. Then I went for K.K., but he's small and quick and vicious. He kept dodging my jabs, waiting for me to tire out. He knew I wouldn't last. Not with an injured arm. The more time I wasted, the farther away you got. So I cornered K.K. into the back of his van. Tied him and his buddy up, back to back. I locked them in there, where they'd kept the kids. No air, no windows, no light. He laughed as I was leaving. Creepy little fucker. He said he liked the irony of it."

"He gives me the chills," I said. "We have to tell the police where to find him. Which reminds me—we have to call Goma. She's putting together a search party—" I stopped in my tracks when I saw the car. "Oh my God, you managed to drive Suzi all the way here?"

She was dented, dusty, and badly banged up. Her bumper was lop-sided, one headlight dangling, the other shattered.

"Ro, is that you?" I heard a mewling from inside the car.

Ro. He called me Ro. I grinned like an idiot. He considered me his friend now. "Bahati?"

He was lying on the back seat, wrapped up in a shiny, metallic emergency blanket, like a potato about to be baked in the oven.

"Are you all right?"

"My eye is still swollen." He peeked at me with the other one. "You don't think it's permanent, do you? I make a living off this face. And I'm very cold. I think I might need a knee replacement. Everything hurts. I can barely move, but I'm so happy to see you. *Oww*," he moaned, trying to shift to his other side.

I shot a concerned look at Jack, but he rolled his eyes. "I'm sure we can ask someone at the orphanage to give you something for the pain," he said. "Until we get you to a doctor. You want to come in?"

"I don't think I can get up."

"Food?" I tempted. "You hungry?"

"No. I don't think I can eat. My jaw is bruised. My nose is bloody. I can't taste anything, and I have this cut right here." He stuck his tongue out for me to see.

"The kids are all waiting for you. The staff, too. You're a hero, Bahati," said Jack. "They want to take pictures with you."

"They do?" Bahati rolled his tongue back in.

"Yeah. But don't worry. I'll tell them you're not feeling up to it. Come on, Rodel."

"Wait." There was a loud rustling as Bahati unpeeled his blanket. "Maybe I can pop in for a bit."

"You sure? You're in pretty bad shape there, buddy."

"I know, but I don't want to disappoint them."

"All right. Come along then." Jack held open the door and stuck out his hand.

"No. Not like this. Pass me my bag. I will go in my Maasai clothes."

"You're not serious."

But Bahati insisted, so we turned our heads and ignored the thudding and swearing as he changed in the car.

"So how did you find him?" I asked Jack.

"I hopped into Suzi, trying to catch up with you, and found the rest of the train, unlinked from the main body. I thought they'd got you. God, Rodel, I kind of lost it. I picked up a couple of tracks and was heading that way when I heard something. I followed the sound until I came upon two tufts of grass. It was Bahati. Sneezing. He'd jumped off the train and covered himself up with dirt to escape the men he thought were still looking for him. It wasn't until he told me you'd managed to get away that I could breathe again."

"I was so worried for you." I cupped his cheek in my palm.

"And me?" Bahati piped in from the car.

"You, too." I laughed, letting my hand fall away. "I'm so relieved that you managed to escape from those men."

"It was a very clever camouflage. You think the kids will want to see it? I have a memento." Bahati held up an uprooted sprig of grass.

"Here. Let me get that for you." Jack took it and helped Bahati out. We supported him as he limped to the gate.

"Name?" asked one of the guards. He already had Jack and me on his list.

"My name is Bahati. Well, that's not really my name. It's my nickname. Or rather, a part of my nickname. I never really got my warrior name, but I'm a real warrior now. I saved my father. He's the chief. And I saved the children and Ro here. I have been invited in, so open the gates. They are waiting for me!" He held his spear out as he said it, in full drama.

The guard quickly confiscated it and left him standing there, with his fist out. Jack inserted the yellowing tuft of grass into his hand, and we waited solemnly as the guard looked from me, to Bahati, to Jack. Seconds ticked before he shook his head and called the office.

"Miss Josephine says you can go in." He unlocked the gates and stood aside.

"See?" Bahati shook the grass at him as he limped by.

The children surrounded him when he entered, cheering as if they were meeting an old friend. Bahati's back straightened, his eyes brightened, and suddenly, he didn't need us to prop him up anymore.

"I think we're okay for a while," said Jack, leading me toward the office, where Josephine was waiting for us. He called Goma while I filled out the paperwork. I could make out the relief and the swearing, the laughter and the threats from the other end of the line.

"How is Scholastica?" asked Jack. "Any updates from Inspector Hamisi about her father?" He was quiet for a moment. "Okay. No. You stay put. I'll see you soon."

I shot him a questioning look after he hung up.

"Nothing on Gabriel yet," he said.

"I already talked to Josephine about him." With her permission, I showed Jack the register and all of Gabriel's entries.

"He's legit," said Jack, flipping through the pages.

"Gabriel?" Josephine's eyebrows shot up. "Absolutely. You had doubts?"

"I wasn't sure what to make of him. So now the question is, where do we find him? His sister is worried, and his daughter is eager to be reunited with him."

"Like I told Rodel, he's building a house in Wanza. You may want to follow up with that."

"I think I'm done here." I slid the pile of paperwork across Josephine's desk. Thirteen children, a gazillion forms. "I filled them out as best as I could, but there's a lot missing. Birth dates, place of birth, name of mother, name of father . . ."

"It can't be helped. We'll try and fill in the blanks." Josephine walked us out to the courtyard, where Bahati was re-enacting how he'd jumped between the freight cars. It was more of a hop, given his bad knee, but the kids seemed suitably impressed.

"You must have some food before you leave," she said.

"Food?" Bahati spun around. "What about the photos?"

"That's a splendid idea. I would love to get some pictures of you with all the children you brought in." Josephine ushered us out through the back gates and went to get her camera.

The lake lapped around us, dotted with purple blossoms floating on mats of waxy green leaves. Boulders lay scattered in the water, some balancing precariously on each other, as if put together by giants playing with pebbles. We lined up against the shore, sixteen of us, brought together like random threads in a tapestry, to meet at this junction, for one big, bright flash of the camera.

"Another!" said Bahati, striking a pose.

I felt the warmth of Jack's arm around my waist as we smiled into the lens. He turned and kissed me as the next flash went off.

"I'm going to wash your hair when we're alone," I whispered.

"Not a fan of the untamed, wind-whipped look?"

"Just returning the favor. And you're wrong. I find it sexy as hell—I can't wait to run my fingers through it."

Jack choked. He actually spluttered. "You should . . ." He coughed to catch his breath. "You should ride trains more often. They seem to have a liberating effect on you."

"Yeah?" I stood on my tiptoes so I could coo into his ear. "I can think of a few other things I'd rather ride."

I'm pretty sure the next photo caught him with his mouth hanging open.

"You're enjoying this, aren't you?" he said through clenched teeth.

"Think of it as payback for playing hard to get, and then disappearing on me." I smiled for the camera.

"You know, two can play this game." His voice dropped a few notches as all five of his fingers slid onto the back of my neck. He grabbed my hair and tugged, holding me immobile. "Say cheese, Rodel."

By the time the next flash went off, I was squirming.

"What's the matter?" he teased, as he traced a long, sensuous line down my back, from my nape to my waistband. "Your English garden can't handle the tropical heat?"

"Thank you. That should do," said Josephine, wrapping it up.

Oh, thank God. I hopped away from Jack, thinking this must be exactly what it felt like to have a corset loosened at the end of the day.

"It's time to go inside, kids," said Josephine. "Say goodbye to your friends."

My throat closed up as they hugged me, one by one.

"*Kwaheri,*" they said. "*Asante.*"

I kissed their snow-white cheeks and held on to them, knowing this was just the beginning. They still had a long, long way to go.

Please, world, be kind to them, I thought. *And if not, just let them be.*

I stood aside as Jack and Bahati said their goodbyes. Something whispered in the trees around us, sending shimmers of peek-a-boo sunlight through the leaves. I walked to the small boulder on the shore and unzipped my backpack. I took a deep breath and retrieved a notebook, letting it fall open to the page where I'd stored my sister's Post-it notes.

It was time to say goodbye.

The lake was mirror-calm, reflecting angel-white clouds against a shimmering blue sky. It was hard to tell where one ended and the other began.

It's the perfect spot, Mo. Free and endless.

I held the three sticky notes and read the first one silently: *July 17—Juma (Baraka)*

Then I lowered it into the water and let go.

Goodbye, Juma. I'm sorry we didn't get to you in time.

I smiled when I looked at the next one: *Aug 29—Sumuni (May-mosi)*

Goodbye, Sumuni. Keep rapping. Don't ever let them silence you.

I smoothed out the last one and was hit with a surge of emotion: *Sept 1—Furaha (Magesa)*

Goodbye, Furaha. We'll never meet because you'd already left with your family when we got there. And you'll never know. Because of you, a lot of lives were saved. We came for you and found the others. Wherever you are, I hope you're well. I hope you're happy.

I sat back and watched the three yellow pieces of paper float away from me. They bobbed gently in the water, sending ripples in ever widening circles until they disappeared, like echoes in a vast valley.

Goodbye, Mo. The tears gradually found their way down my cheeks.

A breeze ruffled through the grass. Wildflowers unfurled slowly, like coral arms waving at low tide. I slipped my backpack on and started walking away. Then I paused and turned around. I'd left my notebook behind. As I bent to get it, a wave broke against the boulder and splashed me.

I sucked in my breath from the shock of cold water on my sun-warmed skin.

Where did that come from? The lake is so calm.

And yet it was all over me—my arms, my hair, my face.

"Look at you," said Jack, when I joined him and Bahati. The kids had gone back inside and the two of them were waiting for me. "You look like you just took a glitter bath."

"A glitter—" I stopped short and held my arms out. Beads of water clung to my skin like little sparkles of silver. "Oh, my God." I laughed. Joy bubbled in my heart as I glanced back at the water.

"What is it?" asked Jack.

"My sister. She filled a balloon with glitter and left it in my closet. It popped and I looked like a disco ball for days. I think she just said goodbye."

Jack and Bahati exchanged a puzzled look.

"Never mind." I grinned. "I'm happy! I'm so happy I could squish you both." I kissed them each on the cheek.

"I don't think so." Jack growled and pulled me back, claiming my lips. My senses whirled and skidded. My arms went around his neck as he lifted me into the cradle of his arms.

"*Oh*," said Bahati, pointing at me, then pointing at Jack. "*Ohhh.*" He backed off with a big smirk on his face.

"I think we've rendered Bahati speechless," said Jack, when he was gone.

"Let me down, Jack." My feet were still dangling off the ground.

"No."

"No?"

"You need to be punished for teasing me through that group picture."

"Jack, no!" I shrieked as he tossed me over his shoulder. "I'll bite! I'll bite your injured arm!"

"Oh, baby." He laughed. "I love it when you talk dirty."

I STEPPED INTO the shower and closed my eyes as the water poured over me. Steamy rivulets cascaded down my face, my hair, my back, dissolving the dirt and grime of the last few days. I inhaled deeply, breathing in the scent of the thin, white bar of hotel soap. I was never going to take the little luxuries of life for granted again.

A puff of cold air hit me as the shower stall opened.

"You're back." I smiled as Jack stood there, gazing at me, his eyes running over my naked body like a warm caress.

"You started without me." He stepped into the shower, completely disregarding the fact that he was fully clothed. One very large, male arm wrapped around my waist as he kissed me, lifting me off the tiled floor.

Hot water, soap, and Jack's special brand of kisses—the ones that sweep you off your feet. Literally.

I could spend my whole day right here.

"Your clothes are all wet," I said, when he set me down.

"I don't plan on putting them on again." He shrugged out of his dusty, tattered T-shirt and trousers, and kicked his briefs to the corner.

The sight of him standing there in all his naked glory gave me a heady rush, until I noticed the purple welts on his body.

"Oh God." I traced the one running down his chest.

"It's nothing," he said. "It looks worse than it feels." He stepped closer, keeping his arm angled away from the water. "They told me to keep it dry." He gestured to the white gauze around the cut.

"And that's it? The rest of you is okay?"

"Would you like to test me out?" My pulse skittered as he pulled me hard against him and nibbled on my neck. I gulped as the full, heavy imprint of his passion reignited memories of our afternoon in the tent.

"Rodel." He cradled my cheek in his palm.

Rodelle. It made me feel like the sexiest woman alive.

"We were impulsive," he said, his eyes pinning me down. "We got carried away in the moment. I should have been more careful. I should have—"

"*Shhh.* We were in the middle of nowhere, and it's not like you carry spare condoms in your wallet. Besides, I finished my cycle a few days before we left for Wanza, so the chances that I'm pregnant are very slim."

He let out a deep breath and rested his forehead on mine. "That's a relief. And yet . . . for a small, selfish moment, when I considered the possibility, it made me unbelievably happy."

I swallowed, thinking how much he'd loved Lily, and how I could totally see him being an amazing father. But I was leaving in a few days, in time for the beginning of the school year, and it was too painful to consider all of the possibilities that could have blossomed with Jack.

Steam rose around us as we soaped each other in silence, skin to slick skin—marveling, memorizing, cherishing. Jack's eyelashes, thick with water; his bold thighs; the way his muscles rippled when he moved; the ends of his hair curled up with lather.

He slung a towel around his hips, wrapped me up in another, and carried me to the bed. The room was worn and sparse, the curtains frayed at the hem, but I sighed in tired contentment.

"A hot shower, soft sheets, a real mattress. Pure bliss." I sat at the edge of the bed as Jack rubbed my hair dry.

"I can think of a couple of things I'd like to throw into the mix." He grabbed a shopping bag that was sitting on the side table and put it in my lap.

"What's this?" I rummaged through it and found an antibiotic cream for his cut, a comb, toothpaste, gum, lotion, and . . . a box of condoms.

"I meant this." He knelt before me, pried the bag from my fingers, and waved the lotion at me. "Lie down," he whispered in my ear. "On your stomach."

My skin tingled as he unwrapped the towel from around me and started kneading my sore muscles in slow, steady circles—my feet, my calves, the backs of my knees.

"*Mmm.*" I snuggled deeper into the pillow. I was more exhausted than I'd thought. I hadn't slept in ages, but I fought the urge to close my eyes. "Did the police pick up K.K.?"

"No. The van was gone by the time they got there. They think the two men who came after you on the train found him and let him out."

An uneasy feeling unraveled in the pit of my stomach. The idea of K.K. running loose was unsettling. "How's Bahati?" I asked. "Is he going to be all right?"

"He's fine. Nothing broken." Jack moved from my legs to my back. I was melting under his firm, sensuous strokes. "Some of the newspaper journalists got a whiff of the story and wanted an interview. He's in the meeting room with them. Lights, cameras, the works."

"That's great." I chuckled. "And Gabriel? Any leads on him?"

"I tracked down the builder who's working on his home." Jack warmed more lotion in his hands before rubbing it over my shoulders. "The construction has stopped because Gabriel hasn't paid him for the next phase. I told him to contact me as soon as he hears from him. Gabriel has put a lot of money into this property. He's not just going to abandon it."

I lost my train of thought because Jack was stroking the sides of my neck, up and down. I was like a pendulum swinging between two states—from relaxation to arousal, and back again. As his fingers worked the knots under my skin, my eyes slid shut.

"Jack," I mumbled, "If you don't stop now, I'm going to fall asleep."

"Then do it. Just let yourself drift off. You haven't slept in ages."

"But time . . . I want to make the most of it." I flipped over and gazed at him.

Something clouded his expression before he blinked it away. "I don't want to think about that. Not right now. Right now, I just want to enjoy this. This feeling. Your skin. Your hair on the pillow. Your sleepy brown eyes."

I put my arms around his neck because I couldn't stand the distance. "Will you do something for me?"

"Anything." His breath was warm against my face. I couldn't help but taste his lips.

"Will you let me comb your hair?"

He laughed, but stopped when he caught my expression. "You're serious?"

"Sit." I patted the edge of the bed and scooted around to kneel behind him. I picked up the comb and ran it through his wet, shoulder length hair in soft, leisurely strokes. He sat stiff and upright, unaccustomed to being looked after. He might have let his barber have a go, but that was different, and I doubted he'd had his hair cut since Lily died.

After a while, his shoulders relaxed. I continued brushing his thick, tawny strands, root to tip, gently untangling his hair in soothing, downward strokes. His head tilted back, and I smiled because his eyes were shut. Every time the teeth raked over a certain spot in the back of his head, he purred and leaned into it.

"That feels so good."

The room turned mellow as the last rays of the sun filtered through the curtains. Warm light hit the side of Jack's face, softening the harsh planes and angles, picking up pale highlights in his beard. He gave himself up to me, up to the tenderness of the act, the soft intimacy of it.

When I was done, he drew the sheets over us and clasped my body tightly to his. We fell asleep, naked and tangled, with no need for words or kisses, too exhausted to think of the goodbye looming over our heads.

I STIRRED AFTER dawn, when the early morning buses turned into a parade of screeching halts outside the hotel. Jack was lying on his side, one hand under his pillow, watching me through lazy, hooded eyes.

"Morning." I smiled. His hair looked different, probably because he'd fallen asleep with it all combed out and a little wet. It had flopped over to one side, making him look like a model for a shampoo ad. *Thick, lustrous, all-day volume.* My smile grew wider. "You've been watching me sleep?"

"I've been stargazing." He traced the curve of my nose with his finger.

It was rather beautiful, the way he felt like all the places I wanted to go. His arms fit perfectly around me, as though they'd been molded by a sculptor, just for me.

"What is it?" he asked, hooking his leg around mine, as I contemplated him.

"When I look at your face . . . this face . . ." I stroked my thumb over the light reflecting off his cheekbone. "I feel like this is exactly where I'm supposed to be."

We started slow—a little drunk, a little dizzy—taking sips of honeyed bliss from dawn-colored lips. The world rolled below us—bicycle bells and newspaper boys, unaware that we were slowly setting the room on fire.

Jack stole the breath from my lungs. He dragged his lips across my hips, tasted my curves, taught me the pitch of pleasure until I was room-spinningly intoxicated with him. And in the heat of electric sighs, when our bodies turned molten and our bones dissolved, it felt like we were made from the same cluster of colliding stars. We clung to each other and sank into the sweet slumber of lovers, drifting in and out of dreams.

When Bahati called to see if we were ready to leave, we got distracted again, until he started banging on our door. The maid scurried in when we finally opened the door. It was way past check-out time.

"Coke for you. Coffee for you." Bahati straightened and handed us the drinks. "I figured you didn't bother with breakfast this morning. Not much sleep either, *huh*?" He scanned our faces and grinned. "It's a long way back, but I'd prefer to drive the whole way myself," he said to Jack. "I don't want you falling asleep at the wheel. I'm going to have my photo printed in tomorrow's paper. Things are finally looking up for me. I don't want to die because you and Ro went at it like bonobos in the night. I mean, it's great and all, but I just got Suzi fixed up as best as I could. A little more work when we get back and then all I have to do is put in the new leather seats you promised. Do you want to see the samples? They had crocodile skin too. Can you believe it? It's a bit nubby. So I told them to . . ."

It *was* a long way back, but I drifted off in the back seat as Bahati chattered on. Parts of me I never knew I had were sore, but sublimely so. Every now and then, Jack glanced at me from the passenger seat. We had a secret language going, whole stanzas hidden in our eyes.

As we drove past Magesa, evening started to settle around us. Jack guided Bahati to the spot where our car had broken down. It was still there, lonely and dusty. We had picked up the spare parts in Wanza, and the ground was finally dry, but it took a while to patch it up. By the time we got back on the trail, the moon was high and Bahati's headlights bounced behind us, all the way back to Kaburi Estate.

"You think they're up?" I asked Jack when we passed through the stone pillars at the gate. Goma had demanded an estimated time of arrival.

"I hope not. It's almost dawn." His eyes wandered over the rows of coffee plants, assessing them out of habit. The tops were starting to turn a silvery pink as morning stirred beyond the majestic peaks of Kilimanjaro.

Bahati parked next to us, and we got out, lugging our backpacks behind us.

Jack fiddled with the keys before shaking his head. "Goma left the door open again."

Bahati chuckled as I stepped inside. It felt good to drop my bags and soak up the warmth of the place. It made me realize how much the farm had grown on me, and how much I'd missed it.

"I think I'll—" I froze as I looked around the living room.

Something was wrong. Something was very wrong.

Family portraits lay smashed on the floor, glass strewn like glittering confetti; lamps were toppled over, cushions strewn, curtains hanging askew.

"Jack, someone's been here . . ." I trailed off when I saw him picking up a blood-soaked bandana.

He straightened, holding it up, his face twisted in dark, dazzling fury. "K.K." He crushed the bandana in his fist and whirled around, racing through the house. "Goma! Scholastica!"

There were bloody palm prints by the door, blood on the floor, blood on the banister, on the stairs. Everywhere.

A primitive alarm began ringing in my head. K.K. had scanned Jack's driver's license. He knew his name. He knew where he lived.

He had come for Jack but had found Goma and Scholastica instead.

Oh God. Scholastica. I shuddered, imagining the moment he'd seen her. He made his living off kids like her. What better way to get back at Jack than steal her from right under his roof? And finish his grandmother off too.

My bones turned brittle. Anxiety filled my veins as we searched the house.

Jack slammed through the kitchen and stopped short. I froze behind him, unable to go any farther, afraid of what I'd see. Bahati hovered behind me as the silence stretched out.

"What the fuck?" Jack swore and stepped forward, his frame no longer blocking my view.

Goma stood there, seemingly unhurt and unaffected, stirring a pan of milk over the stove. Scholastica was seated at the table. They were wearing matching muumuus. It was like we had just walked into a slumber party.

"About time you got here," said Goma, pouring the hot, frothy liquid into a cup and handing it to Scholastica. "Want some?" She waved the pan our way.

We shook our heads and watched as she drained the rest herself and slammed her empty mug on the counter. "*Ah,* much better."

"Are you going to tell us what the hell is going on?" asked Jack. "The place looks like it's been ransacked, and there's blood everywhere."

I sank into one of the chairs, my knees still weak with fright. Jack took the seat across from me. Bahati turned on the tap and gulped down three glasses of water.

"That bastard K.K. barged in here, looking for you. Him and his buddies. Mangy as stray dogs. The look in their eyes when they saw Scholastica. Like they'd hit the jackpot. They wanted to take me too. Figured the old crone might be worth a shilling or two to you.

"We put up a fight, but it was pretty useless. I stopped K.K.

as they were herding us out the door, and said, 'Hey. I know you. I ran into you at the police station.' He peered at me. And then his face lit up. 'Yes,' he said. 'You're the old woman with the crazy rainbow sunglasses. I remember what you said: *Over my dead body.*' That tickled him. He laughed like a maniac. He wanted the glasses, so he marched me up to my bedroom.

"I opened my wardrobe and grabbed my rifle. I don't think I'll ever forget the look on his face when I turned around, and *BOOM*. The fucker was on the floor, clutching his leg. I was loading the gun again, when his men came up, dragging Scholastica behind them. They looked at me, looked at him—bleeding on the ground by my feet, and took off. I stopped them in their tracks. I don't want garbage lying around in my home, so I made them carry K.K. out. I couldn't tell if he was dead or alive. I hope he's burning in hell as we speak." She took a big gulp of milk and shook her head. "Think they can mess with my grandson, come into my home, and steal this little girl from under my watch? The fuckers." She wiped her milk mustache off with the back of her hand and sat down next to Scholastica.

No one said a word. We sat around the table, a little shocked and dazed, as the minutes ticked by.

Then Scholastica finished her milk and slammed her cup down with a *thump*. Mo's frames slid farther down her nose.

"The fuckers," she said, wiping her mouth with the back of her hand, just like Goma had done.

They were the first English words I'd heard her speak. She didn't have a clue what they meant, but she mimicked them earnestly, her face beaming with pride.

Jack got up, opened the refrigerator, and stuck his head behind the door.

Bahati cloaked his laughter in a coughing fit.

I bit down on my lip and stared at my knuckles.

"That's right." Goma patted Scholastica's hand solemnly. "Always tell it like it is."

I RELAXED INTO the crook of Jack's arm and rested my head on his shoulder. He found my hand under the blanket and laced our fingers together. We sat on the porch under a purple sky, on the kiwi green swing that had become our favorite spot. Moon-splashed fields stretched out before us. Behind us, Kilimanjaro watched silently, brooches of opalescent snow shimmering from its lofty peaks. Night bugs hummed, leaves rustled, a dragonfly whirred and fluttered away.

I had always thought of home as a place, where you put down your roots, unpack your collection of mugs with snarky quotes, put up all the bookshelves you want, and watch the rain splash down your windows on wet, gray afternoons. But I was realizing that home was a feeling—of being, of belonging—a feeling that swirled through my veins every time I was with Jack.

"Why so quiet?" he asked.

I shook my head and picked out a coffee plant to focus on. If I spoke, my voice would crack. If I looked at him, my eyes would betray me.

Ask me to stay, Jack.

As stupid and impractical as it sounded, I was ready to give it all up for him. My job. My cottage. My life in England. Because that's what love did. It turned you stupid and made you do things you never thought you'd do.

"Three more days." I kept my eyes on the coffee plant, willing him to make a statement. *Give me something, Jack. Anything to grab on to.*

"We could make it work." He had this uncanny ability to read me, to tune into the frequency of my thoughts. "People have long distance relationships all the time."

"Yes, but not forever." My heart sank. It wasn't what I'd been hoping for. I had always known this is how it would be. He'd told me right off the bat that he'd never ask me to stay, but it still twisted and burned inside me.

"Rodel." He put his hand under my chin, his blue eyes capturing mine. "I'm not ready to let you go."

"I don't want you to, but I'd rather say goodbye now than next year, or the year after, when we're both worn out by the distance. When phone calls and video chats and seeing each other once in a while just doesn't cut it anymore. We'd be okay in the beginning. It would take the edge off, but I'm done with okay, Jack. Okay is existing. Okay is ordinary. And you . . ." I cupped his cheek in a wistful gesture. There was so much I wanted to say to him. "You and me . . . we're too grand, too magnificent to fit into ordinary. I love you, Jack. It's big love. Huge. I can't stuff it in a letter or an email. I'm not okay with that. I'm not an okay girl. I'm an all or nothing girl."

A slew of emotions flashed across his rugged face. Pride. Joy. Sorrow. Heart-rending tenderness. He twirled a strand of my hair around his finger and gave me a poignant smile. "I always knew you'd be trouble."

"Me?" I wanted to sob, but I couldn't allow myself to break down. "Your grandmother blew a man's balls off today."

His laugh was rich and undiluted. It was the most marvelous, catching sound to me.

"My grandmother was fingerprinted, photographed, and let off," he said. "They found K.K.'s body in a ditch. She deserves an award for putting that monster to rest."

"I'm glad he's gone. I think we can all get a good night's sleep."

"They're all down for the night—Goma, Scholastica, Bahati. You should pretend you're sleeping too."

"Why would I do that?"

"To get me to carry you up the stairs, like the last time."

"I knew it! I knew you knew." I covered my face with my hands. "Was I that obvious?" I peeked at him through my fingers.

"Completely." He scooped me up and paused at the door so I could turn off the porch light. "You practically threw yourself at me. Drove me crazy the night the hyenas came, standing before the light in that muumuu so I could see your every curve. You made googly eyes at me over the clothesline. Cornered me in the barn." With each stair, he added to his list. "Kissed me senseless. Fell at my feet—"

"I slipped! I nose-dived into the mud."

"Like I said. You fell at my feet, tossed off your top in the tent, flashed your boobs—"

I smothered him with a kiss. Oh, I knew exactly how to shut him up. And then I proceeded to make him completely lose his train of thought.

TIME. THE LESS you have of it, the more precious it be-
comes. I was stringing every moment I had with Jack like a
pearl on a necklace. Goma caught me, propped up against
the door, the steam from my coffee drifting into the morning air, as
I watched Jack work in the fields. She knew we held hands under
the table, that our eyes spoke words no one else could hear, that
we disappeared for hours and came back with our faces flushed and
bits of hay sticking out of our hair. She stripped my bed, washed
the sheets, and put them away in the linen closet. There was no
need to sneak back into my room in the mornings.

Scholastica's new glasses arrived, but she clung to Mo's, until
Goma caved and called Dr. Nasmo for another appointment—this
time to get new lenses fitted into Mo's frames.

"I'm keeping her," said Goma, after she got off the phone.

"Keeping who?" Jack dried his hands and sat down to eat.

It was lunchtime—too hot to be working outside. It meant a
long break, and Jack knew exactly what he wanted to do with it.
He gave me a devilish grin that set my pulse racing.

"Scholastica. I'm keeping her." Goma poured herself some
water and challenged Jack over the rim of the glass.

"Keeping her?" Jack put his fork down. "She's not like Aristurtle, that you can build a box and keep her in there. She needs school,
kids to play with, a stimulating environment. Rodel promised Anna

she'd get Scholastica to Wanza."

"You really want to take her to Wanza? You saw the place for yourself. Her father doesn't want her living there, either. He's building a house in Wanza so she can go to school there but come home at night. So until he shows up, I'm keeping her. There's no better place for her right now. She's learning the alphabet, she runs around with horses and calves, gets plenty of exercise, good food, and a good night's rest. I've already talked to Anna. She's still trying to find a way to support herself and her kids, so until she's more settled she has no objections to Scholastica living with us."

"Look." Jack leaned across the table and took Goma's hands in his. "I get it. You've grown attached to her. God knows, I have too. Every time I see her, I'm reminded what this place felt like when Lily was around. I don't see why she can't stay here until we hear from her father, but we don't know when that will be. What if he never shows? What if something's happened to him? K.K. wasn't the only guy trading albino kids. What if Gabriel became a problem and someone decided to eliminate him? He could be buried in the middle of nowhere. What happens to Scholastica then? This isn't just a short-term commitment. We've got to cover all the bases and do what's best for her. Even if that means putting our own feelings aside."

The door opened, and Scholastica walked in with Bahati. They were laughing, trying to keep things from rolling out of their hands: potatoes, carrots, and bright red tomatoes, freshly picked from the veggie patch.

"Let's discuss this later," Jack said to Goma, as Scholastica washed her hands and plopped down next to Jack. She unwrapped a paper towel and handed him the biggest, ripest tomato.

"You saved that one for me?" asked Jack. It was plain to see how much they adored each other.

"What's this?" asked Bahati, picking up an envelope from the table. It had his name on it.

"It came for you this morning," replied Goma. "A very pretty Maasai girl delivered it."

"A love letter, Bahati? You've been holding out on us." Jack slapped him on the back.

Bahati didn't take any notice. He sat down, his eyes scanning the paper. When he was done, he looked up with a blank expression.

"Everything all right?" I asked.

"My father . . ." He looked from me to Jack to Goma, still clutching the letter.

Oh no. I braced myself. "Is he okay?"

"My father has summoned me to the *boma*. He wants me to go to the village."

"That's fantastic, Bahati!" Jack let out a big whoop. "The old man wants to make amends. He's inviting you back home."

Bahati folded the letter and slid it back into the envelope. He was wearing a new shirt that showed off his build, but there was something different about him, something more—a new confidence, a new sense of pride. "I've waited so many years for this, for his approval. All I've ever wanted was to feel like I matter to him. And now that it's here, I don't know how I feel. A part of me wants to go to him, but I have a life outside the *boma* now. I don't want to go back and spend the rest of my life living by my father's standards, trying to please him. I'm back at The Grand Tulip next week, and after that newspaper article, I've even had a few job offers. One is for a toothpaste ad. I have to audition first, but I've been practicing." He flashed us a piano-key white smile. It was so dazzling, I could almost hear the *ting* from the glint of sparkle, reflecting off his teeth.

"Oh Jesus." Goma dropped her sandwich to shield herself from the glare. "What the hell did you do?"

"I bleached my teeth. There's no way they can turn me away

now. I mean, who can resist this smile?" He subjected us to another round of his diamond grin.

Ting, ting, ting.

"Do me a favor, Sparkles," said Goma. "Pass me that other envelope." She motioned to the one sitting by his elbow. "This is for you two," she said, taking it from him and sliding it across the table.

Jack and Rodel. It was printed in her bold, shaky handwriting.

Seeing our names entwined on paper, like they belonged next to each other, caught me unawares. I stared at the letters—the thick, horizontal stroke on top of the *J*, the curve that tapered off on the *l*.

"Go ahead, open it," said Goma.

It was a room reservation for The Grand Tulip—all paid for and confirmed.

"I thought the two of you should stay in Amosha tonight." Goma got up and started washing her plate. "Your flight leaves tomorrow morning, Rodel. The airport is right there so you won't have to get up so early."

It was the last night Jack and I would have together. Goma was giving us the time and space to say goodbye.

"Thank you," I said, but she was watching Jack with the whole world in her eyes, like her heart was breaking for him to have to say another goodbye.

She shifted her gaze and smiled at me. "Thank *you* for ridding this place of the grouch that lived here. Remember when you first got here? Oh, Lord. I thought I'd have to live out the rest of my days with Mr. Sourpuss."

"I'm right here, you know." Jack shot her an amused look. "And if you want me to pick up your fiber pills from town, you'd better play nice."

"Senior abuse," muttered Goma.

"What did you say?"

"I said I could do with some cranberry juice."

Jack grinned and got up. "I love you, Goma." He kissed her on the top of her head and gave her a hug. "And thank you for your gift. That was very thoughtful."

A lump formed in my throat as they stood by the sink, Goma's frail form completely engulfed by Jack.

"*Pfft!*" Bahati spewed a spray of water all over the table.

"What the hell?" exclaimed Jack.

"The water." He coughed, pushing his glass away. "It's so cold!"

We stared at him for a moment and then started laughing. Bleaching his teeth had made them more sensitive to heat and cold. Scholastica laughed the loudest as Bahati gasped and sputtered until tears started streaming down her face.

"You think it's funny?" Bahati lunged after her. She squealed and ran out the door. Goma went after them. I followed.

"Let her go," I said, wrangling Scholastica away from Bahati as he caught up to her.

We weaved in and out of the wet clothes hanging on the laundry line. I followed flashes of bare feet between the bed sheets and towels—Scholastica's milky-white toes, Bahati's lean ankles—hopping, darting, finding, escaping. Scholastica was small and nimble. Bahati and I kept getting tangled up in the laundry. The wind carried our ripples of laughter.

"I give up," said Bahati, wearing a pair of Goma's knickers on his face. "But only because my knee hurts." He sat down, his chest heaving, fanning himself with them.

"Gimme those!" Goma snatched her underwear from him and gave him a death glare.

"Good job!" I said, high-fiving Scholastica. I knelt before her and poked her nose. Her arms went around my shoulders and she gave me the tightest hug.

"*Kesho.*" She pointed to the sky.

"Yes," I replied, the words wedged in my throat. "Tomorrow,

I fly. Far away." I held her hand as I straightened. "I'm going to miss you."

Goma and Bahati came around. The four of us hugged in the shadow of the mountain as berry-laden coffee plants swayed around us. Then Goma broke loose.

"Okay. I'm done. My bones can't take any more hugging today. Go." She shooed me away. "Go get packed. I've left a little something in your room. Don't open it until you're on the plane."

"Thank you," I said. "For everything." My heart felt like it was going to snap, so I turned around and headed toward the house. Through the fluttering clothes on the line, I saw Jack watching us. He was standing by the four tombstones, under the acacia tree. Everything stilled as our eyes met. In that one instant, we relived it all—that first meeting on the porch, the way he'd cheated at book charades, the way I'd run from my own shadow in the mist, *next time grab the oh-shit handle,* his teeth grazing my neck, *give me your tongue,* him holding my hand on the train tracks, *I turn around for two seconds and you're at another tea party,* me combing his hair, holding hands under the blanket on our swing. Our swing. Ours.

But our time was done. Except for one more night.

He watched as I walked over to him. I wrapped my arms around him, wanting to soak up the feel of him, wanting it to seep deep into my bones so I could store it in my marrow. We rocked gently, side to side.

As the afternoon sun warmed our backs, I sought out the little tombstone under the tree.

Goodbye, Lily. Every time the sun shines through the rain, I will look for you. I will look for you in rainbows, and I will remember a man who holds the whole sky in his eyes.

23

I STOPPED AT the entrance of The Grand Tulip and scanned the white expanse of the outside wall.

"The first time I saw Bahati, he was standing right here. I thought he was a statue," I said to Jack. He was wearing a button-down shirt with the sleeves rolled up, exposing his strong, tanned forearms. I wasn't used to women staring at him. I'd pretty much had him all to myself. Until now.

As we entered the lobby, heads turned, hair was fluffed, legs tilted, postures corrected. It was as if a hot wind had blown in, bringing with it a heady, intoxicating fragrance.

Down, girls. I lay my hand possessively on Jack's as we checked in. For the first time in years, I had the urge to paint my nails, so they gleamed like sharp little talons. *Keep off.*

They were envious of me. I could see it in their eyes. And yet, jealousy was stabbing at my own heart, because I was leaving and I couldn't stand the thought of him with anyone else.

"Are you okay?" asked Jack, scanning my face.

"Yes." I shook off the blue thoughts that were starting to rain down on me. I had seen the end coming before we began. I had pushed for it anyway. And it was worth every aching, twinging emotion because standing before him right then, I knew down to the depths of my soul: Jack had eyes for no one else but me. And there was nothing more exhilarating than being hit with the full force of that.

"Come on." I dragged him toward the lifts. I didn't want to waste any of our precious time together on empty, useless thoughts.

Our room was on the top level—the third floor, with a balcony that overlooked mounds of bright, pink bougainvillea spilling around a tranquil blue swimming pool.

"Goma must have asked for their nicest suite," I said, taking in the silky bed linens, the bay window with crimson tieback curtains, the lush sitting area, the dressing table, the gilded mirror on the wall. There was a soaking tub in the bathroom, a giant shower cubicle, and gleaming, white marble floors. "Are you noticing any of this?" I grinned, pushing Jack away. He was following me around, taking his own tour. Untucking my top, nibbling my neck, measuring the curve of my waist.

"I notice everything. Like these two vertical ridges that run between your upper lip and nose . . . what's this space called? It must have a name. It fits the tip of my little finger perfectly." He proceeded to demonstrate, and then trailed his tongue over the dip of my cupid's bow. I was getting lost in the magic of his kiss when there was a knock on the door.

"You mind getting that?" he asked, pulling away.

I wasn't sure about the glint in his eyes. "What's going on? You look like you're up to something." Jack was a take-charge kind of guy. If there was someone at the door, he'd want to get it himself.

"Just. Go. Get. It." He spun me around.

I opened the door and saw a porter standing there with our luggage. Behind him was a trio of beautiful ladies carrying bags that were definitely not ours.

"Please come in." Jack swung the door wider and let them in. He tipped the porter while the ladies settled their totes around the dressing area. One of them started hanging garment bags in the closet.

"Jack?" I turned from them to him.

"Rodel, meet Hair, Makeup, and Wardrobe," he said. "I asked them to come in and spoil you. I want you to have a magical afternoon."

"But I . . . I thought we'd be spending our last day together."

"We are, sweetness." His eyes softened as he smiled. "We're going on a date. Just you and me. A proper date. I'll be waiting for you in the lobby when you're done. Don't take too long." His mouth burned a silent promise on mine. "Take good care of my girl, ladies," he said to our audience of three.

"We will, Mr. Warden," they replied.

"I'll miss you." He wrapped his arms around my waist and clasped me in a tight embrace, sweeping me off my feet. I liked being his girl. I didn't want to think of anything beyond that moment.

When he was gone, I turned around and found Hair, Makeup, and Wardrobe gawking after the door.

"Men who pick you up when they hug you," said one of the girls. I didn't know which of them it was, but they all sighed in unison.

I stared at their spellbound faces. They caught me looking at them and cinched up their expressions. There was a moment of awkward silence.

"Well, hopefully it's a man you like," I said. "Otherwise it could be a pepper spray moment."

It took a second before their faces cracked. We all started laughing. It was the perfect icebreaker to the fanciest, most stupendous makeover I'd ever had. Josie, Melody, and Valerie were my fairy godmothers for the afternoon. My hair was washed, snipped, and put in rollers. I was fussed over, colors held against me, palettes chosen, nails buffed, eyebrows tweezed, lips outlined.

"No, thanks," I said to the tray of false eyelashes that Josie held before me. I had images of them fluttering into my drink, or worse, watching Jack through a wonky set as he sat across from me.

"You need to pick a dress," said Valerie, holding up a sleek gown.

"Shoes first. Then dress. Always," said Melody, opening a row of neatly lined boxes.

"This must have cost Jack an arm and a leg." I glanced at the label on the dress. "Are these like a rental?"

Valerie laughed so hard she nearly dropped the gown. "No, honey. No rentals. You get to keep whatever you choose. Our company is very selective about who we work with. We do celebrity weddings, A-list events, charity balls. Top of the class only."

"So how did Jack manage to pull this off?"

Josie stopped in the middle of applying my makeup and held her brush at a slant. "Girl, that man you walked in here with *is* top of the class. Don't tell me you don't know how much he's worth."

"I've never . . . I didn't . . . I thought . . ."

"The question isn't how he managed to pull it off. The question is how he managed to pull it off so fast. We're booked months in advance. When our boss called to get the team in here today, let me tell you, we hustled. So, yeah. Whatever Mr. Warden said to our boss lady, it sure lit a fire."

"I had no idea."

I thought of Jack's muddy boots by the back door, the way he took a damp cloth and wiped the dust off his face and the back of his neck before he sat down to eat. I thought of him cleaning the stalls, talking to the horses, starting his day before anyone else arrived on the farm. That was the Jack I knew. That was the solid, unassuming man I'd fallen in love with. And knowing he wasn't doing it to just make ends meet, that he was doing it because it's what drove him, what inspired him, what defined him, made me love him even more.

"What do you think?" asked Josie, handing me the mirror to

check my makeup.

"I think I want to completely blow Jack Warden's mind to-night." I dismissed the mirror and sat up straighter. "Let's kick this up a notch, girls."

"Yasss!" they chorused around me. "Now we're talking!"

I TOOK A deep breath and checked my reflection. Josie, Melody, and Valerie were gone, but there I stood, afraid to blink, in case the dazzling woman staring back at me disappeared. My hair was parted to the side, chestnut locks falling in lustrous waves around my shoulders. I'd gone for a floor-length black dress with a sexy side slit. It looked demure when I stood still, but every time I moved, it exposed a thigh-high flash of my skin. The cut was iconic, with a deep V in the back and a narrow waist. It fit me like a dream, draping over my curves in all the right places. I took a step forward and stopped. I wasn't used to wearing heels, but I liked the way they made me walk—thrusting my hips and breasts forward, accentuating the roundness of my buttocks.

My eyes appeared bigger and wider—soft gold shadow blended with smudged chocolate brown eyeliner. There was a tingling in the pit of my stomach every time I thought of Jack. It made my cheeks flush and my pupils dilate. My skin glowed with anticipation as I smoothed my dress and turned off the lights.

A date.

A real date.

A real date with Jack.

I waited for the lift, holding my breath. I couldn't wait for Jack to see me all dressed up. And yet, I was wracked with nerves. There was something else too—a sense of urgency to be with him. Our time together was ticking away too fast. I pressed the button again and waited. And waited.

Screw it.

I slipped my heels off and took the stairs. Each step was inlaid with beautiful coconut wood. I could see the lobby as I spiraled down the staircase, holding my shoes in one hand, and lifting the hem of my dress with the other. As I rounded the final flight, the main floor opened up to me. I slowed down, my eyes searching for Jack.

A few guests were seated in plush chairs around intricately carved wooden coffee tables. One of them saw me, bent his head, and whispered something to his companion. Both heads turned my way. Great. I was obviously overdressed. I cringed as I made my way down. More heads turned.

Damn it. Couldn't they have put this staircase somewhere else? Anywhere but smack dab in the middle of the lobby? I stood barefoot on the bottom step, wanting to run back upstairs, when the elevator dinged. As the door opened, I caught my breath. It was Jack, but in a dazzling white shirt and a tailored charcoal jacket that accentuated the frame of his shoulders. His pants were molded to the cut of his thighs and he wore . . . the same pair of worn, dusty work boots.

I smiled and met his eyes, but he stood there, dumbstruck. The lift door shut, swallowing him up again. A second later, it opened, and he stepped out.

"That was . . ." He cleared his throat and pointed to the lift. "That was me, so floored by the sight of you, I forgot to get out." His gaze roved over me again. "You look . . ." He shook his head and tried again. "Wow. You're spectacular."

"You look pretty hot yourself," I replied. His hair was still wild and unruly, but he'd made concessions. He'd trimmed his beard. I could almost make out the outline of his jaw.

He was the kind of handsome that made your heart twist.

"Do I pass?" His eyes sparkled at my unabashed perusal.

"Not sure if the boots go with that fine ensemble, but you'll do."

"Hey, at least I wore shoes. My date showed up barefoot." He crossed the floor and took the heels from my hands. "May I?" He knelt before me and slipped on one shoe, and then the other. My heart took a perilous leap as he brushed his fingers over my ankle before he straightened.

"Ready?" He offered his arm.

I linked my arm through his, and we turned to find every eye in the lobby on us. We'd forgotten there were people around, people who were watching us.

"I feel so overdressed," I whispered.

"They're not staring because you're overdressed. They're staring because they can't help it. Because you're breathtaking. I booked us a table at the restaurant, but now I'm not so sure I want all these people ogling you." He led me across the lobby to the entrance of the restaurant.

"Deal with it," I teased over my shoulder, as the maître d' led us to our table. It was a beautiful dining room—safari-themed, with splashes of crimson and warm wood. Local art adorned the walls. Starched, white cloths covered candlelit tables. "I didn't spend all that time getting ready for room service." I yelped as Jack gave me a sharp, discreet smack on my bum.

"Everything okay?" asked the maître d'. He was an older gentleman, with a thick, groomed mustache and deep lines on his forehead.

"Everything's fine, Njoroge. Thank you." Jack slid the chair out for me before seating himself.

"Good to see you, Mr. Warden. It's been a while," Njoroge replied, handing us the menus. "I'll send someone over to take your order right away."

We sat in silence after he left. I flipped the pages back and forth, not really reading the choices.

"What's wrong?" Jack lowered my menu so he could see my face.

"Nothing, just . . ." I shook my head. I was being petty, and I didn't want to spoil our evening. "It's nothing."

Jack took my menu away and pinned me down with his steely blues.

"Could we not . . ." I crossed my legs under the table. "Could we just . . ."

His expression didn't waver.

"Fine." I sighed. "You used to bring Sarah here." I had forgotten all about it until Jack had addressed the maître d' by name.

"I did." His face was set in watchful dignity. "The last time I came here with my ex was six years ago. We sat at that table." He tilted his head toward the window. "When we left, we both knew it was over. I haven't been back since. It doesn't exactly bring back good memories. But you know what, Rodel?" He reached across the table for my hand. "Everything is new when I'm with you. Food tastes better. Colors look brighter. Music is sweeter. I feel hungry for the world again. I want to go to the places I've skipped, I want to share them with you—show you who I am, who I was, who I can be.

"I'm here, Rodel, not because I like the sugar cookies they leave on my pillow, or the Steak freakin' Diane on the menu. I'm here, in a restaurant full of people, with you, because I can't afford to fall apart, because the thought of you leaving is killing me, so I'm focusing on creating as many beautiful, grand moments as I can for you. I can't give you much else, but I can give you that. And I can't fathom—not for an instant—why you'd be sitting across from me and thinking of my ex, because I sure as hell wasn't. When I'm with you, Rodel, I'm *all* with you."

He'd done it again—sent that ticker tape of emotions all over the place. I felt big and small all at once, like I was holding stars in one hand but sifting through gunk with the other.

"I'm sorry," I said in a low, tormented voice. "I'm sorry I'm ruining our evening." A stab of guilt lay buried in my breast, but there was something more, something I was stifling underneath it all. I wanted him to tell me he loved me. I wanted to hear the words. That was the real reason I was acting like a jerk, and I didn't like the way it made me feel. "And just so we're clear," I teased him with my eyes, "I really like those sugar cookies. They're shaped like tulips, and they taste like heaven."

Jack seemed caught off guard by the quick turnaround, but he threw me an amused glance. His smile had the feeling of indefinable rightness.

"We'd like two dozen of your sugar cookies," he said, when the waiter came to get our order. "To go."

"Yes, sir. Anything else I can get for you?"

"No, that will be all."

"That's it?" I exclaimed, when the waiter was gone. "That's what you're going to feed me? Cookies, on my last night here?" I snatched my hand away from his and feigned outrage. "What about all the beautiful, grand moments? You can't create those on an empty stomach. I think—"

He hushed me with a long, tapered finger on my lips. "Too many words. Too much talking. If I wanted to talk, I'd have invited Bahati instead." He picked up the ribbon-adorned box of cookies that the waiter brought and came around to get my chair. "You ready to leave?"

My skin tingled where he touched it.

Hell, yes. Let's go.

But I sniffed as he steered me out of the restaurant. "That was a cheap date."

"Quit complaining. You didn't want to eat there anyway."

"Wait." I said, when he handed the valet his parking ticket. "I thought we were going to our room. Where are you taking me?"

"On a cheap date." He winked, seating me in the car when

it came around.

We drove away from the hotel and merged into the chaotic traffic of Amosha. The sky was aflame with hues of red and orange from the setting sun. A truck with giant megaphones rattled by us, blaring advertisements in Swahili. Shopkeepers waved phone cards and colorful swathes of *kangas* as people walked by.

Jack parked outside a sorry looking food stall, off the main road. Its fluorescent light buzzed on and off under a rusty roof. "Kilimanjaro Premium Lager" logos hung from the ceiling, held together by clothes pegs on twine. A row of black woks hovered over flames in the front, hissing and bubbling with oil. Battered plastic chairs rested around plastic tables on an uneven floor—half dirt, half gravel.

"Come on." Jack came around and held the car door open for me. "Best *nyama choma* in town."

"What's *nyama choma?*"

"Grilled meat." He steadied me as my heel got stuck in the gravel.

"We are definitely overdressed for this place," I said. Faint fumes of petroleum wafted in from the gas station next to the stall. *Dala dalas* raced by with abandon, and women in bright *kangas* strolled by, carrying all sorts of food on their heads.

"*Jambo,*" the waitress greeted us. She was so busy she wouldn't have batted an eye if we'd shown up in burlap sacks. "What can I get for you?"

"Coca Cola, *baridi*," said Jack.

"Umm . . ." I looked around when the waitress turned to me. "Is there a menu?"

"A Stoney Tangawizi for her," said Jack. He reeled off a bunch of things in Swahili, before sitting back with a grin.

"I have no idea what I'm about to eat. And you're enjoying it, aren't you?"

"Having you totally at my mercy?" said Jack, when the waitress brought our drink order. "You bet. Tonight, you dine like a local. None of the touristy frills." There was a mischievous glint in his eyes as he slid a brown glass bottle across the table, his fingers marking the droplets of condensation that clung to its surface. "Take it slow, baby."

I turned the label toward me, but it didn't give anything away. "What is Stoney Tangawizi?" I asked.

"Tanzanian ginger beer."

"Ginger beer? _Pfft._" I rolled my eyes and took a healthy swig, tilting my head back.

The burning sensation began while I was still swallowing. Hot, effervescent bubbles tickled my nose. My tongue started zinging. The back of my throat caught fire. I slammed the bottle down, tears streaming from my eyes. "The fuck!" I inhaled. Big mistake. It set me off on a coughing spree. More tears. More spluttering. It was ginger on steroids—sweet, bubbly, and fermented, with a pungent kick. And it was good, so good that I took another sip as soon as I'd caught my breath, but this time more slowly.

"Like it?" Jack leaned over and ran his thumb under my eye. It came away black and smudged.

"Great. My mascara is running. I must look like a raccoon." I dabbed my eyes with a napkin to take it off.

"You look exactly the way I'd want you to look after I've made mad, passionate love to you. Except that dress would be on the floor and you'd be wearing nothing but a smile."

It was a heady brand of foreplay, exchanged in the middle of all the noise, the people, the traffic around us. I blinked, flushed and a little lightheaded.

"_Mishkaki wa kuku, samaki ndizi, mbuzi mbavu choma, ugali, maharagwe . . ._" I didn't catch the rest of what the waitress said as she placed heaping platters of food on our table. She held a kettle over a wash bin so we could rinse our hands with warm water before eating.

It was a feast fit for the gods, and it smelled just as incredible: crispy fried fish and plantain, boneless cubes of chicken on wooden skewers with pili-pili sauce, goat ribs so tender that the meat fell clean off the bone, leaving charred bits of salt and chili to savor, a polenta-like dish to counter the flavors exploding in my mouth; bean stew, tamarind sauce, and sips of ginger beer to wash it all down with.

"*Leta chipsi,*" said Jack to the waitress, as I mopped up the last of the plantain. There was no cutlery, so I had to lick the sauce off my fingers.

"So *chipsi* is chips?" I asked, when she brought us a plate of sizzling french fries.

"Yes, you just add the *i* at the end. A lot of English words get assimilated into the local dialect like that."

I nodded, watching two school-aged boys rinse dirty plates by the side of the road before bringing them back to the kiosk. Somewhere across the busy streets, evening prayers blared from a nearby mosque.

"Ready to go?" asked Jack, summoning the waitress as I sat back, staring at the empty plates before us. We'd managed to de-molish everything on the table.

"Wait. I've got this," I said, turning to her. "*Leta billi.*"

If *chips* was *chipsi*, then *bill* must be *billi*. I held my breath, wondering if I'd gotten it right.

"Yes, madam," she said. And off she went.

"I'm getting the hang of it." I shot Jack a victorious grin. It didn't last too long.

The waitress returned with a man by her side. He wiped his rough, wizened hands on his apron and looked at me expectantly.

"You asked for Billy," the waitress prompted after a few

awkward ticks, where I glanced from her to him and back again.

"I'm sorry. I meant the bill."

Billy muttered something in Swahili and stomped off. He was clearly not pleased at having been called away from his grill.

"Would you like to practice your Swahili some more, or shall we get *goingi?*" Jack teased, as he paid our bill.

I exited as gracefully as I could, my heels getting stuck in the gravel just twice. I waved at Billy from the car. Billy did not wave back.

Jack and I kept a straight face as we waited for someone to let us merge back into the street. Then we burst out laughing. Around us, horns honked. Night markets passed by in a blur of kerosene lamps and bargaining. A canopy of stars materialized as we drove away from the heated haze of Amosha.

"Where are we going?" I asked, when Jack turned onto a moon-bleached path between silver cornfields.

"Right . . . here." He stopped, backed the car up into a clearing, and turned the engine off. "Come on," he said, grabbing the box of sugar cookies from the back seat and getting out.

The air was thick and warm with the fragrance of night jasmine. There was a gentle humming around us, like a swarm of bees.

"What's that sound?" I asked, kicking off my heels and following Jack to the back of the car. The grass was suede soft and silent under my feet. "It reminds me of . . ." I trailed off as I followed his gaze.

We were parked by the edge of a stream. A small waterfall cascaded over the rocks on the other side. Silver threads fused and spilled over a gravelly bed in whirls of foam. The moon hung silently above, casting a honeyed sheen over the trees.

"It's so beautiful here," I said. The gurgling, the swishing, the sparkles of shimmering spray—it was like having front row tickets to an illusory concert.

"A beautiful place for a beautiful girl." Jack caressed my cheek. His face held an irrefutable sensuality, but in the moonlight he positively slayed me.

He opened the rear door of his Land Rover and we sat there, my head on his shoulder, our legs dangling out of the trunk as we watched the silky fall of water break over the gleaming rocks. He fed me tulip-shaped cookies, and I breathed in his skin-warmed scent. For a while, it seemed like time had stopped forever. The stars marched across the sky, galaxies whirled around us, and yet we sat still and suspended, not wanting to shatter the magic. It was the kind of magic that comes after a lifetime of searching, when you stumble upon something so perfect, you stop looking, and you say: *Yes. This. I know this. I feel this. I've heard its footsteps echo down the hallways of my soul.*

We turned to each other with kisses that were soft and greedy, reverent and selfish—each one like a pressed daisy to be hidden between the pages of our story. Falling in love with something that can never be is like piercing yourself with a honey-dipped dagger. Over and over again. It's sharp and sweet, beautiful and sad, and you don't always know which when you cry.

"No." Jack kissed the damp corner of my eye. "This is not how I want to remember you. It's not how I want you to remember us."

"Then how? How will you remember me when I'm gone?"

"Like this." He slid the straps of my dress off, first one, then the other. "Your shoulders gleaming in the moonlight. Crystals of sugar on your lips." He brushed his mouth against mine, his tongue tasting the remnants of the cookies he'd fed me. "Your hair, like ribbons of satin over my palms. The thrill of undressing you. Like this." He slid the zip down my dress, exposing my flesh, goosebump by goosebump. "The feel of you in my arms, the way your lids drop over your eyes when I bite you here." His teeth grazed a spot under my ear where my jaw met my neck. "I will remember the perfect oval of your face, the warmth of your throat, the way you hold a pen when you write. Most of all . . ." He cupped my chin, his eyes roving over my upturned face. "I will remember a strange, beautiful girl who liked the feel of old books and drank her coffee sweet. She snuck onto my porch on a gray day and taught me to see in color. She was a thief, my rainbow-haloed girl. When she left, she took my heart. And if I had another, I would give her that too"

It was the closest he would ever get to saying he loved me because those words would bind me, and he was setting me free—free to live out my life, my dreams, my aspirations. He wanted me to find my place in the sun instead of living in the shadow of his life. But in that moment, I didn't want to be set free. I wanted him to ask me to stay. I wanted him to demand it, command it, to leave me with no choice. But he just held me with his eyes, and I learned the power of being all tied up, without ropes or chains.

"I want a clean break." My voice cracked when I said it, but I meant it. "I don't want to spend my days living for phone calls and texts. I don't want to make do with your voice when what I really want is your arms around me. I don't want eyes that can't meet and feet that can't touch. I think that would kill me."

"I know. You're my all or nothing girl. You're grand and special, and so beautiful that my heart aches every time I look at you. I don't want you to settle for anything less. But I don't want to know when you're out with some other guy—someone you meet in a quaint little coffee shop, someone you have brunch with on Sunday mornings, someone who can hold you and love you and fall asleep beside you. I think that would kill me." A ragged breath escaped his lips as he claimed my mouth. He kissed me hard and hungry, like he wanted me to carry the taste of him forever.

"Jack," I said it for no reason, except that it felt right. His name felt like it belonged in my mouth, like it had always belonged.

"I want you naked in the moonlight." He tugged my dress, so

it fell in a puddle around my feet. The rest of our clothes came off in a flurry, fingertips like matches, setting skin on fire.

We made love on a blanket by the stream, slow and gentle, rough and hard, riding the currents of our emotions like waves crashing on the shore. There were flashes of bright sensation— the look in Jack's eyes when he slid inside me, his hands molding my curves, the midnight sky above us, trees swaying around us, the first moan escaping my lips, muscles and tendons dancing to a lover's tango, the silver glow of constellations on our skin, the rush of the waterfall, Jack's harsh, uneven breath, our bodies caught between the intoxication of climax and wanting to extend a moment we never wanted to end. My head rocked back as all the stars in the sky condensed to a single point. Jack stifled my cry with his lips, his fingers digging into my flesh as he hurtled over the edge of pleasure.

We weren't ready to let go so we remained locked in the aftermath of passion. When our hearts calmed and our breaths settled, he smoothed the hair off my forehead and kissed my face. I traced the groove in the hollow of his back. His skin tasted sweet against my fingertips, like the last bits of sugar at the bottom of a cup of coffee. I wanted to savor it. I wanted to drain every last drop and make it a part of me forever.

"What are you doing?" I asked, as he got up and covered me with another blanket from the car. He was kneeling on the ground, fussing around, when all I wanted was for him to come back to me.

"Covering your feet." He cupped my heel and ran his finger down my sole until my toes wiggled. "You have traitorous feet. Tomorrow, they'll carry you away from me, but tonight they're mine." He kissed the tops of my feet softly. "Do they know the way back, Rodel? Do they know that if they ever walk these fields again, they belong to me? Because I *will* claim them. Make no mistake about that."

"And I claim you." I pulled him to me and looped my arms around his neck. "If you're ever in England. And not just your feet. I claim all of you. This, and this, and this, and this." I took inventory of his firm, bronzed body. It would have been funny if we weren't both aching inside.

"I think you missed a spot." He rolled over onto his back and took me with him. "This right here." He placed my hand over his heart.

"Yes. This right here." I lay my head on my favorite spot and closed my eyes.

A chorus of frogs croaked around us, the waterfall cascaded over moss-slicked rocks, but all I heard that last night in Africa, as stars hung suspended above us, was the drumbeat of his heart. *Jack, Jack, Jack, Jack.*

T HE SKY WAS low and somber the next morning, as we drove to the airport, the squeak of wipers un-blurring the world every now and then. A fine drizzle fell around us as we turned in to the drop-off area.

There are moments that remain frozen in time—every sound, every color, every breath, crystallized into vivid shards of memory. Sitting in the idling car with Jack, outside the departures terminal, was one of them. Suitcases clattered over concrete slabs. The smell of diesel hung heavy in the air. Backpackers got off shuttle buses with colorful decals stuck to their luggage.

I conquered Mount Kilimanjaro

Kili—19,340 feet

A sea of faces moved through the doors, under the bright yellow letters of the departures building.

Jack and I watched silently. It was easier to focus on something outside of us. All the combinations, of all the letters, could not form a single word for what we wanted to say. We were circles and spirals and heart beats, rolled up into a glorious mess. We were a bundle of memories parked briefly in the drop-off zone.

"Don't come inside." I took my bag from Jack when we stepped out. "Please." My eyes pleaded with him. "I never learned to cry gracefully, like they do in the movies—with perfect, luminous tears rolling down my cheeks. I look like a withered crabapple when I cry."

"Rodel." He crushed me to him, my name falling from his lips in a hoarse whisper. Another car slid into the spot behind us, its hazard lights flashing rhythmically like the ticking of a clock.

Jack's arms tightened around me. "It's like a piece of me is being ripped away again. First Lily, now you. And yet . . ." His voice softened as he gazed me. "I wouldn't change a single thing. I would do it over and over again."

We said goodbye in the language of ghosts, with unspoken words and haunted longings, oblivious to everything and everyone around us.

"Kiss me hard, then let me go," I said, when the touch of his hand became suddenly unbearable in its tenderness.

I felt the movement of his breath before our lips touched. My heart throbbed at the sweet, savage sensation of his mouth. It was like running without air—breathless and beautiful. I clung to him for a soul-bursting moment, before wrenching myself away and stumbling toward the building. I paused for a beat as the sliding doors opened.

Turn around, Rodel, a part of me screamed.

Don't look back, the other part countered.

I turned. Because I couldn't help it. Because Jack honked.

He was sitting in the car, his palm splayed against the window in a frozen goodbye. Our eyes met through the droplets of water that clung to the glass like little pearls of silver. I retraced my steps, wheeling my bag behind me until I was standing beside his car. Then I lifted my hand and placed my fingers against his. The glass was wet and cold between us, but something warm and powerful hummed in my veins. When I removed my hand, my palm print was etched on the damp window, just like Lily's had been. As our gazes locked, I could feel the connection throbbing between Jack and me through that window. And it was enough. To know, and to have known.

I smiled.

A corner of his mouth tilted up in a way that made my heart skid.

I held on to that image as I walked through the sliding doors and checked in to my flight. As the plane took off, I watched the cars and buildings get smaller and smaller: the pastures where cows grazed, the fields of corn, the mud huts thatched with sheets of corrugated iron. And then the clouds were floating below us like spools of lambs' wool. I reached into my handbag for the little parcel that Goma had asked me to open on the plane. It was a lace handkerchief, tied into a pouch with a jute string. I was almost done opening it when I looked out of the window and caught my breath.

Kilimanjaro rose through the clouds, like a bride of the Gods, its ice-capped peaks glistening like a crown of majestic crystals. Silver mists swirled around the summit, changing and shifting under the rays of the sun. There was something delicate and poignant in the fleeting, moving play of light—the kind of beauty that only transient things can hold.

I blinked back the tears that trembled on my lashes. The mists reminded me of Mo and Lily, of the albino children who appeared and disappeared without a trace, of a love that reached for the summit, if only to kiss it goodbye.

A hot tear rolled down my cheek and splattered on Goma's handkerchief. I wiped my face and untied the knot that held it together. A bunch of M&M's spilled onto my lap. There was a note folded among them. I opened it and read Goma's bold handwriting.

"Chocolate makes everything better," it said.

I laughed. And sobbed. It came out like a strange snort.

"Are you all right?" the lady sitting next to me asked.

"Yes." I dabbed my eyes with Goma's handkerchief. "I just . . ."

I looked at Kilimanjaro and thought of a white manor with a green swing, sitting in the foothills. "I've been on a grand adventure."

"Well, I'm all ears. You must tell me about it."

"I wouldn't know where to start." I smiled at her and stared out the window.

Once in Africa, I kissed a king . . .

25

I FINISHED MARKING the last paper and flipped to the front to tally up the final grade. My pen wavered momentarily as I noted the student's name.

Jack.

Four letters strung together to form a name. Simple. Common. Ordinary.

Four letters that had held no meaning, but that now felt like I had fallen ten stories and hit the ground—*splat*—every time I came across it. How many Jacks had come and gone before him? None had warned of the Jack that was to come, the one whose name would leave me breathless in the middle of the day.

It was July in the Cotswolds, ten months since our rainy goodbye at the airport. Peach colored roses bloomed outside my window. Bees and butterflies darted from flower to flower. It was the end of another school year, my last day at work before the summer holidays. I finalized the exam marks and glanced around my classroom.

"You're still here?" Jeremy Evans popped his head into the room. He was a temp, filling in for the music teacher's maternity leave.

"Just leaving," I replied.

"Me too. You want to grab a drink? I'm heading to the pub for a pint."

"Thanks, but I'm going to pass." I powered down my laptop

and smiled at him. He was cute, with soft brown eyes and dark hair that curled on his forehead.

"Ouch." He clutched his chest. "Shot down again. You'll have to cave one day, even if it's just to shut me up."

"Have a good summer, Jeremy."

"*Ah*. I see what you did there. You just blocked me out of your entire summer. You might as well just shut the door in my face." And with that, he proceeded to drag himself out by the tie and slam the door behind him.

I was still smiling when I unchained my bicycle and headed home. How can you dislike anyone who makes you laugh? I cut through the cobblestone alleys that meandered around honey-hued cottages and little box hedges. Bourton-on-the-Water was a hot spot for tourists in the summer, and the main routes were teeming with visitors. It was a small price to pay for the way I felt every time I came home—the wooden gate, the slate blue door, swathes of yellow flowers spilling out of the window boxes, lavender growing wild against the golden stone.

I secured my bike and collected the mail—bills, a postcard from my parents, flyers . . . a letter from Tanzania. I unlocked the door and dropped the rest of my things on the couch.

I want a clean break, I'd said. And Jack had given me that. I hadn't heard from him since I'd left—no calls, no texts, no emails. Sometimes, when I thought of him on the porch, sitting on the swing and looking up at the stars, bombs exploded in my chest.

Is it you? I asked the letter sized envelope, my heart pounding as I tore it open.

It wasn't. But I laughed when I saw the photo that Bahati had sent. He was on a billboard, looking very debonair in a business suit, modeling a fancy watch. On the back, he'd written: *It's not the big screen I thought it would be, but it's pretty big :)*

A surge of aching pride filled me. Underneath all the fancy

stuff, Bahati was a warrior, every bit as fierce as his brothers and sisters in the *boma*. He had held fast to that tradition of pride and self-sufficiency. Not only had he come through when the children and I had needed him, he had also managed to carve out his own path while earning his father's respect, and more importantly, his own.

I climbed the stairs to my study with his photo in my hand. There, on a corkboard, I pinned it next to the Christmas card I'd received from Josephine Montati. She had stayed in touch, filling me in with updates on the children. I admired her for her tenacity, her dedication, and her passion. She was the kind of person who changed lives. And lives changed worlds.

My eyes fell on the photo she'd sent of Jack, Bahati, and me with the kids. I looked distracted. Jack was grinning.

What's the matter? Your English garden can't handle the tropical heat?

Yes. That was the moment pinned on my board.

How did you do that? I traced the lines of his face. *How did you tug and stretch and grow my heart, and make it sound like sweet, sweet music?*

I unpinned the photo and sank into my chair.

Life is good, Jack. Life is grand. I'm exactly where I want to be, doing exactly what I want to do. I love my job. My students amaze me. They inspire me. They challenge me. It's not always easy, but it's rewarding. I eat croissants in bed, and feed ducks I'm not supposed to feed. I buy overpriced candles and exotic teas. Last week, I went out for a plain white shirt and came home with silky camisoles. I sleep in. I take bubble baths. I think of you every time it rains. In a good way. Not with my withered crabapple face. I'm whole and centered and strong. I'm whole because you loved me for me, not for what I could be to you. And maybe that's why it hurts. Because your love was so good and pure. And it sucks. It sucks because my book boyfriends don't cut it anymore.

You've ruined me, Jack. But it's okay. I'm good, I'm well, I'm freaking magical. But you want to know something pathetic? I've subscribed to all kinds of flight alerts. Every time the price drops on airfares to Tanzania, I get a notification. And every time, I stare at the screen, a click away from getting on a plane so I can see your face again. Because I miss you. Because, so what if you didn't invite me? So what if the memory of me is starting to fade?

That's usually the point I tell myself you're a shithead, Jack. How could you let me go? How could you just go along with this no-contact bullshit and not fall apart like I do? So many times a day. Yup. You're a shithead, Jack. I hate that I miss you. Summer is here, and it's warm and beautiful, and I miss you. I miss you so much.

I held the photo to my chest and closed my eyes. Some circles never close, some wounds never heal. Love is like that. It leaves you forever open, forever vulnerable.

I took a deep breath and got up. It was time to move on, time to open the door and allow myself other possibilities, even though sometimes at night, if I listened closely, I could hear my heart saying *Jack, Jack, Jack, Jack.*

J EREMY EVANS ARRIVED early for our dinner date. The doorbell rang while I was drying my hair, upside down. I flipped it
back, ran my fingers through it, and went downstairs to get
the door.

"Hello, Rodel." It wasn't Jeremy. It was Andy, the estate agent
through whom I'd bought the cottage. He'd called to offer his con-
dolences on Mo's demise, but I had not seen him since I'd returned
from Tanzania. "I was in the neighborhood and thought I'd pop
in, see how things are going. Everything all right with the house?"

"Yes, thanks. Everything's fine. I'm really happy with it."

"Good, good." Andy shifted from one leg to the other. "Well.
I was thinking maybe you want to give it another shot and go for a
drink? The last time was . . . it was terrible, finding out about your
sister like that. I didn't want to rush you, but since I'm in the area
and all, I thought . . . you know. Why not?"

"That's very sweet, Andy." It wasn't going to happen, but he
was so earnest and awkward, I wanted to let him down gently. "I'm
actually waiting for my date. He should be here any minute now."

"Oh." He colored. "That's fine. I was just checking on the
cottage anyway." His eyes settled on the window box. "Nice flowers." He patted them like they were little old ladies. "Well. Have a
good . . . date." He waved goodbye and took off.

I shut the door and went back upstairs. My hair was still damp, but it would have to do. I was putting my makeup on when the doorbell rang again. I glanced at my watch. I still had fifteen minutes. I finished swiping on my lipstick and smoothed my dress. It was a pretty shade of coral, made for picnics and ice cream and sunshine. The skirt flared out and ended just above my knees. I picked up my sandals, grabbed my bag, and headed downstairs.

"I'm sorry, Jeremy. I'm not quite—" My heart slammed in my chest as a black-clad figure straightened, filling the entire frame with his broad-shouldered physique.

Not Jeremy.

Jack.

Jack Warden was standing at my door—dashing and beardless, his thick, tawny hair tapered neatly to his collar. T-shirt, jeans, polished oxford shoes, and a pair of ear buds dangling around his neck—a picture of devastatingly cool urbanity.

He looked good. He looked fucking amazing. And it packed a power punch right to my gut. The shock of seeing him, the shock of seeing him like *that*, with nothing obscuring his face—the square cut of his jaw, the way his lips looked rounder and fuller, his blue forget-me-not eyes, so vivid and real and in my face—it robbed me of my breath. I stood there frozen, sandals in my hand, gaping at him. And suddenly, it struck me. It struck me hard.

"I've been living with a broken heart all this time," I said it to myself, finally admitting the truth, but he caught my words.

A muscle clenched along his jaw. "You know what's heartbreaking?" He slipped his hands into his pockets, as if to keep them from touching me. "It's not when bad things happen to you, or when your life turns out completely different from what you thought it would be, or when people let you down, or when the world knocks you down. What's heartbreaking is when you don't get back up, when you don't care enough to pick up the million broken pieces of you that are screaming to be put back together, and you just lie there, listening to a shattered chorus of yourself.

"What's heartbreaking is letting the love of your life walk away, because you can't give up your work or your home to go with her, because everything you love gets taken away from you. So I'm saying no to heartbreak. Right here, right now. This is me getting back up, crossing an ocean and coming straight to your door, Rodel.

"I can't unlove you. And I can't stop thinking about you. So I'm here to say the words because I never said them and *that* is what's breaking my heart. I'm not saying them to hear it back. I'm not saying them so we can have a happily ever after. I don't know where you're at, or if you still think about us, or if we can even make it work. I'm saying them for me. Because they've been growing in my chest with every breath I take, and I have to get them out or I'll explode. I love you, Rodel Emerson. That's what I'm here to say. This is me, unbreaking my heart. I know it's selfish and thoughtless and just plain arrogant to show up like this, but I couldn't go another day without seeing you."

For a moment, I couldn't breathe. My chest was so full of absolute, unbelievable exhilaration that I didn't want to let a single breath out.

"You're late." The words came out choked and raw. And then I was conscious only of a low, tortured sob as I buried my face in his chest. He gathered me into his arms and held me snugly.

"My date ditched me," he whispered into my hair.

It felt like we were back at the orphanage, saying those words, reliving the intense relief of seeing each other again.

"Speaking of dates . . ." I tried to take a step back when I saw Jeremy approaching, but Jack wouldn't let me go. "Here comes mine."

"*Umm* . . . hello?" Jeremy tapped Jack on the shoulder. "I believe that's my date you're holding." He was a cocky fellow. I had to give him that. Persistent too.

Jack turned around, one arm wrapped possessively around my waist and looked at him. He didn't have to say anything. His massive, self-confident presence did all the talking.

"Riiiiiight." Jeremy backed up and shot me a questioning expression.

"Rodel." Jack kept his eyes fixed on him. "Did you make plans with this gentleman?"

"Yes. We were supposed to go out for dinner. I'm so sorry, Jeremy. Jack just showed up out of the blue."

"Is this a regular thing?" Jack's stance was one of studied relaxation, but his tone had an edge to it. "Are you two dating?"

"No. *Nuh-uh.*" Jeremy let out a nervous laugh. "It's the first time she said yes. But if I'd known you *er . . .*" He gestured to Jack. "Yeah, no."

"So where were you planning on taking my girl?"

"Well . . . there's this nice steak house by the river. It's very . . ." He glanced from Jack to me and coughed. "It's very romantic."

"You made reservations?"

"*Uh . . .* yes. Yes, I did."

"Mind if I tag along?"

"Pardon me?"

"Here's the thing, dear chap . . ." Jack tilted his head toward Jeremy and lowered his voice. "Rodel agreed to have dinner with you. And you, being the gentleman you are, decided to take her to a nice restaurant. And I, being the gentleman *I* am, realize that I showed up unannounced and ruined your plans. Now, I don't expect the lady to switch things around at the drop of a hat for me. At the same time, I'm not about to let her out of my sight. I'm also very, very hungry. Airplane food does not do it for me. So, I'm suggesting dinner. On me."

Jeremy blinked. Then he smiled. "Hell, yes. There's just one thing." He pointed to his Mini Cooper and looked at me. "You think he'll fit in there?"

Jack

27

I FELL IN love with Rodel Emerson somewhere between a tea party in the cradle of Africa and a nameless, roadside food stall with plastic chairs and plastic tables. Maybe it was when she asked me to lock her passport in my safe, and I read her name on it.

I was in love with a girl whose middle name was Harris.

My God, I was irrevocably, irreparably in love with her.

Her charm stole insensibly upon me—slowly at first, and then like a ton of bricks. I can't remember when I started thinking that her eyes were like the smooth river rocks I used to collect as a kid—dark and smoky, with a bright sheen that held me arrested when she laughed, or cried, or got riled up about having an old woman spit on her head. They were always different, always changing, sometimes the color of winter trees at twilight, other times like sunlight shining through Cognac. Her eyelashes were all girl, black and long. They made me believe how the flutter of butterfly's wings could cause a tsunami.

She had the kind of beauty that came from being disarmingly unaware of how pretty she was. Sometimes, I'd turn around and there she was, on her tiptoes, peering out the window at something beyond the horizon. The lines of her body fell into splendid poses, and once you looked at her, you couldn't look away. It wasn't because she was arrestingly beautiful. Wait. I take that back. She was. Hell, the night she came down the stairs, all dressed up, everyone at The Grand Tulip froze. But beyond that, she had an inner simplicity, an artlessness to her speech, her gestures, her smile. People relaxed around her. She saw you. She made you feel like you were someone too.

The first time I knew she was special was when I was heading inside from the fields. I heard her laughter spilling out from the kitchen window and I couldn't help but smile, even though it was just on the inside. Lily had done that to me. Her joy, her laughter, her giggles, used to make me stop and take notice. No one else had the right to make me feel that way again.

I resented Rodel Emerson that day. I resented her for poking holes in my armor, for making me feel anything but the pain that was running like a drug through my veins. I needed that pain, pure and unadulterated, to keep myself going each day. Without it, my knees would buckle and I'd give in to the darkness that was licking at the edges of my soul. I couldn't wait to get rid of the pretty girl with the pretty laughter and the pretty ideas about the world.

But Rodel Emerson didn't leave. And when she *did* leave, she was still always there—in the wind that ruffled the clothes on the laundry line, in the light that touched the soaring clouds, in the rain, in the moon, in the creak of the empty swing at night. And when I woke up, there she was again, in the dew of mist-kissed blades of grass.

I couldn't take a single step without colliding into the ghost of her.

So, I got on a plane. And I got into a Mini Cooper. And I got the most outrageously extravagant bottle on the wine list, as I watched her laugh at whatever her dinner date was saying. This was not a Coca-Cola moment. And she knew it. She knew I was taking in long, slow sips of her—all the parts I had missed and kissed and was going to claim when we got home. It didn't bother me that she'd said yes to this Jeremy fellow, or that he was sitting at the table. I was just relieved that she hadn't moved on. Hell, even Jeremy could feel the sparks zinging between Rodel and me. That's just the way it was, the way it would always be with us.

"Thanks for dinner," said Jeremy as I un-stuffed myself out of his car. "Have a good summer, Rodel."

"I see what you did there." She laughed. "You just blocked me out of your entire summer."

"Yeah. Well, this guy doesn't leave much room for anyone else, does he? But anytime you guys want to take me out for a steak dinner—"

"Never." I thumped the roof of his Mini Cooper. "I'm never getting into this sardine can on wheels again."

"Hey. Take it easy, mate." His voice rose a few octaves before he drove off.

"Sorry," I said, as Rodel linked her arm through mine and we walked into the house. "I didn't mean to leave a dent. Everything is so small around here. The homes, the streets, the cars. I'm used to wide open spaces, not bumping into dainty little things every time I turn around. I feel like a lion in a cag—"

"How could you?" She grabbed my collar and yanked me closer. "You show up unannounced, crash my date, and sit there, eating steak, while a million questions are swirling in my head."

Her lips were so close, I had to focus really, really hard on what she was saying.

"Rodel." My eyes swept over the delicately carved bones of her face. "I've thought about you every day for the last ten months. You think I didn't want to shut the world out the moment you opened the door? I was getting out of the taxi when some guy walked up to your place. I'd considered a lot of scenarios. I got on that plane knowing that things might have changed for you. It didn't stop me though. I had to see for myself. I had to know. But I wasn't prepared for it. When I saw that guy knocking on your door, I lost it. He could have been anyone. He could have been a stranger, a neighbor, a salesman. But in my head, he was holding you, kissing you, living the part I wanted to live.

"I wanted to punch him, Rodel. I wanted to pound the shit out of him. Then he left. And I still wanted to punch him, for blocking you out of my sight. I took a few minutes to steady myself. I had no right to be jealous. Whatever happened when I saw you—if you had someone in your life, if you didn't—it didn't matter. What we had was real. And I wasn't going back without saying the things I wanted to say to you.

"The second you opened the door, I knew—I knew you were still mine. So when that other guy showed up, I saw no point in ruining your plans. It's like when you open a bottle of fine wine. You don't just gulp it down. You take a moment to let it breathe. That's what dinner was about, Rodel. Letting us breathe. Because seeing you again went straight to my head. And right now, all I want to do is this . . ." My mouth swooped down and captured hers.

The taste of her was an anomaly I'd yearned for—sweet and wicked and gut-twistingly sexy, all rolled up in one. God, I'd missed her soft little mouth. I gathered her closer and deepened the kiss. How was it possible for anyone to feel like this? Like heaven in your arms?

"Remember what I told you?" Her hands snaked around my back.

"Baby, I can't even remember my name right now." I nuzzled her neck, losing myself in the scent of her hair.

"I said—" she grabbed a fistful of my hair and tugged my head back, "—if you're ever in England, I'm claiming this." She squeezed my ass, hard enough that she caught me off guard. "And this." She ran her tongue over my lips. "And this." She went where she absolutely should not have gone. All of my restraint left me.

"It's like that, *huh*?" I growled, scooping her up into my arms.

"In that case, let's get you somewhere you can stake your claim properly."

My intention was to carry her upstairs, but there was no way we were getting up there like that. Not on those stairs. I hit my head on the slanted ceiling and ended up shifting her in my arms, which ended up scraping her knee against the wall.

"Fucking small spaces." I let her down slowly, relishing the feel of her curves against me. "Are you okay?" I rubbed my head while she grinned.

"Come on." She grabbed my hand and pulled me behind her. Oh God, that ass.

Her room was exactly like I'd imagined. Cozy and comfortable. Books, pictures, muted walls, wild lavender in a vase on her dresser.

"What's this?" I picked up the paperback on her bed and opened it to the bookmark.

"Give me that." She tried to snatch it from me, but I held it away from her as I scanned the page.

"This is some sexy shit, Rodel." I started reading the scene out loud while she smacked me with her pillow. I held the book with one hand and fended her attacks with the other.

"Stop it!" She was breathing hard, both from the laughter and the flush of her one-sided fluffy combat. She was so beautiful, I stopped just so I could look at her.

"This is what passes for bedtime reading, *huh?*"

She tugged the book from my grasp and slid it under the bed. She was lying on top of me, her stomach moving in and out with the rise and fall of her lungs.

"I've missed you." She traced the lines of my face, her hair falling like a curtain around me. "You're like the broken chapter of my favorite story."

Something fierce trembled inside of me as I tucked one side of her hair behind her ear. How could I explain to her the hunger, the craving, the obsession? The small, sharp memories of her, always at the edge of my brain? I couldn't. So I kissed her. With all the words I couldn't form. My arms locked around her and she melted into me like a sigh.

It was soft, butter-smooth love. Heat rising under our skin. Clothes undone. A string of kisses on her breast. Her legs sliding against mine. The rapture of re-learning her curves. The indescribable fullness of holding her, of watching her body respond to the sensations I was making her feel.

I was hungry for her and hungry to pleasure her. With my hands and my lips and my tongue. I loved the way she came—body arched, mouth open, warm flesh quivering under my touch. Each time she reached her peak, I burned a little more, until the desire to possess raged through my blood like an inferno. There was a brief tear of a foil wrapper, and then I sank into her—deeply, completely.

God. The feel of her body opening up to me, molding around me like a warm, wet glove. Her tongue in my mouth. The way her hands clutched me. The way her leg wrapped around my hip. I bit her shoulder as the animal in me rose. And then it was all primal passion, nothing but the sound of her soft moans. My release should have been quick, but I held on, not wanting it to end. Being inside of her was like a drug. Being inside of her was pure euphoria. I captured the gasp that escaped her as her body stiffened. She was coming again.

"Yes," I growled as she writhed under me. "Fuck, yes." And then I gave in to the explosion of fiery sensations that overtook me, rocking me to the core.

In the aftermath, she slipped her leg between mine and put her head on my chest. I could feel her eyelashes against my skin every time she blinked. It was the tiniest flutter—the softest sensation—but it soothed the hot, brimming ache her absence had left. A wave of completeness washed over me as slowly, gradually, she closed her eyes and fell asleep in my arms.

The light from outside slipped through the blinds and made patterns on the wall. The night was different, so different from the farm. The sound of a lone, passing car, the muted conversations of people walking by, leaves slapping on the windowpane. My toes were hanging off her tiny bed. My head was resting on a ruffled, floral-print pillow. Bobby pins lay scattered on the floor. Perfume and lotion and little jars sat on the dresser. I smiled and drew Rodel closer. She nuzzled into me with a sigh of pleasure.

I was miles from home, but I felt exactly like I belonged.

I WOKE UP early the next morning. For a few long, languid moments, I lay in bed enjoying the warmth of the woman sleeping beside me. My eyes roved over her brow, the small hairs that blended into her hairline, the pink, soft cushion of her lips. I placed the tip of my little finger in the groove between her nose and upper lip. The *philtrum*. I had looked it up. It was mine. It fit me perfectly. Just like the rest of her. Every part of me was made to fit every part of her.

My desire stirred, hot and heavy, under the covers. I wanted her with a craving that knew no depth. She was beautiful and devastating. Just like love should be. I could spend forever in the corners of her mind and never get bored. I could kiss her lips every morning and still not learn all the flavors of her soul. I was gone for this girl—so far gone that it terrified me.

I pulled the comforter over her and slipped out of bed, smiling as she snuggled deeper. We had woken up and gone at it again. And then again. I had exhausted her. In the best possible way.

Take that, I said to the naughty paperback lying on the floor. Then I paused and flipped through it. *Hmm. Maybe we can do this tonight. No. This. This is even hotter. Holy fuck.*

When Rodel came downstairs, I was on the couch, feet propped up, eyeballs deep in a romance novel.

"Really?" She crawled on top of me and kissed me. "I don't

know which I find sexier. You reading this book or the morning stubble on your face." Her fingers traced my jawline. "I'm still not used to seeing you without the beard."

"Does it feel different when I do this?" I pulled her in and reclaimed her lips.

"Wait!" She rescued the book getting crushed between us. "Oh. My. God. Did you bend the corners of my book?" She sat back on her heels and flipped through it.

"Just the parts I think we should re-enact."

"Jack." She shook her head in woe. "You never, *ever* fold a corner over in a book."

"You're so hot when you go all book-nerd on me." Her night-shirt was riding high on her thighs, her lips were pouty, and she was cradling the book as if it were a hurt child. "Do you know—" I flipped her over so she was on all fours, her nose lodged in the folds of the novel "—I have sex with you a lot. In my head. Just like this." I squeezed her sweet ass and rubbed my throbbing shaft over her panties. "Read to me, Rodel. Read to me while I ride you." I pushed the fabric of her panties aside and slipped my finger inside of her. She let out a muffled groan.

"Are you burying your face in that book? Rodel." I tsked. "You never, *ever* manhandle a book like that. This sexy ass, yes." I slapped her full, round cheek. "But the book . . ." I grabbed her hair and tugged so she was looking down at the pages before her. "Read it, Rodel. Unless you want me to stop?" I slid another finger inside her and nipped the back of her neck.

Her voice quivered as she started reading the passages aloud. She kept losing track. I kept reminding her. A little yank, a little spank, to keep her head in the game. Her body squirmed against mine, engulfing my senses, engorging my passion, until the air was thick with hot, heated need.

She opened her mouth to say something, but as I thrust into

her, the book fell away and the only word that escaped her was: *"Un-ghhh."* It was a throaty, unintelligible whisper that was mind-blowingly hotter than all the erotic words I'd made her read.

SUNDAY BRUNCH WITH Rodel, in her kitchen—one that I'd tried to envision many times over the long, lonely months without her. Her kitchen. Her bathroom. What she came home to. What kind of plates she used. What she saw outside her window. Piece by piece, my mind gathered all the little, missing bits like a scavenger on a treasure hunt.

We sat around the weathered island that doubled as her dining table. The paint had rubbed off around its corners and edges. Like everything else, it looked homey and lived-in. The overhead beams, the angled ceilings, the worn patina of the walls—they all took on a soft, bright hue as sunshine streamed in through the windows.

Rodel poured herself a cup of coffee and stirred two heaping teaspoons of sugar into it. She padded over to the refrigerator, stuck her head inside, and began moving things around.

God, did she have any idea what she looked like, bent over like that?

"No Coca-Cola." She straightened and turned around. "Orange juice?"

I grinned. A part of me wanted to tell her to keep looking. "Orange juice is fine." It made me ridiculously happy that she remembered what I liked to drink in the morning.

She took a sip of her coffee and waltzed over to the cabinet to get me a glass. She was pouring the juice when I took the carton from her and set it on the counter. I drew her to me so we were eye to eye, her standing between my legs, as I sat on the stool.

"Good morning, Miss Emerson." I kissed the pulsing hollow at the base of her throat. I couldn't get enough of her. I had lived far too many days and nights without the feel of her.

"It's past noon now." She laughed. "Good afternoon, Mr. Warden."

Her warm, soft lips were intoxicating, but when she swirled her tongue inside, exploring the recesses of my mouth, desire stirred between my legs. But only for a moment, because something else hit me. I reared my head back and frowned.

"What's wrong?"

"Do that again. Kiss me."

"Yes, sir." She grinned and reclaimed my lips, her arms looping around my neck as she kissed me, slow and deep.

"That's weird," I said. "I'm not gagging."

"I should hope not." Her eyebrows arched up. "You're surprised my kisses aren't making you gag?"

"No. Not your kisses." I slid her cup toward her. "The coffee. I can taste it on you."

A light seemed to go off in her head. She took another sip of her coffee and kissed me. This time the flavor of it was hot and strong in her mouth—sweet as hell because of all the sugar she'd dumped into it, but smooth and full-bodied, with a slightly nutty overtone.

"Kona coffee," I murmured against her lips. "From Hawaii."

"Very good." She stepped back and looked at me. It didn't matter where the hell it came from. What mattered was that it hadn't made me sick or nauseated. "Would you like some?" She poured me a cup and watched as I inhaled the aroma of it.

I took a tentative sip and waited for the awful gagging that had plagued me ever since the mall attack.

Nothing.

In fact, my taste buds cried for more.

Coffee. My weakness, my livelihood, my passion. I'd processed close to a year's worth of harvest without a single cup. Tasting it on Rodel, mingled with her sweet breath, had cured me. Or maybe she'd cured me with that first kiss. Or the time she told me she loved me. I would never know. All I knew was that she filled all the aching, gaping holes in my heart.

"Are you okay?" she asked, as I held my coffee and stared at the way the sun picked up the honeyed flecks in her eyes.

"I'm fine," I lied. *Have you ever sat across from someone, fully clothed, and felt them slowly unbutton your heart?* I reached for her hand and squeezed. "I've missed you. So much that my heart still hurts."

"Good." She stuffed a pastry in her mouth. "ImphgladImphnottheomphnlyone."

I chuckled and had some more coffee. "What are we doing today?" I knew what I wanted to do. Absolutely nothing. Except, possibly, to get a bigger bed.

She dropped her pastry and went quiet. "How long are you staying, Jack?"

I didn't know how to say the next part because I knew she'd fight me. "How long would you like me to stay?"

"Ha." She threw me a small smile and went about clearing the counter.

"Hey." I hugged her from behind as she put the dishes in the sink. "Tell me. Talk to me."

"What if I said I want you here, always and forever?" She held her head high, eyes on the windowsill.

I swallowed. She had the guts to ask of me what I had not been able to ask of her. "What if I said okay? What if I said I'd stay? Always and forever."

She stiffened in my arms. The tap dripped little droplets of water into the bowl.

"That's not funny."

"Does it look like I'm trying to be funny?" I nudged her around.

She searched my face with her coffee-bean eyes. "You can't . . . you can't just walk away from the farm. It's your home, your legacy. And then there's Goma."

"Yes, and she kicked my ass for not coming sooner. She said if she caught me moping around the farm one more day, she'd get her rifle and put me out of my misery herself. She threatened to sell her share of the farm and be done with it, if that's what was keeping me from you. She said she wants to go on endless cruises for the rest of her life, see the world, take Zumba classes, and dance on the decks all night, from the money she'd make off it."

A small chuckle escaped Rodel before she sobered up. "She's lying. That farm is everything to her. And so are you."

"I know." I stroked her cheek, wanting to wipe away the look in her eyes, the one that said we could never be. "Sometimes we have to let go of the people we love *because* we love them—because their hopes and dreams lie elsewhere. It's the reason I let you go, the reason I never asked you to stay. And it's why Goma is letting me go, because my heart is already with you, all day, every day. So if you want me, always and forever, here I am."

I'd pictured her eyes lighting up when I told her. I thought she'd go a little giddy. My rainbow-haloed, all-or-nothing girl. But she just stared at me, her eyes sheening over, and it just about did me in. Bloody hell.

"No." I kissed the tip of her nose. "Stop it, Rodel. I didn't come all this way for a crabapple."

She laughed, a little splutter, and wiped her eyes. "I thought you loved all my faces."

"I do, sweetness." I tugged her closer, my arms tightening around her. "And I want to spend the rest of my life learning them all."

She didn't say anything for a while. She just rested her head on my chest and let me hold her.

"I would have stayed." Her words were muffled against my shirt. "If you'd asked, I would have stayed."

My heart swelled with emotion. I knew she would have. She would have given it all up for me. So how could I not do the same for her?

S HE MADE SPACE for me in her wardrobe. She barely had enough of her own. I liked the way my shirts looked next to her clothes—like they belonged.

"It's just for now," she said, leaning back on the bed and watching me like she could read my mind. "I won't let you do it. I won't let you give up the farm."

She was stubborn as hell, and she drove me nuts.

"You're still fighting me on this?" I zipped up my empty bag and stowed it under her bed. "I show up, willing to rebuild my whole life around you, and this is what I get?"

"Hey, you got six inches of closet space That's not too shabby at all."

"Oh yeah?" I grabbed her ankles and pulled her to the edge of the bed, so my hips were nestled between her legs. "How is that fair, considering you get *more* than six inches. Every time."

"Show off." She colored and wiggled away from me.

"Tease." I loved that I could never tell what I was going to get with her. Sometimes coy. Sometimes bold. "I have something for you." I walked over to the wardrobe and reached for the jacket hanging there. "From Scholastica." I retrieved a letter from the inside pocket and handed it to her.

Her eyes lit up as she read it. It was a single sentence that took up the whole page.

"I've been writing to her. It's good practice for both of us."
She pointed to an English-Swahili dictionary on her shelf. "She
writes in English, I reply in Swahili."

I knew that. I drove an hour to the post office in Amosha to
mail Scholastica's letters. I might even have encouraged it. Because
when the reply came, I held it close, all the way back, hoping to
catch Rodel's scent on it.

"What about Billy?" I asked. "Do you write to Billy?"

"I'm never going to live that one down." She laughed.

"Not if I can *helpi* it. But I could be persuaded to forget."

"What do you have in mind?"

"For starters . . ." I sat on the floor beside the bed, facing away
from her. "That thing you do with your fingers in my hair." I leaned
back and gave myself up to the feel of her massaging my scalp.

"So, how is Scholastica?" she asked, rubbing slow circles that
made me want to purr under her touch. "Did Inspector Hamisi
come up with anything regarding her father?"

"Unfortunately, no. Gabriel is now officially listed as a missing
person. We're pretty sure there was some kind of foul play involved,
but we'll never know. It breaks my heart sometimes, when I look at
Scholastica. Her father was an exceptional man. I've always known
about the terrible things that happen to kids like Scholastica, but I
never did anything about it. But Gabriel, he was helping them all
along, quietly, without any kind of compensation, way before any
of us got involved. He probably lost his life for it, and no-one will
ever recognize him for what he did. One day, when Scholastica is
old enough, I'll make sure she knows that her father was a hero.
I'll make sure she's proud of what he did and what he stood for."

"Jack?" Rodel's fingers stilled. "What happens to Scholastica
if you're here? Goma can't look after her on her own."

"Goma won't have to." I turned around and looked at her.
"Josephine Montati offered Gabriel's sister a job at the orphanage.

Anna feels like she's been given the opportunity to continue with her brother's work, and she's looking forward to having her niece back. She's thrilled they can all be together again. We've been working on new housing for the kids and staff. Once that's done, Scholastica will be moving in with her cousins and aunt."

"That's great." Rodel nodded, as if trying to convince herself. "That's really great."

"But . . . ?"

"But you're going to miss her. I can see you're already missing her."

It hurt like hell to let another little girl into my life, and then let her go. As hard as I tried to keep it from showing, I couldn't hide it from Rodel. "This isn't about me. It's about what's best for Scholastica. She'll always have me, but now she'll be with her family, in Wanza. I think that's what Gabriel would want for her. And I'll still be working with Josephine and Anna. It's an ongoing process. Books, supplies, medical care. We need to put all those systems in place."

Rodel chewed on her lip for a while, but she couldn't keep her thoughts from spilling out. "That's just a Band-Aid, isn't it? You can throw all the money in the world at it, but it won't solve the problem. These kids will keep showing up at the orphanage until people start thinking differently, until they stop believing the superstitions about them."

It was true, and I couldn't deny it. I folded Scholastica's letter and put it back into the envelope. None of it was easy. For anyone.

You're needed there, Jack," said Rodel. "Goma needs you. The orphanage needs you. The farm needs you."

"And what about what I need?" Something flared up inside me. "You think this is easy for me? You think I want to be standing here, arguing over stuff that I've turned over in my head every single day? I'm here because *I* need *you,* but if you're going to start piling up the reasons against us, then we might as well call it quits. Right here, right now." I glowered at her and stomped down the stairs. I bumped my head on the ceiling again and glowered at it too.

"Small beds, small closets, small fucking stairs," I growled.

She came down a little while later, holding her handbag and an umbrella. "We need to go to the hardware store." She looked at me expectantly.

"What for?" I was still pissed.

"To get something for the dents you keep leaving every time you come down these small fucking stairs."

It was her way of telling me she wanted me to stay. No more arguments over it.

"What's the magic word?"

"*Pleasi*?" Her Swahili was hopeless, but her voice was soft, and her eyes held a twinkle because she knew she had me.

"Surely you can handle a trip to the hardware store yourself, Harris."

"What did you call me?" Her eyes widened.

"That's right. I know your dirty little secret."

"How did y—"

"Get your cute butt over here and give me a fucking kiss." I patted my lap. "I'm not going anywhere until I have make-up sex. With Harris."

A wicked smile curled her lips. "Oh, you want to meet Harris?"

She slipped the handbag off her shoulder. It dropped to the floor with a *thunk*. She tossed the umbrella and stripped for me, one slow button at a time, giving me little peeks of the lacy bra she had on underneath.

Fuck my heart.

I had the feeling I was really, really going to enjoy meeting Harris.

I T WAS SUMMER, the English countryside was beautiful, and
I refused to take a single moment for granted. I couldn't remember the last time I had days to myself, days that I lavished
on Rodel. We stayed at a quaint bed and breakfast, and woke up
brushing our teeth next to horses munching hay outside our window. We had fish and chips, wrapped up in newspaper. I doused
mine with vinegar. Rodel dunked hers in ketchup. Some evenings,
we sat on Rodel's terrace, watching the golden bricks change from
ochre to copper to cognac-brown in the light of the setting sun.
We chilled at the local pub until the streets were empty and walked
home holding hands and making up lyrics to long-forgotten songs.
I felt a stab of guilt every time I thought about the farm, but it was
up for sale, and I had hired someone to look after the front end of
things until we accepted an offer. Goma started hanging up on me
after a while and told me I was cramping her style.

Rodel's parents came up to see us. We explored forts and pal-
aces, dotted amongst the charming villages. I got the green light
after her father examined my hands. The dirt was slowly fading
from under my nails.

"They're good hands," he declared. "Big, strong, good hands!
Hell, any man that can get my daughter's nose out of those books
gets my vote." He bought me another round of beer, while Rodel
and her mother sang god-awful karaoke under the dim lights.

"Are you sure you're not adopted?" I asked, the morning after they left.

"Mo looked more like them." She stirred her coffee absently. "I wish they'd stayed one more night, especially since today marks a year since the mall attack."

I clasped my hand over hers. We were sitting on the terrace, overlooking the river, with a haze of lavender and roses around us. It was incredible to think that I had survived a whole year without Lily. A lot of it had to do with the beautiful woman sitting across from me.

"Hey." I couldn't stand the sadness on her face. "I forgot to show you something." I turned on my phone and played a video for her.

"Oh, my God." She smiled. "It's Bahati. And Olonana. But Olonana's limping. I guess he never completely recovered from his encounter with K.K.? What are they doing?"

"It's a Maasai ceremony. Bahati is getting his warrior name." I watched the clip with her and explained what was happening.

"And that's what Bahati is wearing?" She laughed. "Designer jeans, designer T-shirt, and an elaborate tribal headdress."

"He's straddling two worlds, and they're both equally valid. I don't think he'll ever turn his back on either. It's who he is, and he's proud of it."

"Oh, and there's Lonyoki, their shaman! What's he saying?" She strained to catch his words. "What warrior name did he just give Bahati?"

"Damn if I know." I chuckled. "He still goes by Bahati. He said it's too much of a hassle to change everything on his social media."

"So, he's okay? He's made up with his father, but he still gets to do what he loves?" she asked, as Olonana and Bahati stood side by side for pictures.

"I guess Olonana figured he has enough kids to let one slip

out of the *boma*. I think he's rather proud of Bahati for finding his own way." I put my phone away, and we finished the rest of our breakfast.

We were about to head back inside when I spotted something floating by in the river. Well, what they liked to call a river. I called it a wading pool. It was barely a foot deep, and the water was so clear, you could see the stones at the bottom. Maybe it turned into a real river farther along, or when it rained. When I thought of a river, I thought of crocodiles lolling on the banks.

"Rodel, there's a rubber ducky bobbing in the water."

"Oh, God." She slapped her forehead. "I completely forgot. There's a rubber duck race for charity, today. I volunteered to help." She glanced at her watch and grabbed my hand. "Come on. We can still make it."

Throngs of people were already lined up on the footbridges that spanned the river. Some of them were in the water, trousers rolled over their knees, as bright rubber ducks got launched off one bridge and made their way serenely toward them.

"The suspense is real, Rodel. I'm not sure I can handle the tension."

"Go sponsor a duck." She pushed me toward the table next to hers. "I'm going to be a while."

I would never, ever in a hundred years have thought I'd say the words that came out of my mouth next, but I said them. For her.

"I'd like to sponsor a rubber ducky, please."

"That'll be ten quid." One of the volunteers took my money and handed me a duck. "Good luck, mate."

I held the little plastic toy in the palm of my hand. It stared back at me with its orange beak. "All right, little fellow. Show me what you've got." I found a spot to launch my duck off. People seemed to just part for me. I took it as a good sign. My duck was a badass. Rodel waved at me madly as I stood there, towering over everyone else on the bridge.

"Don't let me down in front of my woman," I said to my duck, as I held it over the water, waiting for the next launch signal.

"Excuse me, sir." A heavy hand fell on my shoulder. "I'm going to have to ask you to stop right away."

I turned around to face a solemn policeman, with a baton in his hand.

"We've just received a complaint," he said. "Apparently, there's an ancient bylaw which says that the river and village green cannot be used on Sundays for fund-raising purposes."

I scanned the area and noticed police cars all around us. Uniformed officers were pulling people away from the bridges and scooping yellow, plastic birds out of the water. Rodel was folding away her table.

"No rubber ducky race?" I asked.

"I'd advise you to let it go, or face arrest."

For a moment, I considered letting my little duck go.

Run. Swim free, my friend.

I could claim I misunderstood the policeman's instructions. But I pulled my duck out of the water and straightened. "It's a little heavy-handed, don't you think?"

"Just doing my job." He seemed embarrassed.

"Everything all right?" Rodel walked up to us and stopped by my side.

"He won't let me play with my rubber ducky, Rodel."

"It's okay." She smiled at the officer and started pulling me away from him. "I've got him."

I held on to my duck as she steered me toward a tearoom across the bridge.

"This is your solution to the atrocity we just witnessed?" I had to stoop to enter the establishment. "A tea party?"

She ignored me as the waitress sat us down at a table by the window. We watched the police drag the ducks away in fishing nets and lock them up in their vehicles.

"I'm sorry you had to see that," Rodel said to my duck, turning it away from the window.

My shoulders started shaking. I couldn't contain the great booming laughter that rolled from my mouth. I had been holding it back for too long. Rodel's face split into a grin. And then we were hunched over the table, laughing until our ribs hurt. Around us, polite patrons held their sandwiches mid-air, watching us like we'd lost our minds.

"No." I shook my head when the waitress finally got the nerve to come up to our table with a teapot. "Coffee for me."

I could finally drink the stuff. Nothing else was going to cut it for me now.

Rodel ordered for us and sat back in her chair. "I love when you laugh." Her voice was soft as she gazed at me. "You know what's amazing?"

"What?"

"That we're both sitting here laughing, a year to the day that we lost Mo and Lily."

Our hands met silently across the table and held, taking comfort in each other.

"I called Sarah today," I said. We hadn't talked since Lily's funeral, but I knew she missed her just as much as I did, and today of all days, I felt the need to reach out to my ex.

"And?"

I shook my head. "I don't think she's ever going to forgive me for what happened to Lily."

Rodel squeezed my hand softly. "People will love you. People will hate you. And it always has more to do with them, than it does with you."

We sat in comfortable silence, lost in our thoughts, until our food arrived.

On the way home, Rodel nudged me into a newspaper shop. "Let's go in here."

Metal signs and fridge magnets hung on the walls. Porcelain dolls were lined up in a glass display case by the cash register.

"I'll be right back. You look around," said Rodel, making her way to the back of the store.

I tinkered with the wind chimes while I waited for her.

"Ready!" she announced.

I turned around and froze. Her face was almost lost behind a bouquet of six yellow balloons.

"Do you still keep them in your study?" she asked.

"Some people like to keep flowers in their room. I like yellow balloons."

"Well, come on then." She dragged me out by my hand.

"Where are we going?" The sight of her walking down the street like that, reminded me of Lily running ahead of me in the mall, holding her balloons. It did something to my heart.

The banners from the ill-fated duck race hung over us as she led me back to one of the arched stone bridges that spanned the river. The crowds had dispersed, and the river stretched out before us. A few tourists sat on the grassy banks. Beech, willow, and chestnut trees swayed in the summer breeze.

"Here." Rodel handed me the balloons as we stood on the bridge. "For Lily."

My throat clogged up as I took them from her. I picked three of the strings out and gave them to her. "For Mo."

Her eyes turned bright with unshed tears, but she gave me a smile. "Together?"

"Together."

We let the balloons go and watched them drift away into the sky. It was paradise-blue, infinite and endless.

Something floated up inside me, light as a feather, as the balloons soared higher and higher. Lily's last words: *See you on the other side.*

"See you on the other side, baby girl," I repeated mine to her.

Rodel looped an arm around my waist as the balloons disappeared from our view. I kissed the top of her head and we started walking away from the bridge.

"Excuse me, sir." A heavy hand fell on my shoulder.

I turned around to face the same policeman from earlier.

Fuck this shit.

"Let me guess," I said. "There is an ancient by-law which says no balloons on Sundays?"

He held his hand out expectantly.

"*Ah.*" I held out the rubber ducky that was tucked under my arm. "We weren't going to put it in the water."

If anything, he looked even sterner.

"Really? Not even in my bath?"

He cleared his throat and gave us a curt nod. "Very well, then. Carry on."

I waited until he was off the bridge before giving my duck a squeeze and honking after him.

"Jack!" Rodel slapped my arm.

"We saved one." I held the chubby little bird before her. "We need to return it to its natural habitat."

A BUBBLE BATH.

But just for the duck and Rodel. I couldn't get in without all the water overflowing.

"Small fucking tub," I said, as I dipped the sponge into the water and rubbed her back.

"No one said love is easy." She leaned her head over the edge and looked at me, upside down.

"Big love, you said." I repeated the words she'd said to me on the swing, the night we'd returned from Wanza. "Huge, you said." I brushed my lips across her forehead. "You left out the small spaces part."

Her laughter was like bright, cheery dandelions upon the field. I couldn't get enough of it. I'd do anything to make it happen again and again.

She slid back up and went quiet on me. "I miss Tanzania."

"It's just a plane ride away. Say the word and we can visit. Any time you like." I poured water over her soapy shoulders.

"No." She stilled my hand. "I don't mean to visit. Today, when I saw you release those balloons, I realized that you were with me when you should have been with Lily. Under that tree. By her side. If Mo's body had ever been recovered, that's where I'd want to be. I don't have that, but you do. And it's not just Lily. It's your parents, your grandfather, your whole family."

"Let's not get into this again, Rodel." I started getting up.

"You're not listening." She clamped down on my wrist. "I said *I* miss Tanzania. I love this place," she gestured around us, "but Tanzania . . . it changed me. It was like discovering something I didn't know I was searching for. I haven't been the same since. I would have stayed, Jack, but I couldn't just jump in, not one-sided like that. I needed you to hold my hand because it was scary, because I couldn't do it alone." She traced the silver scar on my arm, a reminder of my confrontation with K.K. "I miss Goma and Scholastica and Bahati. I miss the earthy, musky aroma of the land. I miss the snow-capped peaks and the baobab trees. I miss the wild jasmine on the porch. I miss the potholes and Stoney Tangawizi. I miss the frustration, the anger, the wonder, the excitement, the tranquility."

I listened to her quietly. I knew exactly what she meant. Tanzania was in my blood, my skin, my bones. To hear her say she missed it scared the hell out of me, because it opened up possibilities I had never dared to hope for. It had always been either Rodel or the farm. And I had picked one. Home was wherever she was, and it didn't matter if I banged my head on the ceiling each time I went down the stairs. I was that crazy for her.

"I'm in a bit of a bind because I've committed to the mortgage here." She was babbling, more to herself than to me. "I could sell it, though. And hand in my resignation at the school. But what would I do at the farm? I'd have to find a job. But we're in the middle of nowhere. Then again, what would you do here? I know you. You won't be able to sit on your hands for long, doing nothing."

"I could grow lavender," I interrupted her stream of thought. "We could have a lavender farm. I know the earth and I know the sky. Between the two, I can grow almost anything. We can have babies with pink, round cheeks. Rubber duckies all over the place. You can continue teaching. Or not. Whatever you want."

"Babies." She smiled. "With you." Her eyes had a faraway look, as if she were imagining their little faces. "Paint me another picture, Jack." She closed her eyes and leaned back. "But this time, in Tanzania."

"I could keep the farm. You could keep the cottage. It would be our little love nest. You'd pick coffee, and put up with a cranky old lady. Your boss would demand all kinds of inappropriate things from you. The hours would be long. The salary would be peanuts—just enough to make payments on the cottage. We'll visit Scholastica. Bahati can sit in the back with Goma, but to her left. She's half deaf in that ear now, so that works out great. We can make babies with pink, round cheeks. Rubber duckies all over the place. You can home-school them, and maybe some of the other kids too. They travel a long way to get to school right now. You could teach them how to think, instead of what to think, so when they grow up, they're better people than us. But it would be your call. Whatever you want."

The yellow ducky bobbed as Rodel remained silent, her eyes

still closed. The top of her nipple peeked out at me through the bubbles. Wet strands of her hair disappeared under the surface. A soft curve touched her lips. Wherever she was in her head, it was a good place.

"Yes," she said, when she finally opened her eyes. "I want that very much."

"Which part?"

"All of it. I want it all with you. Here. There. It doesn't really matter." She came up to the edge of the tub until I could feel her breath on my lips. "But right now, when I opened my eyes, the picture that stayed with me was a green swing on the porch of a beautiful, white house. That's what's tugging at my heart. So that's what I'm going with. Let's go to Tanzania, Jack. Let's give it a shot."

There was genuineness and excitement in her voice—a spark of something that left me with no doubt that it was what she wanted, not for me, but for herself. Turns out she was an adventurer, after all—an explorer, just like the rest of her family. She was ready to take a leap with me, and it made my heart grow impossibly larger.

I captured her wet lips and was overwhelmed with the need to absorb her, to soak her in through every pore of me. I shrugged out of my clothes and got into the tub, first one leg, and then the other. Rodel squealed. The rubber duck honked as I squished it. Water spilled all over the floor.

It was slippery and uncomfortable and completely crazy, but we laughed because we were high on love and the fumes of endless possibilities.

"Hell, yes," I growled, my teeth grazing the soft, creamy expanse of her neck. "Let's go to Tanzania. But I hope you remember what I said. If you ever set foot there again, I'm going to claim you. You're mine, Rodel Harris Emerson. All mine."

31

ON THE DAY of our wedding, Aristurtle ran away from home. Scholastica had taken him out of his box so she could clean it. She turned around, and he had busted loose.

"Good for him." Goma adjusted her fedora. No feathery, flowery hat for her. "If *you* lived up to 150 years, you wouldn't want to spend it in that shit box either." She lifted the half-curtain in the kitchen and clucked at the search party that was supposed to be looking for him:

Bahati, the best man and honorary maid of honor, taking selfies in his sponsored suit.

Scholastica, our flower girl, twirling through the coffee plants in her new dress, while her Aunty Anna chased after her with a hat.

Anna's kids, playing hopscotch in the dirt, white socks rolled up in their shoes.

Rodel's parents, trying to talk Olonana into selling them his earrings.

"Aristurtle could crawl up their leg and bite them in the ass, and they wouldn't notice," said Goma. "And you." She turned to me and tried to adjust my tie, but she couldn't quite reach the knot. "No peeking in the living room."

Hair, Makeup, and Wardrobe were holed up in there with Rodel—the same girls who'd come to the hotel. I couldn't wait to see Rodel in her wedding dress, but holy crap, how long was this taking?

Goma chuckled as I paced the floor. "Jack . . ." She trailed off and patted the chair beside her.

"I wish your grandfather were here," she said, when I sat down. "He'd have been so proud. Your father and mother, too." She stared at the table and nodded absently. "And Lily . . ." Her voice cracked as she said it. A lump formed in my throat. I put my arm around her and pulled her in. She laid her head against my shoulder, and we shared a sweet, silent moment.

"I'm tired, Jack," said Goma. "But seeing you and Rodel together gives me new breath. You better make some babies soon. Not for me, of course. I hate babies. Screaming, pooping, useless little things. But just so you can go fuss over someone else and leave me the hell alone."

"I don't fuss over you."

"Oh yeah? I sleep in a couple of hours and you're tiptoeing outside my door. I'm not going to croak in my sleep, Jack. That's not my style."

I chucked. "Well, you might be putting up with one of those screaming, pooping, useless little things soon."

"No!" Goma slapped my arm. "Yes? Tell me!"

"Careful. I might start thinking you actually care."

"I just want to know so I can plan my cruise around it. I'll be back when it's out of diapers and sleeping through the night."

"You're not going anywhere, Goma. You're going to need someone to change your own diapers soon."

"Shut your filthy mouth." But she grinned and looked at me like she always did—like I meant the world to her.

"We're ready!" One of the girls popped her head out of the living room. Josie. Or Melody. Or Valerie. I could never get it right.

I tried to say something but ended up grinning like an idiot. Rodel was on the other side of the wall. Ready to walk down the aisle.

"Thank you," said Goma, piping in for me. "We'll start getting everyone to the barn."

We'd cleaned out the barn and moved the animals to the sheds. String lights and chandeliers hung across the wooden beams. Most of the guests were already seated when we entered. Bahati stood by my side as we waited for Rodel. Jodie, Valerie, and Melody walked in first. Bahati's phone pinged. He glanced at it quickly and typed a reply. Across the room, another phone went off. One of the girls that had just entered jumped in her seat to silence it.

"Which one is it?" I asked Bahati.

"No idea what you're talking about." He turned his phone off and gave me a cheeky smile.

Scholastica was up next. Her smile was as big as the moon as she headed toward me, forgetting to scatter the flowers as she came up. I chuckled as she presented me with a basket full of petals. She'd saved them all for me.

And then Rodel walked in, and the whole world stilled. It had been a year since we'd returned from England, and she still managed to steal my breath away. Her shoulders gleamed as she stood in soft silhouette against the entrance. She wore her hair down and held a single lily. She was a vision in the dress that Goma had sewn for her. It was knee-length, with a fitted bodice and a tulle skirt that flared out from the waist. The hemline wasn't completely even, but no one wanted to challenge Goma's eyesight.

Rodel's father probably escorted her down the aisle, but everything else faded. I had eyes only for her. It seemed to take forever for her to reach me.

Come on. Come on.

When she finally got to my side, I wanted to skip ahead to the part where I got to kiss her. Delicate blooms of jasmine were tucked in her hair. I wanted to pick one and run it up and down the graceful curve of her neck.

"I turn around for two seconds and you're in the middle of a tea party," she said.

"You like?" I smiled.

Around us, guests were gathered on small, round tables. Teapots and tiered trays sat on burlap table runners.

"A tea party on a coffee farm." She smiled back. "I like."

The next few hours passed by in a blur. Renegade hens crashed the wedding party. Rodel discovered that a lot of the tea was actually booze. Olonana got tipsy and hit on Goma. Josephine Montati gave us a wedding card signed by the children from the orphanage. I danced with Rodel's mother. Bahati danced with Hair. Then Makeup. Then Wardrobe. There was no telling which one he'd been texting. Inspector Hamisi wanted to know if the circuits were set up to handle all the extra lights. The Maasai *morans* that had come with Olonana had a dance-off with the farm hands. Scholastica and Anna's kids stole sips of adult tea when no one was watching. Olonana's mother spit on us.

As the sun began to set, I pulled Rodel into the stall where she had first kissed me. There, as the golden light fell on her, I aimed my Polaroid camera at us.

"Wait!" She fished for something inside her bodice. "I've been waiting to use this all day." She pulled out a Post-it note, on which she'd written our wedding details:

August 11th—Jack & Rodel (Kaburi Estate)

She held it between us as we smiled into the camera.

We watched the picture develop, our faces appearing on the milky film like a painting coming alive through the mist. Two bright, overexposed faces—black suit, white dress, a yellow note between us.

This is what it looks like when you wander somewhere between the sand and stardust, and meet a piece of yourself in someone else.

My lips found their way instinctively to hers and I kissed her. My wife. My rainbow-haloed girl.

"It's good, Mrs. Warden." I lifted her off the ground and spun her around.

"The photo?" She giggled, flushed and a little dizzy.

"The photo. Your smile. Life. You. Me."

"And baby makes three," she said softly, as I set her down.

My heart lurched like it always did when she mentioned the baby. I placed my hand over her tummy in a silent vow to the little life growing inside and felt a circle close around us. My greatest loss had led to my greatest love. Hearts were broken, and hearts were healed. Lives were lost, and lives were saved.

As I tucked our photo into my wallet, next to the one I kept of Lily, I noticed the triangular flags that had been captured in the frame. They were part of the jute banner behind us, hanging from the beams. Together, they spelled out the words on Rodel's bracelet, the one that Olonana's mother had given her:

Taleenoi olngisoilechashur.

We are all connected.

"What is it?" asked Rodel as I looked around the barn.

"You ever wonder what we'd find if we could pick up the threads back to the point where things unravel, where paths cross, and lives pivot, and people come together?" I took her hand as we rejoined our guests.

That night, the lights blazed on until dawn in an old, red barn at the foothills of Mount Kilimanjaro.

Epilogue

MO EMERSON FLIPPED through the travel magazine as she sat in the optometrist's waiting room. Dr. Nasmo's office was in the lower level of Kilimani Mall, across from the food court. Her appointment had been a few weeks earlier, but she'd been away with her friend Gabriel, so she had rescheduled.

And what a day I picked, she thought. Through the glass doors of Dr. Nasmo's office, Mo could see a crowd of people gathered around a makeshift podium.

"What's going on out there today?" she asked Christine, the receptionist.

"Some kind of political meeting. A convention for supporters of John Lazaro."

"Who's he?" Mo had seen his name on posters and signs around Amosha, but she hadn't paid any attention. The elections were coming up in October, but her volunteering gig would be over by then. She didn't know where she'd go next, but that was the thrill of it. She could close her eyes and point to the map for the start of a new adventure. The possibilities were endless. Mo thrived on the adrenaline rush of the unexpected. It made her feel more vibrant, more alive than anything else could. It was the one thing her sister, Ro, could never understand. And yet, if anyone gave her hell over her choices, Ro was the first one to step in and defend her.

"John Lazaro?" Christine looked up from her desk. "If you ask me, he's a dirty politician, but he's rich and powerful, and he's been making all the right promises."

"Hmm." Mo went back to the article she was reading:

Get Paid To Travel: Become A Travel Photographer.

Yes, she nodded, talking herself into her brilliant new calling. She was no photographer, but she could learn. And then she wouldn't have to mooch off her parents when she fell short, halfway around the world. Well, maybe just one last time—for a good camera. And lenses. And some classes. *But after that, watch out, world.*

She got her cell phone out and snapped a picture of the resources listed in the article. She would have torn the page off, but
she liked Dr. Nasmo too much for that. He was a sweetheart, and
someone she looked up to. She'd met him at the orphanage in
Wanza. He toured a lot of the rural areas, giving free eye exams
and glasses, but it was his work with the albino children that he
claimed was the most rewarding. Mo had witnessed the joy of it
herself, the first time she'd seen the expression on a child's face,
when the whole world had come into sharp, clear focus. Naturally,
he was the first person she thought of when she realized she'd
neglected her own checkups for way too long.

The door to Dr. Nasmo's office rattled as a young woman
tried to make her way in with a stroller.

"Here." Mo held the door for her. There was a little boy, fast
asleep in the stroller.

The woman thanked her and checked in with Christine. "Hi,
I'm here to get fitted for contact lenses. My name is Zara Ayadi."

"Thank you." Christine checked her name off. "Please have
a seat. Dr. Nasmo is running a little late today. He's with a client,
but he'll be done soon."

Zara sat next to Mo and turned her stroller so she could keep
an eye on her son.

"Batman fan?" asked Mo. The little boy's face was painted in
the trademark black and yellow logo.

"Not really. Isa doesn't know Batman from The Joker." His
mother laughed. "There's free face painting for the kids today.
This is what he picked." She slipped one of her flip-flops off and
massaged her foot.

"How long until the big day?" asked Mo.

"A few more weeks." Zara rubbed her pregnant belly.

The shrill ring of the office phone jarred Isa from his sleep.
He opened his eyes and blinked, trying to orient himself.

"Dr. Nasmo's office," Christine answered. "Lea, how many times have I told you not to call me on the work phone? Are you in the mall?" She listened for a few ticks and sighed. "Okay. No, it's fine. I'll see you at home. But for God's sake, hold on tight when you're on his motorbike. No, you don't. You read books on the back of that steel contraption. It's not safe. Just humor me, okay? Yeah. Love you too." She put the phone down and rolled her eyes. "Sisters," she said to Mo. "She was supposed to meet me today, but she's decided to go off with her boyfriend."

"I have one of those. A sister, I mean. The boyfriends come and go." Mo grinned. "It's the other way around for us. I'm the one ditching her for hot dates."

Isa was now wide awake, and fussing to get out of his stroller. He stared at Mo with big, round eyes.

Someone came out of Dr. Nasmo's room and stopped at the desk. "I'm all set. He said you can send in the next person."

"Okay, thanks." Christine pulled out a file and got up. "Mo? Dr. Nasmo will see you now."

Mo looked at the pregnant woman who was struggling with her toddler. "Why don't you go first?"

"Are you sure?" she asked, trying to soothe him with a pacifier.

"Absolutely."

"That's very kind. Thank you so much!" She gave Mo a grateful smile and followed Christine into Dr. Nasmo's room.

"How long will they be?" asked Mo, when Christine returned to her desk.

"About twenty minutes."

"I'm going to get some coffee. I'll be back in a bit."

The door shut behind Mo, as she stepped out. John Lazaro was up on the podium. Flanking the platform, on all sides, were lines of security guards. Their uniforms were different from those of the mall guards, and they were heavily armed.

Blimey, thought Mo, as she walked past the gathering. *He's not pissing around.*

She scanned the fast food restaurants in the food court and decided to get her coffee from the café upstairs. John Lazaro's words were blaring over the amplifier, mingled with the chatter of unaffected shoppers and mall music. She preferred her coffee a little less noisy.

Mo took the elevator upstairs and passed a balloon vendor. He whistled at her and inflated a long, pink balloon in her honor. Mo had that effect on men. She was used to it. Maybe it was the colorful clothes she wore, or the flirty skirts, or the big, fun pieces of jewelry that jangled as she walked. But there were exceptions to the rule. Men who remained unaffected. Like Gabriel Lucas.

Mo mulled it over as she sat at one of the tables inside the small café and drank her coffee. Gabriel was different. He was intense and broody—an enigma she hadn't been able to solve. She had first noticed him at the nightclub that all the volunteers from Nima House frequented. It wasn't just his good looks that set him apart. He wasn't like any of the other locals. He didn't talk. He didn't dance. He just sat there and got rip-roaring drunk.

Eventually, she learned that he had a daughter and sister in Rutema. There was no work for him there, so he took odd jobs in Amosha. He never said what he did, but he traveled a lot. When he told her that he was going to Dar es Salaam, the largest city in Tanzania, Mo had begged to tag along. She wanted to stroll along Oyster Bay, and spend money she didn't have at the shopping center. It was on that trip Mo learned about Scholastica and the situation with albinos. A friendship developed between the two, and when Gabriel proposed a plan that would work for them both, Mo had agreed.

Mo finished the rest of her coffee and glanced at her watch. *Perfect timing.*

She stepped out of the café just as a tall, striking dish of a man, holding a bouquet of bright yellow balloons walked by her.

Hello. Mo did a double take. She caught a brief glimpse of his profile—square jaw, strong nose, thick, dirty blond hair. Rugged and handsome, with powerful shoulders that bracketed a lean, athletic physique. She couldn't help but get sucked into the wake of his trail. It wasn't just the flurry of balloons rustling behind him; it was the whole massive presence of him. The air swirled in his aftermath.

Damn. Mo inhaled the faint scent of his cologne, as he exited through the main doors. _I should hang out at the mall more._ She made a mental note to tell Ro about him. He looked like he'd stepped right out of one of her books. Mo wasn't sure what kind of books Ro was reading these days, but she was certain her sister would have stopped long enough to stare.

Mo took the elevator to the lower level. The doors opened and closed like they were waiting for an entire busload of seniors to get on and off.

So slow, thought Mo, as she got in. _But still better than that packed escalator._

She hummed as a piano solo piped through the speakers.

When the doors opened again, it was to an entirely different set of sounds.

Gunshots. Screaming. Chaos. Panic.

All hell had broken loose while she was in the elevator, and Mo found herself smack dab in the middle of it. She had no idea what was going on, but she knew it was bad. She made her way to Dr. Nasmo's office, but one side of the door was shattered, and she couldn't see anyone inside. Gunfire rattled through the air, first to the right of her, and then to the left. It was coming from all around.

Mo dropped to her knees, deafened and disoriented. There was no time to think. She crawled under a table in the food court and covered her ears. Fear, like she'd never known, welled up in her throat, but she swallowed the screams. She jumped as a bullet grazed one of the chairs next to her. She was too open, too exposed.

Her eyes darted around—past the flurry of feet that were running by her: white trainers, leather sandals, manicured toes, little pink shoes. There was a room beyond the food court, off to the side. No one was coming in or out of it. Mo wasn't sure if heading there was a good idea, but she knew she had to get as far away from the sound of gunfire as she could.

She made a dash for it, half rolling, half crawling, until she got to it. It was empty—rows of folding chairs, some toppled over, arranged before a stage. The shuddering sound of her breath echoed around her. She leaned back against the wall, hugging her knees.

"Over here," someone said. "Get in here."

She looked around, but couldn't see anyone. Then she spotted a slit in the fabric at the base of the stage. It was an elevated stage, with a skirted bottom to hide the scaffolding. The perfect place to hide.

"Hello?" Mo crawled inside. It was so dark her eyes took a while to adjust.

"*Shhh*," said a figure sitting on the other side. "Don't be afraid. My dad will be here soon. He'll make everything okay. He always does." It was a little girl, with her hair tied up in a ponytail.

"Your dad?" Mo swallowed the lump in her throat. The girl couldn't have been more than seven or eight, but her faith in her father was so strong, that she was reassuring a grown woman. "Where's your dad?"

"My teacher said he went to drop off the balloons. She told me to go with the other kids, but then he won't be able to find me. I know he'll come to get me. He's always in the front. Right there. See?" She pushed the stage skirt aside and pointed to the chairs.

"Yellow balloons?" asked Mo. The man with the balloons, that had stopped her in her tracks. "Your father was holding yellow balloons?"

"Yes! Did you see him?"

"I did." Mo sat back. She'd seen him leave the mall, minutes before the chaos erupted. Even if he made it back inside, she had no idea if he'd make it to his daughter unharmed. "I'm sure he'll be here soon."

"Why are they doing it?" asked the girl. "What do those bad men want?"

Mo took a deep breath. She was wrestling with the same question herself. "I wish I knew."

They were whispering in the dark, between violent cracks of gunfire. Their insides clenched with each shrill, sporadic barrage of horror. But in-between, they pretended as if they were meeting under different circumstances.

"What's your name?" asked Mo.

"Lily. What's yours?"

"Mo."

"You're pretty. I like your glasses. Are you married?" Lily paused at the sound of shattered glass. Something crashed. There was a moment of silence and then the hoarse howling of people. "I think my father should get married," she continued. "He misses me when I'm away. I know he's lonely, even though he has Goma."

"Who's Goma?"

"My great-grandmother. She made me this skirt." Lily smoothed the circle of her tutu.

"It's beautiful." Mo touched the fabric and felt small, sharp shards of regret assail her. She should have called her parents more. She should have gone home for Christmas. She should have mailed Ro postcards and silly knickknacks. Suddenly, she had the overwhelming need to reach out to her family. Her parents were in Thailand, but Ro would be in her flat. For once, Mo was thankful for the one steady constant in her life—her sister.

The space under the stage glowed blue as Mo powered up her phone. She noticed a bunch of missed calls. Someone had been trying to reach her, but she had missed them in all the chaos. She dismissed the notifications and dialed Ro's number. It rang a few times, and then went to voice mail. Mo moved to the other side, away from Lily, and lowered her voice.

"Ro, I'm in Kilimani Mall. A shit storm just broke out. Something bad is going down. There are gunmen everywhere. I'm hiding under the stage, in some kind of hall. There's a little girl with me. She's the only thing keeping me sane."

"Who are you talking to?" asked Lily.

Mo put her hand over the phone and turned to her. "It's my sister. In England."

"Oh. Tell her not to worry. Tell her my father will be here soon and then we'll be okay."

"Yes, sweetheart." She held her tears in check as she spoke into the phone again. "We're going to wait it out. I think it's safe here, but if I don't . . . if I don't make it, I just want to say I love you, Ro. Tell Mum and Dad I love them too. I don't want you to worry when you listen to this message. We'll probably laugh at this someday. It'll be another one of my crazy stories, like when I thought I was going to die on that ferry in Australia." She paused as urgent footsteps entered the hall. "I have to go now," she whispered. And then, because it sounded like a goodbye, and she didn't want her sister to panic, she added, "I've taken all the chances, Ro . . ." She trailed off as the footsteps came closer. When they stopped outside, a few feet from the stage, Mo hung up and held her breath.

"That's my daddy!" said Lily, springing into action.

"Wait. We don't know that for sure. Lily, wait!"

But Lily slipped out of her grasp.

For a few tense seconds, Mo sat paralyzed under the stage,

waiting for confirmation of a happy reunion between Lily and her father. It never came. There was nothing. Not a sound, not a shuffle. Mo felt the chill of impending doom, crawling down her spine. It wasn't Lily's father. Someone else had barged into the hall. Mo had no idea if Lily was face to face with the enemy. All she knew was she couldn't leave that little girl alone out there. And so Mo crawled out from behind the stage skirt and put on her bravest face.

Small, insignificant details became suddenly vivid, as if her mind was trying to grab on to things, to keep from slipping over the edge. The dark birthmark on the back of Lily's ankle. The frayed hem of the man's jeans. Her gaze swept over his torso. Up, up, she stood, taking Lily's small hand in hers as she straightened. Then her eyes met the man's and she gasped.

"Gabriel?"

"Mo!" His whole body slackened with relief. "God, Mo." He embraced her in a tight hug. "I was on the escalator, on my way out, when I saw you take the elevator down. I tried to call you. I've been looking everywhere for you. Thank God I found you! We need to get out of here." He started ushering Mo and Lily toward the door.

"No!" Lily pulled her hand away from Mo's. "I'm not going anywhere without my daddy. You go."

"I'm not leaving you," said Mo. "Why don't we all just stay?" She turned to Gabriel. She had no idea what he was doing in the mall, but she was relieved to see him. "It's safe here. We're away from everything. We can hide under there." She pointed to the stage. "Let's just wait it out."

"It's *not* safe here. Nowhere in the mall is safe. Trust me, Mo. We need to move. *Now!*"

Something about Gabriel's tone gnawed at Mo. "Lily, get back inside and wait for me. I'll be just a minute." She waited until Lily disappeared before pulling Gabriel aside. "What's going on? What's going on out there?"

"It's John Lazaro." Gabriel's words were clipped and urgent. Mo knew she was testing his patience—she knew she could trust him, but she wasn't about to follow him blindly into the chaos. She had a decision to make, not just for herself, but for Lily too.

"It's an assassination attempt on John Lazaro," Gabriel continued. "He's done some things—lots of things—and the people he did them to want him dead. It's business and politics, all wrapped up. If Plan A fails, they'll go to Plan B. Either way, he's not leaving here alive."

"So, let them fight it out. Let's just wait here. Plan A or Plan B. What does it have to do with us?"

"Because!" Gabriel clenched his fists. "Because I'm Plan B, Mo. If John Lazaro's security team gets him out of that food court alive, this whole place blows up."

Mo opened her mouth and shut it. "I don't . . ." She shook her head. "What are you saying, Gabriel? You're not making any sense. Are you saying you're involved in this . . . this assassination attempt?" This was her friend. He was a good man. She *knew* him. And yet, the part of him that had always eluded her, the part of him that had remained an enigma was coming into focus. A weight settled in Mo's chest. She found it hard to breathe.

"I tried, Mo," he said, his Adam's apple bobbing at the look in her eyes. "I worked two jobs. Day in, day out. But I wasn't getting anywhere. I needed money. I needed money to get Scholastica to Wanza. I needed money to build the house. I needed money to save the kids. Gas money. Food money. I was running short all the time. Then one day, I was sitting at the bar, and someone offered me a job. It was simple. Pick up a shipment and drive it somewhere, no questions asked. I couldn't believe the amount he paid me. So, I took on another job. And then another. And I haven't stopped ever since."

"I get that," said Mo. "I get it, Gabriel. We all do what we have to. But what does *this* have to do with any of *that?*"

"Today . . ." He glanced at the ceiling, as if he couldn't bear to meet her eyes. "Today, I picked up a truck and drove it to the mall. It's in the underground parking lot. I met a guy in the food court and handed him the keys, just like I'd been told to."

"So?" Mo wanted to shake him. He was talking in circles. "How is that Plan B?"

"The truck I drove? It's packed with explosives, Mo. Someone is rigging John Lazaro's car as we speak. If he tries to get away, they'll blow it up, and everything else along with it. That's why we have to leave. They're still fighting, which means John Lazaro is still alive. And as long as he's alive, as long as there's a chance that he'll slip out, we're not safe here. We're not safe anywhere in this mall."

"No." Mo's thoughts were jagged and painful. "Gabriel. No. All those innocent people."

"Exactly!" Gabriel's eyes flashed with something wild and fierce. "All those innocent people. Do you know what John Lazaro does? He drinks albino blood. He thinks it makes him powerful and invincible. He thinks it will help him win the election. I just did my job, Mo. I did what I always do. I delivered the goods. But if I'm completely honest, I *want* John Lazaro to die. I want him to die before any more innocent people lose their lives, including my daughter! The rest of it, I'll have to live with. I'll have to turn a blind eye, just like everybody else does, to the injustices that go on right under their noses, because they're powerless, or afraid, or profiting from it. And if I burn in hell for it, then so be it. At least Scholastica will have one less monster coming after her."

They were both crying, Mo and Gabriel, with tears streaming down their faces—Mo trying to come to terms with what she'd just learned, and Gabriel trying desperately to make her understand. Then slowly, tentatively, they moved toward each other, eyes searching eyes, probing the depths of friendship and betrayal.

"You came back for me," said Mo. "You could have left me, but you came back."

"I could never have left you. It was never a choice."

Mo sobbed in his arms. Gabriel Lucas. He was both the angel and the devil.

"We need to leave now," he said. "Let's get the girl and go."

"That might be a problem. Lily is convinced that her father is going to come and get her."

"Let me have a go." Gabriel walked over to where Lily was hiding and peered under the stage skirt. "Lily, what's your father's name?"

There was no reply. After a while, she asked, "Where's Mo?"

"I'm right here, Lily. It's okay. You can tell him."

"My dad's name is Jack," she replied. "Jack Warden."

"How about you come out of there, and we call your dad. Would that be okay?" Gabriel coaxed Lily out. "That's right. Good girl. Now. What's his number?"

Lily called out a string of numbers but trailed off. "I think that's when I dial from Cape Town." She tried again, but her face fell. "I'm not sure what the rest of it is. My mummy always dials it for me."

"That's okay. We'll call the operator. She'll be able to tell us."

It was amazing how calm Gabriel was with her. Mo knew that it was taking everything for him not to swoop her up and carry her outside, kicking and screaming. It would be too much of a risk though, especially if she tried to break loose and got caught in the line of fire.

Mo glanced at her watch. It seemed like they'd been there forever, and yet it wasn't long at all. Everything seemed to stretch out—each breath, each word, each tense, weighted moment, as Gabriel tried to get through to Jack. Mo knew the exact moment when Gabriel decided they were wasting precious time. His eyes changed as he spoke into the phone.

"Yes, operator. That's him. Can you please put me through?" He waited a while before continuing. "Hi, Jack? I'm in the mall with Lily. She's waiting for you to come and get her. Where are you? I see. No, she's fine. Of course. I'll let her know. We'll see you soon." He ignored Lily's attempts to grab the phone and hung up. "I'm sorry, sweetheart. We don't have time for that right now. You can talk to him soon. You were right. He's on his way. He's almost here, but he said it will be faster if we meet him at the safe place."

"The safe place? Where's the safe place?"

"Come with me. I'll get you there." He held his hand out to Lily. She stared at it for a few beats and then looked at Mo.

"I'm right behind you," said Mo. "We'll all go together."

As soon as Lily placed her hand in Gabriel's, everything changed. Everything slow became fast again. It was like they had slipped through another dimension. They were back in the midst of chaos, except there was less of a crowd now. Those who hadn't fled were sprawled on the floor, hurt or dead—it was hard to tell—while the two parties continued exchanging fire.

Gabriel spun around when they got to the escalator. "It's been blocked off." He picked Lily up and made a dash for the lift. "Come on, Mo!" But there was a stack of tables and chairs blocking it too. John Lazaro's enemies had used his own gathering against him. All the exits and stairwells had been blocked.

"Shit!" exclaimed Gabriel.

He scanned the lower level. John Lazaro was holed up behind one of the fast food counters, flanked by his men. They were shooting blindly in all directions. Bullet holes sprayed the walls. Bits of mortar flew into the air.

"The parking lot," said Gabriel. "It's our only way out."

"But his car's in there."

"We either stay in here or we go out there. Either way, we're taking a chance."

"Keep going!" said Mo, following closely behind him.

"Is my daddy going to be there?" asked Lily.

"Yes," replied Gabriel. "We're meeting him at the safe place. Remember?" He let her down and knelt before her. "Now, I want you to run as fast you can, okay? The faster you run, the faster you can see your daddy."

Lily nodded and held her hand out to Gabriel. "Can I run with you?"

There was something about Gabriel that drew her to him. Maybe it was because he was a father too. Whatever Lily sensed in him, it seemed to soften his heart. Mo's heart caught in her chest as Gabriel took Lily's small hand in his.

"I'll try to keep up," he said.

And then they were running through the parking lot, toward the ramp going up. Their footsteps bounced off the concrete walls, echoing with their breath. They were halfway up the first ramp when they heard the throttle of an engine revving up. There was a loud screeching, a spinning of the wheels as the car reversed out of its parking spot. The sharp, zing of bullets on metal followed, and then the sound of a car driving toward the ramp.

"What's the matter?" asked Lily, when Gabriel stopped in his tracks. "Let's go! We need to get to the safe place." She tugged his hand.

Mo and Gabriel exchanged a look. If that was John Lazaro's car, about to come around the bend, they were out of time.

Suddenly, a deep calm settled over Mo. For the first time in her life, she just wanted to stand still—for these last few seconds. They were hers, and they were glorious. She could feel the thunder of her heart, the air rushing in and out of her lungs. It was beautiful—being alive. It was enough to know and to have known.

Together, Mo and Gabriel ushered Lily to the corner, where one ramp met the other.

"This is it," said Gabriel. "This is the safe place. I'm going to call your father and let him know, okay?" He punched in some numbers. Mo held Lily's hand as he spoke into the phone. "Hello, Jack? We're here. Yes, Lily's right here, too. She's a very brave girl. You must be so proud of her. Hold on, I'll tell her . . ." He turned to Lily. "Your daddy says he'll be here very soon, and he loves you very much."

"Can I talk to him now?" she asked, holding her hand out like she was claiming a prize. There was no one at the other end of the line, but Gabriel let the phone slip from his hand.

"Of course," he replied, a flicker of something bittersweet crossing his eyes.

"What about you?" asked Mo. "Aren't you going to make that call?"

"Nobody knows I'm here, Mo. Not Anna, and not Scholastica. It's better that way. I don't want them to live with the shame of knowing what I've done. I don't want that to be my legacy to my daughter. It's ironic. I did it all for Scholastica, so I could keep her safe, so I could give her the life she deserves. And now she's going to grow up without me. If she grows up." His eyes welled up.

"*Shhh.* You're a good dad. And you've done a lot for other people's children too. You've risked your own life to get them to safety sometimes. Someone will step up. Someone will make sure Scholastica is looked after."

"Daddy?" Lily stared at the phone. "He's not saying anything." She handed the phone back to Gabriel.

"Maybe he got cut off. Let's try again." Gabriel pretended to dial Jack again. "It's ringing now. Here you go."

As Lily bent her head over the phone, it was impossible to ignore the sound of the approaching car.

"When?" Mo asked Gabriel.

"I don't know."

Mo gave him a slow, wistful smile. "Let's save one more?"

Gabriel stared at her for a few still beats. "Let's."

They cocooned Lily between their bodies, knowing that the blast would destroy everything within its radius. But maybe, just maybe, they could take the brunt of it for Lily.

As the car sped up the ramp, Mo and Gabriel caught a brief glimpse of John Lazaro in the back seat. They braced themselves, forehead to forehead, arms around each other, shielding Lily in the middle.

"Daddy?" said Lily. Her face was all lit up as she spoke into the phone. "I'm in the safe place now."

Author's Note

Where do stories come from? How do they form and flow and find their way into our world? How do we take sparks of inspiration and bind them between the covers of a book, project them onto the big screen, or transform them into the notes of our favorite song? The creative process is a magical thing that lets us take thoughts, ideas, and feelings—those ethereal, intangible pieces—and condense them into reality. I cannot begin to explain how it works because it's different for every one, every time, but I can take you behind the scenes and show you the events, people, and circumstances that inspired this book.

After I finished my last novel, *The Paper Swan*, I knew two things. One, that my next book would be set in Africa. Two, that it would be a love story. I let it go and waited for that spark, that rush, that knowing, that sets you sailing on a new adventure.

A few weeks later, I had dinner with Dr. Nasmo[1]*, who had just returned from Tanzania. Dr. Nasmo is an optometrist who was born in Tanzania but lives in the U.S. As a child, he suffered from poor eyesight, a condition that went uncorrected until a volunteer mission came to his village and fitted him with glasses. So impactful was this gift of sight, that he based his career around it. He now makes annual trips to Tanzania to help prevent blindness and vision impairment by providing free eye exams and glasses in rural areas. He is an inspirational figure, and I always look forward to the times when our paths cross.

On this particular trip, Dr. Nasmo had visited an orphanage for children with albinism. Tanzania has one of the highest

1   * *name changed to protect privacy*

concentrations of albinos in the world. People with albinism lack pigment and usually have a number of eye conditions, including poor vision and sensitivity to light. Ninety-nine percent of the kids that Dr. Nasmo examined at the orphanage needed vision correction. As we flipped through the photos from his trip, he showed me a video of an albino girl playing with a piece of string. She dropped it and attempted to pick it up several times, but failed, because she couldn't find it.

Vision is not the only issue that children with albinism struggle with in parts of Africa. Thought to have magical powers, their body parts are bought and sold for thousands of dollars on the black market, for use in potions said to bring wealth and good luck.

I could not sleep that night. The powerful images I had seen kept flashing before my eyes. I recalled a similar night, when a friend had sent me a news article on the Westgate Mall attack, also in East Africa, where I lived for many years. Somehow the two events got linked in my head. When I got out of bed the next morning, something had crystallized from all the bits and pieces that had been circling my mind. Although the circumstances around the tragic Westgate Mall incident were vastly different from the fictional Kilimani Mall attack, a story had started to form.

It was not a story I wanted to tell. It felt too big and too real, and I didn't know if I could do it any justice, so I stored it away. But it kept knocking and knocking until I opened the door and let it in.

Aside from the conception of the story, the following pieces of truth have been woven into the fiction:

- The villages on Mo's sticky notes are named after real victims of albino attacks.

- Amosha is a fictional place, derived from the towns of Arusha and Moshi, in the Kilimanjaro region.

- Josephine Montati's name is inspired by a woman who started a non-profit organization to help children from crisis zones get custom prostheses for missing limbs.

- The illegal rubber duck race in the Cotswolds is not fiction.

- John Lazaro is named after two albino contract killers in Tanzania.

- Scholastica is the name of one of the children in Dr. Nasmo's notes from the albino orphanage.

- Aristurtle is the name I gave my little brother's tortoise when we were kids. My brother kept losing him and we would tiptoe around the apartment until he was found.

Ultimately, this book is a work of fiction. I have sought to entertain and inform through the filter of my experiences, imagination, encounters, and research. It is not my aim to depict or represent any given event or situation.

Last but not least, my thanks to the flame of mad magic that burns in us all, and that connects us in wonderful, unknown ways.

With love,
Leylah

About the Author

L EYLAH ATTAR IS *a New York Times, USA Today,* and *Wall Street Journal* bestselling author of *53 Letters For My Lover, From His Lips, The Paper Swan,* and *Mists Of The Serengeti.* She writes stories about love—shaken, stirred and served with a twist. Sometimes she disappears into the black hole of the internet, but can usually be enticed out with chocolate.

CONNECT WITH HER AT:

www.leylahattar.com

For exclusives and information on new releases,
sign up for Leylah Attar's mailing list:
www.leylahattar.com/subscribe

Acknowledgments

DR. NASMO, THIS story would not have been possible without that chance meeting with you. Your work changes lives. What an incredible privilege it is to watch that unfold.

Hang Lee (*By Hang Le*), your covers are pure magic. They speak to me without saying a single word.

Lea Burn (*Burn Before Reading*), my fantastic editor, thank you for working through the holidays to meet the deadline. I am knitting you a scarf with all my redundant commas. It is nice and cozy and will wrap around you many, many times.

Christine Estevez, I can't imagine this journey without you. Thank you for proofreading, and seeing me through another book. I like holding hands with you.

Christine Borgford (*Type A Formatting*), my phenomenal formatter—always meticulous, always on the ball. My books aren't real until you've worked your wizardry on them. And that feeling when I'm holding one of your beautiful eARCs or paperbacks for the first time? That's all you!

Soulla Georgiou. Here we are. And what a ride it's been. Where do I even begin? Thank you for your unwavering support, your friendship, and for putting put up with me even though I refuse to use my cell. I love you mucho, mucho!

Mara White, my immense gratitude for filling in the blind spots, and sharing your vision and insight. Love always.

My agent, Amy Tannenbaum—thank you for your invaluable input on this project, and for standing in my corner.

K. Larsen, Layla Boutazout, Lisa Chamberlin, Luisa Hansen,

Priscilluh Perez, Saffron Kent—with great affection and appreciation for your early feedback on these pages.

To the countless readers, dedicated bloggers, and book lovers
who spend hours reading, reviewing, and sharing, thank you is not
enough for all the things you do. You are the pulsing beat of the
book community. You are what keeps it fresh and vibrant and alive.
You inspire me to keep writing, and to write better.

To every person who has taken the time to contact me, made
beautiful art out of words that have touched them, poured their
hearts into creating book-related tokens, I am immensely humbled,
and grateful for your gifts of kindness.

My author friends, I can't tell you how many times I have
picked up one of your brilliant books and wished I could write
the same magic. You inspire me, not just as writers, but by being
the brave, generous, inspiring souls that you are—everyday, in so
many ways. It is impossible to list you all here, so from my heart
to each of yours, thank you.

Big love for the little band of Leylaholics Book Nook—I may
not be able to squeeze you all in here, but my heart is fully ex-
pandable, and sometimes it sounds like an accordion. So you get
music too.

A big shout out to the BBFT crew, This is Indie / This is Romance, and all the wonderful collaborations that I am fortunate
and honored to be a part of.

My friends. My life is rainbowier because of you. And smileyer.
I can make up words and you still know what I'm saying. I love
you more than all the dead people in Game of Thrones. I mean in
number. Because they're dead so they can't really love you. Also,
they never met you. Unless you count that one time Amanda met
Jason Momoa. That she keeps reminding us of. Bish.

My son. The best, brightest corner of my life. I am so proud
to be your Kuriboh.

My husband. My sweet, amazing, incredible man. I fall in love with you more every day, and we've been at it a while now. Thank you for making me breakfast every morning, and for not giving up on Funny Face Egg. You looooove me.

$15.00

7/17

73259735R00217

Made in the USA
Columbia, SC
08 July 2017